SAVAGE HEARTS

Shifters of Darkness Falls Book 4

JASMIN QUINN

Savage Hearts Copyright © 2020 by Jasmin Quinn. All Rights Reserved.

All rights reserved. No part of this book may be reproduced in any form or by any electronic or mechanical means including information storage and retrieval systems, without permission in writing from the author. The only exception is by a reviewer, who may quote short excerpts in a review.

Cover designed by Jem Monday Publishing

This book is a work of fiction. Names, characters, places, and incidents either are products of the author's imagination or are used fictitiously. Any resemblance to actual persons, living or dead, events, or locales is entirely coincidental.

Visit Jasmin's website at https://jasminquinn.com/

First Printing: August 2020
Jem Monday Publishing Inc.
ISBN Paperback (Amazon): 9798680039748
ISBN e-book: 9781999037192

 Created with Vellum

ALSO BY JASMIN QUINN

Running with the Devil

The Darkest Hour (Running with the Devil: Book 1)

Secrets inside Her (Running with the Devil: Book 2)

Black Surrender (Running with the Devil: Book 3)

Without Mercy (Running with the Devil: Book 4)

Hard Lessons (Running with the Devil: Book 5)

Courting Trouble (Running with the Devil: Book 6)

Shattered (Running with the Devil: Book 7)

Past Sins (Running with the Devil: Book 8)

Wild Card (Running with the Devil: Book 9)

Fallen Angel (Running with the Devil: Book 10)

Mr. Master (Running with the Devil Book 11)

House of Shadows (Running with the Devil Book 12) (November 27, 2020)

Shifters of Darkness Falls

Basic Instinct (Shifters of Darkness Falls: Book 1)

Fierce Intentions (Shifters of Darkness Falls: Book 2)

Alpha's Prey (Shifters of Darkness Falls: Book 3)

Savage Hearts (Shifters of Darkness Falls: Book 4)

Primal Heat (Shifters of Darkness Falls: Book 5) (February 26, 2021)

Unbroken

Unleashed (Unbroken Book 1)

After Dark

In collaboration with Nikita Slater

Collared: A Dark Captive Romance

Safeword: A Dark Romance

Chained: A Forced Mafia Marriage Romance

Good Girl: A Captive BDSM Romance

Hostile Takeover: An Enemies to Lovers Romance

Standalone Books

First Blood Moon Novella

Bless our hearts, that we may hear,
in the breaking of the bread,
the songs of the universe.

— *UNKNOWN*

INTRODUCTION

Shifters aren't easy – to know, to be, to live with. They're a fragile contradiction: part wolf, part human, all shifter. They're ruled by instinct and governed by convention.

Darkness Falls, a small British Columbia community, is nestled in the northernmost access to the Rocky Mountains where the rugged wilderness, the vast back-country and the lakes, rivers and streams are untouched and pristine. The area is well-known for its fishing and diversity of wildlife, including moose, black and grizzly bear, mountain sheep, goat, caribou, elk, lynx and of course, wolf. This is how Darkness Falls thrives – its raw nature is a lure for tourists and shifters alike.

Many come to visit, some don't leave.

Darkness Falls is a haven for shifters and too many things can go wrong.

Humans and shifters working together, playing together, fucking together. The four packs that claim territory around Darkness Falls try to be civilized, try to work with each other and the humans to co-exist and protect the community, but in the pack, human rules don't apply and where pack justice is concerned, the lines between humans and shifters get blurred.

It's dark in Darkness Falls, even when the sun is shining.

Shifters of Darkness Falls is a paranormal contemporary romance suspense series with no cliffhangers, no cheating, and HEA. All books are standalone but are connected by common characters and themes.

PROLOGUE

Cherime stood on the edge of a cliff and let loose a long shrieky echoing scream. Well, maybe not a scream, more a howl. No… not that either. A howl-scream was what it was. She repeated it twice more. Yes, definitely a howl-scream. And why not? This was the happiest day of her 18 years of life. It was the end of June, school was out forever, and she was alone in her secret sanctuary in the mountains of the Darkness Falls region of northern British Columbia.

Where to start?

First, she dusted the flat top of the good-sized boulder that was the sole rock in the middle of the clearing, then carefully perched herself on said boulder so as not to get the ass of her white daisy dukes dirty. Next, she stretched her long, tanned, and well-toned legs out in front of her and admired them. They were shaved and silky, tapering to shapely ankles and sexy bare feet.

She was in the mountains in her favourite hang-out spot for when she wanted to be alone. This little piece of paradise was a neutral area that sat just outside the territory of the Mountain wolf shifter pack, which she avoided because her brother, Raff, beta to the Lodge pack, told her to.

They're uncivilized assholes who will drag you off by your hair, use you, and toss you out, he grumbled to her all the time.

She never once pointed out the irony of his words considering he was just as uncivilized as any other male shifter she'd ever encountered, and went through women like they were cheap cans of beer.

None of that matter today. She didn't want to think about Raff, or her sister, Mara, or Mara's new guy, Connell. She also wasn't going to think about the Lodge pack, or Lucien, the sexy new alpha who barely acknowledged her, let alone returned her teenage angsty feelings.

What she did want to do was enjoy the day for what it was. The first day of the rest of her life. "School's out for summer! School's out forever!" she sang at the top of her lungs. Yeah baby, she was so ready to put in place the plans she'd been thinking about ever since she found this private little paradise.

She raised an invisible glass of champagne and toasted to freedom, to her future, and to this awesome wondrous piece of the world she lived in. Draining the airy champagne in a single guzzle, she refilled her fake hand-shaped glass, then winged the empty imaginary bottle over the cliff.

Tossing back the second glass, she threw it at the rock wall behind her, pretending she was drunk and wincing at the illusion of shattering glass. She flipped her long dark hair over her shoulders and shaded her eyes with the flat of her hand. The view up here was to die for. Literally, she thought as she eyed the unfenced edge of a cliff that ended at least 20 metres below on a hard bed of slate.

She could see for miles, nature at its finest, unmolested

and virginal. Northern BC, the Yukon and Alaska were her jam and she'd never leave this area, unlike some of her friends, who were gearing up to head to Vancouver in the fall to get book smart.

There was a college in town if she should have a sudden urge to learn something she couldn't find on the internet. With a population of about 5,000 humans and shifters, Darkness Falls was a tourist draw that was nestled in a valley surrounded by mountains, vast forests, a snaking highway that led towards the Yukon and a majestic waterfall that the town was named after. She could see her pack's territory, the Falls Lodge, a tiny tract of green hemmed by old-growth trees, with little cabins like smudges of paint only slightly marring the masterpiece.

She slept up here sometimes, in the back of her beat-up old jeep, which she managed to maneuver through the trees, hollows and dips after she cleared rocks and a few logs out of the way. Other times, when the weather suited, she shifted and slept under a huge old growth western red cedar, which sang lullabies of past generations of shifters when the breeze ruffled its boughs.

This area was perfect: hidden and private with the right number of trees and rocks, a freshwater stream, and enough level ground space to pitch several tents. All she'd need to do to was build a solid fence at the edge of the cliff, so none of the idiot schoolgirls fell over.

She grinned as she thought of Mara, who would scold her for being so negative about high school girls, but Cherime had a right to call them idiots. She used to be one: getting a hangnail was an apocalyptic event, the girls she considered friends were also her worst enemies, and she expected the world to revolve around her. Graduation didn't much change her behaviour, but at least she was self-aware enough to recognize the teenage drama for what it was.

With the grad ceremony over, hats tossed in the air, and teachers looking forward to the summer break, she was now the holder of a useless piece of paper that made her sister weep with happiness. Was it worth it to graduate high school to make Mara happy? No, nope, nada. It had been a torturous prison sentence and Mara was the cruel warden, practically dragging Cherime over the finish line.

Cherime had checked out in grade 10 anyway, preferring to study boys over math. School was overrated, a government hoop she needed to jump through to earn a scrap of paper that would ultimately do nothing for her future. She was never leaving Darkness Falls, never going to university to get a degree. She had all the skills she needed to survive in the world of shifters, and a reasonably functioning head on her shoulders to turn her vision into a reality.

She stood, swaying a little from the champagne, hands on hips, her gaze sweeping her future. This was going to be the Falls Lodge Glamping spot – well one of them anyway. She had two other locations in mind depending on the time of year and weather.

No one knew about her plan yet; not Lucien, Raff, or Mara. They'd scoff but give in to her because it would be the only way to shut her up. At first, they'd think it was harmless, and then eventually, they'd thank her for having the will to implement it.

Without doubt, her glamping trips were going to put Lodge Falls on the map and attract thousands of people from around the world.

CHAPTER ONE

Eight years later

Cherime hated glamping, she hated this stupid mountain-top spot, and she especially hated snowstorms in June. The cold wind howled around her, whipping her long purple hair into a Medusa-like frenzy around her face as she stared helplessly at the tatters of her meticulous planning.

"We have to go!" Aubrey Powell shouted in Cherime's ear, her squeaky voice seized by the wind and carried away. Aubrey was a little thing, even for a human. Short in stature, light-weight, with arms and legs that lacked muscle tone. Right now, her lips were turning a light shade of blue as she quivered in her flip-flops.

Cherime and her wolf both scoffed. Humans were so fragile; a little cold breeze and they were shivering through their bitching. Still, as much as Cherime didn't want to agree with the schoolteacher, Aubrey was right.

There were nine girls on this glamping trip, all soon-to-be graduates from Darkness Falls Secondary School. Cherime had implemented graduation glamping trips several years ago to modest success. The school district subsidized them and the girls who signed up for the almost-dry, usually boyless event had nothing but great things to say when they emerged from the mountains four days later, dolled up like they were beauty queen contestants.

This time round there were eight human girls and one shifter female plus Aubrey and herself. "They're turning into smurfs." Cherime laughed at the girls, who were varying shades of blue as they huddled together with their shifter schoolmate for body warmth.

Their discomfort didn't stop them from chattering like magpies, punctuated with the occasional, "I did not!" and "Shut up!"

Aubrey didn't seem to find the blue humans as funny as Cherime. Instead, she pointed to the dark, low-hanging clouds. "If we don't pack up now, we're going to be stranded. What the hell are we going to do then?"

Wow, the prim little schoolteacher said a swear word, if hell counted as a swear word these days. "Fine!" Cherime felt belligerent.

Nature was a prick, a mischief maker, a jerkass sonofabitch that she'd never forgive for this. He messed with her all the time and the problem was that the only way she could get revenge was to leave the garbage, water bottles, food wrappers and other such crap behind. Of course, she wouldn't, and the bastard knew it. Unlike math, protecting the environment was ingrained in her.

"Let's go," she shouted to the girls. "Get all the tents down and packed up properly."

None of the girls moved, though a couple looked up.

Cherime wrinkled her nose at them. "Get your asses moving, now! It'll warm you up!"

Aubrey gave her the stink eye as the little human

snowstorms. They came on without warning and sometimes lasted days. If Cherime had known this was in the forecast, they'd have gone to the glamping site near the Lodge. But daddy nature obviously bribed the weather reporter to tell lies, although she went to school with the idiot. He didn't need bribes to be wrong.

"This is the last of it." Aubrey was breathing heavily from the exertion as she shoved a tent into Cherime's arms.

Cherime pushed the tent into a tiny crack of space and then slammed the back door shut. "Let's go!" she shouted, which wasn't necessary because the girls were already huddled inside the bus, blankets around them, shaking like they were in a Stephen King novel.

Cherime rolled her eyes as she climbed behind the steering wheel and fired up the bus. "Jesus, you girls are pussies. It's a little fucking snow."

Aubrey climbed into the passenger seat and struggled to close the door as a gust of wind caught it. "Language," she muttered as she strapped herself in. To the girls, she barked, "Seatbelts everyone!"

The back-up sensors beeped as Cherime rolled the bus out from under the trees where it had been parked, then she put it in drive and moved it forward. "You've got a sexy, dominatrix, schoolteacher vibe going on there, girlfriend. Give me an hour and a private school uniform and I could turn you into one sexy brotherfucker."

Aubrey threw a stabby glance at Cherime. "Keep your eyes on the road and get us home, please."

Cherime shrugged as she steered the van down the quickly disappearing trail that led from the glamping site to a rough gravelled road. They were a couple of hours out of Darkness Falls on a good day, and as the wind and snow picked up, visibility dropped and so did Cherime's speed.

It took her almost 30 minutes to navigate the short trail, then once they were on gravel, she crawled along, the snow slick under the tires of the bus, the road no longer visible. The wind was knocking the bus around and Cherime was sure that any minute she was going to crash into a tree or drive off a cliff. Either way, she figured she was about five minutes away from killing them all.

She threw a quick glance at Aubrey, who was white-knuckling the tops of her thighs, her face pale, her lips pressed together.

Aubrey caught her looking. "We're all gonna die," she muttered.

Cherime nodded. "Yeah, I think so too."

Aubrey seemed disappointed in Cherime's response and her forehead creased into wrinkles she was going to regret by the time she was 40. "Do you know where we're at?"

Cherime wasn't sure they were still on the road. "Somewhere between *Schitt's Creek* and *Fucked up Avenue*."

Aubrey opened her cell phone and tapped on it. "No bars. We can't even call for help."

"No one could come to our rescue right now anyway. We're on our own, Little A."

The ominous words settled between them and it was as quiet as an empty library in the van. The girls in the back were huddled together, fingers clinging to armrests and blankets. Their feet simultaneously braked whenever Cherime did.

After about the tenth time Cherime almost lost control on the slick snow, Aubrey leaned in and quietly said, "We've been driving almost two hours. We're going to run out of gas before we get anywhere. And if that happens, we're toast."

"More like freezer burnt," Cherime replied, but

Aubrey was right. "Even if we did have the proper winter gear, it wouldn't be enough to keep us alive in these temperatures." Cherime jerked the steering wheel, barely avoiding a tree. "We could stop, and I could shift. Go for help."

Aubrey shook her head. "And leave us alone? No way. That might give the girls the idea that it's okay to walk out of here." She glanced towards the windshield. "Like you said, no one can come out and help us anyway."

Shut down and rightly so, but annoyance trickled through Cherime anyway. "Okay, then what? I don't hear you coming up with any solutions."

"What's that?" Aubrey pointed to a sign that was several yards down on what appeared to be a trail. "I can't see it in this snow. Slow down would you."

"If I go any fucking slower, the turtle will win the race again." Cherime pressed the brake until the bus rolled to a stop, then shoved the gear shift in park and got out. "Everyone, stay inside," she barked as she slammed the door and trudged down the trail to the sign. *Mountain Shifter Pack Community Hall. No Trespassing.*

The wind wickedly laughed in her ears as she took a deep draw of the cold air. She had a short list of things to avoid. Number One: Mountain shifter pack territory. Number Two: Ren Ketkah, the Mountain Shifter Pack's alpha. Number Three: Tequila.

She returned to the bus, slammed the door as she climbed behind the steering wheel, shoved the bus in reverse until it was at the entrance to the trail then shifted into Drive and made a right turn onto it.

"What does it say?" Aubrey squinted at the barely visible sign as they passed it.

Cherime grimaced, momentarily forgetting Vogue's beauty advice on frown-lines. "No trespassing."

It took another 30 minutes of crawling forward on the *maybe-it's-still-a-trail* trail while the girls chattered too loudly, excited about their possible survival. Cherime bit her tongue to stop herself from screaming at them and Aubrey was as stiff as an ice sculpture, except for her lips, which were wordlessly moving.

The van ran into the gate – literally, because Cherime didn't see it in time to stop – and everyone cheered as she let a little tension go. She pried her fingers from the steering wheel, pulled them into fists, then stretched them out again. After doing this a few times, she shoved the bus into reverse and backed up several feet.

Aubrey knitted her brows. "Want me to open the gate?"

"No," Cherime growled as she gritted her teeth and pressed the gas. The tires spun briefly, then the vehicle surged forward, splintering the wooden gate as it crashed through. It careened into what may have been a parking lot. As it neared the building, Cherime hit the brakes hard and flipped the steering wheel to her left as the bus slid on the snow.

The community centre loomed close as the bus skated forward, but Cherime spun the wheel again and slammed the brakes, coming to a full stop next to the door of the community centre.

The screaming stopped, there was a beat of silence, and the cheering started.

"Your chariot has arrived!" Cherime whooped, adrenaline coursing through her body, her heart beating too fast and her wolf doing a Snoopy jig. "Let's get this bitch unloaded. This glamping trip is back on track!"

The girls piled out of the bus, chattering and laughing, their near-death experience already forgotten. A shaky

Aubrey turned to Cherime, her pale face now the colour of ash. “What if the Mountain pack finds us trespassing?”

Cherime shrugged, more confidence in her voice than she felt. “If that happens, I’ll handle it. Besides, a storm like this? No wolf in his right mind would be out running today.”

CHAPTER TWO

Ren loved the snow, and these late spring storms were his version of paradise. His wolf was like a puppy, playing in the white stuff as the wind howled around him. A big-ass, black moody mother-fucker of a puppy, but nonetheless, it was jumping around like it was on crack.

It plowed through the snow, oblivious to Ren's silly internal monologue, racing around trees, over rocks, loping through streams. In wolf form, he was impervious to the cold, and the blinding snow was a mere inconvenience. Sure, his senses were blunted, but then so were the senses of potential attackers, and he was likely the only predator fucked up enough to be out in this weather. When storms got bad, animals dug themselves in. Not Ren, but he wasn't an animal, he was a shifter, considered a human, but with unique genetic makeup.

His wolf didn't give a shit who thought what of him. It wanted to sprint, run madly, but his piece of the mountain didn't have much room to do that, because his cabin was deeply ensconced in the boreal forest that surrounded his territory. Rocks, trees, and deadfall offered a difficult obstacle course that, on a good day, he enjoyed sprinting through, but not on a day like this when the snow covered all sorts of hazards that could trip him up and snap a leg.

To unleash his need for speed, he made his way to a secondary road that connected to the trail that led to his cabin. He could race flat out on the road without fear of slamming into a tree or running off a cliff.

It was his freedom: being in wolf form, being in the snow, hearing the howling of the wind as it whipped around him. Alone, solitary, merging with nature without all the foolish trappings of the human world.

He was alpha to his small pack of Mountain shifters, and he never denied his heritage. He was born alpha, would be alpha to the day he died. When that blessing came, he would return to where he came from, back to the arms of his real mother, not the bitch who abandoned him to fend for himself as a pup.

His pack? They were Mountain for a reason. Like him, his shifters craved solitude and nature. Their homes were built among the trees, separated by several kilometres, and they generally saw each other out of necessity rather than by design. They lived off this land, kept their distance from the township of Darkness Falls, and enjoyed their blessings. They were hunters, traders, mountain dwellers.

Darkness Falls offered them sanctuary, safety, and respect, which is why the pack had claimed territory where it did long before he came along and took over. The three other shifter packs in the area mostly left the Mountain shifters to themselves, and his pack preferred the fringe over getting too involved in shifter politics.

He stopped mid-stride and let loose a long joyful howl, then waited for an answering one. Nothing. Of course not. His beta, Oz, might have been out and about, but he was on a sabbatical after his fucking human mate pissed off the wrong shifter and got her throat torn out. Ren felt a moment of guilt over his shitty attitude towards the now-dead trouble-maker, but couldn't sustain it. Not in this incredible weather.

He launched himself forward, slamming through the snow like an out-of-control plow, then, as he turned the corner towards the pack's community centre, he stopped in his tracks. What the fuck? Hard to see in the blowing snow, but with his shifter eyes, he could make out a filmy grey cloud coming from the smokestack. He glanced around him, then sniffed the air for scents and strained his ears for sounds. Nothing because mother nature was in control. At least for the moment.

He slipped into the trees and padded forward, keeping an ear and his nose on his surroundings as his eyes held steady in the direction he was going. Maybe it was one of his pack members, stranded in the storm. Most likely Flint and his family, the twin boys still too young to shift.

He couldn't think of a reason anyone else would be on his territory. The pack rarely had visitors and the community hall was practically the end of the decent road. Anyone coming through the mountains this way had a death wish, the deep-rutted dirt road nothing but a trail, easy to get stuck or drive off the side of the mountain. Easy to get stopped or crushed by a rockfall or avalanche.

As he reached the edge of the trees, he crouched and peered through the snow. When the gusts dropped, he could make out a vehicle. By the glimpses he caught, it appeared to be a handi-dart bus, of all things. What the fuck would a handi-dart bus be doing on his mountain? Maybe stolen, because his brain couldn't conjure a scenario where old people with walkers and wheelchairs would be driving up the mountain for fresh air.

If it were thieves, then he would need to be cautious.

He wasn't afraid of humans – check that – he wasn't afraid of anything. Well… not entirely true. He was highly uncomfortable around cats, the fucking little fearless ones that meowed at him when he was in town. He hated those fuckers.

Cats aside, he was a predator, and he wanted to assess the situation before he stormed the castle. They could be shifters, not humans, and while that wouldn't stop him from ripping off their limbs, he'd prefer not to add another welt to the fading scars that littered his body.

He crept forward, watching for lookouts, but was pretty sure if there were any, they'd be too frozen to move. *Who the fuck steals a handi-dart bus, anyway?* As he reached the door of the hall, he pawed his muzzle and shook his body, letting loose chunks of snow that had formed on his fur. When he was satisfied, he shifted and stretched out, all 6'6" of him.

He loved his human form almost as much as his wolf form. Mother Nature knew he'd have to be big and strong to survive alone in this world, and so she gave him what he needed. Strength, power, and an arrogance to match. Unlike many shifters, who felt constrained by their human forms, he felt formidable and sometimes even invincible.

Still, in human form, with no fucking clothes, even as a shifter, he was freezing his ass off. He carefully pushed the unlocked door open, then silently shut it behind him. It pissed him off that the door hadn't been kicked in – meant one of his pack had left it unlocked.

Noise assailed him first, voices so high-pitched his wolf thought it was being tortured. Then the gag-inducing scents, which almost brought him to his knees. Manufactured shit, perfumes and other goop almost concealing the body odors. Some shifters, most humans, all female.

But one scent stood out. One that woke up his brain,

perked up his wolf and made other body parts stand at attention. Cherime Montana was on his territory.

"Fuck," he whispered under his breath as an eight-year-old memory assailed him. This girl was not going to be happy to see him.

So be it. He hadn't asked her to drive a handi-dart bus and a bunch of girls onto his territory. Nope, she invited herself, so she would have to live with the consequences.

He strode into the hall and surveyed the scene before him. Females, all of them, dressed and made-up like hookers right down to the fucking stilettos on their feet. There were eleven in total, but Cherime was a queen among her subjects. Taller than all the girls, wearing a white flowy dress that dropped to mid-thigh, hair regally piled on top of her head in what appeared to be a beehive, or something poofy like that.

Was her hair purple? Jesus fucking Christ, why'd she go do that to her gorgeous mane?

"What the fucking hell!" he roared. The talking abruptly stopped, and a couple of the girls shrieked when they saw him. Most of them covered their eyes but peeked through their fingers to get a good look. He didn't deny that his size and nakedness would make them curious, but the sight of his dick alone would probably ruin them for all other men. A human woman Cherime's age stood frozen, her jaw hanging as she stared at him.

And Cherime. She tilted her head and studied him, her eyes sliding over him slowly, the smile she'd had on her face when he stepped in slowly dying.

CHAPTER THREE

"What the fucking hell!" The deep voice of the male split the noise in the hall like a swinging axe. The conversation crashed and burned as all eyes turned towards the massive naked shifter who had entered the hall like a raging bull.

Hot fucking damn! Those were Cherime's first thoughts as she saw Ren, the sexy Mountain alpha standing in all his naked glory before her glamping group, arms crossed over his chest, legs splayed wide, the impossible-not-to-notice goods swinging low between his thighs. She hadn't exactly forgotten how marvelous his body was – what woman could? She'd expected more grey hair, some saggy muscles, maybe erectile dysfunction. But nope, eight years hadn't changed a damn thing. In fact, they made him hotter, if that was possible

Yeah, he was the shifter she remembered. His glorious height, his chiselled muscles from all the hard work he never seemed to stop doing. His beard, long and untidy, reached down to his chest, his long hair was an uncombed, badly cut mess falling past his shoulders. His sledgehammer hands, his muscular arms and his fucking cock, huge like the rest of him, semi-saluting her now. His dark gaze held hers, his generous lips puckered into a frown.

Was he happy to see her? Cherime couldn't tell by his face so she glanced at his cock again. It seemed to be responding, but there were 11 of them. Maybe he was still interested in the nubile young things.

She glanced at Aubrey, who stood motionless, her mouth gaping, her eyes glued to his Adonis belt's landing point. All the girls were now openly staring, except Bella, whose angry glare was pinned to an oblivious Trixie. Cherime shook her head. She'd never understand girls who didn't like cock, especially the one belonging to Ren.

She decided the best way to deal with this Mountain shifter was to match his belligerence. "What are you doing here?" As she stepped past the girls who were in her path, he took a few steps towards her.

It was always like that when they were in the same room. Magnets drawn to each other like they were opposite poles of the earth. That didn't mean it was a good thing. "It's my fucking hall, Wolverine. Start talking."

Wolverine. Fuck. His nickname for her eight years ago. Bastard, bringing it up like it was yesterday. "We were on a grad glamping trip. The storm hit and we couldn't get down the mountain, so we sought refuge in your dusty, broken-down barn."

He eyed the other shifter girl. "No fucking way are you and that puppy staying on my territory." He turned to Aubrey. "And you." He took a threatening step and Cherime moved her body to block him from getting close to the teacher. He was a full head taller than Cherime, so he pretty much looked right over her and skewered Aubrey with his glare. "I don't want any fucking relative of Adrienne's anywhere near my pack."

Aubrey managed a gasp, but that was all.

Cherime, however, wasn't going to be intimated by Mr. Meany. In fact, he deserved an ass-kicking for being so insensitive and she was just the woman to do it. She raised her hand and slapped his face. "Try to at least pretend you have a human side, you bastard," she seethed as Ren caught her wrist in his hard grip. "Aubrey's still grieving her loss and besides that, she's no Adrienne."

Ren sneered at Cherime. "Yeah. This one doesn't seem to have her legs permanently pried apart."

Aubrey gasped again. The woman needed to work on her comebacks. Cherime decided to model correct shifter behaviour – she raised her other hand and slapped Ren again. He grabbed that wrist and gave her a little shake. "Stop hitting me."

"Then quit being a prick." She jerked from his grasp and put some space between them. Her body was starting to want things that had taken her years to stop yearning for. Her wolf too – no bloody common sense, dismissing everything that happened back then.

She had no need to worry. Ren's next words were a cold shower, thank the earth. "You all have five minutes to pack your gear and get the hell out!"

He was so snarly and aggressive that the girls and Aubrey scattered, grabbing the glamping supplies and food and throwing it haphazardly into a box. Apparently, they preferred death by freezing or car-crash mangling over Ren's wrath. Cherime had no such wish.

"Stop!" she bellowed. "This bully is not going to force us to go back out in the weather."

Everyone froze, looking uncertainly at Cherime.

"I think we should leave, Cherime," Aubrey said in a whispered voice only a shifter could hear.

Jesus, teach had no sense of solidarity. "We're not going anywhere!"

"To hell you aren't!" Ren towered over Cherime, his face dangerously close to hers. "You can't fucking stay here!"

He was so frustrating. "Why? Why can't we stay?" She lowered her voice as she clutched at his arm. The upper arm. The one with the perfect bicep that both hands couldn't even begin to circle. "You send us out there in that storm, it's a death sentence. No way we'll make it down the mountain in this weather."

Ren stretched his head from side to side, his neck cracking. "What are you doing up the mountain in the first place? On my territory?" He dropped his voice as well so that they couldn't be overheard, even by the nosy female shifter who was shuffling around behind them.

Cherime shook her head instead of rolling her eyes. Play passive, girl. Big, bad wolf likes to have his dick sucked. "Not on your territory. We were glamping at my lookout point. You know, the one where you reverted to a caveman the first time you saw me."

He narrowed his eyes and flared his nostrils. Cherime knew exactly what he was doing – he was scenting her, taking her in, stroking his memories. "The one where we fucked," he said.

She blinked. "It was more than fucking!" Oops, too loud. It was typical of the asshole to pretend that he hadn't shattered Cherime's heart. He did that every single fucking time they crossed paths, which wasn't all the often. He knew what he'd done to her: took her virginity, toyed with her, then abandoned her.

"Still have the emotional maturity of a peanut, hey? I figured you'd have outgrown the drama and stopped playing the broken-hearted little girl. It might have worked for you back then, but now, baby, you've been far too busy to pretend I mattered to you."

"You don't know anything about me and what I do or don't do!" Cherime raised her voice again, ignoring the fact that their argument just went public. "So fuck you!"

"Seriously? That's how you're going to play this? You got a bus full of girls and you've decided a shitty attitude is going to win me over?"

She took a pull of air to settle herself, knowing Ren was right. Fighting with the bastard wasn't going to get her what she needed. "I'm sorry," she said in a soft voice, sliding her hand over the chiselled peaks and valleys of his chest. "Why don't we take this into your office?" She circled a nipple and moved closer so that her leg was brushing his cock. Based on the steel rod pressing against her, he was liking what she was doing. "Got your attention, do I?"

Ren reached down and adjusted himself, then stroked upward on his cock like they were the only two in the room. "What are you offering, Wolverine? A fuck in exchange for me sheltering you?"

"Why not?" Cherime retorted in a moment of temporary insanity. Every time she saw Ren, she walked away from him emotionally wrecked. "After all, it's just fucking."

"Oh my god!" Aubrey's shrill voice invaded Cherime's stupor. "It's bad enough he's naked, Cherime. But come on, you have an audience." She placed her hands on her hips as she huffed out an angry breath. "And an impressionable one at that. In what world is offering sex in exchange for what we need a good method of negotiation?"

Cherime rolled her eyes at Aubrey. "Pretty much every world. Don't be such a prude."

Ren grabbed Cherime by the upper arms and gave her

a shake. "Don't you fuck around with me. It might work on all the other men in your stud barn, but I'm not interested in a fuck and run."

"Double standard, asshole? You can fuck around whenever you feel like it, but I can't?" Cherime shoved hard against his chest with the flat of her hands. When that didn't move him, she slammed her stiletto heel into his foot.

"Sonofabitch!" he roared, but instead of retreating, he kicked her feet out from under her.

She landed solidly on her ass, the pain jolting her tailbone. "Oh my god, what's wrong with you?" she shrieked as she scrambled upright.

"With me? What the fuck's wrong with you?" Ren was holding up his foot and peering at the bruise that was quickly forming. Being naked in that pose was maybe not the best idea.

"What the fuck's wrong with both of you!" Aubrey's schoolmarm voice slammed through the room. The puny human stood a few feet from them, hands balled into fists. The scowl on her face said everything—she was at the end of her rope. "You." She pointed at Ren. "You're not going to turn us out in this storm. That would be murder, plain and simple, and while you may be king of your castle, the humans and the other shifter packs won't take kindly to that kind of behaviour."

"Shit," Cherime muttered as Ren took two steps towards Aubrey and loomed over her. The room and all the girls in it held their breath. Cherime too. And her wolf.

Aubrey stretched her neck back, her bravado fading as she unsuccessfully tried to hold Ren's fiery glare.

Ren's voice held a deadly edge. "Fucking little human female, thinking I give a shit about your pretty human rules. That's the problem with both you and your sister –

thinking you're smarter than me because I'm a Mountain shifter. Wonder what else the two of you have in common?"

Cherime scrunched her face as tears formed in Aubrey's eyes. *No, no, no. Never let them see you cry.* "Leave her alone, Ren." She stepped between them. "Aubrey and I are responsible for the safety of these girls, so it's only right that we look out for them anyway we can."

He twisted his head towards Cherime. "Negotiate."

"What?" Cherime and Aubrey gasped at the same time.

"You heard me. I want something in return for letting you stay, and a quick fuck in one of the closets isn't going to cut it."

"We could give you a makeover!" One of the girls playfully suggested.

"Good idea!" and "Yes!" and "He could use one!" rang out along with giggles. The girls were no longer taking Ren seriously, which was not really the direction anyone should go with Ren.

Ren didn't move, his deadly stare aimed at Cherime. "They stay, you come home with me."

Cherime's jaw dropped. "Go home with you? Like to your cabin?"

"Yeah." He turned his head towards one of the windows, the pane frozen over. "This shit's going to last a few days. You warm my bed until it's melted, the rest can stay here."

Cherime took a step back, bumping into Aubrey, who took a step back. They did this two more times, then Cherime shook her head. "No, nope. Not going to happen. You want a bed warmer, take Aubrey."

Aubrey gasped. "I'm not a sheep you can throw to the wolf."

Cherime rolled her eyes, noting that Aubrey could dish it out pretty good when her hackles were up. "Clever. How long have you been holding on to that one?"

"You, Wolverine," Ren interrupted. "You and me. Either that or all of you get out."

Cherime raised her face to the ceiling as if the exposed beams might have the answers she needed. "If I come back with you, there's no sharing a bed. I'll stay. We can talk, I'll even cook for you, but hands off my body. You had your chance and you blew it."

Ren grinned. "If my recollection is right, you were the one doing the blowing."

Asshole, dickhead, sonofabitch alpha bastard. "I really hate you."

His smile dropped, but it wasn't remorse in the depth of his eyes. It was anger. "Don't matter how you feel about me, bear bait, as long as you come home with me. When the storm passes, you can come back and return these squatters back to Darkness Falls."

Aubrey interjected herself. "You're not going to coerce her into sleeping with you."

"Stay out of this, Aubrey," Cherime muttered. "I can handle this oversized gorilla."

Aubrey shook her head. "No. I can't in good conscience let you leave with this lunatic."

The lunatic in question growled. "She comes with me, or you all go now."

Aubrey narrowed her eyes. "And if we refuse to leave? What're you going to do about it?"

Ren threw back his head and bellowed a laugh. "Jesus fucking Christ, you've not been around shifters much, have you, mini-mouse? What I'll do is pick you up two by two, carry you outside, and dump your asses in the snow."

Aubrey crossed her arms over her chest, her eyes

holding a hint of uncertainty, but she was still not willing to back down. "You can't take on all of us at once."

"Stop, Aubrey," Cherime muttered. "He *can* take us all on at once." She didn't think Ren would do his worst, which was shift and slaughter them, taking out the female shifters first, then destroying the humans. The problem is she didn't know Ren well enough to know what his black heart was capable of.

"I don't believe it," Aubrey exclaimed.

"Want me to show you?" Ren wasn't giving an inch.

Cherime decided to end the impasse. "I'm going with Ren," she said quickly.

"No!" Aubrey squeaked.

"Don't worry, mini-mouse." Yeah, that was a good nickname for the teacher. "Ren and I have a history. I can manage him for a couple of days."

Ren smirked liked she'd made a joke. "Oh baby, that's precious. Let's go."

Cherime stared around. "How? You came as your wolf."

Ren stared at her. "Nothing gets by you. Did you forget how to shift?"

Cherime shook her head. "But I'll have no clothes or makeup."

"Won't really need clothes. If I recall, you weren't exactly shy back then. Not now either, from what I hear."

Cherime narrowed her eyes at the massive shifter. "You're ticked off because I didn't wait for you to change your mind all these years?"

Aubrey cleared her throat. "Okay, Cherime. Go with him but come back when the storm ends so we can get out of here."

Pissed at Ren, Cherime kicked the puppy instead. "I wasn't asking you for permission!"

Aubrey ignored Cherime as she turned to Ren, her voice taking on that shrill school-marmish tone that only dogs could hear. "And you, Mr. Ren. You keep your hands to yourself unless the lady invites you to touch her."

Ren narrowed his eyes as he glanced the around the room. "Lady? What lady?"

Fuck you! Cherime hauled off and slapped him again.

CHAPTER FOUR

Of all the community halls in all the world, Cherime had to walk into Ren's. Eight fucking years and he'd managed to more or less avoid her, other than a couple of accidental meetings. But now, sharing the same space with her brought the past flooding back. A past that never should have happened, but shit, she looked damn fine all dolled up like she was going to a New Year's Eve bash.

Over the years, they'd kept their distance like they had restraining orders against each other. She was a handful then and it appeared she hadn't changed a bit. He didn't mind a strong woman, but Cherime was like a wild horse. He knew the only way he could tame the girl was to break her, and something like that would ruin her spirit.

He stole a glance behind him at the snow-white wolf following him through the blizzard. How was it possible that this female shifter was so perfect? She embodied an alpha's mate, her human side on the sharp edge of primacy and her wolf, glorious and proud.

She caught him looking and snarled, baring her teeth. It took him back to the first time he'd laid eyes on her.

It was late June, same time of year as now, but the weather was hot that day, the sky cloudless. He had been on a solo run and he'd strayed off territory to the hard-to-find overlook that he thought no one knew about. Her scent attracted him first – a heady combination of heather, crocuses, and the lightest aroma of salt underscoring it all. He was drawn to it like a bear to a beehive.

When he'd come out of the trees and seen her, he was hooked. She was sitting on a boulder, her long tanned legs stretching out in front, arms behind her, elbows locked so she was leaning backwards, lush breasts pointing towards the sun. Her head was tilted back, her face skyward, eyes closed. A sleek cloud of long ebony hair fell in soft curls almost to her ass.

Two seconds was all he had before she knew he was there. With the grace of a panther, she'd bounced to her feet and turned in his direction. She was so stunning his wolf almost jumped her. Everything about her was firm and ripe, like a fresh peach waiting for him to come along and pluck her. Young though, with the face of an angel despite the scowl.

He was a bastard of a wolf: big, black, ugly as sin and proud of it. Covered in scars from run-ins with other shifters, two bears, and a pack of wolves, and she hadn't so much as flinched as she inspected him. Instead, she scented the air and the scowl gave way to curiosity and something more, something heated.

"Shift!" she commanded.

He didn't. Instead, he stalked towards her, teeth bared, a low growl in his throat. He'd been a pike caught in a gill net, too stunned to try to escape. But he was also an alpha and females didn't command him.

When she realized he wasn't going to do her bidding, she had ripped her tank off, no fucking bra, then dropped her shorts and panties. "Who the fuck are you?" she panted, then shifted and leapt at him, landing on his back and biting down. He'd been caught off guard. Most male shifters didn't have the balls to take him on, and this sultry white wolf had him by the scruff of his neck and was trying to shake him.

Ren sighed as his memories scattered. Cherime had moved up so she was parallel to him, defying the pack order, even if she wasn't part of his pack. Then she sped up and raced past him. He sprang, landing on her and slamming her to the ground.

She was a squirmer, wiry and fast, but he had the advantage of expecting her aggression this time, and rolled them so she was belly up and he was pinning her with his paws around her neck. By instinct, he locked his jaw on her throat and bit gently. *Turtle, you fucking princess, before you get hurt.* Silly, pointless thought. She hadn't turtled back then either. Instead, she'd battled him until they were both exhausted. He didn't want that now, not out in the storm, but he couldn't let her think she had the upper hand.

She struggled, barked aggressively, scratched at him with her claws, gouging him, heating his wolf. So fucking reckless. He bit harder until he broke her skin, until he was suffocating her. She shifted under him and he lost his grip.

"You fucking bastard!" she spat as she brought her hand to her neck, then looked at the blood on her fingers. "You broke my skin."

He shifted too, his body on hers, pressing her into the snow. In this temperature, they could only stay in human form for a few moments or they'd freeze off their bits and pieces. Ren was attached to his and didn't want to lose any of them. He had to make this fast. "What the fuck is wrong with you! You think my wolf is going to roll over and play dead to a challenge. You know better than that!"

"Fuck you!" She shoved at his chest, tried to knee him in the balls, tried to scratch his face.

He grabbed her wrists and yanked them over head, then sat up and straddled her. His dick was the hardest it had been in eight years. It wanted her; he wanted her. That was clear as it laid out on her belly pointing its way to her mouth. All he had to do was shuffle forward a few inches and he could shove it between her tits and thrust. Problem was he'd have to let go of her hands so he could squeeze those firm ripe mounds together, and that might lead to his dick getting broken.

"Shift!" he commanded, like she had eight years ago. "And get your ass behind me so we can get the fuck out of this storm."

She shifted suddenly, then twisted and scrambled out from under him and raced off into the thick veil of snow, her white coat blending and disappearing.

Ren stood, his chest heaving from his lust. "You get your ass to my cabin, Wolverine," he bellowed into the storm. "If you're not there when I arrive, I'll sacrifice your fucking glampers to the devil!"

He shifted and followed her scent. Yes, it was sheeting snow, the cold and wind fucking with his nose, but this was Cherime and he always knew when she was nearby. She'd heard him yelling at her. She was headed to his cabin.

CHAPTER FIVE

Cherime padded up to Ren's cabin. Same old cabin as it was eight years ago except more rundown. Back then, she was excited to be here. Back then she was young, naïve, in love. The first time she saw Ren, her first glimpse of him in his wolf form stole her breath. Her back had been to him, the breeze blowing against her, so she wasn't aware of his approach until he was almost on her.

Her heart almost tore out of her chest as the biggest wolf she'd ever seen hovered behind her. He was breathtaking, black fur, scarred and hardened. His liquid eyes were pools of tar, so deep that if she fell into them, she'd never escape. His scent, overwhelmingly masculine and she wanted… no… needed to see his human from.

"Shift!" she had demanded as she jumped up from her rock. The wolf ignored her. Of course, it did. She was a female commanding a male shifter and this shifter, she knew without being told, was alpha. He stalked closer to her and she shifted because she had no choice. In human form, she was far too vulnerable.

She couldn't let him know how cornered she felt, or he

would have taken that as compliance and asserted his dominance. It was better to come out swinging, which is what she did. She launched on top of him, grabbing the nape of his neck as she catapulted over him.

They'd struggled, an aggressive prelude to what was sure to be a passionate mating. After he pinned her, made her submit, he headed into the trees, expecting her to follow. She had, because she was 18, already in love, knew this was her man, her wolf, her mate. Back then, she had stars in her eyes, like every other teenager on the planet.

But Ren wasn't gentle, romantic, or loving. His behaviour had helped her realize that romance was bullshit and male shifters were no different than human men when it came to relationships. She'd thought they were a pair-bond, but what did she know at her age? Sure, he'd made her heart pitter-patter, her legs go weak, her body lustful, but so what? How could he be her fated mate and treat her so badly?

Cherime shivered as she shifted, then let herself into Ren's unlocked cabin, barely stepping past the threshold before she froze. Clearly a man lived here. Dirty dishes filled the sink and were strewn across the counter, the floor hadn't seen a broom in weeks, and winter gear was scattered everywhere.

Mud boots lay abandoned in the middle of the single room that housed the kitchen, dining area and living room, and a deer pelt stretched out on a drying rack, pushed up against the kitchen counter next to a loaf of moldy bread, two rotting tomatoes and an apple with a bite taken from it. And fuck if the air didn't smell like Ren, but not in a good way.

She felt Ren's heat on her back as she tried not to gag and stumbled forward when he gave her a gentle push. As he closed the door behind him, he grabbed her waist, turning her so she was shoved up against the door. His hard face twisted into a scowl as his hands slid from her waist upwards to her breasts, which he groped from the bottom, squeezing like he was testing peaches.

On the bright side, he hadn't tackled her outside in the storm. Nope, he was kind enough to wait until they got inside his stinky cabin. She wrinkled her nose and pushed at his chest, trying to ignore the hard peaks and valleys of his muscles. "Hands off the goods! I said I'd come back with you. I didn't say I'd fuck you."

He released her breasts and pressed his hands against the door, either side of her head. "That was implied."

She dropped her body and slid under his arm, striding deeper into the dump. "You really gotta work on your seduction technique. Feeling a girl up before you offer her a drink doesn't cut it in this day and age. And this cabin – no offence but the place should be condemned. It's disgusting." She brought her thumb and forefinger up to her face and dramatically plugged her nose.

He gazed around as if trying to see it through her eyes, then turned back to her, a frown deepening the ridges of his forehead. "Forget about the cabin. What the hell is wrong with you?"

"What are you talking about? Can't you smell this mess?"

Ren seemed to realize that he should at least make an effort to tidy up as he picked up his mud boots and chucked them out the door before slamming it on the gale of wind that tried to improve the living space. "I'm talking about the way you challenged my wolf out there. You know better than to take the lead on a pack run. One of these days you're gonna mess with the wrong shifter."

"That day already happened a long time ago." Painful memories swamped her, and she went on the attack. "That out there," she jabbed her finger at the door. "That wasn't a pack run because you and I aren't a pack. You're not my alpha! You're not my fucking mate! You made that clear enough."

She hated the emotion bubbling up in her. Ren was the only one who had the power to destroy her. Whenever she saw him in Darkness Falls, or even a glimpse of his truck, or a mention of his name; it would send her sideways, sometimes for days. Being in his presence, so close to him, she was going to splinter if she didn't find a way to deal with her need for him.

He closed the space between them, but this time didn't touch her. His cock though, was stretching toward her like a heat-seeking missile. "Pretty words that mean nothing. My wolf doesn't do logic – you're fucking lucky I have it well-trained." He jabbed a finger to her chest. "You better have a goddamn talk with your wolf and explain the lay of the land, because I only have so much patience. And my wolf? It has fucking none."

Cherime wanted to take a deep breath but thought the stink would knock her out. "I'm not afraid of you."

"You should be!" Ren stomped into the kitchen like an enraged bear and lit the wood burning stove, then added water and coffee to the percolator and set it on the burner.

"Right. I'm shaking in my..." She looked down at herself. "...my skin."

He twisted, fury on his face. "I don't want to break your spirit, but you're pushing me." He slammed past her into the bedroom.

Eight years ago, this man had led her back to this cabin. She was an 18-year-old girl; he was a 30-year-old man. He took her virginity, then broke her heart.

Now she was here again. Same cabin, same man, but not the same girl. She felt her wolf panting inside her, wanting this man, wanting what he could offer, what he refused to give her back then. But it was too late, wasn't it? Back then, she would have given up everything to be here with him. But now, staying here with this uncivilized giant, in a stinky cabin, off the grid, away from her friends, her pack, was a non-starter. She had a life now, any trace of the starry-eyed teenage girl in love gone, along with her innocence.

With Ren in the bedroom, the quiet of the cabin lulled Cherime for a few precious moments. No shrill teenage voices, no aggressive masculine growling; simply the crackle of wood, the howl of the wind and the hiss of the percolator.

She made the mistake of pulling the tainted air into her lungs, ruining her moment of peace.

When Ren returned, he was wearing a pair of faded, ripped jeans, button opened and unzipped, his semi playing peek-a-boo. She let the air out in whoosh and a cough. The man had no business being that sexy.

If he had any notion of the affect he had, he didn't show it. Instead, he tossed a faded grey T-shirt at her. "Cover yourself or I can't be held accountable for what I do next."

She deftly caught it and raised it to her nose. Clean, thank god, and sun-kissed, the residual scent of Ren in the fabric. She slipped it over her head, and it draped mid-thigh, swamping her like a badly-hung curtain. Cherime was tall and curvy, but she had nothing on Ren. No one did and that thought got her all worked up again. "Thanks," she mumbled.

"Coffee's ready," he grunted as he headed into the kitchen and fumbled around the dirty dishes to produce two coffee cups. He looked inside one, then turned it over and tapped the bottom of it.

Cherime watched in horror as something fell out. "What was that?"

Ren shrugged. "A dead earwig. Edible if you're hungry."

Oh my god, what was wrong with him? "Is my cup at least clean?"

Ren exaggerated his survey of the kitchen, a dark expression on his face. "I don't have clean dishes at the moment, and besides, Wolverine, you don't have a cup. I'm going to let you borrow one of mine."

Cherime gag-coughed. "Nope. I want a clean cup."

Ren looked up from pouring the coffee. "Then do the dishes."

"I'm not your fucking housekeeper!"

He shrugged as he brought a mug over to her and handed it off. "Then don't do the dishes."

He cleared the couch of books, towels, and a pair of stinky socks with a swipe of his hands, then dropped himself onto a cushion, patting the other. "Sit, baby. Let's talk."

What to do? If she sat, it would appear as though she was obeying him. On the other hand, if she stood there, she'd look like a fool. But sitting next to him, she'd forget to be mad. But there was no where else to sit, except on a lone kitchen chair that was covered in all sorts of shit. Maybe even literally.

She momentarily forgot that the cup in her hand was once the death pit for an earwig and took a sip of the coffee. It was no latte, but it wasn't too bad. Chewy though. Coffee grains and… oh, ugh. "I can't drink this." She carried the cup to the kitchen and set it on the counter.

He sighed. "If I'd known I was having royalty over, I would've had the servants clean."

"Next time, make it so." Cherime took a few tentative steps into the barely liveable living room and sat on the edge of the cushion next to Ren, keeping her posture stiff, her hands folded in her lap so her wolf understood there would be no jumping of the bones. "What do you want to talk about?"

He stared into his cup, then took a gulp of the coffee. "Remember when we met?"

What a stupid question. "Vaguely."

He snorted. "You were so fucking young. If we'd stayed together, I would've ruined you."

Cherime hated the direction the conversation was headed. She didn't want a stroll down memory lane. She wanted a decent cup of coffee in a clean cup. "We'll never know, will we?" Was that bitterness in her tone? Probably. She should be over him by now, but he had been… or was… probably still was… her mate.

"I thought about you a lot over the years, Wolverine. Of how we ended things. There's no else like you in the world, you know that right?"

What was with the *we* word? "*You* ended things. It was your choice." Cherime turned her face from him so she could get away from whatever emotional bullshit he was dipping his toe into. She had girlfriends when she needed to have intimate discussions. She didn't need this blustering fool to talk about the feels with her. "Are you on some sort of 12-step program?"

Ren gritted his teeth as a muscle near his jaw ticked. She was pissing him off, which was a good thing. Better brawling then getting mushy. That's how girls got hurt. "What I'm saying here," his tone was edged with frustration, "is that maybe we should talk about the whole mating thing again."

Blood roared in Cherime's ears as she jerked to her

feet. Yeah, the brawl was about to start. "Are you fucking kidding me? Mate with you?" She kicked out at the coffee table and it tipped over; dishes, books, a frog buddha crashed to the floor.

Ren stood too, tugging at his beard as he glared. "I said talk!"

"We talked, you asshole!" Shit, screaming already. This didn't bode well for the future of their disagreeable little love nest. "Eight years ago. Actually, we didn't talk. You talked." She paced away, tugging at her hair and letting the pain in her scalp settle her. "You told me I was good for a fuck, but I needed to go back to my pack." She twisted back to face him, pinning him with a glare. "Remember that?"

Ren ran a hand over his mouth and down his beard. "Because two days in and you were already planning the mating, the babies. You had fucking stars in your eyes thinking we were in love. Look at me." The reach of his arms as he swung them widely reminded her of his power. "I'm nobody's happy ever after."

Cherime refocused on his beard so she could pull a couple of coherent thoughts together. "I *was* in love with you, Ren. I was young, but not fucking stupid. I knew what I was getting into."

"No, you didn't!" His bellow echoed off the walls of the cabin and made Cherime flinch. "Being fated mates doesn't mean we're a good match. Just means we'd have strong offspring."

"I know what it means! I don't need a fucking mountain man telling me shit!" Cherime shouted back. "You were going to be my one and only until you kicked me to the curb. So fuck you, Ren. You had your chance."

Something she said pissed him off. She could see it in

the set to his face, the fury in his tone. "How many others, baby? Since us. How many men?"

"None of your fucking business, *baby*." She couldn't believe he was asking her that question. "*We* are not a thing, and even if we were, it's still none of your fucking business."

For a solid wall of rock, he was swift and graceful on his feet, invading her space as he cupped the sides of her head and walked her backwards until she was against a wall. From there, he tested the strength of his fingers on her neck, squeezing with enough pressure to show Cherime his restraint. With his other hand, he grabbed a fist full of hair and forced her head back, so her face was pointed to the ceiling, with him looming over her.

"We are whatever I say we are!" Bullshit alpha words but Cherime's response was cut off as he dropped his mouth to the base of her throat, to one of the puncture marks he'd put there earlier, and sucked at it, lapping with his tongue, pulling the flesh between his teeth. Then he brought his lips to her ear, his hot breath causing chills through her body. "I want you. I've always wanted you. Now that I've got you back, I might not let you go."

Words she had wanted to hear from him for so long. Words that kept her awake at night, invaded her dreams, kept her from moving on to her own happy ever after. Ren coming back to her, telling her he was wrong. That she was it for him. Years she waited, and now… finally… except… he needed to suffer. She shoved at his chest. "You're too late. I'm not interested."

He dropped his hands and lurched back, like her words were bullets. "Too good for me now?"

She stared around the cabin, wrinkling her nose as she inhaled the moldering scent. "Yes."

CHAPTER SIX

This was not how he'd planned it. None of it. He'd constantly thought of Cherime over the years. An ache that wouldn't go away no matter how much he self-medicated with other women. He liked his peace, his place in the mountains, his pack, but he wanted a woman to share it with and not just any woman. He wanted Cherime.

Eight years ago, he wasn't looking for companionship when he'd found Cherime, but after those few days with her, everything changed. He tried to forget her, sought company elsewhere, but it seemed no woman measured up to his Wolverine. Over time, he came to terms with the biggest mistake of his life, forcing Cherime to leave. That solidified the decision that was always surfacing; he would either spend his life with Cherime, or he would spend it alone.

Seeing her in the community centre, standing tall and proud, her long legs, her shapely ass, reminded him of what he was missing. And now, having her in his home, her intoxicating scent tying him up in knots, her beauty giving him tunnel vision. It made every moment they'd been together come crashing back. He wanted her, needed her with desperation, and the years had only made his longing for her grow stronger.

But she was a tougher version of the girl he'd fucked eight years ago. A woman now, a warrior. Not someone he could approach in public without it becoming a fierce battle, so he never did. Instead, he waited patiently for his opportunity, or at least that's what he told himself. Deep inside of him, he thought maybe the chance for them had truly passed.

Then fate forced his hand, led him to her, and now he finally had his second chance, but he was blowing it because he was a fucking alpha male, too proud and masculine to grovel. His wolf was no help, pacing inside him, reminding him he was the king of the mountain, that he took what he wanted. Even Cherime couldn't say no – except she had.

First fucking impressions were down the toilet. His cabin was a disaster. No one came over except Oz's mother, Tess, and sometimes Felan, the daughter. They treated him like family, especially Tess, who bustled around and cleaned up when she visited. Clearly, she hadn't dropped by for a while.

Tess preferred he come to her home, where she could feed and fuss over him. He was fine with that. It meant he could do what he liked to do without having to worry about doing the shit he wasn't interested in. Like washing the fucking dishes. But the purple-haired princess wasn't having it.

And then there was her pissiness. How could someone stay mad for eight years? Any grudges he had, he solved quickly by removing them from the face of the earth. That way he didn't have to hold on to them. Mind you, if

Cherime had tried to remove him, she would've gotten seriously hurt. "If the cabin's the problem, that's easy to fix. I can clean, expand, get a freshwater set-up so you don't have to haul water from the stream."

Cherime shot him a puzzled look and he wondered what he said wrong this time. By the deadness of her eyes, it appeared she was gearing up to tell him. "The problem with us isn't fixable. You used me, treated me like shit and tossed me aside." She shrugged like it was nothing to her anymore as she wandered into the kitchen and shuffled dishes around. "Also, I don't haul water. You get the water, get it heated and I'll do these dishes for you. But only because there's nothing else to do up here. She glanced around and shuddered. "No TV, no music, no internet. How do you even survive?"

Fucking purple-headed woman. "I hate your fucking hair." Then he flicked his head to the door. "There's water out back." He met her aggressive stare. Most females would drop their eyes, be hurt by his insult, but not this one. He didn't scare her and as much as he wanted to see her tremble, he didn't want to scar her for life.

She crossed her arms. "You do not hate my hair. You love my hair. Maybe not the colour, but I remember how much you loved it." She aped Ren as she flicked her head towards the door. "And while you're fetching the water, bring in some more wood. It's going to take a lot of hot water to clean up this pig sty."

Ren had enough of her sass, but rather than sass back, he stomped out of the cabin to the wood pile, bare-chested without shoes. Frostbite wasn't nearly as bad as Cherime's ass-chewing. She was right, loathe as he was to admit it. The cabin needed cleaning and she shouldn't have to eat off dirty dishes. He thought about his bedding. It hadn't been changed in at least a month, maybe two. Picturing

Cherime in his bed, he decided clean sheets were far more important that clean dishes.

He grabbed an armload of wood that was stacked in an open shed and hauled it into the cabin, enjoying the scrape of the bark on his bare chest, pretending it was her nails digging in as he fucked her.

Cherime was in the kitchen, sorting through the mess, stacking the plates. She looked up when he approached. "Why is the deer hide drying out here? You have a perfectly good spare room." She pointed to the room near the front door as if he had no idea what room she might be referencing. "Why don't you put it in there along with the rest of your gear?"

He dumped the logs in the bin next to the stove and straightened up. "Because I don't fucking care where it is."

She shoved her hands on her hips and looked up at him. "Well, I do fucking care. It's stinking up the cabin so bad my wolf fainted. Shove it in the room, open the window, and close the door."

Her logic was sound, but fuck he hated being bossed. "It won't dry if the room's too cold."

"The storms gonna pass and it'll be warm in the cabin. You should be dragging it out in the sun anyway. And all this gear. Put it in the room so we can move around."

"We only need to move from the kitchen to the bedroom." He smirked as his eyes slid down to her chest.

"Huh!" She tossed her head. "Speaking of the bedroom, where are you going to sleep while I'm here?"

He grinned, couldn't help it, the sleeping arrangements were nonnegotiable. "I was thinking inside you; maybe on top of you or pinned under you. Whichever way you want, Wolverine. You choose."

Cherime rolled her eyes. "Maybe you should take me to Oz's momma and let me hang out with her and Felan.

You want a second run at me, maybe you should think about courting me. And that means no living or sleeping together until you learn to play nice."

Why the fuck was this slip of a woman getting the best of him? He didn't take lip, didn't take orders. "We're sharing the bed. It's the only option you've got."

She lifted the side of her mouth. Clearly, the conversation wasn't over. "Water. I need water."

"Right!" He turned and stalked out the open door.

"Food too," she called after him. "It's been a day from hell, and I need to eat!"

"Me too!" he grumbled as he heaved a tub of water off the ground. "Was thinking you were gonna be my dinner."

CHAPTER SEVEN

Cherime didn't want to do it, but she had no choice. She had to make the cabin liveable or she wouldn't be able to settle down. An agitated Cherime was a cranky Cherime and when she was cranky, she forgot how to be clever. She was more than likely to attack Ren over his rudeness, which would lead to wrestling, which would stoke the fire that had been simmering inside her since he walked into the community hall.

She was overheated, feverish, feeling him in all her e-zones, which was a huge problem. She needed to keep a cool head and to do so, she needed to make this cabin habitable or shift and sleep outside. Ren wouldn't let her do that though. Wolves were high on the predator list in northern BC, but bears topped it and they were out of hibernation, hungry and horny. Cougars too. Ren might be a bully and a bastard, but he had protective instincts. Or maybe that was giving him too much credit. Maybe it was all about possession and ownership with him.

She sighed as she dusted her hands and headed into the *Master's* bedroom. It was surprisingly spare given the riot in the main room. A dresser shoved in a corner, a huge unmade bed, a bear rug on the floor. A rifle leaned against the wall in one corner of the room, a crossbow and a quiver of arrows next to it.

Shifters were hunters, but generally hunted in their packs. Guns weren't really needed. But part of the Mountain pack's economy was the trade in furs, so she supposed a gun, bow or traps would do less damage than the ripping of teeth.

Her thoughts were scattered by loud cursing in the kitchen and she poked her head out to see Ren shoving a tub on the stove top, the water slopping over and drenching the front of his jeans. "Careful," she teased as she approached him. "You're going to put out the fire."

He pulled a breath into his lungs as he stalked towards her, grabbing her upper arms and crushing his body against hers. "We need to establish who the alpha is here." A hard, aggressive kiss followed as his fingers found her jaw and forced her mouth open so he could sweep the inside of it with his tongue.

Holy fucking hell's bells, she'd forgotten what it was like to be kissed by him. No, she hadn't. It would be impossible to forget the heat and ice that he evoked, stroking up her spine, making her shiver and streaking to her pussy, making her warm and wet. No one kissed liked him. Not a single other male in the world and she'd sampled enough to know.

She grabbed at his head, her fingers curling into his hair, and dragged him closer to her, her tongue sparring with his like they were fencing. His hard length pressed against her as he pinched one of her nipples, making her sweet spot clench in desperation.

She had a choice. Let him have her, and if he took her, that would be it. She'd be all in. Or stop now, while she still had a brain in her head. Her wolf was all for making the deep dive but a faint voice in her head reminded her that Ren had once crushed her heart and could easily do it again.

A thunderous crash from outside made the decision for her as it shook the house. They jumped apart and Ren twisted, taking off outside.

Cherime followed him to the door and watched as he quickly disappeared in the blustery snow. Probably a tree toppling over, she thought as she returned to the kitchen, licking her lips like they were coated in chocolate. He tasted so fucking good, so unique, and her stomach did that flippy thing it did when… uh… no… it didn't do that flippy thing with anyone else but Ren.

The water was starting to bubble, and she tried to lift the tub off the stove. She couldn't budge it. She shivered at the thought of Ren's strength. It was such a turn-on being in the arms of a man that big and strong, knowing she'd be safe and protected with him.

She felt the idea all the way down to her toes as she imagined them wrapped together in each other's arms as the storm raged around the cabin. Naked, the heat of their bodies keeping them warm, his large hands on her breasts, her stomach, her back. Caressing, squeezing, exploring.

Her nipples peaked as she shivered, then Ren entered the cabin, shaking the snow off his hair and beard. "Tree toppled over. Figured it was going to drop soon. Had it marked for cutting down." He shrugged. "Guess I don't have to now."

She glowered at him for interrupting her fantasy, talking about men shit she wasn't interested in. "Water's ready. Can you pour some into the washtub?"

He entered the kitchen and grabbed a pot, ladling the

heated water into the washtub on the counter. "Not really a problem solver, are you?"

She narrowed her eyes at him. She'd thought of doing it that way, but really wanted to see the strain of his bi-ceps as he heaved the tub up. "I'll wash up these dishes. Maybe you could move your shit into the spare room?"

The steam rose between them, literally, as he added another pot of water. Cherime was still feeling the throbbing in everything below her neckline and had to restrain herself from reaching out and touching his massive chest.

"Sure, Wolverine. How do you want to do dinner? I have a few stores, but usually hunt for the protein."

Cherime sighed as she added some generic dish soap that looked like it doubled as hand soap, if the grungy fingerprints on the bottle were any indication. She didn't usually hunt… as in never. Yes, she was a shifter, didn't mind getting her hands dirty or sinking her teeth into the neck of a scared bunny and sampling the warm blood, but her human half preferred dining. Her pack, the Lodge pack, was all about civility. After all, they made their living interacting with human tourists. "Will there be anything to hunt in this weather?"

Ren grinned. "Probably not.

Cherime rifled through the cabinets. "So what were you planning to eat?"

"You."

The flutter in her belly made her face flush warm, but she needed to stay strong. "I'm off the menu, Ren. I said I would come back with you, spend the weekend, but I didn't say we were going to bump uglies."

Ren stared her down and she managed a full 14 seconds before she dropped her eyes to his pecs. This male was unholy. His muscles were carved in granite, rock solid hunks of sexy, and the hair on his chest was a thing of beauty, not a full-blown fur rug, but certainly enough to force Cherime's hands into fists to stop her from reaching out and curling her fingers into it.

If she did that, then the next thing she'd do was trace her fingers down the furry fun trail that was framed perfectly by his Adonis belt, sexily exposed because his jeans hung loose on his perfect hips. And once she was down there, she wouldn't be able to resist tracing each side of the sexy vee, which would lead to the opening in his button-fly jeans, where her fingers would slip through his dark patch of pubic hair to his super-sized McSausage, which she would then find herself feasting on.

She blew out a huge exhale and stepped back from him. "It's too hot in here. Let's go get us some bunnies for dinner."

She shed the shirt Ren had supplied and quickly stepped outside, shifting almost immediately. Like always, the shift centred her, cooled her down, brought her back to the few senses she had. She was always a happy girl in wolf form, but she tried to temper it a little around Ren. His wolf was big, burly, and as grumpy as he was. He was all alpha, whether wolf or man: dominant, demanding, and expectant.

He joined her as she dropped in the snow on her haunches, her tail waving at him like it was attached to a flagpole. *For god's sakes, Cherime. Don't be so obvious.* But she couldn't control the joy of being at Ren's cabin, watching as the alpha god shed his clothes and shifted into his huge wolf.

Shifters were like cocks. The size or colour of the human form didn't influence the wolf form. Big shifter males could be average-sized wolves, and smaller male shifters were sometimes big wolves. Colour was a factor too, and Cherime was a good example of that. She was tall, curvy with almost black hair and coffee-bean coloured eyes when she was in human form, but her wolf was flawless snow white with blue eyes. She was somewhat slight in her wolf form, which she didn't mind. It made her fast, agile, and graceful.

Ren was big in human form, his skin a deep brown, his eyes the colour of molasses. In wolf form, he was black with tufts of greyish white on his underside. His massive size made him king of the mountain, and his eyes, which were currently settled on her, were dark and devilish.

She knew he wanted her submission, wanted her to go belly up, but that wasn't going to happen because if it did, he'd take control and she'd lose any self-restraint she had left. She'd shift to human form, then he would, and they'd likely bang one out right where they were, in the snow with the storm raging around them.

She briefly met his eyes, then dropped hers, standing up, letting her tail marginally droop, and emitted a soft whine. Combined it told him she wasn't submitting, though she would follow his lead. Of that there was never a doubt. She had enough shifter instinct to know that her wolf would acknowledge and respect the alpha no matter what her human side wanted to do.

She couldn't tell what he was thinking because he didn't move a muscle, didn't change his stance, didn't shift his eyes off her. Maybe he hadn't liked her response, because he knew, too, that she wasn't giving into him. She hadn't needed to be coy, instinct overruled her.

She waited, lowering her head slightly, and he finally turned and headed into the trees. Her wolf leapt forward, and she knew it was trying to pounce on him, take him down, play with him. She sharply coiled around and tried to land on her feet, but gravity won, and she thumped belly down in the snow, her front and back legs splayed to her sides.

Ren turned and watched as she scrambled to her feet, shaking the snow off her fur. Goddamnit! She glared at him and he bared his teeth. The asshole was laughing at her.

Daylight waned quickly in the mountains and the blizzard obscured the last few rays as darkness descended. Cherime trailed after Ren for over an hour as he rooted out prey and chased it down. He was all hunter: focused, intent, quiet. It was a sexy sight as he glided through the snow toward rabbits, gave chase if they ran, and despite his size, he was fast, graceful, and tenacious.

The first rabbit he caught was a good sized one, brown fur easy to spot against the whiteness of the fresh snow. The poor thing didn't have a chance as Ren clamped down on its throat with his huge teeth and broke the neck as he choked it.

Cherime sat on her haunches and waited. The alpha always fed first, then his mate if he had one, then the rest of the pack. It was like that with wild wolf packs, and shifters in wolf form had similar instincts. He'd eat the fresh kill, they'd hunt for more, and he would eat until he was satisfied, leaving the scraps for her.

Except that wasn't what happened. Ren picked up the rabbit by its scruff and carried it back to Cherime, dropping it in front of her.

What the hell? Was this a test? What did he want her to do? He held her eyes, then glanced down at the rabbit with a nod of his head. She whined, indicating she was not comfortable with his feed-the-female-first routine, but he ignored her. Leaving her with the rabbit, he padded away and disappeared into the blizzard.

She waited a couple of minutes for his return, then

decided instincts be damned, she was starving, and the fresh kill was too enticing to resist. She tore into the rabbit and ate almost all of it. When she was finished, she rubbed her snout in the snow over and over again. Blood contrasted horribly with her white fur and she didn't want Ren to see her with a dirty muzzle.

CHAPTER EIGHT

Ren laughed inside at the surprise in Cherime's eyes when he dropped the rabbit in front of her. He wasn't playing games.

Despite how wolfish he seemed, he had a human side with human instincts. Most male shifters used their wolves as an excuse to dominate. Ren didn't have to. He dominated no matter what form he was in – not only others, but also himself. He wasn't a wolf. He was a shifter and had free will over his instincts and the self-discipline to exercise it.

He considered himself a leader and yeah, at times he led with brute force, but as Mountain shifters, his pack members needed to be exceptionally strong and hardy. His ego, temperament and stubbornness served him well in a crisis, over the long winter, and during pack hunts. But he was also a man, currently with a woman who made his heart rate increase whenever she was near, and no fucking way was he going to eat first while she watched.

He left her behind, knowing she'd find him after she chowed down, and continued his hunt, catching, killing, and eating three rabbits before she caught up. She gave a yip as she came out of the trees, letting him know she was there, though that wasn't necessary. Despite the howling wind, his keen hearing tracked her movements and not even a raging snowstorm could hide her addictive scent; it was that strong of a pull.

He turned from the rabbit he'd been tearing into and watched with wonder as she entered the glade. Such a vision, in wolf or human form, though he truly did hate the purple hair. Maybe after spending enough time with him in the mountains, she'd stop with the colour.

He picked up the remains of his rabbit and carried it to her, dropping it front of her. She whined and backed away, conveying that she was full. He was too, at least for rabbit. Watching as she warily studied him, he stepped closer to her, nuzzling her neck, inhaling her warm, spicy fragrance. It hadn't changed over the years – it was as intoxicating now as it had been the first time it drifted to him on the breeze.

He sniffed the traces of blood on her snout and didn't resist his wolf's urge to lick her muzzle. She stood, letting him lick her clean and then returned the favour, her tongue lapping at him. Finally, she stepped back and turned, heading toward the cabin. He quickly overtook her and reclaimed the lead.

Yeah, he might let her feed first, but no fucking way was she leading him anywhere.

Back at the cabin, they shifted and quickly went inside, Cherime slipping into the T-shirt almost immediately, as if she were shy. He donned a loose pair of sweatpants, not to make her more comfortable but because his dick didn't seem to understand that the lady had said *no*. In Ren's mind though, that meant *not yet*, which was maybe why his cock was in a constant state of readiness.

Cherime seemed introspective as she walked into the kitchen and scooped a cup of water from the tub on the stove and drank it down. "Want some?" She filled her cup again and turned towards him.

He didn't want her waiting on him. "I can get my own." As he entered the kitchen, she scooted around him and over to the couch.

"I'm kind of cold now."

"Yeah," he grunted as he guzzled several cups, then brought a full one to the side table next to the couch. "I'll get a fire going."

He already had a stack of wood and kindling set up, ready to be lit. He arranged the fire every morning when he needed to. It was a mountain man's number one rule – be ready for anything.

Once the fire was roaring, he joined Cherime on the couch. She had her feet tucked up under her, her water cup in hand, her long hair flowing over her shoulders and covering her chest. The only thing that would make her more goddess-like was if she were naked. He started to open his mouth to say so, but she filled the silence before he could.

"Why'd you do that?" she blurted.

"Do what?"

"You know. Feed me first. Why'd you do that? It's not natural." Ren could see her confusion as she looked down at her cup of water.

"We're shifters, but we're not animals. My pack and I share in the spoils of the hunt equally, though we don't often do hunts together. I'm surprised you even have to ask, given you're the least wolf-like shifter I've ever encountered."

"It's weird, Ren." She glanced up at him, her eyes seeking answers.

"Doesn't happen in your pack?" He was curious now about how Lucien ran his pack.

"The males most often go on the hunt, but then it's generally for food for the restaurants and pack dinners. If we want fresh kill, we hunt on our own."

"What do the skirts do while the cavemen go out and get dinner?" He meant it to be funny, but based on Cherime's scowl, he thought maybe his timing was off.

"Don't be sexist! They keep the Lodge running, the tourists happy, and everything else in between."

He bristled. "I wasn't being sexist." He changed the subject before Cherime explained all the factors related to his sexism. "So your pack never does activities together?"

Cherime turned to face him, pressing her back against the arm of the sofa. "We usually have Sunday dinner meals on a regular basis, but in human form, eating with knives and forks and napkins." She paused for a few seconds. "Sometimes pack runs. Rarely though."

He had an image of Cherime naked in front of her male pack members and possessiveness flared up. He didn't know why he was getting so hot about her male pack members seeing her with no clothes, except any fucking man in the world would take one look at the amazon on his couch and lose their shit.

He reached across the cushion and yanked her to him. The cup she'd been holding flew out of her hand, splashing water down her T-shirt, soaking through the fabric enough to make it cling to her perfect globes. Her nipples, which had previously been hard little points, now stood up like tent pegs.

"Don't!" she shrieked as she brought her hands to his chest. Fucking soft palms stroking across his pecs until she curled her fingers into his hair and grabbed on for purchase.

He wrapped his legs around hers and dragged her with him as he slid off the couch onto the bear rug that was spread out on the planked floor. "I don't like the idea of other males looking at you."

She grunted as he rolled on top of her, carefully flattening his body so he didn't crush her to death.

"Get off me, you jackass!" She thrust her hips up to try to throw him off as she took a swipe at his face with her nails.

"Fuck, baby, don't do that. Feels too much like you want me." He sat up, his knees straddling her hips as he grabbed her wrists and shoved them on either side of her head. She was magnificent, pinned by him on her back on the bear rug, the purple in her wild hair barely discernable in the soft light of the fire, her chest heaving as the pulse in her neck ticked rapidly. He dipped his head and kissed her gently, tasting her lips with his tongue, the sweetness of her saliva. Her rapid breath warmed his mouth and he sucked it in along with her natural scent.

"Ren, I'm not ready for you," she protested but her body was slack as she stared up at him.

"Close you eyes and let me kiss you."

She quivered under him as she drew a breath and let her eyelids droop.

Ren wasn't sure if she was submitting, but he didn't hesitate. He returned his lips to hers and voraciously took them, too hard, too fast, but he couldn't stop. His mouth slid to her cheek and he kissed along her jawline to a sweet spot under her earlobe. The shiver that racked her body made him greedy and impatient. He wanted to worship every inch of her body and his dick was in full agreement as he brought his mouth back to hers.

She moaned as he deepened the kiss, releasing one of her wrists and wrapping his hand in her hair, pulling her face closer to his. He scented her growing desire, which stirred his frustration at the layer of clothing separating them.

He sought out her breast and as he squeezed the supple mound, she jerked her lips from his and turned her head.

"Get off of me, you asshole. Now!"

Fuck, too much too soon – he should have taken it slower, used his mouth until she was writhing under him, begging to be fucked. Before complying with her demand, he framed her face with his hands and drew her eyes to his. "This is gonna happen, Wolverine. You know we're destined to be together."

Tears sparked in her eyes as her face reddened. "Yeah. I know we are, Ren. I knew it eight years ago when you rejected me. Why would I risk my heart a second time?"

Ren lifted to his knees, still straddling her, but leaving enough room for her to flip around and crawl out, which she immediately did. "What do you want from me, Wolverine? An apology? I'm not sorry about what I did back then. You were a frivolous, giggly teenage girl, not mate material, and my pack would have eaten you alive. The only regret I have is the eight years of fucking that you gave away to all the other men."

She kicked out at him so quickly he was unprepared for the blow to his face. The contact was hard enough to shove him backwards, making him thump down on his ass. "You can't help yourself, can you! The hunt – that was bullshit, playing games, pretending you were a gentleman? All you're trying to do is get into my pants." Her foot shot out again, but this time he dodged in time. "That shit isn't sustainable. This—" She waved her hand at him and wrinkled her nose like he was a bad smell. "This is the real you, crude, rude and all fucking alpha."

He stood and towered over her, willing his aggressive

wolf to settle, but he couldn't contain it. He grabbed her by the hair and forced her backwards until she thumped up against the kitchen counter. Shaking in rage, he held himself back from striking her.

What the fuck was he doing? He didn't hit women.

The tension in him made his hands shake as he pointed a finger into her face. "Don't ever do that again, for fuck sake. You know better than to wake the beast. You got something to say, use your fucking words!"

"I used my fucking words!" Cherime swallowed, twisting her body to get out of his grip and away from his menacing fist. "You think you know so much about me, making assumptions about who I am. Even back then, you decided you knew everything about me. And now, you got it all figured out again. All these years that passed, you never once asked me how I was doing. Never checked in on me." She swiped an arm across her eyes, then checked it for wetness. "Why the fuck would I think you gave a shit about me."

"Sure, dump it on me. I'm the dick that threw you out so it's my fault we didn't reconnect. That has nothing to do with all the fucking around you've been doing. Guess you were getting lots of practice."

A huge gasp fell out of her mouth and she reared back to slap him, but he jerked away in time, and turned from her, tugging at his beard to keep his hands from circling her neck. He needed some distance, or he'd do something he'd regret. He wasn't a man of violence despite his size and demeanor. He didn't have to be because no one fucked with him.

Except Cherime, who brought the savage out in him. There never seemed to be a happy medium. Her next words, hurled at him like hunting arrows, proved that. "You crushed me, you bastard. You're right that I was just a kid with stars in my eyes, thinking the ground you walked on was sacred. You broke my heart when you kicked me to the curb." Tears trailed down her cheeks and she turned sideways, trying to hide them as she swiped at her face. "There are ways to break a girl's heart without destroying it." Her voice cracked.

Her crying was gutting him, and he needed to harden her back up before he said something he'd regret, like *sorry, babe, my bad*. "That why you fuck around so much?" Despite feeling like the prick he was, it worked.

Her eyes flashed fire, her face reddened, her fists clenched. "None of your fucking business what I do in my spare time."

Maybe he should have gone with the apology because her words further inflamed him. "You seem to have a lot of spare time."

"Don't be so fucking arrogant. You and every other asshole in town think I'm some sort of insatiable sexual siren. You could walk into Becker's…." She stopped and blew out a breath. "I'm not going to defend myself to you."

"No. Of course you're not. You don't have a defense."

"Who've you talked to, Ren? About me? All anyone ever hears are the bullshit rumours where one guy says I'm a slut, and they pass it on. But no one ever says, yeah, I've had a piece of that."

"Doesn't mean they didn't."

She stalked up to him, her teeth bared as she got in his face. "That's because I sleep with decent men who don't kiss and tell. And fuck you anyway. I can do whatever I want. I don't answer to anyone."

Her words, all of them, were logical and on point. She was a gorgeous, sexual, independent woman who dressed provocatively and gave as good as she got. It'd piss guys off when she rejected them. And she would.

He should apologize, but he hated apologizing. Instead, he grunted, "Bedtime."

Cherime tilted her head, confusion at the 180-degree shift in their battle. "I'll take the couch."

Ren nodded, his gut clenching at the thought of the beauty sleeping in the same space with him but not in the same bed. "Figured." He entered the bedroom, then emerged with a quilt, which he carelessly tossed at her.

She caught it deftly and sniffed it. Apparently, it met her criteria. "I need a pillow too."

He only had two pillows because he never had guests overnight. He grabbed one off his bed and threw it on the couch. "Anything else, princess?"

She wrapped the blanket around her body and dropped on the cushions. "Not a fucking thing."

Ren pursed his lips, forcing himself to close the bedroom door without slamming it. *Not a fucking thing.* He deserved that.

CHAPTER NINE

It was impossible for Cherime to settle down, wrapped in a blanket that smelled like Ren, lying on a couch that was infused with his scent. Her anger, hurt, and hormones were a raging quagmire of bubbling out-of-control lava. Her wolf paced restlessly within her, pushing at her to go to him, bow down to her alpha. Thank the earth she had a human side, one not so easily persuaded.

It was beyond reason that he thought she should be the one to reach out to him over the intervening years. He'd crushed her and it had taken her two years before she would even look at, let alone sleep with, another man. All she'd wanted was Ren and without him, she lost her spirit.

Strangely, it was her wolf, pining for Ren, that woke her up. It became restless, caged in, needed more than she was giving it. Once she cracked open the self-imposed cage around her heart and set herself free from the hold Ren had on her, she was able to embrace her independence.

Her words and attitude protected her heart and the casual, don't-give-a-shit air she adopted attracted men. A lot of men, so many that she could pick and choose. She embraced who she was: a sultry, sexy bitch who could throw down with the boys and fuck them into a coma. Why the hell should she apologize for who she was? Or feel guilty because Ren didn't approve.

She wasn't about to lie and pretend she was a born-again virgin so Ren could sleep at night, thinking he was the only stud in town. She was a woman in her prime who liked sex and men, in that order, though she was never in it for the long-term. Ren had broken the part of her that would willingly risk her heart. Besides, she couldn't get Ren out of her head, even when she had her legs wrapped around someone else, and until that happened, she wouldn't commit to any other male.

She rolled onto her stomach, groaning and pressing her face into the pillow. It smelled like Ren. Everything in this cabin smelled like Ren. It was unavoidable. His home, his world, screamed who he was down to his core: alpha, stubborn, unbending. Pissed at her because he had wanted his woman to pine for him.

Small towns and wolf packs were hard on a girl's reputation. She wasn't nearly as sexually active as everyone made her out to be, but she was a target because of the way she dressed, the way she talked, the words she said, and the way she said them. She didn't have a harem of men on rotation. She only slept with one guy at a time and usually it lasted until he got too serious.

She's had dry spells and, at times, deliberately created a bubble around herself, hiding away for a month or two and missing Ren. Usually that happened after she ignored the signs that the male that she was seeing wanted more than the casual encounters she was comfortable with. She'd dump him, he'd get pissy, and the rumours would flare up again.

Over the years, she had considered leaving Darkness

Falls to get away from her relentless obsession with Ren, but her home, her family, her life was here. And she was as stubborn as a girl could be. Ren wasn't going to run her out of town. The sonofabitch could rot with the deadfall before she'd give him that kind of satisfaction.

She tossed and turned for what seemed like hours, then finally fell into an exhausted sleep, dreaming about Ren, wanting him, needing him, waking up to find her hand between her legs, her fingers stroking her damp pussy.

She jerked her hand away from herself and sat up quickly. She needed to settle down or Ren would scent her desire and be drawn to her like a bear to a beehive. The idea of him savaging her made her nipples ache and her need for him spin out of control. "No fucking way," she whispered as she knocked the quilt to the floor and scrambled from the couch in record time. The cold morning air invaded the cabin when she flung open the front door.

The storm had settled somewhat in the night, but it was like Cherime's appearance woke it up, and as she stepped into the snow the wind whipped up, howling its displeasure, swirling the snow around her, battering her. Tilting her face to the clouds, she bent her elbows and raised her arms so the middle fingers on her fists were pointing skyward. "Universe, you fucking bastard! Do your worst – freeze me to death!"

Ren appeared at the door she'd left open, hair and beard askew from what appeared to be a much more restful night than she'd had. Her gaze got stuck on his body, his muscular bare chest, his honed abs, his sweats hanging low on his slim hips, showing off that fucking perfect vee. Every inch of him screamed alpha.

"What the fuck are you doing?" he shouted as the wind howled alongside him.

"Saying my morning prayers and getting some fresh

air. I'm not coming back inside until you move that fucking deer hide into the spare room!" Her words were lost on a gale that turned the snow into a blanket that practically obscured her from Ren.

Then he was there, looming in front of her, a cranky set to his face. His huge hands gripped her waist and he hoisted her over his shoulder, strangling her thighs with his strong arms. "Goddamned crazy woman," he grunted, carrying her back into the cabin.

"Put me down, you animal!" She punched him in his perfect ass and kicked him in the thigh, landing one hard enough to make her toes curl up. To her satisfaction, it also made him grunt.

Her ass thumped down hard on the floorboards as he unceremoniously dropped her and strode to the kitchen. "What the hell was that about?"

She climbed to her feet and dusted off the back of her T-shirt. "You mean my chanting to the pagan gods? I was checking in with them to see if today is the day that they're going to rain hellfire and brimstone down on you." She wrinkled her nose as she glared at the drying deer hide. "Put that thing in the other room."

The stove hissed as Ren set the percolator on the top of it. He turned towards her. "Say please."

Please? Say please to him? Not even if she were Oliver Twist asking for more gruel would she say please to him. She stalked over to the drying rack and examined it. "I'll do it myself." She hated that she lost the clash of wills, but ridding the main room of the noxious deer hide was far easier than saying please.

His laugh was derisive. "Can't bring yourself to ask nicely, Wolverine?"

Fuck you. She heaved the rack up and headed to the

spare room. "Can't bring yourself to apologize, alpha-man?" she sneered.

The doorway was covered by a hanging blanket and she brushed it aside as she stepped inside. The spare room was used as a storage room: several tools and axes were shoved in a corner, a couple of huge trunks sat under a window, boots stood on the floor and winter gear hung on hooks. A couple of animal pelts were pinned to the wall. One appeared to a wolverine.

She huffed at the sight.

There was ample room for the drying rack and other clutter that was taking up the main room. She moved a couple of pelts from the top of one of the trunks and set the drying rack on top of it. Warm air rose, and the hide would dry faster this way.

She dusted her hands as she took a step backwards to view the result and bumped into Ren, who had somehow snuck up on her. He immediately wrapped his arms around her body in a bear hug and kissed the top of her head. "I'm sorry, baby."

Fuck no, he wasn't apologizing. If he did that, all would be lost. "Sorry doesn't cut it."

"I know," he replied with a mocking tone. "I should have moved the pelt myself."

She elbowed him hard in the ribs, and he loosened his grip enough to allow her to slide under his arm and leave the room. "Asshole," she muttered. Her wolf seemed to be on board with her for a change as it sniffed its displeasure at the alpha's light treatment of the issues between them. In the main room, Cherime curled up on the couch and wrapped the blanket around her legs.

She watched as Ren tramped to the kitchen, grabbed two cups, and swished them through the cold water in the wash basin that she had yet to use. She'd have to heat the water again, so she could wash up the dishes and gain a semblance of harmony in this living space.

"Why's your cabin so untidy?" she asked, as he poured the coffee into the cups he'd dried.

He carried the mugs to the couch, handing her one, then seating himself next to her. "Because I have more important things to do than dust and wash windows."

His comment drew her eyes to the windows. They looked like they hadn't been washed in forever, and the dust in the room was so prolific, she thought maybe it came with the furniture. The floors needed sweeping and washing, and the kitchen needed a serious scrubbing. The couch was old, the cushions flattened, nothing comfortable about anything.

All the clutter in the room clearly made this a bachelor pad. A handsaw sat next to several screwdrivers and wrenches; an axe settled on top of stack of newspapers so old they were curling at the edges. There was room enough for a small dining table, but the space was filled with books, old shoes and clothes, a wooden bar stool with a broken leg. Paint cans.

This was the same cabin Ren had brought her to eight years ago. Back then it was well-kept, neat inside. Looked like a home. Rustic, yes, but he had talked about digging a well, installing pipes. Making it solar-powered, so there was electricity.

He'd told her about his plans to build a bathroom, a heated shed for his work, a covered car port for his vehicle. Maybe he'd been trying to impress her, but she didn't think so. She wondered what happened in the intervening years for him to let it go to hell.

"This place is barely habitable, Ren. Maybe if you cleaned it, aired it out, you'd feel more settled inside."

He took a sip of his coffee as he followed her eyes to

the mess in the corner. "I'm settled just fine, Wolverine. I didn't bring you here to nag me."

"Then why did you?" Stupid question or utterly profound? She wasn't sure.

The couch wobbled as he shifted his body so he faced her. "You know why. Thought maybe you'd be of the same mind I was."

She dropped her gaze to her coffee as her stomach twisted into tight little knots of need. "Why would you think that? Despite what you've heard, I'm not easy. I don't sleep with every male I come across. Second, we might be pair-bonded, but that doesn't mean we're compatible." She gazed around his cabin. "If we mated, you'd expect me to live here." She shuddered.

"Who said anything about mating?" he growled.

Cherime blinked back tears at his hurtful words. "What you're saying is that I'm here for a few rounds of burying-the-hatchet? That's all I mean to you?"

Ren didn't meet her eyes as he took a sip of his coffee. "That would be a good start, don't you think? We barely know each other, so it might be worth taking the time before we decide whether we'll be able to live happily ever after."

"We don't need to fuck to know that will never happen. We can barely tolerate each other in the same room, let alone a lifetime of this. I'm not the girl you screwed over eight years ago, but I can't deny that what you did had a huge influence on who I am today." She contemplated the run-down cabin and added, "And I'm thinking you, too."

The scowl that had been creasing his forehead deepened as his dark eyes flashed their fury. He stood up and stalked towards the front door. "Don't fucking play mind doctor with me. You got nothing to do with my current state of affairs."

Cherime twisted on the sofa to catch him kicking off his sweatpants. "What're you doing?"

"Going for a run," he barked. "Got better things to do than spend my time talking with you."

That didn't even make sense, but she knew she'd pushed a button and felt a perverse satisfaction at getting under his skin. She decided to grind a little more. "You want me?" she yelled after him. "You better figure it out!"

CHAPTER TEN

Ren stayed away most of the day, drifting from cabin to cabin, checking on his pack, making sure everyone was sheltered, had enough wood and stocks to get them through the next day or two. He figured that the storm would blow itself out sometime tonight. It was nearing the end of June and it wouldn't take long for everything to thaw and return to normal.

In between his visits, he thought of Cherime's last words. *You figure it out.* He shouldn't have brought her back to his cabin. The second he saw her in the community centre, he should have turned tail and run for the hills.

Every fucking minute of every fucking day for eight years, the memory of them together, of what he did to her, haunted him. If he hadn't figured out what to do about it by now, then he probably never would. He'd had her once, forced her out, and now, he had a second chance, but he was fucking it up because talking about feelings and shit like that wasn't a strong suit of his. It stripped him of his power and that was something he couldn't let go of.

When he returned to his cabin, it was late afternoon,

snow still falling, but the wind was less frenetic as the day darkened. An unfamiliar scent greeted him as he stepped inside, and he wrinkled his nose in distain as he sniffed the air and stared around his cabin. The dust and clutter were gone, floors swept, and even the windows looked like they'd been washed, at least on the inside.

"It's called clean," Cherime snarked from behind the washtub in the kitchen. "Unfamiliar to you and won't last unless you actually keep it up." Her hair was braided into a long thick plait that hung over one shoulder and inexplicably made Ren's dick try to get a closer look. An added factor in his growing lust was his T-shirt on her curvy body, the wet fabric clinging to her soft mounds as she splashed around in the washtub, cleaning a plate. She was biting on her lower lip as her big brown eyes grazed over him appreciatively.

Her beauty struck him in his stomach and groin. She was a demi-demon with a heart in need of mending. He ached for her in a way that wasn't natural. All the things he could say to her, should say to her, but didn't know how. Instead, he stalked up to her and tugged her braid. "This is a good look on you. All we need is for you to be pregnant, and you'd be perfect."

She flipped a wet hand up and jerked her braid out of his hold, ignoring his provocative statement as her expression went from neutral to pissed faster than a fox chasing a rabbit. "You have nothing to eat in this place and I'm starving. Did you at least bring back food?"

He didn't let her temper dissuade him from running a finger over her cheek, sliding up her temple, and tracing her perfectly arched eyebrow before pinching the lobe of her ear. "Nope. Wasn't out hunting. Checked in on my pack to make sure everyone was managing."

Something about that statement made her madder as

her frown deepened. He had no doubt she was about to tell him exactly what the problem was. "Nice of you to think of them," she grumbled before turning away from him and laying a clean coffee cup upside down on a towel.

He ran his hand down the side of her head, so fucking hard not touching her. "Was thinking of you the entire time."

She dropped her chin to her chest, something suddenly fascinating about the dishwater. "And yet, you forgot to feed me."

He grinned at her cute little pout. "Are you hungry, Wolverine?"

"What do you think?"

"I think you should've went hunting." He sidled away from her a few inches so he could get the blood flowing back up to his brain. "Lots of small game around."

She clenched her teeth as she rinsed another cup and banged it down on the towel. "I don't hunt."

He threw back his head and laughed. "If you're a shifter, you're a hunter."

"You're the male, you're supposed to feed me." She glared at the dishwater.

He leaned into her as he looked into the washtub. Nope, nothing in there that was as interesting as he was. He placed a finger under her chin and raised her head so she had no choice but to meet his eyes. "According to you, I'm not your male."

She sucked in a breath. "Then perhaps I should go back to my girls."

"Run back with your tail between your legs? Still storming outside. How you gonna get them down the mountain?" The question was moot; he wasn't going to kick the girls out into the storm no matter what, but Cherime didn't have to know that.

"Fuck," she said under her breath as she yanked her head to the side so he wasn't touching her anymore. "I need to eat, Ren. I get hungry."

He decided to let her off the hook. "We'll go to Oz's mom's. She's expecting us."

Cherime washed and dried a plate, then added it to the growing stack of clean dishes drying on the towel. "She'll be expecting *you*. And how're we getting there? Shifting? Great first impression showing up naked and uninvited."

Jesus, why couldn't she be agreeable for once? "I'm the alpha of the pack. I show up at someone's door for dinner, they're going to open it and welcome me and whoever's with me."

"That doesn't make me less naked."

"Grand time for you to go all shy on me, Wolverine." He headed towards the bedroom. "I'm gonna change the sheets on the bed, so you have one less thing to complain about, and then we'll head out. Since you're my guest, the least I can do is make you more comfortable."

"That still doesn't make me less naked," she called out after him.

"Felan will lend you some clothes," he grumbled.

Oz's sister could be as prickly as Cherime and he wondered how the two would get along. He figured they were close enough in age that they would have been in school together. That didn't mean they'd been friends.

He stripped the blankets and sheets off the bed and shoved them in a corner, then opened the bottom drawer on his dresser and pulled out his only other set of sheets. He'd give Cherime the bed tonight and stretch out on the bear rug in front of the fireplace until she felt guilty enough to invite him to sleep with her. That'd be all it would take.

His wolf huffed his indignation. *Quit fucking playing games and take the girl. You're a fucking alpha. Act like one.*

Ren told it to shut up. He was playing for keeps this time and needed to be smart about bringing Cherime around, not a prick who shouted orders and made threats.

Cherime's querulous voice called from the kitchen as he shook out the bottom sheet and placed it on the mattress. "Could you do something with that stinking hide, too? The smell isn't going away just because it's in the spare room. I'm getting close to tossing it out of the cabin."

He poked his head through the bedroom doorway, a menacing growl to his voice. "You toss out my deer hide, and I'll wrap your body in it and throw you off the side of the mountain."

"I'm shaking," she sneered as she returned her attention to the dishes.

CHAPTER ELEVEN

The cabin was as close to civilized as Cherime could get it, save for the fucking deer hide, which Ren seemed unnaturally attached to.

She took a last satisfied look as they headed out the door to get some good grits, as Ren affectionately called it, from Oz's mother.

Cherime was somewhat of an expert on the Mountain pack. As a teenager, back when she thought Ren was the man of her dreams, she'd practically hunted him. That's what a teenage girl did, wasn't it? Meet a hot guy, become obsessed and learn everything about him, until she'd internalized his routine. Cherime had done the stalking part for sure, even after Ren rejected her.

Oz's mother, Tess, took Ren in when he first arrived in Darkness Falls at the tender age of 15. Ren and Oz became best friends, and Tess and Felan became his family. Problem was, Cherime wasn't all that fond of mama's boys and Ren certainly seemed to still be suckling at the maternal breast, or whatever Tess was to him.

Oz's sister, Felan, was a couple of years younger than

Cherime. Cherime remembered her from high school. Felan was a mouthy, difficult chick entering grade 10 when Cherime started grade 12. Cherime didn't much like her because Felan was brash, a little mean, and didn't know when to shut up.

Yeah, all these years later Cherime recognized it for what it was – a case of the pot calling the kettle black. Cherime also knew that Tess, Oz's mother, was widowed young when Oz was a child. Tess had mated again, Felan's father, but that ended badly, though no one ever said what happened. He was the devil himself according to local gossip, and also the alpha of the Mountain pack until Ren took over. She thought maybe Ren had killed Felan's old man but there was never talk of a challenge.

Cherime wasn't sure of the timeline and Ren wasn't much interested in talking about his personal life. He'd never asked about hers, either, and she wondered if he spent any amount of time thinking about who she was or where she was from.

She, along with her brother, Raff, and sister, Mara, had been orphaned when she was 10 years old. Mara was just 12, but fortunately, Raff was old enough to take over the parenting role. Except he wasn't much of a parent, wasn't interested in two girls who were fast becoming women, and didn't know what to do other than to interfere when males came knocking. She and Mara did an okay job of raising themselves, which Cherime didn't mind because it was better than some interfering do-gooder from the pack taking over.

Her life had improved when Lucien challenged the pack's former alpha, Otzoa, and won. Lucien was a good alpha who ruled with a healthy dose of aggression, but it was offset by his good heart and smart brain. He was what the Lodge pack needed. He was what Raff had needed to help settle him. And Trist, Raff's mate, a weak little Omega, seemed to have the magic touch, somewhat taming the savage beast within him. Trist was growing on Cherime, a little like a fungus, but still, once in a while, the girl showed backbone.

And Cherime's dead parents? She side-stepped every single conversation about her parents whenever it came up. She was angry at them for what they'd done – dying in a car crash before they were done raising her. It wasn't rational or logical, but her emotions told her head to fuck off and it did, repeatedly. She knew that Mara and Raff were tight-lipped too, so she didn't think many people knew their story. She didn't think Ren knew or even wanted to know. He never asked her questions, never tried to make an emotional connection.

The storm was settling as they neared Tess's cabin, but by the scent in the air, it was far from over. These late spring storms took on a life of their own, sometimes lasting days, knocking out power lines and cell towers. She doubted anyone even noticed her absence. Maybe Lucien, but Mara was in hiding, still grieving over her lost life when her philandering mate died. And Raff? He was tied up with Trist and their twin boys. He had no room in his life or his heart for his baby sister.

Lucky for Cherime, she was an armadillo, her shell so hard that she could weather anything that daddy nature threw at her. Well, almost everything, she thought as she glanced at the biggest, baddest, blackest motherfucking wolf she'd ever seen in her life. Then he shifted into the biggest, baddest motherfucking mountain man she'd ever laid eyes on. She sat on her haunches and peered up at him, taking in every inch of magnificence. Without a doubt, he was going to be her undoing.

The door behind him opened and Ren turned towards

it as Cherime peeked around him. Tess and Felan were peering out from the brightness of the cabin, curiosity in their eyes.

"Tess," Ren said as he scratched the top of Cherime's head like she was his pet dog. "We got company."

Cherime shifted and straightened up. "Hi." She couldn't help but grin widely at the surprised expressions on the women's faces.

Felan found her words first. "Cherime. Wow! Last person I expected to be on our mountain."

Yeah, right. Their mountain. "Got stranded by the storm. Ren helped me out."

Tess stepped back into the cabin and gestured to Cherime. "Well, come in." To Felan, she said, "Get Cherime something to wear."

Ren was already shrugging into jeans and a T-shirt as Felan flipped around and headed to what Cherime presumed was her bedroom.

"Smells good in here. What's for supper?" he asked as he zipped himself into his jeans, smirking when he caught Cherime admiring the bulge at the apex of his thighs.

"Venison stew. Was going to grill steaks, but…." She let the sentence trail as she waved a hand towards the window. "Crazy weather."

Ren ambled his big body familiarly over to the large stone fireplace, smouldering cinders in the hearth, and added a fir log. "Stew's perfect." He stirred the glowing ash and Cherime got caught up in the flexing muscles of his back and biceps. And his ass in those jeans—she was practically salivating.

"Hey Cherime." Felan stuck her head through her bedroom doorway. "Come on in. See what fits."

Cherime reluctantly tore her gaze from Ren, Felan's words reminding her of her current state of nudeness.

"Thanks." The word came out too husky. She needed to settle down or everyone in this cabin would know how needy she was.

She caught a glimpse of the bathroom as she walked towards Felan's room and felt relieved – no pun intended – at the glimpse of the porcelain toilet and freestanding shower. At least the cabin that Tess and Felan lived in was civilized. Tidy, bright, and cozy with running water, electricity, and a gas stove. Maybe she should bunk here while she waited out the storm.

"How's it going?" she asked as she entered Felan's domain. "Haven't seen you in a while."

It was a typical bedroom without all the frills that Cherime's room had. It was spartan like Ren's, meant for practical purposes. Mountain shifters were a different breed, that was for sure. Hardier even than other shifters, pragmatic men and women who found utility in everything they had. If it didn't have a purpose, it didn't have a home.

Still, Felan wasn't a total freak. A couple of framed watercolours graced her walls and the top of her dresser held a few trinkets.

Felan shook out a light long-sleeved jersey. "It's wrinkled but should work." She handed it off to Cherime, then looked her up and down. "You always did have a smokin' body."

Cherime shrugged as she slipped the sweater over her head. "You're no slouch."

"Sure," Felan replied as she picked up a pair of sweatpants and tossed them at Cherime. "Men really dig chicks who can disembowel and skin a deer in less than an hour."

Cherime yanked the sweats up over her ass. "Maybe you should keep that softer side to yourself."

Felan fingered a pair of socks. "What're you really doing out here?"

Cherime shrugged. She wasn't about to explain herself to Felan. "Thanks for the clothes." She walked back into the main room to see Ren and Tess talking, their heads bent together intimately. The conversation stopped when they saw her.

Tess pulled a stack of dishes from an overhead cabinet and shoved them into Ren's hands. "Is Oz home yet?" That was a funny question given that Tess was Oz's mother.

"Haven't seen him." Ren set the table, handing Tess back an extra plate. "Guess he needs more time."

"Where'd he go?" Cherime sidled up to Tess and took the cutlery she was holding.

Tess turned to the stew, stirring it a few times. "It's ridiculous! He's still hung up on Adrienne. Even dead, she's got him all twisted up in knots." She turned the burner off and donned a pair of oven mitts.

"Fucking disaster is what she was," Ren agreed.

Cherime wanted to say something, defend a woman she didn't know. It wasn't Adrienne's fault that a psycho shifter asshole raped and killed her. Wasn't Aubrey's either as she thought back to Ren's anger at the community centre, basically having a hate on for the schoolteacher because she was Adrienne's sister.

"Supper's on," Tess called as she carried the pot of stew to the table. "Cherime, have a seat."

Cherime stood uncertainly. Shifters were territorial, even within their own packs, and she knew without being told that the family had their designated chairs. She glanced Ren's way. "Which chair?"

He grinned his trademark mean, toothy smirk as he approached her, then reached past her and yanked out a chair. "Sit here, Wolverine."

"Stop with the fucking nickname," she muttered as she

sat down and pulled her chair up to the table. She wished he wouldn't smile, wouldn't talk, wouldn't breathe. It was all turning her on, and she didn't want to be turned on in front of Tess and Felan. They'd know, hear her elevated heartbeat, sense her agitation.

"Stop being so prickly," Ren countered as he took the chair at the head of the table, to the left of her. Of course, he would – here, at the hall, in any of the other pack member's homes. He was the alpha, the king of the castle.

Tess sat at the other end of the table and Felan pulled up a chair next to Cherime. Cherime sat with her hands in her lap waiting for Ren to serve himself, but instead, he leaned his elbows on the table and intertwined his fingers, bringing his hands to his face and closing his eyes.

Holy fuck, they were going to say grace. Cherime glanced at Felan to make sure Ren wasn't playing a practical joke, but both women had followed suit. So Cherime did too.

Ren's low growl made her shiver.

"Bless our hearts, that we may hear, in the breaking of the bread, the songs of the universe." He lowered his hands, winked at Cherime and reached for the stewpot.

CHAPTER TWELVE

It wasn't easy to unsettle Cherime so Ren basked in the expression on her face after he said grace. A frown played at her lips as she studied her place settings as if they were valuable relics. He decided to add to her discomfort by ladling some stew onto her plate before he served himself and passed the pot to Tess. Yup, it worked.

Cherime's face suffused in red as she glanced side-eyed at him under her dark, luscious eyelashes.

"Bread," he rumbled as he passed a woven basket filled with slices from a freshly baked loaf. "Tess makes the best."

"I made the bread," Felan interjected, then affectionately smiled at Tess. "And it's as good as mom's. She taught me well."

Ren glanced at Cherime as she took a slice. Her expression had moved from embarrassed to almost grief. *What the hell?* Maybe she was missing her mom, wanting the mother-daughter bond that Tess and Felan shared.

He realized this was something he could give her – neither of them had parents and within Cherime's hard shell was a woman crying out for affection. He imagined her in his arms at night, her back pressed against his chest as they spooned. His groin tightened at the thought – it would have to be after they fucked a couple of times, because he'd never be able to hold her tenderly until he had his fill of her supple curves.

He shifted his thoughts away from Cherime in his bed before he split the seam on his jeans. Tess was a good distraction, as she treated him and almost everyone else in the pack like they were her children. Sure, she was overinvolved in their lives, but she had a generous spirit and enough love to go around. He squeezed Cherime's knee under the table but let go as Cherime jerked it away and tossed him a side-eyed glare.

He noticed Tess curiously eyeing Cherime. The woman already suspected that he and Cherime were more than friends, but didn't want shows of affection to lead her to the wrong conclusion about the degree of their relationship.

Cherime was going to be his mate one way or another, but despite his earlier fantasy, he wasn't under any illusion that this would be a match made in heaven. She was too prickly to be anything to him but a woman to warm his bed and a mother for his children. His heart protested his evaluation of the future and he tried to reason with it.

Yeah, she was the sexiest woman on earth, but she was shifter-soft, preferring the materialistic trappings of her human heritage over her shifter instincts. She was the only woman for him because they were pair-bonded, but fate didn't equate to love or any other human concept. Wolves mated for life out of necessity. They had their family and stayed together as a unit until one of them died. Didn't mean it was sunshine and roses.

Cherime would learn what it meant to be with him. She was old enough now, she was ready. It was time.

He took a large bite of stew and washed it down with a gulp of beer. As usual, Tess and Felan's cooking didn't disappoint. The baked bread smelled like safety, warmth, love, and his gut groaned in anticipation. He generously buttered his slice, then folded it over and sopped up some of the stew gravy and shoved half of it in his mouth. This is why he came to Sunday dinners. For the food and the family.

Cherime buttered her bread and took a bite, fluttering her eyelashes as she chewed. "I haven't had bread this good since… I don't know… maybe never."

"They must bake bread at the lodge," Tess replied as she took a sip of water.

Cherime nodded. "They do. Rye, rustic, all the requisite authentic recipes, and the tourists love it. But it's still done up in the big, shiny kitchen with trained chefs. It's a facsimile of the real thing." She raised her slice in the air. "This is the real thing."

Ren grinned to himself as he inhaled the stew. Cherime was right – Tess knew how to cook and had passed that knowledge to Felan. It was time Felan mated and had children of her own to pass down their precious shifter traditions. For the sake of their survival, it needed to happen. Too many shifters were leaving the lifestyle, lured by the lies of the city, the bullshit promises that life was better with HDTV and internet.

Speaking of prickly, Felan didn't much like the topic whenever it was raised, but since Cherime was here and he felt playful, he thought it might be fun to stir the pot. "Met your mate, yet, baby sister?" He considered her as much a sister as Oz did, which made their relationship comfortable rather than awkward.

Tess tsked as Felan turned to Ren, a scowl wrinkling her forehead. "We're not having this conversation."

Yeah, they were. "Who's going to pass your Mom's recipes on if you don't have kids?"

"If and when I meet the asshole of my dreams, I'll let you know." She picked up her fork and shoveled a bite of stew into her mouth.

He felt like a lazy cat playing with a mouse. "You're not getting any younger, Felan. Time you settled down."

Her fork clattered against her plate as she tossed it down. "Holy hell, Ren. Why don't you settle down? You're practically ancient compared to me."

Yep, she went there, but he expected her to retaliate and Cherime being here made him a prime target. Ren shrugged nonchalantly as he reached for another slice of bread. "Why do you think I brought Cherime for dinner?"

Cherime choked and carefully placed her fork on her plate. "I already told you this isn't happening." Her angry eyes were willing him to shut up.

He leaned into her, so close that she flinched as his breath stroked her cheek. His voice was the growl of a chainsaw. "It's happening, Wolverine."

Cherime put a few inches of space between them as a deep blush suffused her face. "This isn't the time or place for us to be having this discussion."

Felan, sensing an opportunity to steer the topic away from her, interjected, "Cherime's older than me, so it makes sense that you two mate and have children. Then I'll be auntie and pass the knowledge on to your kids."

"I'm not dead yet!" Tess joined the discussion as she wiped her mouth with her napkin. "I'd like to have grandchildren to pass on the knowledge myself." She turned to Cherime, her eyes softening. "Ren is like a son to me, and it would be wonderful for him to settle down with a good woman."

Ren noted that Tess hadn't explicitly sanctioned

Cherime as the *good woman* and Cherime appeared to pick up on that too. She pushed back her chair and stood. "I hate to break it to all of you, but I'm not mother material or mate material, or even girlfriend material. I can barely feed myself most days of the week. I eat at the Lodge restaurant when I get hungry. Almost all the time!"

"Sit down!" Ren ordered gruffly, seeing the wild look in Cherime's eyes. She was about to bolt, and he didn't want to have to chase her. Well, he did if the twinge in his dick was any indication, but not in front of Tess and Felan.

She ignored him, which was pretty much what he expected. "I can't breathe in here." She ran a nervous hand through her hair and headed to the door, which she shoved open, letting a cool rush of air invade the warmth of the cabin. She glared back at Ren. "You're a fool!" The door banged behind her as she fled.

"You fucked that up well and good, didn't you?" Felan smirked at Ren as he shot to his feet.

Goddamn prickly woman, running out on him like that. Now he had to go after her. "She and I will mate – it's just a matter of time."

Felan stood, flipping a lank of light brown hair behind her shoulder. "Why, Ren? Why her? You know she's not right for you. Look at her! She has purple hair and manicured nails. She can walk on stilettos in the snow better than most people can walk in mukluks. I bet she doesn't even know how to tie them."

That brought him up short. He'd thought Tess might've protested his choice of mate, but Felan was usually laid back around him. "Jealous, sister?"

She narrowed her eyes at him. "I'm not freaking jealous, you Neanderthal. I'm looking out for you. Cherime's okay, but let's be honest; the girl would let your baby drown in a swamp before getting her designer skirt dirty to save it."

"Felan!" Tess gasped and rightly so. His alpha status demanded respect from everyone, including the women he considered family.

Ren waved Tess off, though. If Felan had something to say, best get it off her chest before Cherime officially joined the pack as their alpha's mate. "You don't know her like I do." He recalled the vision of her in his cabin, barefoot, wearing his T-shirt, dragging the deer hide out of the main room.

Felan shook her head at him. "Don't know what's wrong with you showing up for dinner with Cherime in tow, but you need a reality check, pal."

His temper was starting to fray, which meant it was time to put some space between him and his so-called sister before he said something he couldn't take back. He turned towards the door. "I gotta go find her."

Felan rolled her eyes. "I'll go. You stay and visit with mom. You haven't been here in weeks and with Oz gone too, it's gotten a little lonely for us."

Ren felt an arrow of guilt and was torn between staying and chasing after Cherime. "Can't trust you not to be a bitch to her."

"We're talking about the same woman, right? She might be too fancy to fit in with us, but she's almost as mean as you are. Besides, maybe we'll bond, and I'll see the light."

Tess moved next to Ren and circled his forearm with her hands. "Stay, Ren. Let's talk. Felan will find Cherime and bring her back."

Ren pulled his beard. Staying would be better than chasing after her, which was probably what she expected him to do. "Yeah. Okay." To Felan, he said, "You fucking treat her with respect, you hear me?"

Felan tossed him a passing glare as she stormed to her bedroom. Moments later, she returned, naked, with a leather pouch hanging around her neck. "I can't believe any of this." She rolled her eyes and disappeared out the door.

Ren made his way back to the table and sat down. "Didn't mean to disrupt supper."

Tess shrugged as she picked up her fork. "Hard to resist the call of the wolf inside you. If she's the one, your wolf knows it. You gotta get her, then, Ren. Felan's right about you getting older. You need offspring to pass your legacy on to."

Ren let out a heavy breath. "Cherime's different. It's gonna take some finesse to convince her and you know I don't have a soft bone in my body."

Tess shrugged as she toyed with her fork. "She's close to her heat cycle, Ren. I can sense it. It might come early; stress sometimes does that."

Ren considered Tess. He wasn't much interested in the political side of being alpha and neither were most of his pack – that's why they lived in the mountains. Tess, though, had shining moments where she gave shrewd advice that helped him and the pack deal with the human side of their heritage. This was not one of those instances. "Not going to happen that way. I'm not going to trick my woman to get her to stay."

"Don't be so noble, Ren. If you're fated mates, then it'll happen sooner or later. What's wrong with moving up the timeline?"

Ren shook his head. "We're talking about Cherime. She's difficult, unforgiving and she'll resent me for the rest of my life if I take advantage of her." He decided not to raise the fact that he'd already done so eight years ago, which is why his woman was out running in the snow instead of relaxing beside him in the warmth of this house.

Tess fingered her water cup as she made a poor attempt to look contrite. "You're right, I guess. But you know you won't stand a chance of resisting her if she starts her heat cycle."

"It's not going to happen that way," he snarled, soundly shutting Tess down with his tone.

CHAPTER THIRTEEN

Cherime trotted through the snow, letting her wolf dictate the direction. It seemed to want to turn around and head back to Ren, and she went in circles for a few minutes, trying to get herself to run a straight line.

The Mountain alpha was a like a lodestone, drawing her to him. It had always been that way, those torturous eight years, sensing him when he was near, which was rare, but it happened more often than she wanted.

They'd ended up at the town's watering hole, Becker's, at the same time three times. Three times she had to force herself not to climb him like he was a eucalyptus tree and she was a koala bear. His complete disregard for her presence threw up another wall of resistance. The hurt cut like a knife when he didn't acknowledge her, didn't even look her way. He would have known she was near, his awareness as heightened as hers. It wasn't something shifters could simply shut off, especially when the fates conspired against them.

Now, with the snow muting her senses, she finally convinced her wolf to move in a straight line. She aimlessly tracked through the trees without an end plan, though she certainly knew where she wasn't going.

The night air and the darkness settled her enough to let her mind wander to that first time, after they arrived at his cabin, the same cabin he still lived in. He had her in his arms before they were inside, his lips on hers, his hands all over her body.

She had been so young, so excited that this magnificent, brutal man wanted her. Not once did she think to stop him.

When he said, "I want to fuck you," she'd nodded.

That was all he needed. Words disappeared as he picked her up and carried her to his bed, tossing her on it and flattening himself on top of her.

"Ren," she whispered. She couldn't resist him. He was her mate – that lightning bolt that hit the moment she saw him. He'd touched her, stroked her, licked her, his lips finding her nipples and sucking on them, gentle at first, then hard, and only when she cried out, did he relent.

He'd stroked her pussy, already wet, but his touch near her opening drove her crazy. And his thumb on her clit, teasing it relentlessly as she bucked and moaned under him.

He was hard, magnificent. His chest sprinkled with dark hair, thickening over his hard abs, trailing down to his super-sized erection. It made her mouth water, the size of it, the hardness of it. Wanting her, needing her. She reached to touch it and he let her explore him as he thrust inside the grip she had around it. His fingers were driving her insane, teasing her clit, circling her vagina relentlessly as she climbed higher.

"Inside me, please," she had begged.

"I like when you beg," he'd growled low-throated, then he lined his cock up and slammed inside of her.

She'd been wet enough to take him, but it was her first time and he'd ripped through her hymen without thought. "Fuck!" she shrieked.

He slowed his thrusts, but still pumped. "Let it happen."

She lay under him while he fucked her, the pleasure trying to fight its way over the pain. "I can't," she'd mumbled, and he slid out of her, his fingers seeking out her clit, his eyes holding hers as he played with her, bringing her pleasure back up until she was begging again.

This time, when he entered her, he held himself back, not spearing her, but gliding inside slowly until he bottomed out. Then withdrawing. "Better?"

She'd nodded. She couldn't form words, couldn't think rationally. Her body took over, her legs wrapping around his waist as she met his thrusts. When she came, it was explosive. Nothing like self-love. This male became everything to her in that moment. He owned her – body and soul.

Over the next two days, he took her countless times. "I'll never get enough of you," he'd whispered that last night.

The following morning, something changed in him. He didn't touch her or hug her, barely spoke to her. "Time to go home, baby."

"What?" It was so out of the blue that, at first, she didn't understand what he meant. "I thought this was home."

He repeated himself, this time a harsh undertone in his words. "Time to return to your pack, Wolverine. You and me won't work."

"But we're mates." Fat wet tears rolled down her cheeks and dripped off her chin. She loved this man; they were meant to be.

"We're not official until I mark you. You're too young. This, what we had, it was a nice distraction, but this isn't me." There was no tenderness to his words, to his tone.

She was stubborn and difficult even back then. "Then who the hell are you?" She wore the anger, embraced it, and it helped her tears to dry.

"I've been holding back so I don't break you. You're too much of a princess. We can't work."

"Fuck you, too!" she'd shouted. There were more words, more yelling, hurtful things that erased the beautiful moments of the previous two days.

When she refused to go, he literally tossed her out of the cabin and slammed the door in her face. She remembered standing in the yard, shouting obscenities at him until he stormed outside and gripped her by the neck, squeezing until she got dizzy. "Go," he ordered as he released her.

That time, afraid he might kill her, she listened.

It was the last time they'd said anything meaningful to each other until this week. And now he wanted her after all this time? After what he did to her, put her through. Fuck him!

She sat in the snow, hearing the soft pads of an approaching wolf. Not Ren. She knew his gait, his scent. His everything. It was Felan.

Oz's sister nuzzled her neck. Pretty wolf, patches of white and brown. Hazel eyes. Felan let out a yip and then turned, not back in the direction she'd come, but deeper into the trees.

Cherime's wolf didn't sense hostility, so she followed until they reached a solid wall of rock with an overhang that clearly served as a shelter. There was wood and a firepit, and a crate that resembled a trunk right down to the hinged lid. The latter was tucked up against the stone wall under the overhang. Packaged together, it was a nice little place of refuge.

Felan shifted first and Cherime followed.

"Nice place you have here." Cherime watched while Felan pulled some twigs, dry moss, and a few pieces of firewood from a neat stack next to the crate and set it up in the firepit.

"My place, though others use it too." She motioned to some cedar boughs. "Bring them closer. They're softer to sit on than the rock."

Felan pulled a lighter from the leather pouch around her neck and ignited the kindling, then added more sticks and moss until the fire was in full flame.

The cedar boughs were dry and fragrant and Cherime inhaled deeply as she dragged several over and arranged them near the fire, then settled on them. Felan sat down next to her, then fished inside her pouch again and produced a joint. "You smoke, don't you?" she said.

Cherime closed her eyes. "If you weren't a Mountain shifter, you'd officially be my new best friend."

Felan grinned as she lit the joint, took a heavy drag and passed it to Cherime, who took a pull, then another, and one more, before giving it back. Alcohol had nothing on weed in terms of mind-altering substances. A few glasses of wine might get Cherime buzzed, but her body, like most shifters, metabolized the alcohol too fast to do much of anything. Weed, however, was tripping.

They chain-smoked two joints and Cherime felt the tension leave her shoulders. "Thanks for this." She tossed the last of the joint into the fire.

"Thought you needed something after big bro's show."

Cherime giggled at the rhyme. "What the fuck is wrong with him?"

Felan traced a finger up her toned calf. "He's an alpha,

which is an automatic pass for being an asshole."

Cherime closed her eyes, letting the high wash through her. "Yeah. Can't figure him out at all."

"Why don't you want to mate with him?"

Cherime wondered at Felan's motivation for asking. What to say? *Your asshole alpha took my virginity eight years ago, strung me along for two days, then literally kicked me out of his life?* No, that sounded too pitiful and self-absorbed. Besides, Felan didn't need to know how much Ren sucked. "I'm a city mouse and he's a country mouse." *More like a rat.* "He wouldn't leave his pack to live with me in Darkness Falls. He'll expect me to move in with him." She paused. "Have you been to his place?"

Felan nodded with a smirk.

"There's no running water, no electricity. No Wi-Fi. I'd die if I all I had was my phone for social media. I need my tablet too. And a TV. A smart one." She stopped as she considered what else. "I like to shower everyday too, and he doesn't even have an indoor bathroom. I'd have to haul and heat the water, then bathe in it, which I don't mind, but it's not great for washing hair. I suppose he could rig up an outdoor shower, but the water would be cold." She met Felan's amused eyes. "I like warm showers," she finished feebly.

"You don't love him?"

The invasive question struck her hard. The L-word. She had loved him back then, and even after he broke up with her, her heart was full of him. Those two days with him, it had been a honeymoon. Day three, he'd shown his true colours. Cherime sighed. "I don't know him, Felan. We don't know each other. All this fated mate bullshit. I'm not even sure what that is."

Yes, you are, her wolf interrupted.

She ignored it. "How can we live in the same area for

years and only now find each other?"

Felan turned towards the encroaching darkness, the snow falling softly. "Your heart's pounding like you've just run up the mountain. There's more to this story than you or Ren are saying. But I get it. Whatever's going on is between you and Mr. Big."

Cherime poked a cedar bough with her big toe. "Yeah."

The silence settled awkwardly between them for a few moments, then a cry in the distance drew their attention.

"Someone's out there." Felan's hushed voice held caution.

Cherime stood and swiped at her ass, clearing it of residual cedar needles. "Yeah. Male. Human. Sounds like he's in crisis."

They shifted simultaneously and Cherime let Felan lead the way. This land was the Mountain shifter's hood and Felan was much more in tune with the environment up here.

It didn't take long to track down the source of the cry because the cool air held the scent hostage, easily leading them along. As they circled a large boulder, they saw him, flat on his back in the snow. A lone male, definitely human, underdressed for the weather and night chill. A faint smell of copper. He was hurt, but not too badly unless he had broken a bone.

He was lucky, too, that Felan and Cherime were nearby. His cry and scent might have attracted far more deadly predators out looking for a midnight snack.

Better shift, Cherime thought, and then did, striding towards the guy. Felan followed suit. He didn't notice them until they were practically on top of him. Weird – it was like he was in a bubble, flakes floating from the sky, but not touching him. "Need help?"

He jerked in surprise and swiftly sat up. His eyes rounded like full moons as he saw the two females in front of him. He probably hadn't expected all the lush curvy nakedness showing up in the dark. His lips formed a big O, but no sound came out of his mouth.

"Who are you?" Felan demanded, her brows knitted as she flipped her long brown hair behind her shoulders.

He gave his head a little shake. "Dexter." Maybe he thought he was dreaming. "Are you two for real?"

"What happened?" Cherime ran her eyes over him. Blood was seeping from a cut on his forehead and a bump was forming, but neither injury appeared lethal.

"Why are you naked?"

Answering a question with a question seemed to be all they were doing. It wasn't getting them anywhere.

Felan seemed to think so too as she huffed and crouched down, grabbing him by the collar of his light windbreaker and yanking him to his feet. "Answer our fucking questions. Who are you and why are you out here? And where else are you hurt?"

He sucked in a breath and fell on his ass when she let go of him. "Sorry ladies. Or princesses of the forest. You're both so beautiful, I thought the bump on my head was making me see things."

Felan turned to Cherime with a serious frown on her face. "I'm going to eat him if he doesn't stop talking."

"You just ate," Cherime retorted, trying to lighten her up. The girl needed to grow a sense of humour. "You eat him, you'll get bloated."

Dexter chuckled, clearly not picking up on Felan's hostile vibe. "Please don't eat me. I'm stringy." He sighed as he rubbed one of his knees through his jeans. "I'm Dexter Hayes. You probably know my brother, Jackson?"

Felan crossed her arms under her breasts, making them perkier than they already were. "Nope."

"Never heard of him." Cherime was enjoying the game. At least it was taking her mind off Ren.

Dexter's focus got stuck on Felan's chest. "I was coming to Darkness Falls when the storm hit and my truck got stuck, so I decided to walk in."

Felan snorted. "Sounds like bullshit."

Cherime decided to throw him a bone. "Dexter Hayes, as in Chief Jackson Hayes?"

His lips formed a pout. "Acting Chief is my understanding, but yeah. Heading to Darkness Falls for a visit with my brother."

Cherime tilted her head as he talked. No elevated heartbeat, no pheromones suggesting he was lying about anything. Either he was the coolest male on earth, or he was telling the truth. "Are you hurt?"

He nodded. "Yeah, took a fall. Twisted my knee and banged my head as I went down. I don't think anything's broken."

"I'm surprised you're still alive. It was fucking stupid of you to head out walking in this weather." Felan again. "And shouting like that. You're lucky we were in the neighbourhood and not a grizzly or black bear."

"Yeah, no doubt you're right. But you know how it is." He shrugged like it was no big deal. "I got tracker in my blood. I always end up where I want to be, mostly in one piece."

"Get up." Felan commanded. "We'll take you back to my place."

Dexter offered them a captivating grin that did zero for Cherime. The guy was good looking, had a sexy vibe, a subtle charm, but he had nothing on the big mean shifter she and Felan were about to introduce their new friend to.

CHAPTER FOURTEEN

Two walked away; three came back.

Ren had been standing outside waiting for Cherime and Felan to return and was taken off guard by the man they were supporting as they walked. An unreasonable wave of anger rolled through him at the realization that the fuck was seeing Cherime naked. He wasn't exactly excited that Felan was parading around with her tits out too, but it didn't move him into the murderous rage he was trying to talk himself out of.

"What the fuck's going on?" he demanded as he stomped to the group, yanking the soon-to-be human corpse out of the females' grips.

"He was—" Cherime started.

"Get some clothes on! Both of you!" When they didn't immediately respond, he roared, "*Now!*"

The girls scrambled by him and he felt a slice of satisfaction that Cherime finally did something he said without turning it into a protracted debate.

As the slam of the cabin door echoed in the dark, he

grabbed the lapels on the male intruder's jacket. "Talk, bitch. What the fuck are you doing here?"

Tess called out to Ren as she reopened the door and let the light spill out, illuminating him and his human victim. "For god's sake, Ren. He's clearly hurt, not out to take advantage of the girls. Bring him inside."

Ren narrowed his eyes, scenting the newcomer. He seemed harmless enough. Nothing indicating any aggression. "You heard the woman. Get your ass in the house."

He jerked his hands from the jacket, turned and stalked into the house, the new guy limping behind him like a one-legged pansy-ass jerk-off. There was something off about the asshole, but Ren couldn't put his finger on what.

The guy was wiry, six-feet – Ren guessed – of hard, lean strength. Long black hair in a single braid down his back, brown skin. Too smooth: that was it. Smiling at Tess like she was a warm sunbeam on a cold day, his face unlined like he'd never been outside a day in his life.

Cherime and Felan came out of Felan's bedroom as the new guy kicked off his boots. Ren pointed to the sofa. "Sit there."

"No!" Tess protested. "He needs some warm food in him." She pulled out a dinner plate and cutlery and set it at the table. In Ren's fucking place! Goddamn it! He bit his tongue though because he didn't want to sound like a whiney brat.

The shit smiled wider. "I'm Dexter." Asshole had a name. Wasn't that special?

Ren waited for Dexter to sit, then stepped closer, crossing his arms, widening his stance so he was looming over him. "What the fuck are you doing on my mountain?"

"Thank you, ma'am," Dexter murmured to Tess as she ladled the stew onto his plate and handed him the breadbasket, refilled with warm slices of bread. The smells made Ren hungry all over again.

"You're welcome. I'm Tess, by the way. That there is Ren. He's alpha of our pack."

Dexter tipped his head respectfully towards Ren, then moved his gaze to the women. "And these lovelies?"

Ren carefully unclenched his fists so he wouldn't be tempted to sledgehammer Dexter through the floor. "None of your fucking business," he growled.

"Ren," Tess warned in scolding mother mode. "My daughter, Felan." She pointed towards Felan, who nodded. "And that's Cherime, Ren's mate-to-be."

"Oh, for God sake!" Cherime exclaimed as she folded her arms across her chest. "I'm not—"

Ren growled loudly. "We're not going to have that conversation in front of this jackass."

Dexter was in mid-bite but lowered his fork to the plate. "Perhaps I should go."

Tess's lips pulled downward. "Don't be ridiculous. Where're you going to go in this weather? You'll freeze to death."

Felan rounded the table and stood next to Ren, emulating his stance. "How come you haven't already frozen to death? You were flat out on your fucking back in the snow."

"That's enough!" Tess snapped at Felan. "Stop with the cursing. You two are the worst I've seen."

Ren glanced at Cherime, who was leaning against the wall next to Felan's bedroom. She hadn't moved from the spot, hadn't said a word since Ren cut her off. As much as he hated Tess calling him out, the woman was right. He wasn't going to get information out of the guy by threatening to kill him, because a hollow threat was a useless threat.

"Yeah. Okay." He yanked out the chair Cherime had previously used and flipped it around so he could straddle it and lean his arms on the back. "Dexter." He rolled his tongue around the name and decided he hated it. "Maybe you should talk more, eat less."

Tess narrowed her eyes. "Maybe you need to talk less, so he can talk to you."

Ren frowned at Tess. He loved her, but sometimes she forgot he was the alpha. "Tess, take a break," he growled in warning. "Help Cherime and Felan clean up." He hardened his expression, so she understood there'd be no more backtalk.

She was astute enough to get the message.

She caught Felan's eye and flicked her head towards the kitchen, then moved to the stove. Cherime didn't move from where she was standing, and Ren decided not to challenge her. If Tess wanted Cherime's help, he had no doubt that Tess would let her know.

He turned to Dexter. "Waiting."

Dexter swallowed the bite of bread and licked the butter off his lips. "As I told my pretty rescuers, I was headed into Darkness Falls to see my brother, Jackson Hayes. You know him?"

Unfortunately, Ren did. With Oz, his beta, out of town, Ren was sitting on the Integrated Territorial Crime Unit to represent his pack. Right now, with the death of the independent shifter female, Tia, they were meeting too fucking much. "Yeah. RCMP Chief."

"Acting Chief," Dexter corrected with a slight scowl.

Ren was losing his patience, of which he generally had little to start with. "Whatever."

"Right." Dexter nodded. "Got caught in the storm and abandoned my truck. I decided to walk in. Must've got disoriented. Fell into a hole obscured by the snow. Twisted my knee and hit my head." He pointed to the bump on his forehead.

Ren glanced at it. "Where were you coming from?"

Dexter took another bite of the stew and mumbled around it. "Reserve."

Ren narrowed his eyes as he stared down the asshole. "Huh. Not how I'd come in from the reserve, given that Route 97 leads right into Darkness Falls."

Dexter lifted his shoulders in a half-shrug. "Yeah, but I'm a journey kind of guy. Coming in over the mountain, making the trip last a couple of days. Camping under the stars."

Ren couldn't detect a lie from the guy. Not an elevated heartbeat, not a twitch to indicate he was hiding anything. Nerves of steel. "Takes you right through my territory."

Dexter plastered a friendly smile on his face. "I don't recognize your territory."

Ren bellowed a laugh. "You fucking human. Doesn't make you less dead."

Not even a slight increase to the pulse. This fuck was as cool as they came. "Your territory is respected by other shifter packs. That's between you and them, how you want to settle it. But me. I'm a human, which means I can wander wherever I like unless you own the land, and even then, given that I'm First Nations, it's questionable."

Shifters had been roaming the land as long as wolves had, a lot longer than Aboriginals, but Ren wasn't about to get into a debate about how colonialism had fucked up both their respective worlds. "Weather's died down. Think you should leave."

"No!" Felan and Tess chorused.

"Doesn't mean the road's passable," Tess added. "And he can't walk with a twisted knee. We'll fix him up and he can stay the night."

Ren glanced at Cherime. Her eyes were almost glassy and the intensity of her focus on him made his head spin, his wolf whine, and his dick hard. What the fuck was going on with her? "Cherime and I aren't staying over, and no one knows if this jackass is full of shit."

"I don't sense a lie," Felan said. "Besides, big bro, even though mom and I are delicate female shifters, I'm pretty sure we can handle one puny human male who can't even walk."

Ren felt grumpy at all the push back he was getting. "Fuck me for not wanting you murdered in your sleep."

"I promise no harm will come to these lovely ladies." Dexter threw a wink at Tess. "Thank you for inviting me for the night. It's much appreciated."

Felan pushed off the counter she'd been leaning against. "If you're done eating, I'll wrap your knee and fix up your head." To Ren, she said, "Why don't you take the missus and head home."

Ren wanted to throw Felan through a plate glass window. "Yeah. No point in trying to talk you stubborn women out of anything." He turned to Cherime and nodded his head towards the door. "Let's go."

She grasped the hem of her jersey and started pulling it up over her head. "Not here," he roared, making everyone flinch, the cool asshole included. "Outside, where the bastard can't see you."

Cherime shrugged her shoulders and sashayed out the door like she was an old-time hooker in a saloon full of men. Ren was furious at her, at all of them. He was a goddamned alpha – where the fuck was the respect?

CHAPTER FIFTEEN

Something was wrong. Cherime had never been sick in her entire life. Not once, not even a cold. It was the hardy shifter blood, but also good genes. Colds and flu flushed through her system without so much as a sneeze.

While Ren interrogated Dexter, Cherime felt too wobbly to do anything but lean her back against the wall and watch the scene in front of her unfold. She couldn't move, couldn't talk. Couldn't have helped in the kitchen, even if she'd wanted to, which she didn't. She felt like she was burning up inside, sweating a little, stomach churning, head fogged. She couldn't concentrate on the conversation taking place. Her sole focus was Ren. How male he was, his body so big and hard, his attitude wary and protective, with a savageness that rolled off him in waves.

She was weak with desire for him. It was overwhelming her so much that she didn't dare move or she'd embarrass herself by throwing herself at him. Not in front of the relatives, she kept reminding her wolf, who was pacing inside her, agitated, panting. Needing relief.

Then he snarled at her for attempting to take off her

shirt in front of Dexter. That kind of possessiveness was unusual in shifters. Unlike humans, shifters weren't embarrassed or uncomfortable with the bodies they were gifted. They didn't generally strut around naked, but packs couldn't be packs without pack runs. And pack runs didn't happen in human form. Thus, shedding the clothes in front of other pack members was as natural as breathing air.

Even so, the shift happened fast, because the human side was bold and curious and easily turned on. Like now, Cherime thought, as Ren shed his clothes in front of her, his human body so fucking sexy that she thought she might have drooled a little on Felan's shirt.

"Hurry up," he barked before he shifted.

Thank god. She had been about to jump his bones. Her wolf wouldn't do it, that's not how it happened with shifters. Nope, their wolves ran together, hunted together, sometimes played, sometimes dominated, but it was purposeful. The human side, that was where the desire was, even if her wolf felt it. She handed Felan's clothes to her with a murmured, "Thank you."

"You're welcome," Tess replied. "And come back with Ren again." She smiled widely.

Felan rolled her eyes. "Yeah. Drop by anytime you're on the mountain."

Cherime nodded and shifted, then raced after Ren. She needed to find him, be near him. His scent was overwhelming her senses and she had no trouble catching up. He was racing through the snow, dodging trees, stumps, deadfall, not faltering. Cherime, on the other hand, felt like she was stoned. Maybe it was the blunts she'd smoked earlier with Felan, but that should have worn off by now. Unless it was super weed. B.C. bud at it's finest. No. Cherime knew her weed like a hypochondriac knew his drugs. Not even B.C. bud would keep her stoned this long.

Whatever the case, she had to slow her pace because she kept stumbling over herself. She wanted to stop and call for Ren, but she knew that if she did that, it would stall her from getting what she wanted, which was Ren on the floor in his cabin, his cock inside of her.

Go! Go! Go! her wolf urged.

Fortunately, she could follow Ren's trail like a bloodhound; otherwise, the haze in her head might have led her astray. Relief flooded her when his cabin came into view. She shifted as she bounded into the yard, then raced inside the cabin. Ren was tugging on a pair of jeans and when he saw her, he threw a T-shirt at her.

"Ren," she mumbled, trying to catch the perfect toss and missing because her eyes were crawling over all of his manly parts. The T-shirt fell at her feet. "I don't want to get dressed. I want you, Ren. I want us together. I want it all." Was that desperation in her voice?

"Stop, Wolverine." He backed up to put more space between them. "You're not thinking straight and I'm not either. You're so enticing, I won't be able to stop myself from fucking you."

Cherime shrugged her shoulders. "Why would you want to stop yourself?" She kicked the T-shirt out of her way as she advanced him, swaying her hips like she'd done at Tess's. "Feel me. Feel how much I want you." She grabbed his hand and tried to guide it to the wetness between her thighs.

He yanked out of her grip and slid by her, holding his body back from brushing hers. A garbled "No" fell from his mouth as he ran straight out the door.

She followed him, shouting at him from the doorway. "What's wrong with you?" Why did she sound so needy?

She didn't do needy. Not for any man. Except Ren. Yeah, she needed him.

"You're in your heat cycle," Ren hissed as he stood in the snow, his feet bare. "We can't be around each other right now. I can barely resist you at the best of times. Now, though. No way." He took a deep breath and a shudder raced through him.

Cherime shook her head, in part to clear the fog so she could concentrate, but also because her heat cycle was a week away. "I'm not in my heat cycle. And even if I was, I never get horny. Well, I do, but not like this." She followed him into the yard, but he scrambled back from her.

"This… we're together, baby. Meant to be, so you ovulating around me makes us both out of our minds with lust. We can't fucking do this."

Cherime tried to grab him, but he twisted away. "Yes, we can!" she moaned. "I'm saying it's okay."

"No. I'd be taking advantage of you. I want you, yeah, but it has to be on your terms."

"Didn't you hear me? I'm saying it's okay! I want you; I want this." A wave of desperation hit her hard and she squeezed her eyes shut and her legs together. "Please! I can't not do this. I have a fever; my blood is boiling. I feel like I'll die if I don't get some relief."

"Fuck!" Ren yanked his hair as he paced in the snow. "Cherime, you'll hate me in the morning."

"I've never hated you, Ren. Not even when you tossed me out." She hoped the little lie might speed things along. At least she was still in the right frame of mind not to tell him she loved him. "I just need a little sip of you, a shot to get me through the next few hours. My heat cycle doesn't usually last longer than 12 hours."

Ren considered her, tamping his feet to keep them from freezing. "What if we can't stop?

Cherime thought about tackling him in the snow. He was as vulnerable as she was right now; her ripeness would be his downfall. "You said you wanted us to mate. So what if I get pregnant? It was going to happen anyway."

Ren blew out a breath and Cherime could tell he was caving.

"Please," she simpered, her eyes begging him. "I need you."

He took several steps towards her. "Maybe if we do everything but fuck."

"Yes!" Why hadn't she thought of that? She raced up to him and grabbed his hand, guiding it to her pussy.

He wrapped his huge paw around her wrist. "Inside!" Like she had a choice as he dragged her behind him and slammed the door shut.

In the bedroom, he picked her up and tossed her on the bed. Ignoring the whoosh of air that escaped her lips, he clutched her ankles and maneuvered her ass to the edge of the mattress, then dropped to the floor and shoved her knees over his shoulders. Wrapping his arms around her thighs and holding her too tight, he attacked her pussy with his tongue, inhaling her scent at the same time.

She came quick and hard, she was that needy. Her body shuddered as the orgasm ripped through her like the rush of a waterfall. Her pussy clenched, her womb pulsed, her toes and fingers tingled, and her head almost exploded. She wasn't done throbbing before she wanted a second helping. No, not a second helping. What she really wanted was him buried deep inside her. She was desperate with need. Her wolf, her womb, cried out for him.

He was still lapping at her wetness, his tongue burrowing onto her vagina, then replaced by one of his fingers as he brought his lips to her swollen clit. She almost leapt up off the bed as he sucked and prodded the sweet spot inside her. Another minute, and she came again, her hands clutching his head, mashing his face into her pussy.

"Fuck!" she screamed. "Ren, please, please." She didn't know why she was begging because he showed no signs of stopping.

She grabbed at his arms as he stood and grabbed her ankles, sliding her body around until her head was hanging off the mattress.

"My turn," he growled, kneeling on the mattress, her head between his thighs, his hard cock teasing her lips. He guided himself into her mouth and she took as much as she could, sucking it in to the base of her throat. She grabbed the root of his cock and did her best to circle it with her fingers. Too fucking thick, but it didn't matter. She had a grip on it. She had control.

Her need for him quivered through her as she sucked him in and out. He seemed to know she needed him again and fumbled his way to her clit, stroking it gently at first, and then pinching so hard, she jerked her ass and almost clamped down on his cock, which made him squeeze harder. "Watch the teeth," he snarled.

He fingered her as he let go of her clit. Blood rushed in and she went off like a bomb, but this time there was no milking her. Instead, he gripped the sides of her head, his fingers clutching her hair as he thrust deeper, faster, holding himself at her throat until she struggled for air and then giving her a few precious seconds to breathe before roughly pounding her mouth again.

"Ren," she gasped when he pulled out. "I can't…"

He flipped her over, her ass in the air. "I need to fuck you."

"Oh God, yes!" Cherime screamed. All good sense was gone. All she wanted was to feel his cock deep inside her.

He shoved his fingers in, then withdrew them, circling her anus, using her desire as lube.

What? No! Well, maybe. How far gone was she? Nope, not that far gone. "No!" she struggled away from him, her need slightly ebbing as he lost his grip on her. "No fucking way."

He snatched her by the waist and hauled her back while she clawed at the covers, trying to inch out from under him. "Baby, I got to."

"No, you don't! No one has ever touched me there."

Ignoring her, his fingers explored her rim, lubing it, softening it, but she felt the heat of his anger as he leaned on her back, practically flattening her. "Let's not fucking talk about how many males you did these past eight years."

"Fucking judgey," she grunted as she futilely struck back at him with her feet, kicking mostly air. Her aggression was enough to get him to flip her to her back. He shoved her legs up towards her head, then grabbed her wrists and dragged her arms under her knees so she was basically giving her legs a hug. He pinned both wrists with one of his humongous paws, then returned his attention to her ass.

She couldn't contain her desire as he circled her, softened her, probed her. He slid his thumb to her clit, toyed with it enough to get her bucking and screaming and then used her desire against her by lubing her ass.

"I'm surprised your ass is still virgin."

She grunted as he slid a finger inside. Only to the knuckle but it stretched her, and the pain of it braided with her pleasure until she was breathing hard again. Big cock, big hands. Ren was a monster.

"Don't believe everything you hear," Cherime rasped as she tried to jerk her ass away from him before she started liking what he was doing too much. It didn't help anyway, because he leaned his body on her legs, shoving them closer to her head, further immobilizing her.

"You telling me you haven't earned your nickname?"

What nickname?

He shoved two fingers inside her pussy, none too gently, and she moaned at the sensation of fullness. His breath warmed her ear as he loomed over her, finger fucking her. "I don't think I can wait."

Those words, his thumb pressing the rim of her ass, the supposed nickname: all served to somewhat douse her heat. "Yes, you can. You're not doing this, Ren. We're not committed enough to bring a baby into this world."

He moved his head so his face was overtop hers. "That's why I'm gonna fuck your ass." His expression was hard, lustful, adamant.

The guy was an eternal optimist. She liked his fingers where they were at, deep in her vagina, and doing it any other way seemed… well… it seemed ass backwards. If he couldn't accept that she had a *No Entry* sign back there, then too bad for him. "You will not fuck my ass, Ren. I'll swallow your cum, but that's as far as I'll go with you tonight."

He snorted a derisive laugh. "You have one hard limit, do you?"

Her desired waned. "What exactly do you think you know about me?" She used all her strength to break his grip on her wrist, then rolled over to the other side of the bed and off, backing up until she bumped into the wall.

He shoved himself to his knees, eyeing her from the bed. "Your nickname is Cherry-Popper because you pretty much fuck anything on two legs."

It was like her heat cycle flash-froze. "What the hell are you talking about?" Why didn't she know about that nickname? Why would anyone call her that?

"I heard you love the barely legal boys. That you take your fucking seriously, making sure you take advantage of those teachable moments." He was sneering, angry at her for something he had no business being angry at, whether it was true or not.

The burn of tears made her blink at the unfairness of it. "Go to hell, you hypocritical sonofabitch! You tossed me out eight years ago and you're judging me for having a life?" She ripped at her hair with her fingers, using the pain to calm her fury. "Did you stay celibate all these years? No women in your past?"

"Not the same number!"

"You have no fucking idea what my number is!" She wasn't a saint, but some men talked through their asses, making up shit to appear almighty. And women could be as mean, even when it was none of their business. And why, why, why was she defending herself to Ren? "It's none of your fucking business!"

"It is my business because you and I are going to mate and as an alpha's mate, you have a reputation to uphold."

"Let's do it, then!" she hurled at him. "Perfect time for you to take advantage of me. I can't resist you; you can do anything you want to me. So do it!" She folded her arms across her chest and hugged herself. She was near tears, but crying now would give away too much of her power.

He was the only male in the world that did this to her. Eight years ago, she had cried for weeks, her self-worth brittle, her heart broken until she iced it over, looking at men as something to do, someone to do, when she needed a distraction.

"Fuck," he snarled as he stomped out of the bedroom.

She stayed against the wall, listening to him curse and slam things around. Then he reappeared, his hard body, his pulsing cock, his dark pubic hair drawing her attention.

She felt the lust again, grabbing at her, overwhelming her. "I can't be here with you," she moaned as she grabbed her head. "Why isn't this controllable?"

Ren tilted his head back, squeezing his eyes shut, his face creased like he was in agony. "I can't control it either. I don't know what to do."

She edged around the bed, then sprinted past him. "Maybe I should go back to the community centre."

Ren grabbed her before she reached the front door. "No fucking way are you going out on your own in the dark."

A wave of desire almost buckled her knees and she yanked herself out of his grip. "Well then what?"

Ren's eyes darted around, as if a solution would materialize. Finally, he said, "We gotta separate. That'll settle us both down. I'll leave for the night. You stay here." He stalked to the door, turning before he opened it. "I'll be back tomorrow. Maybe you'll be out of the cycle by then."

"I hope so." Cherime hugged herself.

CHAPTER SIXTEEN

Ren ran for an hour, not to exhaust himself, but to put distance between him and the she-devil in his cabin. He settled once he was far enough away that he couldn't scent her, but the pull was still there. His mate in his cabin, ripe and ready to take his seed. It spoke to his primacy, his instincts, his need to propagate.

He loped through the snow, sorting out his emotions. The further he got from her, the more the rational part of his brain returned. He regretted lashing out at Cherime for the reputation she'd built for herself in his absence. Guilt wasn't a sentiment he often burdened himself with, because he didn't often sweat the big or small stuff. He had a hot temper, yeah, but it quickly blew past. Ego, also yes, but that was pure alpha instinct. So was his need to protect his pack, his territory, his mate.

The problem was he unreasonably felt betrayed by Cherime. Over the years, every time he heard of her exploits, it had made him want to storm the fortress and carry her back to his castle. But that's where he left it. He'd never followed through on the desire to force her to his will because of pride – doing so would be an admission of the mistake he made when he broke it off with her the first time round.

He had taken her, made her his, then rejected her, and he had lived with the consequences ever since.

He saw a rabbit and gave chase, but without enthusiasm so the bunny got a reprieve. A few fallen trees offered a shelter of sorts and he picked his way to the centre of them and curled up. He could doze in and out, but sleeping wasn't an option. Grizzlies were hungry this time of year and he'd be a perfect morsel out here all alone.

He doubted he'd do much more than nap anyway. After the show-down with Cherime, his mind and his wolf were on permanent simmer. His wolf wanted him to go back to the cabin, fuck the woman senseless, plant his seed, and mate with her. His brain, on the other hand, was still regretting everything he'd said and did.

His relationships with other females were simple. He found one he liked, they hung out for a day or two, enjoying each other's company. Never in Darkness Falls, never on his territory. He sated his needs when he was on the road, on a trading mission, in the spring and fall.

He didn't try to convince himself he was good-looking. Maybe as a young man, he had the goods, but now, he was weathered, his nose broken a couple of times, scars across his torso. His ragged beard hid another on his neck, put there by a momma bear that took exception to Ren wandering between her cubs and her.

But good-looking and attractive didn't always equate. Female shifters saw him and wanted him. Whenever he walked into a tavern, he had his choice because he was a big, strong, alpha. They were warm bodies he could sink into, take pleasure from, but none were Cherime. No one lit him up like that girl. Sometimes he wished he'd never met her because then he wouldn't know what fireworks felt like.

He sighed and pawed his muzzle. What if he'd kept her all those years ago? What if they'd mated? He would have been her one and only – no past, no rumours, no other men to fuck with his head. He'd have children now, would have rebuilt his cabin, made sure it had everything they needed to raise a family. And Cherime would be his queen, supporting him, loving him without the hostility and anger.

He curled tighter into the snow and closed his eyes and dozed.

CHAPTER SEVENTEEN

After Ren left, Cherime paced the cabin, her mind at war with itself. She knew the second he was beyond her scent range because her body stopped thrumming and her wolf settled down.

Heat cycles were a funny thing in a female shifter's life. In packs, the cycles generally synced and happened like clockwork. Females knew when their cycle was about to happen, and the unmated ones secluded themselves inside their homes.

Mated ones didn't have to. They definitely had the pheromones, but the mating mark was as much a repellant to other male shifters as it was an aphrodisiac to the male mate. It was the only time a female shifter could get pregnant. Humans were the same. They had their own cycles and ovulated, but they'd lost touch with their instincts as they evolved, so unless they were monitoring their heat cycles, they didn't know they were fertile.

If a male shifter impregnated a female shifter, then they would be required to mate. It was an old practice that died hard, but maybe it was necessary. Shifter life could be difficult, with many children orphaned because of the savageness of male shifter instinct. Fight to the death was not all that uncommon among shifters, and fights between shifters and other prey animals was also a regular occurrence. Shifter pack mentality ensured that children were traditionally raised, even if the parents weren't around to nurture them.

Packs were also dwindling because many left, leaving behind their shifter heritage. And more and more young ones gave in to the lure of the city and formed urban packs, which all but abandoned the old ways.

Independents still existed, though. There were three in Darkness Falls, drawn to the town due to the shifter population, and the town's acceptance and tolerance of the four packs that claimed territory around it. These were shifters who followed tradition, but for some reason were either abandoned by or left their packs.

Cherime tried to sleep, but the thoughts whirling around in her head kept her from settling, so she puttered instead. She made Ren's bed, heated water, washed some of his clothes and pinned them up around the cabin.

The work kept her from noticing the passing hours, and as the day dawned, she finally dropped in exhaustion and fell asleep. When she woke up, the sun was high in the sky and she was still alone. She didn't know at what stage she was in her heat cycle. It could last anywhere between 12 and 24 hours. That's why females were sequestered for 48 hours. Overkill, but effective.

She slipped on a clean T-shirt of Ren's, wondering if he was colour-blind. Everything he owned was grey, black, or white. Still, the thought of him wearing an emerald green tie over a light pink shirt under a fitted suit jacket gave her a fit of giggles.

She fired up the stove and got the coffee perking. *Better*

than Ren's, she thought as she cradled her first cup and took a sip. A wave of relaxation settled inside of her for the first time in days, and she sank into the cushions on Ren's couch.

It was so quiet out here – bird calls and leaves on the trees rattling in the slight breeze. The storm had passed, the day was warming, and the snow would melt quickly. Her glampers would be happily glamping and awaiting her return.

She searched inside her for the usual desire to be part of the fun, but it seemed to have disappeared. She felt calm, collected, even content.

Then Ren walked in.

The moment their eyes met, her stomach twisted, her body quivered, and her pussy melted. She set the coffee cup down and stood, facing him. He stalked over to her, grabbed her face between his palms, pulling her to him, and slamming his mouth on hers with a desperate, needy kiss as he swept her with his tongue, robbing her of breath and good sense.

She kissed him back, her hands cradling his face as she jumped up his body, circling his waist with her legs. He flipped them around, knocking over the coffee table and spilling the coffee as he carried her to the bedroom and fell on the bed, his body crushing hers as his fingers sought her pussy.

"Still wet, baby."

"For you, yeah." It'd been 18 hours since she started her cycle. Surely enough time had elapsed. This time the wetness was due to her attraction to Ren, nothing more.

Ren's breathing was harsh, the hair on his chest brushing her nipples as he inhaled and exhaled. She shivered as he drew his lips down her neck, then his tongue, far more in control than yesterday, which had been a frenetic exchange of lust and hostility.

She tilted her face toward the ceiling and squeezed her eyes shut, cherishing the sweet silkiness of his lips as they trailed over her skin. His hot tongue darted out and tasted her, goosebumps trailing in its wake. His scent was a combination of moonlight and earth and it spoke to her primal, savage core.

"Oh god!" she hissed as he rimmed her belly button with his tongue, then dropped his hand between her legs and flicked her clit with his thumb.

"I want you, baby. I want to sink down deep into your cunt, fuck you until you can't walk."

"Yes!" Cherime gasped as he slid a finger inside her. "In me now, Ren. I want to come while you're fucking me." She was quivering in anticipation. Ren, the man she had always wanted, was going to fuck her. Would they eventually mate? Would she move up here with him? Would they have babies?

Fortunately, her wolf intervened. *Shut the fuck up with the thinking, Cherime. Get your groovy on.*

Ren flipped her over onto her belly, then pulled her up until she was on her hands and knees. He held her hips as he guided himself inside her, easing into her a few inches before slamming home.

"*Fuck!*" Cherime screamed, not sure what to feel. So big, and even as wet as she was for him, she felt split apart.

He eased back and thrust again, this time gently. "You okay, Wolverine?"

"Yeah," she panted, her desire overwhelming the stretch of her walls. And his pelvis, bumping up against her ass, the connection between their bodies. It was too fucking amazing!

"Damn you're tight," he grunted, leaning over her

back and supporting himself with his hands on either side of hers, his hips pistoning as he thrust.

His cock rubbed against the sweet spot inside her, forcing her close to the edge. She cried out and Ren laced his fingers through hers as he sped up his thrusts, his hot breath on her head, his chest hair rough against her back.

"Oh god, oh god," Cherime chanted. "More, again. I need…."

He knew what she needed, letting go of her hand and fumbling for her clit, finding it, teasing it as his groans increased. "Fuck!" he shouted as Cherime came on a cry, her pussy pulsing hard around his cock, gripping it like a turtleneck sweater.

He came deep inside her, ramming his cock until he was emptied. "Fuck!" he repeated.

After a heartbeat, he slipped out of her and flipped to his back, his breathing heavy and uneven as Cherime dropped to her belly, cradling her head with her arms, still pulsing inside.

It was amazing being with Ren again, better than anything in the world. She had never been fond of the idea of fate, even if her shifter heritage was deeply immersed in the lore, but the way she was feeling, maybe there was something to the idea that free will was a passenger, but destiny was the driver.

The silence between them lingered until it became unbearable for Cherime. Ren was not the tall, dark, and silent type. He was tall, and dark, but verbal, even if the words were often blunt and gruff. She'd had enough of waiting for him to speak first. "What now?"

He shifted onto his side and pulled her hair, forcing her face to his, making her flip to her back. He gently kissed the corner of her mouth, his tongue tracing her lips, probing at the seam. She opened to him and he tumbled inside as his hand slid to the back of her neck, grasping it as he deepened the kiss.

He moved from her lips to her cheek, then to her ear. "I need a nap," he whispered, his warm breath stroking the shell of it.

Seriously? "Don't you think we should talk?"

He flipped to his back and closed his eyes. "Not now, Wolverine. I barely slept last night. I want to either sleep or fuck." He raised his head and glanced at her face. "We can fuck first. I'm up for round two."

Cherime scrambled out of his reach and stood. She felt his cum leaking onto her thighs, mixing with her desire. "Go to sleep, you ass."

He was already snoring as she stomped from the room.

CHAPTER EIGHTEEN

Cherime washed up with cold water, then stepped outside, shading her eyes from the sun. Nature was so unpredictable, especially this far north and at this elevation. Snow covered everything, big drifts against the house and the outhouse, but it was wet and drippy and she could hear chunks of the white stuff sliding off trees and thudding to the ground.

Why did Ren live here? Why not somewhere else, where a well could be dug and water piped in, a home could be solar-powered. Somewhere with a few amenities supplied by the beautiful world they lived in.

Her stomach twisted as she thought of mating with Ren. After he rejected her all those years ago, she had considered moving to Vancouver. Despite her bravado, she didn't have the courage to do that. She could've faced down big bro and sis, even talked them into letting her make a short-term move, but what she couldn't do was leave the safety of Darkness Falls.

This was her world and regardless of her love of glamour and social media, she grew up in a pack that embraced the natural environment and practiced shifter traditions. She wasn't worldly, despite her attitude, and she'd be a freak in Vancouver or anywhere that wasn't Darkness Falls.

She sighed as she took a few steps into the snow. She was a freak anyway, but at least she had friends here. That hadn't happened easily, either, and she owed her crazy circle of friends to Trist, Raff's mate, and Honi, formerly of the Lodge pack, but now mated to the alpha of the Dominant pack.

Her heart lurched in her chest as she thought of her girlfriends. That's what she was missing right now – a friend. She needed a woman to talk to: one who she could trust enough to share her past. Her mind settled on Aubrey, the mousey little schoolteacher. She was perfect because she wouldn't share if Cherime asked her not to. She didn't know her all that well, but she somehow understood that Aubrey was honest and trustworthy.

With a doubtful backward glance at the cabin, she shifted. She didn't owe Ren anything, and if he was serious about mating with her, he could come find her. She wasn't soft and feeble. She was a warrior who stood her ground and fought for what she believed in. There'd be no mating with her until Ren grovelled the appropriate amount and agreed to her demands. No more sex, either. Only talk, agreement on the future. If they couldn't find common ground, then they couldn't be together.

Her heart hurt as she faced that truth. He was the only male for her and if they weren't together, she'd likely never mate with another. Eight years, she had tried to find someone to replace him in her heart, but it was futile. The only time she felt whole was when she was with the Mountain alpha shifter.

She stopped and sniffed the air to make sure there were

no predators close by. Bears didn't typically attack wolves, but the snow might confuse them into thinking it was time to get ready for hibernation. She didn't know for sure, but it seemed like a reasonable conclusion.

The Mountain pack's community centre wasn't far off, and less than 30 minutes later, it came into view. Cherime hoped the roads were passable because she needed to get the girls packed up and home to their parents, who would likely be milling around the Lodge with pitchforks and torches.

The town would send the plow up the mountain to dig everyone out, and given the lateness of the day, they'd likely already made it this far.

As she rounded the corner of the community centre, she froze. The handi-dart bus was gone, the melting snow betraying the tire tracks headed for the main road. She followed the path and when she arrived at the highway, saw a large swath of plowed road, enough to get the bus down the mountain.

Well fuck! Aubrey left without her.

Cherime's temper blew through her. Why the hell would that feeble little teacher abandon her? Just when she thought she could trust the bitch.

She ran back to the centre, shifted, and stepped inside.

Yeah, they were gone. Everything was gone, the centre now a cold, empty abandoned warehouse. To get back to Darkness Falls, Cherime would now have to run home in wolf form and she hated doing that. It would take her several hours of picking her way through trees, rocks, and other shit, but what else could she do?

Her wolf got up in her face. *Turn around and go back to your mate.*

"No!" Her voice echoed in the empty hall. "Haven't

you been listening? If Ren wants me, he's going to have to earn me."

She slammed her way out of the hall, shifted again and headed towards Darkness Falls. She cursed her way down the mountain and was still steaming when she finally arrived home. Other pack members saw her in wolf form. Some waved, others stared. She loved her white coat, couldn't even to begin to figure out how she'd inherited it, but it was impossible to hide. She was a rare wolf, no two ways about it.

She shifted and stepped inside her cabin. She was home, where there was hot water, electricity, and Wi-Fi in abundance, not to mention a bed with clean, 400-count cotton sheets. When she had the chance, she was going to burn the cheap flannel shit that Ren used.

She guzzled a large glass of water to settle her thirst, then showered, washing the grime of the last few days off her body. Enjoying the warm water flowing over her, she shampooed her hair with her favourite floral scented color-protectant shampoo, then conditioned it to bring back the shine and colour of her purple highlights.

She stood under the stream until the hot water ran out, then wrapped herself in a towel and refilled her water glass, drinking down half before seating herself on the sofa and tackling her nails. They were destroyed. As she removed the polish she thought about Ren and his way of living. Their lifestyles were so at odds, how could they begin to find a happy medium?

He'd never come out of the mountains, never give up his pack. It was tradition for the female to join her mate's pack, and eight years ago, she was all in. But now? She had a home, a pack that she was comfortable with, a job that kept her engaged, and friends and family close by.

The thought of family perked her wolf up. It had been

missing Mara. It had – Cherime hadn't. Mara was still grieving for Connell, the fucking bastard who cheated on her and tried to kill Eva Blakely. Seven months had passed, and for a while, Mara had seemed to be getting over it, but then she'd had a setback a few months ago and hadn't been at a pack dinner, meeting, or her job since.

Guilt wracked Cherime as she tackled the rough edge of a nail with her file. She hadn't seen Mara for two, maybe three months now. It was too depressing to go to her house and talk to her. Last time she'd been, Connell's stuff was still there, and Mara threw her out for suggesting that they toss it in a pile on the front lawn, light a match and invite the rest of the pack over for a wiener roast.

Mara hadn't found it funny when Cherime said, "We can pretend we're cooking his dick, over and over again."

By the time she was done her nails, she had a laundry list of things she needed to do: visit Mara, get a manicure, and give Aubrey hell for abandoning her on the mountain. And Ren, he didn't get to be in her thoughts. The asshole fucked her, then rolled over and went to sleep. He was lucky she hadn't ripped his throat out.

She thought about payback to those who had wronged her as she dressed and headed to Falls Lodge. All those calories she'd burned these last few days made her ravenous. She needed a big steak, mashed potatoes, gravy, and a mug of beer. Her stomach cramped at the thought of beer. Wine then? Also a resounding no as her stomach rolled over. Whatever. Too much activity and dehydrated, she thought. More water then. Her stomach gurgled in agreement.

Fuck, she couldn't get a break.

CHAPTER NINETEEN

Ren knew Cherime was gone the second he opened his eyes. Her honey-sweet scent lingered in the air, but it was not nearly as strong as it would have been if she were close-by.

He rolled to his side and ran his hand over the sheet where she'd lain, missing her already. His loneliness swamped him, but he knew he had no one to blame but himself. He'd acted like an asshole this morning, using her for his relief and then falling asleep. In his defence, he'd been exhausted, and needed a little shut eye or the conversation would have turned into another rager.

The pendulum swing of emotions when they were together was out of control. They fought, they fucked, they fought again. There didn't seem to be an in-between.

He got out of bed and fired up the stove, setting the percolator on one burner and a kettle of water on the other. He needed a cup of coffee first, and a wash, then he'd track her down. Maybe she was out for a run; the waning day was spectacular and called to him too.

After the coffee and the wash, he stepped outside and

shifted. He tracked her scent to the community hall, but it was abandoned. The bus, the girls, Cherime were gone. The full moon seemed to share in his subdued mood, and he lifted his muzzle to it and let out a long mournful howl. Close by, the answering howls of a pack of wolves pulled him back to himself. He was Ren, alpha Mountain shifter. He'd find his mate, bring her home, and keep her here.

On return to his cabin, he brought down a deer and gorged on it, then left the remains for the pack of wolves who had answered his call. Next time he and Cherime were together, it wouldn't be just fucking. Next time, he'd mark her to make sure she and the rest of the world understood who she belonged to.

CHAPTER TWENTY

Dexter Hayes crossed his arms over his chest and leaned against Felan's truck, waiting while the beautiful scary female shifter had a few last words with her mother. She could be a real asset if she were corruptible. Nice height, nice curves, legs that went on forever. Not afraid to show them off as they stretched seductively from the cut-offs she was wearing. She seemed not the least bit uncomfortable around him, but still suspicious as fuck, unlike her mother, Tess, who seemed to embrace him like he was her long-lost son.

He wasn't exactly son material and besides, the daughter was too hot. He couldn't tap Felan if he thought of her as his sister. The biggest problem was not the suspicions of the gorgeous wild wolf. No, the problem was that Felan was about to drive him into Darkness Falls and drop him off at the RCMP station. Despite the bullshit he'd fed the mountain shifters, he'd been coming into Darkness Falls over the past year – not to visit his pain-in-the-ass older brother, but to attend to a little side business.

The fucking snowstorm threw a solid wrench into his

plans. He had an important meeting today, and not with the cops. Sure, eventually, he'd hook up with Jackson, but not until he and his partner agreed on the details of their plan. They could use the cops to their advantage, and Jackson was perfect, because though he and Dexter didn't much get along, they were still blood, and his cop brother would protect him should things go south.

Felan came out of the cabin, her hips moving seductively and her tits jiggling as she approached. His cock woke up and he started to stir the air to mask his lust, but let the breeze go when he caught the smirk on her face as she rounded the truck and climbed inside. He wasn't a monk and the pretty girl seemed to be of the same mindset he was.

He popped into the passenger seat and barely got the door closed as she hit the gas and rolled the truck around. She steered out of the yard and took a sharp left onto the secondary highway without looking in both directions.

"Jesus," Dexter breathed, gripping the holy shit handle as the tires squealed.

"No one was coming." Felan opened her window and let the cool breeze inside. "I'd have heard."

"Doesn't hurt to take a look." He tried to settle his heartbeat, realizing the bitch had scared him intentionally.

She rolled her eyes as she smirked again. "Next time, I promise I'll look… oh wait. There won't be a next time."

All the things Dexter wanted to say to this mouthy she-devil. She didn't know him, not a fucking thing about him. No one did, except his partner in crime. Not even Jackson.

Dexter didn't take no for an answer, though *not right now* was a viable option. "Doesn't hurt my feelings," he grunted as he looked out at the trees, dismissing Felan from his thoughts and settling them on his brother.

Jackson Hayes, Acting Chief of the Darkness Falls

Royal Canadian Mountain Police detachment. The fucker had their father's temper and their mother's self-righteousness. He could be mean, demanding, a total prick, but he had brains enough to pick and choose his moments. He had everyone fooled: their mother, their tribe, and everyone in Darkness Falls, including the shifters.

The biggest problem was that Jackson was like a born-again Christian, once as wild and out-of-control as Dexter, but Sandy Ivers, their stepfather for a whole five minutes, influenced him to ditch their people and his family and join forces with the white people. Jackson didn't even see that he was the token Indian, getting ahead in his career because of the colour of his skin and his native heritage. No way he'd be running the Darkness Falls RCMP detachment if he were anyone else.

Between Jackson and their mother, Dexter grew up frustrated, angry, and rebellious. What the fuck did they expect? Jackson abandoned his roots, making his home in Darkness Falls, pretending he was a fucking saint. He could have been a tribal cop, but that wasn't good enough for him. Nope, he was all about the bigger and better things.

Jackson epitomized the modern native with his bristly haircut, his GQ clothes and his fucking white friends. Yeah, his heart had bleached out, though the fucker denied it. When he came home to the reserve, he would swagger around like he was the king of rock and roll and all the rest of his nation would worship the ground he walked on, thinking he was a wise man, not some asshole who left them all behind.

To settle his mood, Dexter thought about how useful his brother's ego was going to be because, despite the antagonism between the brothers, Jackson and Dexter were blood. Dexter was always careful to swallow the full extent of his bitterness when he was around Jackson, but his brother still pressed his buttons.

"How long're you going to be in Darkness Falls?" Felan's sweet-as-honey voice invaded his thoughts.

"As long as I need to be." Dexter knew he sounded short and changed his tone to charming as he added, "Unless I have a reason to stay, like a gorgeous female shifter with a hot body."

Felan glanced side-eyed at him. "They're plenty of those around."

"But not with your attitude," he countered.

"Or my ability to kick human ass." She pressed harder on the gas as she flashed him her signature smirk.

Dexter laughed, his mood lightening at her easy comeback. "I don't mind a good tussle. Besides, don't underestimate me. I'm fairly good at ass-kicking too."

"You're in shifter country, pretty boy. Not really a fair match."

Dexter took a breath as he nodded. What the pretty she-devil didn't know was that he had a few tricks up his sleeve, which he'd honed over the years. Rare gifts from his native heritage. He knew of only one other like him. His fucking brother.

Dexter decided to throw it out there. "We should stop and get to know each other better."

"I already know you well enough, cowboy."

Fucking cowboy. The woman knew how to launch a low-blow. He'd have shown her exactly who he was if she hadn't been driving like a maniac off her meds.

"I got a war axe that says otherwise, bunny cheeks." He didn't really know what the current insult was for shifters but thought she wouldn't much like being called a rabbit with fat cheeks.

Felan snorted, Dexter laughed, and they bantered their

way to Darkness Falls. As she slowed the truck to the speed limit, he almost asked her to let him out on the main street but decided that he had better connect with Jackson before word got out that he was in town. No point starting this trip with big brother interrogating him.

As Felan pulled the truck up to the RCMP front doors, he thanked her for the ride and again for Tess's and her hospitality. "Hope to see you again."

He wasn't lying, even though she rolled her eyes at him as she shifted into gear. He watched the truck fishtail back into traffic as he thought of all the other things that he had to do in Darkness Falls, including hooking up with his partner and discussing the future.

The RCMP precinct was central in Darkness Falls, but on the main route that blasted through town. It had a good-sized lot with lots of parking space currently not in use.

Dexter strode into the lobby and up to the security windows, which were open. A tall blonde with a long pony-tail glanced up from the desk she was sitting at, then stood, a smile on her face.

Fake smile, Dexter thought. "You must be Eva." They sure grew gorgeous women in this town. He wondered if it was something in the water.

The smile transformed into a real one. "I am. How do you know that, stranger?" She had a flirty lilt to her voice.

"Jackson talks about you when he comes home."

"Oh!" Eva's eyes danced with excitement. "You're Dexter! I see the resemblance now!"

Not a way to win him over. "Yeah, side-by-side, we look more alike except for the hair and build." He touched his flawless cheek. "And his scars, broken nose, and crooked lips."

She let loose a playful laugh. "I knew you were the better-looking brother."

"Wow, despite you and Jackson being friends, I think I'm gonna like you." He wasn't lying either. This one was a nicer version of the woman he'd just left.

"You'll regret it," a female voice said from behind, causing both Eva and him to jump. He turned to the sight of a small woman who was all hair, eyes and attitude, standing with her arms crossed, eyeing him suspiciously.

"Where'd you come from, Leah?" Eva asked, seeming pissed that her and Dexter's flirting was interrupted.

Dexter's senses were honed enough to know that Leah was a shifter though he had never seen one as small as she was. She wore a loose faded yellow T-shirt and rumpled jeans, with old sneakers on her feet. Untamed was his first impression. Shifter women were all wild, but this one seemed almost feral.

Leah rolled her eyes towards Dexter. "Do you want to have the sex talk with her? I've tried to explain it several times and she still doesn't get it."

"Ignore her." Eva glared. "She's a menace."

Leah lowered her face and stared up like she was Jack Nicholson in The Shining, catching first Eva's eyes, then Dexter's. "Ignore me at your own peril. I bring advice, secrets and good gossip."

Eva fell for it. "What gossip?"

"You're pregnant!" Leah announced loudly. So loudly that a door in the back opened and a couple of officers stepped out, one of them Jackson.

Eva's face turned red as she fumbled open the security door, and skated into the lobby, grabbing Leah by the upper arm and hauling her out of the precinct.

"Help!" Leah shouted before the door closed on her. "Jackson, get her off me."

Dexter turned back to Jackson, who didn't appear at all concerned about the little shifter's state of health.

"Dexter." Jackson's greeting lacked warmth and enthusiasm.

Dexter nodded. "In the flesh and blood, brother."

CHAPTER TWENTY-ONE

Cherime slept like she'd been on a five-day bender, she was that exhausted. She woke-up stiff and thought she must have been numb the day before not to feel the soreness. It was everywhere: deep inside where Ren had pounded into her, bruised lips from his kisses, sore scalp from the hair pulling. And her muscles, from Ren's use of her, but also the other activity. She couldn't remember the last time she'd run for hours in wolf-form.

That made her mad all over again. Fucking Aubrey Powell, abandoning her on the mountain with the mean Mountain alpha. That kind of behaviour stopped now – she was making a new girl rule. No abandoning friends, no matter the situation.

Cherime made herself a latte from her single cup coffee brewer and guzzled it down as she got dressed. She had spent the last three days either naked or in T-shirts. She was about to become the queen of mean and to do that, she needed to dress the part.

She started with sexy lingerie. A purple lacy thong and matching bra, then her brand new designer skinny jeans that fit her like a glove, followed by a clingy camisole top that dipped low and exposed the tops of her breasts. She threw on a filmy coverlet that hung open, added bangles to her wrists, a property collar to her neck, and silver hoop earrings. Her hair flowed wavy and free and her makeup was as subtle as a tree falling through a rooftop.

She smacked her purple lips as she regarded herself in the mirror. "Perfect," she announced as she reached for her shoes. Her wolf groaned like it always did when she wore four-inch stilettos. It didn't seem to mind the makeup or dye in her hair, although it preferred being naked as much as possible and hated shoes, all shoes.

You're out of touch, Cherime told her wolf.

Or you are, the bitch snarked back.

It was not quite 11AM when Cherime arrived at Aubrey's apartment and banged on the door. No answer and locked, she discovered when she rattled the door handle. "Dammit," she muttered, as she scanned the hall as if the answer to her problem would materialize in front of her.

Low and behold, it did. A gnarly old woman poked her head out from the doorway across the hall. "Aubrey's working," she snapped ungraciously, as if Cherime was causing a disturbance.

Cherime huffed a breath. "I knew that." She'd kind of forgot school was still in session. The graduation ceremony was always early; a tradition to get over with before provincial exams. It was bullshit for some kids. If they didn't pass their exams, they didn't graduate, even if they walked across an auditorium stage and got what appeared to be their diploma.

Whatever.

When she had graduated high school, she'd felt emancipated. Back then, the thought of never returning to the walls of Darkness Falls Secondary was like getting out of prison after serving a 12-year sentence. Now, as if her parole had been revoked, she was heading back to the school, acid burning her stomach at the thought.

High school had sucked. While Darkness Falls was well-known for its shifter population, humans still outnumbered shifters. There were maybe 125 shifters in the area, most in packs, some independents in town. But the population of Darkness Falls was around 5000. She had been one of two shifter graduates in her class and was quickly pegged as a snob and a trouble-maker by the teachers and many of the students.

She had hated gym and sure as hell wasn't interested in sports or the fat-headed boys and girls that thought they were future gold medalists. Her skills as a shifter would have pumped up the girls' basketball and volleyball teams, but once she told the jocks she wasn't interested, she became a pariah, dead to them unless they wanted to test her patience, which they did enough to get her suspended on two separate occasions.

The nerds ignored her because she wasn't smart enough, and frankly, she wasn't needy enough to hang around them anyway. The group of goth students thought she was too posh and full of herself, and admittedly, she was. Big mouth, bad attitude and tough as nails, which even back then, sported an awesome manicure.

The boys liked her well enough, but they were boys and she'd outgrown them in grade 10. The other shifter in her class was a male, part of the Dominant pack and a jock. They despised each other.

And the fucking teachers, always telling her to sit up straight, pay attention, act like a lady. Eight years later, most of them were still teaching at the high school because they had no other skills. Even their teaching abilities were suspect, but it was Darkness Falls. The young, eager ones came, stayed a year or two, and then fled to the south.

Cherime cut short her rumination as the tires on her SUV kicked up gravel when she made a sharp right into the teachers' parking lot. She slammed into the Vice-Principal's reserved parking spot. Jerk of the decade, VP Jasper, had wanted nothing more than to be principal when Cherime was in high school. Nothing had changed – he was still VP, but more bitter and unyielding.

She knew because Principal head-up-his-ass Berkowitz got her cornered at Becker's a few months ago, dead drunk and handsy now that she had *blossomed into a woman.* His words made her laugh, though it might have been the weed she was smoking. Ugh. He was like 60 years-old. Kept calling her a good girl and telling her how beautiful she'd become since high school.

He wasn't wrong, but even if he was the last man on earth, she'd rather make a meal of him than fuck him. She shuddered at the thought. Ugh again.

Locking her SUV, she strode through the front doors of the high school like she was the boss and immediately caught the attention of the school secretary, Mrs. Abbot the Rabbit, as she stalked past the office.

First stop was the science lab, or at least that's what it used to be, back in the day. She wondered if Mr. Proctor was still the teacher. Proctor was cool, but a bit of sadist when it came to homework assignments and tests.

Mrs. Abbot scurried after her. "Miss! You need to sign in at the office." Wow, bunny didn't recognize her, maybe getting old and the memory was failing. Or still afraid of Cherime, which didn't seem fair. Cherime only threatened to tear out Abbot's throat once, and got a three-day suspension for it. Raff was so pissed at her he'd made her shovel shit for the days she was off.

Nothing was fair, but she'd learned her lesson; the next time she was going to tear out the throat of one of the school staff, she wouldn't tell them ahead of time.

She ignored Mrs. Abbot as she threw open the science lab door.

Mr. Proctor was still there, but the former hottie was now sporting a bit of a beer belly and a nose that suggested he had a drinking problem. He looked in her direction as did his roomful of students.

"Cherime!" he exclaimed in surprise. At least Proctor remembered her. But if he was teaching science, Aubrey was teaching something else. She should've paid more attention to what Aubrey talked about, but fuck, conversations about teaching, students, and school subjects ranked right down there with eating salads, listening to instrumental music, and watching any movie with John Travolta in it.

She slammed the door on the science lab and stormed to the next room, the door of it standing wide open. English. Yep, Ms. Beckett was still the teacher, still wearing clothes two sizes too small. Didn't anything ever change around here? Beckett turned towards her and narrowed her eyes, transporting Cherime back ten years, when Beckett had disapproved of Cherime's outfit the first day of class in grade 11. Apparently, her shorts were too short.

She'd gotten detention that time. A week's worth for complying with Beckett's request not to wear cut-offs by taking them off right then and there. Cherime had never been sure if it was because the thong she'd been wearing under the shorts was virginal white and completely sheer, or if was because she suggested Beckett's ass wouldn't fit in shorts even if the bitch wore the right size.

Fat shaming a teacher was apparently a no-no, though Cherime felt set-up by the whole thing. She was giving fashion advice, following Beckett's request, exercising her rights to freedom of speech.

That time Raff threatened to send her to Alaska to live in an igloo with the Eskimos. After the sensitivity training she was required to take, she realized that Raff needed the course too, but when she explained his erroneous use of the term Eskimo, he made her clean the horse stalls, which threw the horses into a frenzy because they hated her. It was mutual.

"Ms. Montana," Beckett sneered, her voice hostile. "What bad deed did I do to have you grace me with your presence?"

Cherime glanced inside the classroom, the students staring at her like she was an alien from another planet. She smirked at the boys, who were sitting there with their jaws falling open. Some of the girls were also looking at her in awe. A couple of females weren't so pleased and Trixie at the back threw her a small wave.

Girl looked good with her pink hair, shorts and tank, and three-inch wedges on her feet. Despite Raff and Lucien's dislike of Cherime's glamping trips, the four-day weekends were an obvious success.

She brought her eyes back to Beckett. "Looking for Aubrey. I thought you would've retired by now."

Beckett narrowed her eyes. "I'm thirty years away from retirement."

Cherime did the calculation in her head and it didn't equate, but math had never been her strongest subject. "My bad," she countered as the students tittered.

"Aubrey who?" Mrs. Abbot had been hovering behind Cherime, her hands clasped together in front of her like a… well… a rabbit, except rabbits couldn't wring their paws. Were there such things as shifter rabbits?

Her mind snapped back to Mrs. Abbot's question when Mrs. Beckett cleared her throat.

Aubrey who? Good fucking question. "Aubrey Something. She's a teacher." Oh yeah, Powell, the dead girl's sister.

"Are you telling me that you're friends with a school teacher?" Beckett's superior tone was about to earn her an ass-kicking.

Before Cherime could respond, Trixie spoke up. "Ms. Powell is a middle school teacher."

Cherime jerked her head towards Trixie as did everyone else in the in the room. "Then what was she doing with us on the glamping trip?"

Trixie flushed as other students started to titter. "We needed a teacher-supervisor and couldn't get a high-school teacher to come along."

Cherime stepped further into the room, her eyes sweeping it. "You fucking judgey jerks!" she said to the gasps of Beckett and Abbott. "You little piss-ants are about to head out into the big, bad world where your attitude will get you crushed. And you'll deserve it." She pinned Trixie with her eyes. "You boys are gonna wish you had fucked that gorgeous girl when you had the chance, because you're going to marry one of these stuck-up females, have a couple of babies, then your wives are gonna get shrewish, difficult and start to look like their mothers. You boys are going to fart at the kitchen table, grow a beer belly, and expect to be thanked for cleaning out the fucking dishwasher.

"Cherime, stop this minute!" Beckett huffed, but Cherime ignored her.

"Little Trixie there is going to be pole-dancing down at the Zoo and you're all going to want her, but can't have her, and regret how you—"

"Ms. Montana!" An officious voice interrupted her tirade. Cherime jerked around. Yep, Mr. Berkowitz, principal extraordinaire himself. "Would you mind stepping out into the hall?"

Cherime was transported back to her high school days; her guts coiled around her kidneys and squeezed. Just fucking great, now she had to pee. She looked back at the students. "I was done here anyway." She turned, straightening her back and raising her chin in the air as she strode from the room.

THE RCMP STATION house was en route to the middle school that Aubrey apparently taught at. As Cherime approached it, she checked her speedometer and braked slightly. Inside she was simmering. Why would Aubrey masquerade as a high school teacher if she wasn't one?

At least this time, getting kicked out of high school didn't result in a suspension. Well it did, if Berkowitz's warning to call the police if she came back was any indication. But she had no plans to return to Darkness Falls Secondary – EVER!

She rounded a corner and caught a small figure running across the RCMP's parking lot, waving her arms like an air traffic controller. It was Leah, little shifter wannabe. No fucking way was Cherime going to stop for that trouble-maker. Cherime pressed the gas, then braked hard to the irritation of the driver behind her if the blare of the horn was any indication. Leah was running because Eva was chasing her. What the hell had Leah done now?

Whatever it was, Cherime made a split-second decision to choose Leah's side over Eva, who had been instrumental in getting Cherime handcuffed (which kind of turned her on, if she was being honest), was also human and baked horrible muffins. She reached across the console and flipped opened the passenger door as a speedy Leah dove in and slammed the door behind her.

"Go, go go!" Leah gasped-yelled from the floor of the passenger side.

"I'm going!" Cherime peeled back into the smattering of traffic.

Leah popped her head up and looked behind her. Eva was standing on the sidewalk yelling and waving her fist. "Thanks. She's fast for a human."

Cherime smirked as she ran a yellow light and made a left across oncoming traffic. "Or maybe you're slow for a shifter."

Leah sucked a huge breath into her lungs and climbed onto the seat, fastening her seat belt. "Not slow, but she has stupid long legs."

"Everyone has stupid long legs compared to you."

Cherime wasn't wrong in her assessment of Leah. The latent shifter reminded Cherime of a pixie the way she flitted around, small for a shifter and even most humans, she couldn't have been more than 5 feet, she was energetic, always doing things a little outside the norm. She was a latent shifter, which meant she couldn't shift even though she had a wolf inside her. More sensitive than most shifters, she picked up things before others did, even if her nose often led to trouble.

Leah stretched her feet out in front of her and looked down at her legs. "At least they're proportionate."

Yeah, Leah was Leah, gave it back better than most people could dish it out, all fun and games, but not always thinking things through. Like the time she stole Gideon's truck, which resulted in Cherime, Leah, Trist, and Honi getting handcuffed and arrested.

"What'd you do now?" Cherime asked as she braked for a red light.

"Nothing. I was talking to Eva about her pregnancy and she went apeshit on me." Leah rolled her eyes as if Eva had overreacted.

The light turned green and Cherime rolled forward behind a car whose driver was making a career out of going through the intersection. "Eva's pregnant?"

"Yeah, maybe a month."

"Shit, Leah, did she know?"

"Oh yeah." Leah widened her eyes and nodded her head. "I barely mentioned it and she went ballistic. Hormones, I guess."

"Huh." Cherime twisted her lips to the side. She and Eva were frenemies if that was still a thing, but at least Cherime was sensitive enough to understand that Eva might want to wait to share the news. "Was anyone with you two when you mentioned her pregnancy?"

"Jackson and Dumb and Dumber were there, and Jackson's brother, Dexter." She flailed her hands as she turned to Cherime. "But why would that be a problem?"

The Chief and the two assholes who had arrested her, Dagmar something and Adam Cole, who always seemed a little too fond of Cherime. "Maybe she didn't want anyone to know yet." Cherime was irritated that she was defending Blondie, and at Leah for being a brat. "It's a private thing and has implications for Eva's career. And the first few months are when the fetus is at its most vulnerable."

Leah looked down at her hands. "Oh." She glanced out the window as Cherime pulled into the Darkness Falls Middle School.

These names were so imaginative, Cherime thought as she guided her SUV into a parking spot. "Now she has to explain herself to Jackson and put up with that idiot Dagmar's asshole remarks."

"Stupid of me to do that. I'll make it up to her." Leah flipped open the door and jumped out. "What're we doing here?" Apparently, the conversation about Eva was over.

Cherime headed towards the front door with Leah trotting beside her like a guard… uh… puppy. "I've got a little ass-kicking to do."

Leah clapped her hands as they entered the building. "Sounds like fun. How can I help?"

Cherime turned towards Leah, worried that the latent shifter might get them arrested again. "I don't need your help. I've got this."

"Okay." Leah shoved her fingers into her jean pockets and trailed behind Cherime to the office. "I'll watch then."

"You do that," Cherime concurred. Watching seemed benign enough.

The school secretary, a red headed female with super breasts, greeted them. "Hello. How can I help you?"

"Are those real?" Leah pointed to the woman's chest. It was a fair question but still….

"Do you not have any filters?" Cherime didn't have many herself but there were some things that went without saying.

"Of course, I have filters." She returned her attention to the secretary's chest. "Your breasts are fabulous, even if they're not real. May I feel them?" She cupped her hands and reached across the counter.

Red turned red and took a quick step back. "Thank you. They're real and no, you may not feel them."

Cherime had to give the woman credit for maintaining her composure, and to Leah for asking permission. "I'm looking for Aubrey Powell."

Red narrowed her eyes. "She's in class. Is she expecting you?"

Cherime said, "Yes."

"No," Leah replied at the same time, clearly forgetting that she was a tag along.

Cherime glared at Leah. "Could you please just stand there and look pretty without moving your lips."

Leah sighed. "I could do that." She flipped her unevenly-cut brown hair like a diva. "Question is, will I?"

Cherime bent at the waist and hissed into Leah's ear. "You will or I'll twist you like a pretzel." To the secretary, she said. "Aubrey is expecting me. I'm a guest – a former student and graduate, now a successful businesswoman. It's the old *be cool, stay in school* rallying cry."

Leah snorted. "And I'm a fashion model in my spare time."

The secretary ignored them as she checked the schedule. "Ms. Powell's room is 203 on the second floor. The stairs are down the hall."

"Fabulous," Cherime said as she stalked from the school office, her anger at Aubrey somewhat deflating as her irritation at Leah grew.

"I loved middle school," Leah said as she tramped up the stairs next to Cherime. "There was always so much to do and lots of after class activities."

"Ugh," Cherime murmured. "Why would you want to spend more time in school than you had to?"

Leah shrugged. "I just liked it here."

When they reached 203, Cherime flipped open the door and strode into the room like a queen about to address her royal subjects.

Leah followed her but headed over to a student's desk and sat down on the top, turning to the young boy who was seated at it. "You don't mind, do you? I need a front row seat. This is gonna be an awesome showdown."

The boy shook his head, his eyes darting to Aubrey, who had been writing on the chalkboard when the shifters entered, but was now facing Cherime, a startled look on her face. "Wha… Cherime…?" She glanced at her class. "Ms. Montana, I mean. What are you doing here?"

"Well, Ms. Powell." Cherime strode past Aubrey, running her finger along the edge of the teacher's desk, which was placed at an angle in the corner of the room. She turned dramatically. "I'm here to ask you why you fucking deserted me!"

Leah leaned towards the boy, her eyes bright with laughter. "Told you."

Aubrey's jaw dropped. "Cherime, this is not the time nor place for this discussion."

"*Now* it's not the time nor place. This is the fucking conversation we should have had in the mountains, before you abandoned me."

Aubrey held her hands in the air, palms facing Cherime. "Stop swearing in front of the students."

Aubrey was such a little schoolteacher. Cherime rolled her eyes and addressed the class. "Hands up if you've never heard the word *fuck* before."

Not a single student raised their hands. "Annnnduh, hand's up if you've never said the word *fuck* before."

Again, not a single hand went up except for Leah's, who smirked when Cherime glared at her. Cherime nodded at the class as she returned her attention to little Ms. Priss. "As I was saying, why the fuck did you drive off without me?"

Aubrey's eyes darkened as she clenched her jaw. "What the heck was I supposed to do? Wait until mid-August for you to show up? The weekend was over, and I had a job to get back to." She swept her hand out at the class.

Leah leaned into the boy. "Now you're a job. How's that make you feel?"

Cherime caught Leah's eye and shook her head. "Zip it, Leah. Your job is to sit and stay." Back to Aubrey. "You could have waited a few more hours."

"I did wait!" Aubrey exclaimed defensively, "But when you left with Ren, it seemed like the deal was you were going to stay in the mountains for several days."

Leah addressed the class, the glee on her face making her eyes sparkle. "Ren is the alpha of the Mountain shifter pack, in case some of you aren't familiar with pack politics."

Aubrey turned to Leah as if she'd just noticed her. "Why are you here?"

Leah shrugged. "I'm a runway model."

All heads turned towards Leah, as the class tittered.

"You're a runway model?" A tall girl with long blond hair asked sceptically. "I'm taller than you."

Leah hopped off the desk and strode across the front of the classroom, ignoring Cherime's murderous scowl. "Yes," she said as she leapt up on Aubrey's desk, standing with her hands on her hips as if she were Supergirl. "I'm also a spy, currently undercover as a short, scruffy companion to a successful businesswoman. I'm much taller when I'm not in disguise."

"Leah, get down off my desk!" Aubrey snarled, then turned to Cherime. "And you. Outside, now!" She pointed her finger towards the door.

Cherime shuddered as high school memories flooded her. Fucking teachers. She hated them. She turned and headed for the door, Aubrey following.

"I'll take over class while you're gone, Ms. Powell,"

Leah called. Then to the class, she said, "You may call me Ms. Kävik. The L is silent."

Aubrey slammed the door, muffling Leah's voice. "What the hell, Cherime?" she snarled. "You can't come to the school and disrupt my class. This could have waited until later."

Cherime felt emotional, which was not something that often happened to her. Her throat hurt from swallowing the tears threatening to leak from her eyes. "You up and left me."

Aubrey's face fell as she picked up Cherime's distress. "Did Ren hurt you?"

Yeah, when it came to Ren, she was an emotional train wreck, but physically? He was rough and dominating, but he hadn't done anything she wasn't willing to do. "No." She felt deflated. "I don't know what's wrong with me."

"I don't either, but maybe you need to go home and reflect on your actions. Coming to my school is not appropriate."

Cherime stretched her neck. She thought maybe she had something against small women, which would explain her difficulty with Leah, and now, Aubrey. But she liked Trist, and Trist was little too, so it couldn't be that. "Don't talk to me like I'm one of your students."

A flash of anger crossed Aubrey's face. "Are you kidding me! My students are better behaved than you!"

Cherime pouted as she crossed her arms. "So what should I do now?"

"Oh my god," Aubrey exhaled, her composure appearing to crack. "Go home Cherime! Stay there and get your head together."

Cherime stepped back, thinking maybe Aubrey was right. "Fine, but this isn't over."

Aubrey rolled her eyes as she reached for the doorknob

to her room. "Yes, Cherime. It is over." She tried to turn the knob on the door, but it wouldn't budge. "What the hell! She locked it!"

Cherime smirked as Aubrey slammed her hand against the door. "Open the door, Leah!" she yelled, apparently forgetting they were in a school.

Payback was a bitch, Cherime thought with a grin as she strolled away.

CHAPTER TWENTY-TWO

Cherime left Aubrey to contend with Leah.

The day wasn't that bad after all, she thought, as she detoured to the grocery store and shopped for snack food and wine before returning home.

She opened the bottle of wine and poured herself a glass as she put away the crackers and dip, the bag of chocolate, and the tortillas and salsa. She wasn't a complete savage as she pulled out a loaf of sliced bread, some hazelnut spread, and a dozen eggs.

Looking down at the eggs, she felt weepy. They used to be little embryos, unborn chicks that never had a chance to unfold their tiny wings and soar to the top of a chicken coop, using their little peckers to eat so they could grow strong and lay their own nests of eggs.

She inhaled deeply to control her emotions as a few tears spilled down her cheeks. Something was horribly wrong when she was crying over eggs.

Aubrey was right; Cherime needed to be home, spend some time alone and sort things out. Her frantic race to challenge the schoolteacher was more avoidance of the topic of Ren than anything else. If she kept busy hatching plots of vengeance, then her tangled thoughts and emotions would stay in the background.

She kicked off her stilettos, then plopped down on her sofa, rubbing her tired feet. For the most part, it had been a super-duper day. Leah could be a riot at times, especially when she was pestering Eva. The cop and the latent were like weird bickering sisters, but there was also affection between the two of them.

Mara's and Cherime's relationship was the exact opposite – they didn't bicker anymore because Mara wasn't talking to anyone, and even before that, her sister's idea of friendliness was holding the door and letting Cherime enter the lodge first. Trist, though, she was a font of sweetness and caring, and Cherime was so happy Trist had mated with Raff. She was the younger sister Cherime never had.

The tears started again as her wolf called her a liar. She'd been mean to Trist at first, not because she was jealous or anything, but because little sis was the omega of the pack, and Cherime's instinct was to bully her. She didn't anymore. She liked Trist's hugs.

A big fat tear rolled down her cheek and plopped into her glass of wine. Yeah, that's what she needed. Wine – she was a happy drunk, though the most she ever got from alcohol was a little buzzed, unless it was imaginary booze, which she drank a lot.

The thought elicited a smile and she brought the wine it to her lips, but her stomach rebelled. "C'mon," she moaned as her wolf whimpered. It didn't want wine either and usually it was a lush.

Maybe a puff then, something to help relax her, but she didn't move off the couch. Her body was saying no and her wolf was saying no.

"Fuck," Cherime said as she placed the wineglass on the side table and glared at it. Then a thought struck her. She jerked up from the couch and grabbed at her hair, replacing her glare with what she imagined to be a look of utter horror and fear.

Fuck, oh, fuck, oh fuckity fuck. She was pregnant. Her stomach rolled over and her knees felt so wobbly, she sat down again, reaching for her wine to help settle her, then stopping mid-grab. That explained all the emotional shit and her body's aversion to alcohol and drugs. She closed her eyes and searched inside her, trying to connect with the tiny bean. Not so hard to find, it was nestled in her womb laughing its little head off at her disbelief.

She wondered if Leah had known she was pregnant, though it had barely been two days. And Leah wasn't one to keep her mouth shut, the evidence of her encounter with Eva proving that.

Shifters were more receptive than humans when it came to their bodies. Trist said that she knew the moment she conceived. Her wolf became joyful, and she became more sensitive to scents and motion. Her emotions were a carousel, constantly circling; she couldn't drink alcohol or eat certain foods, and the morning sickness started almost immediately.

It was inconceivable that Cherime hadn't realized it before now, but she'd been on a rager, her focus outward, not reflective. She closed her eyes as she ran her hand over her stomach. This baby, hers and Ren's. She'd still been fertile when they had sex, and this little by-product was about to throw a wrench into her life.

Once Ren knew about the baby, he'd insist they mate immediately. She shivered at the thought, certain that her pregnancy would only intensify the problems between them. She'd have to avoid him until she sorted out the situation, because he'd know the moment that he got close to her.

She groaned as she covered her face with her hands. She and Ren would be a disaster – they couldn't stop yelling at each other long enough to have a friendly conversation. And speaking of Titanic-sized catastrophes, she wasn't mother material, not for a baby. Chicks were conceivable, but a shifter baby? Her nurturing skills were sorely lacking.

She stood again as her heart thumped like a drummer in a high school marching band, and reached up and squeezed her chest to try to alleviate the panic-sized pain. Her mind staggered back to Trist. The omega had recently given birth to two twins. No. Just twins, not two. Well, yes, two babies, but one twin. No… that wasn't right either. FUCK!

Babies, babies, babies.

Shifters often had twins, even triplets. It was a thing for them, nature's way of bolstering their dwindling population.

Her stomach growled at the same time her wolf did. Jesus, she was in this alone, her wolf not the least bit interested in the human emotions that were swirling through her.

Feed us, it snapped.

Right. Babies needed feeding. She thought about heading to the lodge for a healthy meal but didn't think she could maintain her composure. What if someone sensed her pregnancy or worse, what if she got all hormonal and started crying?

In the kitchen, she threw a pan on the stove and tried to crack an egg, but she felt like a monster thinking about eating the embryo inside the shell. Instead, she made four toasts and slathered them with hazelnut spread, opened the bag of tortilla chips, and set it next to the jar of salsa.

Part-way through the meal, she had to stop. Why had she made so much? Sure, she had a hearty appetite, but she'd fed it yesterday. She'd barely done anything today to expend the kind of calories on her plate if she didn't count all the ranting and raving earlier.

Maybe it was the baby wanting to be nourished. Tears prickled in her eyes at the thought of the little fellow reaching for its bottle. She shook off the image. How the hell was she going to do six months of these swinging emotions?

No, not six, her wolf corrected her.

Right, it was nine months. Nine fucking months during which time her boobs would swell, her body would bloat, and she'd have to pee every five minutes.

She clutched at her stomach, rubbing her hand over it. But at the end, it would be worth it, wouldn't it? She'd have a little baby that she could nurture and love. Who'd love her back, until he became a teenager wanting to play basketball, wanting her to come to his games, needing money, borrowing the car. Yeah, the little jerk would attach conditions to his love, and she'd give in all the time.

She clutched at her chest again.

Maybe she was having a heart attack, maybe she should call Ren and tell him. Rip off the Band-Aid. No, nope. Better to avoid him for a while. But Lucien and Raff would make her tell him once they knew who the father was. Sure, they were rival packs, but shifters had a code and besides that, Lucien sure as hell wouldn't shelter another alpha's baby.

She shoved the last of her toast away and massaged the back of her neck. Sleep was what she needed. The day's excitement coupled with the cement mixer of emotions churning inside her were enough to exhaust her. She stripped off her clothes, washed her face with olive oil soap, applied a thick layer of night cream and crawled into bed. The moment her head touched the pillow, she was asleep.

Hours later, she startled awake. She knew dawn was breaking even though it was still dark as black ink outside. As she rolled over, she also knew the baby was gone. She lay on her back and stared up at the ceiling, conflicted over the loss. Hollowness seeped through her, an emptiness that she hadn't anticipated.

It happened to women all the time without them realizing they were pregnant. The womb would either reject or absorb the fetus before anyone was aware of the condition. The female might spot, she might not, but the moment often came and went without knowledge that something had transpired. No biggie.

But those were human woman, not shifter females. Not Cherime, who was pregnant, but didn't want to be, but now that she wasn't, ached inside from the emptiness she felt. Her emotions seemed back in control, except for the guilt. She'd wished the baby away, made it feel unwanted and let it go. A nameless, faceless, sexless pup that could have grown up to be a mighty shifter like its dad. An alpha shifter.

She trembled at her loss and thought it strange that she was so despondent. If this was how she felt now, she couldn't even begin to imagine the pain a female would experience miscarrying a few months into her pregnancy.

For the rest of the day, Cherime went into autopilot, showering, scouring her bathroom, cleaning her house. Day two was more of the same as she tried to keep her mind from dwelling. On Day three, she talked herself out of the house for a long walk and by day four, she was ready to re-enter the real world.

Getting out and about didn't mean her heart didn't still hurt, that the loss didn't affect her, that her guilt had disappeared, but emotionally, she was better. And there were other reasons for her to get her act together. Ren had been texting and she hadn't been responding. The longer she waited to return his text, the harder it would become. She needed someone to talk to. Not about the baby – okay, maybe about the baby, but mostly about Ren.

Mara was a hardass, but she was the only one Cherime could think of. Trist wasn't a viable option because, while she could keep secrets, she couldn't hide them. Raff would know something was up and bully it out of her. Shit would hit the fan and Cherime wanted to avoid the stinky stuff as long as she could.

Besides, it was time to reconnect with Mara. At least that would be her reason for the visit, she decided, as she walked to her sister's cabin. The snow had all but disappeared, the muddy trail was now hard-packed again, and Cherime's wedges got a little dusty, but that would be easy to clean up.

As for Mara, Cherime would tell her that it was time for her to rejoin the land of the living. She would even apologize for being a neglectful, self-involved sister, and vow to change.

She grinned at her silliness as she lightly rapped on Mara's door and twisted the handle. Of course, she wasn't going to change, but maybe she could soften her edges a wee bit. Those were her thoughts as she made her way inside and saw Mara hovering in the kitchen looking as surprised as Cherime felt.

"Cherime!" Mara croaked, her eyes round as saucers.

That wasn't the only thing round, as Cherime stared at

Mara's belly. Her enormous pregnant belly. "What the hell, Mara?"

"Shit!" Mara shoved her hair off her face and turned towards the living room, as if turning her back would make Cherime unsee the basketball Mara swallowed. "What are you doing here?"

That hurt and she let it leak into her voice. "I'm your sister. Why wouldn't I come over for a visit?"

Mara scowled as she lurched over to the sofa and awkwardly sat down. "Oh, I don't know. Because you never do."

Cherime sat in a chair opposite Mara and stared at her stomach. She couldn't drag her eyes away from it. "Is this why you've been hiding out? Because you're pregnant?"

Mara placed a protective hand on her belly as she started crying. "Yes. I didn't want anyone to know."

Cherime felt her eyes rolling towards the ceiling. She straightened them out before they got stuck. "Kind of hard to hide indefinitely." Her mood flipped a switch as the initial shock of Mara's condition passed. The untidy emotions were back – the guilt, the conflict of losing her barely-there baby.

And now, Cherime finding out Mara was pregnant, both of them having the same thoughts about keeping the pregnancy hidden. Cherime realized how irrational her thinking had been. "Who's the father?" She had an image of Ren and Mara together and almost doubled-over as her stomach clenched. *Please, please, don't let it be Ren,* she begged silently, despite knowing the possibility was practically nil.

"Connell," Mara said, wiping at her ever-increasing tears.

"Connell?" Cherime echoed. "What the fuck?" Connell – fucking dead, cheating, murderous brother-in-law, who almost killed Eva several months ago. Seven months ago, to be exact.

"I've been pregnant several times over the past few years. Lost each one really early on, so I didn't think that I'd carry this baby either, especially after everything that happened with Connell. But it stuck and here I am." She keened with sorrow.

Cherime felt herself responding to Mara's sadness with irritation. "What's the problem? You finally get your baby." No one had ever accused her of being counsellor material.

Mara grimaced as she swiped at her eyes with her hands. "Why would I want Connell's baby?"

Cherime stood in agitation. "Shut up! Don't say that in front of your child. It'll sense it's not wanted." She marched over to the kitchen table and grabbed a tissue box from it, then shoved it at Mara.

Mara stared at Cherime in surprise as she inelegantly grappled with the box. "What's gotten into you?"

Cherime sat again, crossing her legs and trying to stop frowning. "Nothing," she muttered. "You're talking about my nephew or niece."

Mara shook her head. "I know. It's just… you know… after everything with Connell…."

Fuck! "Not *everything with Connell.* He cheated on you and tried to kill Eva. Maybe killed Adrienne Powell. He's dead." Someone needed to be the hard ass. "Time to face it, Mara."

A deep angry flush infused Mara's cheeks, which would have been more effective if she didn't have to turn her body and use the back of the couch to stand. She tugged her shirt down over her belly as she faced Cherime. "You think I don't know! I live with it every day! His betrayal, his death! And now, because of this," she pointed to the bowling ball, "I'll have to live with it for the rest of my life."

Cherime stood too. "This baby is you, Mara. You can hate it because Connell is the father or you can love it because you're the mother. And you can make it all yours, however you want to raise it."

Mara's shoulders sagged. "You think I haven't been telling myself that for months? You've known for five-minutes, Cherime. Five minutes! And you have all the fucking answers, don't you?"

Mara was a softer version of Cherime most days of the week, and Cherime felt like biting back, but she swallowed her retort. She returned to her chair and placed her elbows on the arm rests, her fingers digging into the cushioned fabric. "I don't have any answers." Fucking tears were threatening again. *Don't cry. Not now.* "I want to support you however you need, unless you plan to abandon it."

Mara sucked in her breath. "Abandon it? How the hell does a shifter abandon a baby? Unless I take off, have the baby and leave it on the doorstep of a church."

"Which you won't," Cherime stated bluntly as shock rippled through her at her sister's thought processes. She almost added that she would tell Raff and Lucien, but she left that off. For now.

Mara slumped down on the sofa and covered her face. "No. I'll suck it up, have the baby. The pack can raise it."

Cherime shook her head, her resentment rising again. "You'll raise it. The pack will help you raise it."

"Sure," Mara said faintly as she dropped her hands to her thighs. A layered silence settled the tension and both sisters let it linger for a moment.

"Mara." Cherime leaned forward, placing her elbows on her thighs, and letting her clasped hands hang between her knees. "I know I'm not easy and despite that, you've been a good sister to me. It's my turn to help you out. What can I do?"

Mara sniffled and wiped her nose with a tissue. "Uh… I guess…." She stopped, drew a breath. "Thank you. I do need you. I wanted to tell you months ago, but I couldn't bring myself to say the words."

Cherime reached over and touched Mara's knee. "It's okay. I'm here now. Anything you need, I'm here for you."

Mara stared down at Cherime's hand, then wrapped her fingers around it. "I need two things, I guess." She met Cherime's gaze. "Will you come with me to tell Raff and Lucien?"

"Of course." That was an easy one.

A smile tugged a Mara's lips. "The other thing, it's a little more complicated. I want you to be with me when I deliver the baby."

Fuck, not that. Please. Anything else. "Uh, are you sure you want me there? Wouldn't Trist be a better birth coach? After all, she's been through it."

Mara shook her head. "I want you there. My sister. We don't do enough things together. It's time we changed that."

Cherime tried to see it from Mara's point of view, but it wasn't materializing. "Maybe we should start small, like meeting for coffee."

Mara half-smiled. "Cherime, please. Do this for me."

"Okay," Cherime lied, thinking she'd be conveniently involved in an MMA fight with a bear when Mara started her labour. "When are you due?"

"Late July, early August."

Cherime's eyebrows jumped in surprise. "That soon! How have you managed to conceal this from everyone?"

Mara shrugged as she looked down at her hands. "It was winter, I wore big sweaters and then as I got bigger, I pretended I needed time and space to get over Connell." Tears spilled over. "I guess I wasn't really pretending."

Cherime thought she should go to her sister and hug her. People needed physical contact, and Mara had been alone with this burden for months, but she couldn't make herself move from her chair. They weren't a cuddly family, and Mara definitely didn't like close contact. Maybe it was why Connell— *Stop thinking that bullshit, Cherime.* Connell was a fuck, that's why he cheated.

Risking rejection, Cherime moved to the couch and pulled Mara into an awkward hug. "I'm sorry this happened. I'm sorry I haven't been here for you."

Mara sniffled and laughed, letting Cherime cuddle her. "You're as insensitive as the males. If you were touchy-feely, you would have known the day I returned to work."

Like Leah.

Both Cherime and her wolf laughed at the thought of Leah being sensitive. "Yeah, I guess I can be a little self-absorbed." She gave Mara a squeeze and stood. "Have you seen Coop?" Jared Cooper was a local doctor, but also a shifter. Though he was part of the Dominant pack, he served all the shifters in the area and even some humans because he was that well respected.

Mara shook her head. "No. I haven't seen a doctor, but especially not Cooper. He'll tell Gideon, who will tell Lucien."

Must be pregnant hormones because Mara was supposedly the smarter sister. "Coop is a doctor so he can't violate your privacy or he'd lose his license." Cherime felt irritation rise in her. She'd just lost a baby she'd barely carried, and Mara wasn't caring for the one she was toting around. "We're going to see him."

"If I get seen—"

"For god sakes! You're gonna get seen eventually. Or

are you planning on having the kid here by yourself? I'm going to get Lucien and Raff to come over so they know what's going on, and then I'll call Coop and set up an appointment for you."

Mara pursed her lips and crossed her arms, throwing some serious narrow-eyed shade at Cherime but she kept her mouth shut.

"I need air. I'll make the calls outside." Cherime stomped out of Mara's house and inhaled a deep calming breath. It was little wonder that Mara was able to conceal her pregnancy. In winter, the pack went into semi-hibernation mode because tourist season was over, so it was bare-bones staff until March, when they started gearing up again. Even the pack dinners became infrequent after the holiday season, and were only held when there was pack business to discuss.

Wishing she had brought a blunt with her, she pulled out her phone and dialled Raff. It made sense to call him first because he was the big brother. Even so, sometimes the family connection with Raff irritated Lucien, the alpha. Pretty much everything Cherime did irritated Lucien. Today was going to be no different.

"Hi." Raff's deep impatient voice stormed the phone line.

"Hey, bro. Need you at Mara's."

He was silence for a heartbeat, then a cautious, "Why? Is she okay?"

"She's not dying if that's what you're worried about. But no, she's not okay."

"I'm on my way," he grunted.

"Wait!" she said quickly, because Raff was not big on social conventions and would hang up without a goodbye.

"What?" he growled at her in his typical fashion.

"Can you call Lucien? He should be here too."

"Yep," he hung up.

Cherime stared at her phone with a frown. It was as easy as a brief phone call to get Raff to come to Mara's rescue, no questions asked, and Cherime wondered if he'd be that quick to respond if she was in trouble. Probably not. But Cherime was a problem-solver. She had to be because she always seemed to find herself in problems of her making.

She flipped open her contact list, found Coop's clinic and pressed the phone number. Iris, his human assistant, picked up. "Dr. Cooper's Health Clinic," she said like she had a million things to do and a phone call was a major inconvenience.

"Hey, Iris. It's Cherime Montana."

Iris's voice softened. "Hey, Cherime. Long time no see."

Iris was the kind of woman who judged her self-worth based on her friends and she liked to count Cherime among them, although Cherime couldn't fathom why. Nonetheless, Cherime had nothing to lose by being nice.

What the hell? Did she just think that?

Maybe she was still hormonal. "Yeah, I hear you, girl-friend. I need an appointment for Mara as soon as she can get in."

Cherime could hear tapping in the background as Iris took a moment, then the receptionist said, "Everything okay?"

Curious kitten, and Cherime knew Iris had a right to ask, but no way was the grand reveal happening over the phone. "Yeah. She's got a female problem that needs checking." Understatement of the year! "Probably needs a half-hour appointment."

"Well, she's in luck. Dr. Cooper had a cancellation this

morning, so I can fit her in this afternoon around three o'clock. Will that work?"

"You're a doll. See you then." Cherime ended the call and went back inside. "Raff and Lucien are on their way here and we have an appointment with Coop at three.

"I like the way you say *we*." Mara was in the kitchen making tea, which Cherime despised.

"You want me in the delivery room, then I better be in on the rest of the shit." She flipped the fridge door open. "Got any wine?" Her little peanut was gone, no longer forcing temperance, and Cherime needed something stronger than tea to deal with the storm that was coming.

"No. I'm pregnant so why would I have wine?"

"No alcohol at all? Raff and Lucien won't want to drink that weak herbal shit."

Mara opened an upper cabinet and pulled an unopened bottle of bourbon from it, passing it to Cherime. "I bought it for Connell the day before...." She stopped and sniffled.

"Perfect!" Cherime ignored Mara's grief. She unscrewed the cap, pulled three glasses from an overhead cabinet, and poured a couple of fingers into each. She caught Mara's watchful eye. "What? I'm only going to have one, then after this showdown, I'll go home and change. I'm not dressed for a doctor's appointment."

Her comment made Mara smile for all of two seconds before the slam of a truck door sobered them both up. "Shit," Mara whispered as she started to tremble.

"Go sit on the sofa. I'll do the meet and greet."

Mara hurried off as fast as her bulk would permit as Lucien opened the screen door and stepped inside, followed closely by Raff.

Side by side, these two male shifters were so fucking hot that they had their pick of women. Raff was taller than

Lucien by a couple of inches and leaner and meaner. Both were strong, built like gods, with leadership emanating from them.

Raff was already mated to Trist, the omega of the pack, which was meaningless now since she was Raff's mate. He loved her in a way that sometimes ripped Cherime's heart out. It's what she wanted. To be loved like that.

Lucien wasn't yet mated, and she'd never understood why not. The male was perfect. An alpha with an even temperament and strong sense of fairness. Sure, he was gruff, had a temper like any male shifter, Cherime often on the receiving end of it, but he was also reasonable and open to suggestions. Their pack was strong because of his 21st century approach to organization. They were a team, and under Lucien's guidance, the Darkness Falls Lodge had become an A-list destination.

"What's going on?" Lucien said to Cherime as she handed them each a glass of the bourbon.

Raff glanced around the kitchen. "Where's Mara?"

Cherime took a sip of her bourbon and willed herself not to cough. She was all about the wine and pretty drinks and wasn't ashamed of it. Even so, she could slam the hard stuff when she had to, but it went down easier when she was buzzed.

"In the living room. I need you two to stay calm when you see her – don't be your usual reactive selves."

Alpha and beta shot her the same hostile glare. They didn't like being told what to do.

Too fucking bad. "I'm warning you, hold on to your tempers. No upsetting her."

She didn't wait for them to agree as she turned her back. They wouldn't anyway because they were stubborn male shifters.

She led them into the living room and sat down next to Mara, taking her hand and lacing their fingers together.

Raff and Lucien stared at Mara or more accurately, her protruding belly.

"What the fucking hell?" Raff growled.

Mara dropped her eyes and said to her stomach, "I'm pregnant."

"No shit!" Lucien barked, tossing his shot, then in a bourbon-roughened voice, said, "How come we're hearing about this for the first time?" He shifted his glare to Cherime as if it were her fault.

"Hey," she snapped defensively. "I just found out too. Apparently, I'm as insensitive as you guys."

"Whose baby?" Raff looked like he was calculating in his head, trying to sort out how far along she was.

Mara sighed as she shifted her ass to get more comfortable. "It's Connell's. I didn't realize because I was so emotional over his death and… and the stuff with…." She choked on the name. "That woman. And then when I did, I couldn't talk about it with anyone. I was waiting for one of you to notice."

Lucien scratched his head as he stared at Mara. "That's bullshit, Mara." He marched into the kitchen, poured himself another shot and returned, taking a gulp. "It's on you to tell us."

"Why?" Cherime piped up. "Just because we're a pack doesn't mean Mara has to explain her pregnancy to you."

Lucien disagreed. "It's exactly why she does. This baby is a member of the pack and we all have a role in raising it."

Cherime rolled her eyes. *Here we go with the whole it-takes-a-village bullshit.*

Raff seemed to be taking it more personally than

Lucien. "I'm fucking family, Mara. Why the fuck didn't you talk to me?"

"She's talking to you now!" Cherime exclaimed, watching Mara's face redden. The woman was barely holding it together.

Lucien glared at Cherime. "Did she lose her hearing and her ability to speak? Shut the hell up!"

Cherime held Lucien's glare for a good seven seconds before she dropped her eyes. It was a new record – Ren was bringing out her alpha bitch.

Mara came to Cherime's defence. "Don't take this out on her! It doesn't matter why I didn't say anything. That's my business. I'm saying it now. Baby's due early August I think."

"You think? Haven't you been to a doctor?" Lucien took another drink.

Cherime opened her mouth to answer, but Mara elbowed her in the side. "I've got an appointment this afternoon."

Lucien nodded. "I want an update when you get back." He drained the bourbon and set the glass on a side table. "Time for you to come out of hiding. Expect you back to work tomorrow." He glanced at Cherime. "Why aren't you at work?"

"I was working all weekend," she lied. "On the glamping trip. I figured I could take a couple of days off in lieu."

"How'd you pull it off in the snowstorm?"

Cherime shrugged, keeping her own secrets. "We came down before the storm hit and camped out at Aubrey Powell's apartment. She was the teacher-chaperone." She kept talking, telling them minutia about made-up events. Over the years, she'd found that talking about her glamping trips was a fantastic way to clear a room.

It did its job this time too as Lucien shook his head at her and left the house with a bang of the screen door.

Raff turned to Mara, tenderness in his eyes. "You gonna be okay?"

Mara turned to Cherime, tenderness in her smile. "Yeah, I've got my little sister helping me."

Raff rolled his eyes. "Shit. That kid doesn't stand a chance." He was still muttering as he left.

CHAPTER TWENTY-THREE

Ren was cranky. To be fair, Ren was always cranky. He'd been in and out of Darkness Falls all week, trying to track down Cherime so they could talk. It was driving him crazy not knowing where she was or how she was doing. She hadn't taken his calls, wasn't returning his texts.

Was she safe? Did she piss off someone? Or worse, was she with someone else? The last thought made him murderous. There better not be anyone else or he'd kill the fucker and chain Cherime to the bed for the rest of her life.

A few deep breaths helped to settle his thinking. She wouldn't want anyone else but him – that's what made pair-bonds so strong.

His wolf disagreed, reminding him that according to the rumours she'd had plenty of men in the intervening years before they reconnected.

He acknowledged that it was a double-standard, thinking it was okay for him to fuck women, but not okay for her to do the same with men. That kind of thinking didn't sway him from his connection to her. She was his, always was, always would be. He could let go of the past as long as she understood that she belonged to him, and there'd be no more fucking around.

It wasn't the only reason he was in a mood. He was also pissed at Oz, his beta, for still being out of town on his so-called personal journey. Christ, what was wrong with shifters these days with all the namby-pamby bullshit?

Adrienne Powell wasn't worth grieving over and he couldn't care less that she was dead. Did that make him a monster? Probably, but he wasn't about to pretend otherwise. Murdering her had never crossed his mind, and in retrospect, he wondered why not? Didn't matter though, she'd pissed someone else off enough to have her neck ripped apart.

Now he had to act civilized because he was sitting in for Oz at the ITCU meeting, the topic of which would be the murders of Adrienne and an independent shifter named Tia. Whoever decided on the 1PM time needed his or her ass kicked. It was the middle of the fucking day and made it useless for him to get anything done, given the travel time in and out of Darkness Falls.

He bet it was Eva, Aztec's human mate. There was another fucking reason to be pissed. Aztec had been a member of the Mountain pack before he was lured away by the bloody blonde siren, and a fucking good one at that, rejecting the alpha status of his own pack so he could stay with Ren's pack.

His wolf grinned viciously as it pointed out that Aztec came back to Darkness Falls for his booty call, not Ren.

Right! Aztec was happily mated, like Ren should be, if only he could track down his damn fated mate.

As he stepped into the RCMP precinct, he reminded himself to appear unhappy about Adrienne's death, to behave himself around Eva and Raff, and not to threaten to kill Gideon's new beta.

His wolf raised its eyebrows.

Ren told it to fuck off.

He hadn't much liked the Dominant pack's previous beta, Varg, who apparently was now alpha of a Northern Alberta pack, but the new one? Weston Hawke was too young, too smug, and too arrogant. The fuck hadn't yet earned the right to be that conceited.

Gideon probably saw this as an opportunity to mould the kid into what he wanted in a beta without having to watch his back. Rumours held that there were always fireworks between Gideon and his former beta, because Varg had an independent streak and a chip on his shoulder, though no one knew why.

Ren was last to arrive to the meeting, the rest of the group standing and sitting around the conference room. Jackson strode towards Ren, his hand extended. "Nice to have you here, Ren."

Ren took Jackson's hand because that was the polite thing to do and grunted something that sounded like, "Thanks," but his wolf translated it as *this is so much fucking bullshit.*

"Help yourself to coffee." Jackson indicated the carafe and various unmatched cups sitting on a table against a wall. "We're about to get started."

Ren observed the other participants as he poured the RCMP swill into a mug with the words, *my java lets me espresso myself.* Weston Hawke was seated next to Aztec's mate, Eva. He was tall, not fully bulked out yet because he couldn't have been more than 23 or 24. Male shifters came into their prime in their 30s, and this shit still had a babyface with patchy whiskers.

Eva was laughing at something Hawke said. If Aztec

could see this, he'd solve the Hawke problem quick, and permanently. It was hard to believe Aztec let his mate work with all these males. The guy needed a refresher course on how not to be a female's bitch.

Raff from the Lodge pack was there too, seated several chairs away from Eva and Hawke, looking like someone shit in his mouth, his gaze glued to Hawke. It appeared that Raff and Ren had something in common after all.

Ivan Polski sat opposite Eva near where Jackson had his paperwork scattered. The Russian greeted Ren with a nod, his heart rate elevating as Ren held his eyes. Ivan Polski was the resident forensic expert, a cop in his own right, and currently filling Jackson's shoes as staff sergeant while Jackson filled in for the chief.

Ascena wasn't anywhere to be seen, but he knew she wouldn't be.

Ascena was the *alpha* of an all female pack, a place of refuge for female shifters who were on the run from their packs. Her pack was protected by the Lodge and Dominant packs. No one messed with her women or they'd answer to Lucien and Gideon, brother alphas of the rival packs. It was like a fucking soap opera around here. And their protection was bullshit anyway; it hadn't saved Tia from her fate.

He dropped in a chair on the opposite side of the table from Raff. No fucking way was he going to get up close and personal with that asshole. It seemed the feeling was mutual as Raff glared at him.

Jackson pushed the same sheet of paper at him that everyone else already had. A fucking agenda, with a neatly typed numbered column. Why the hell did they need an agenda? Waste of time and taxpayers' money, not that he paid taxes.

Jackson cleared his throat. "Let's get this meeting started, so we can get on with our day."

Ren focused on Jackson, finding the cop interesting. Jackson looked like his brother, Dexter, but also didn't. Both were around six feet tall and lean, but Jackson came across strong, hard, and all business. Dexter, on the other hand, with his long hair and pretty-boy looks, gave the impression of trouble.

Between Ren's few interactions with Jackson and Oz's respect for the cop, Ren had a lot of insight on him. Jackson knew how to handle shifters, had the right instincts to take over the leadership of this precinct. He was a human alpha, and while there were plenty of them around, few could or would take on an alpha shifter. Jackson, however, was a rare exception.

He trained his eyes on the cop, so he wouldn't get sidetracked by Raff or Hawke. He was too volatile right now, not hearing from Cherime. The wrong look and he wasn't sure he'd would be able to restrain himself from savaging the assholes.

"Thanks for coming in," Jackson said. "Sorry about the postponement. These late spring storms mess everything up." He looked down at the agenda. "You all know Weston Hawke, Gideon's new Beta?"

Ren nodded at Jackson, not Hawke. He didn't look to see what Raff did, but he could scent the hostility in the room. Jackson would be sensitive to it, too.

"Thanks Jackson." Hawke's big-man grumble grated on Ren's nerves. "Where's Oz?"

Was the asshole talking to Ren? He shifted his gaze to Hawke for a few seconds. Indeed, the fuck was looking at him expectantly. "None of your fucking business," he snarled, which should have shut down the new young beta, but the shit was glaring like Ren had hurt his feelings and wanted retribution.

He turned back to Jackson, catching Raff's sneer at Hawke on the way by. Fuck, he hated having something in common with the fucking beta of Cherime's pack. Her name in his head shot an arrow into his gut, making it clench. Raff and Cherime were more than pack members, they were siblings.

Eva piped up. "Can we move this along, Chief? Or we're going to need a bathroom break." She stared meaningfully at Jackson and he nodded, a slight smirk bending his lips.

"We haven't met for a while and we've been spinning our wheels over Tia's death. We were good to pin Adrienne's death on Connell and even Tia's disappearance. Forensic evidence hasn't given us much and eyewitness reports are notoriously unreliable."

"What the fuck are you talking about?" Raff interrupted. "Are you suggesting that what Trist said was bullshit?"

Jackson's expression was less than friendly. "Not suggesting anything, Raff, but the big factor in Trist's attack was that the wolf was grey. The attack was in the dark—"

Raff started to interrupt but Jackson held up his hand. "I know shifters have fantastic eyesight, but your sight isn't any different than mine when it's dark.

Ivan popped in with an explanation no one was interested in. "Cones and rods in the retina are light-sensitive. The cones need plenty of light to activate colour vison and there was a rainstorm that night – so not a whole lot of light to work with. What may be grey in the dark, might be another colour in the light of day."

Ren sighed, missing his mountain, his cabin, and Cherime. Not necessarily in that order.

"So why the fuck are we discussing this months later?" Raff growled.

Jackson's voice held exasperation. "Because we have no fucking idea who killed these women."

Ren suppressed a grin at Jackson's profanity. Didn't take long for the alpha inside the cop to show up and shove professionalism into the back seat. "Thought it was Connell," he said gruffly.

Eva jumped into the fray. "Here's where we're at, which is no where, actually. Last year, Trist was kidnapped by Rusty, who was killed by Raff." She stopped for a second, her throat convulsing, swallowing tears if the flush to her face was any indication. Trist hadn't been the only victim of Rusty's attack. Eva had gotten ripped up by psycho shifter too.

There was shuffling and throat clearing as the men waited for Eva to compose herself.

It didn't take her long. "We thought it was possible for Rusty to be Adrienne's killer, but then Tia disappeared and… well… Connell." She stopped, shook her head, and stood. "I need a bathroom break."

They all knew where she had been heading with the story. Connell had been having an affair with Tia before she went missing. Eva found out about it while she was investigating the disappearance and questioned Connell, who then tried to kill her. The town crazy, Simon, saved Eva by bashing Connell's head in. Then Tia's body was discovered in a cave behind the waterfall. Frozen, marked. Same MO as Adrienne's murder, but with more finesse.

"Tia's murder links to Adrienne's, but we can't trace the murders back to Connell. No proof he knew about the cave behind Darkness Falls and he seems to have an alibi for Adrienne's death, as much an alibi as any of us have. His wolf wasn't grey." He glanced at Raff. "Though we're not ruling him out on that basis."

"Don't forget the partner theory," Eva said as she re-entered the room, rubbing a strong moringa scented lotion on her hands that made Ren sneeze. Why the hell would she do something so hare-brained in a room full of shifters?

Hawke pulled out her chair, throwing an overly-familiar smile at her as he helped her to sit. Raff glared at Hawke and Ren realized Raff was protective of the blonde cop for some reason.

This bullshit was why he liked the isolation of the mountains.

"What theory?" he grumbled, grabbing a tissue from the box Ivan shoved at him and loudly blowing his nose, returning Eva's glare with one of his own.

Jackson took over. "Adrienne was clearly killed by a shifter, her throat torn out. Tia, we don't know who was involved, but she froze to death after she was starved for god knows how long. In both cases, no shifter scents were present. How does that happen if only a shifter's involved?"

"Are you sure that the throat was torn out by a shifter?" Hawke asked his first stupid question.

Ivan furrowed his forehead at Hawke. "As sure as the forensic evidence and my expertise. But in case that's not satisfactory, I got a second opinion from Dr. Jared Cooper. I'm sure you've heard of him."

Credit to Hawke that he merely nodded. "Coop and I are practically best friends," he said, returning the sarcasm.

Ren's grumpy was growing. "So we're nowhere, is what you're saying. What's the point of this meeting?"

Jackson considered him with narrow eyes. "A reminder

that there still might be a killer or killers in the vicinity of Darkness Falls preying on women and so far, we've got nothing. I don't want us sitting on our hands, waiting for another woman to go missing."

"Right," Hawke said, then stopped talking as if that were the only word his brain could conjure.

Ren heaved a sigh. "So you're saying that a shifter did the damage while a human disposed of the bodies? That doesn't make any more sense than anything else I've heard. Humans stink too." He caught Eva's eye with a smirk.

She tilted her head at him and sneered, "Not like wet furry dogs."

Ren chuckled at her taunt. "Clearly you haven't been between the legs of a female shifter. Best fucking scent ever."

"Whoa!" Hawke jerked to his feet, his fists clenched like he was about to defend Eva's honour.

"Enough of this bullshit!" Jackson snapped as he shoved his chair back and stood.

Ren glanced at Raff, who hadn't moved a muscle, but the grin on the beta's face was telling enough. Raff was in full agreement with Ren. Of course, Raff didn't know that Ren was referring to his sister, Cherime. Might be fun to mention that.

He turned to Wolfe instead. "I'm not going to fight you, you motherfucker. Gideon loses any more betas and we're going to have to change your pack's name to the Pussies."

Raff threw his head back, his laugh resounding off the walls while Jackson dropped back in his chair and rubbed at his temples.

"For Christ sake," he muttered.

"I need to pee again," Eva said as she stood and left the room.

The meeting broke up shortly after and Ren headed out the door without saying goodbye to anyone. He was almost at his truck when his name on Eva's lips made him pause.

He turned towards the blonde female, who was striding across the parking lot. She and Cherime had similar characteristics, but it ended at the height and curves. It was almost like Eva embraced the shifter side of life, while Cherime embraced the human side, with her high heels, posh clothing, and purple hair. Eva had an earthy vibe, came across as a strong woman. Any other human and he would have scoffed, but he understood why Aztec was attracted to this woman.

Still, if her intention was to call him out for his earlier behaviour, he wasn't about to go easy on her. "What?"

She didn't shrink from his hostility, though her discomfort of him flitted across her face. She crossed her arms in a defensive gesture. At least she respected his power. "I heard you met Jackson's brother, Dexter."

"Yeah," he said, waiting impatiently for her to get to the point.

"Could you tell me how you came across him? Felan dropped him off and left, so all I have is what Dexter told Jackson."

"Jealous?"

Eva narrowed her eyes but maintained her composure. "Not jealous. Weirded out, you know? I can't get a handle on him."

Ren did know. He wasn't exactly weirded out, but definitely there was something off about a guy tramping through the mountains in a snowstorm, then smiling at Felan and Tess like he could guarantee multiple orgasms. "Cherime and Felan stumbled across him during the snowstorm. He'd twisted his knee. Claimed he was coming into

Darkness Falls to visit Jackson and got caught in the storm, decided to try to walk out."

Eva looked at the pavement, a thoughtful frown creasing her face. "I didn't know Cherime and Felan were friends."

Ren tilted his head. "That's what you got from this? Shouldn't you be more interested in why Dexter was wandering around my mountain in a snowstorm?"

Eva snapped her eyes up to his. "Yes. Right. Dexter. Why was he?"

"How the hell would I know? He's smooth as fuck, had Tess and Felan eating out of his hand the minute they laid eyes on him."

"But not Cherime."

"Cherime had better things to eat." He knew he should shut the fuck up, but it didn't matter because it wouldn't take long for word to get out about him and Cherime. The little group of glampers would make sure of that.

Eva grinned widely and he bared his teeth.

"Don't be a fucking gossip, Eva."

"Of course not," she protested. "I'm happy for Cherime is all."

"Sure you are. Anything else?" He jangled his keyring.

Eva's smile dropped. "Jackson and Dexter are family, so Jackson will have a hard time seeing past his brother's story. Don't know what Dexter's up to, but I doubt it's simply about him missing his big brother. I've been here four years, and this is the first time Dexter's visited Jackson."

"That you know of."

Eva raised her eyebrows. "I know everything about Jackson. This is the first time."

Ren pulled open the door and got in behind the wheel of his truck. "A little advice, Eva. You keep acting the way you do around with other males, you're going to push Aztec over the edge."

She scowled. "Aztec isn't an asshole like the rest of you guys."

Ren chuckled without mirth. "Yes he is, and one of these days you're gonna go too far."

He slammed his door in her face and gunned it out of the parking lot.

CHAPTER TWENTY-FOUR

Cherime and Mara were in the waiting room of Coop's clinic. There were a couple of other doctors in town, human assholes too good to share a clinic with Coop. It was a prejudice that shifters were used to facing and no one got overly pumped up about it. Shifters had their own sets of biases against humans.

Mara elbowed Cherime and nodded towards a sign on the wall that told patients to please turn off the sound on their cell phones so as not to disturb other patients. Cherime sighed as she reached in her purse and clicked the phone off. Stupid human rules.

There was another shifter female in the waiting room and a young human boy and his mother. The female shifter was an unknown, probably from Ascena's pack, and didn't give Mara a second look, so that was a good thing. The human mother was texting on her phone and ignoring the kid, who was coughing up a lung.

Cherime and Mara exchanged judgey glances, forgetting their earlier conversation about how unwanted the kid inside Mara's womb was. Cherime's eyes burned as she thought of what her future could have looked like if she had a little Ren sitting next to her. Mind you, they wouldn't be in a clinic because shifters didn't catch flu or colds, but her little guy could have stepped on a rusty nail.

Yeah, that's what happened.

He was out playing with Trist's twins at the campgrounds while she and Trist drank wine and gossiped. The boys were playing close to some old planks from a recently torn down hut – the stupid house where Connell and Tia met for their trysts.

Huh, Trist sounded like tryst.

Anyway, little Ren stepped on a board and a rusty nail went through his shoe and into his foot. They raced to the clinic, Trist calling Coop while Cherime drove. Trist's kids, Shadow and Scout, were in the back seat with little Ren between them, keeping him calm. But he didn't need babying over something as minor as a nail hole because like his daddy, he was brave and stoic. Not even crying, which made his mama proud. They got to the clinic and he walked in by himself, with the twins flanking him in case….

"Mara, Dr. Cooper's ready for you." Iris's voice jolted Cherime from her fantasy. Mara was trying to stand and Cherime leapt to her feet and lent a hand. Her pulse was rocketing from the path her thoughts had taken, from the shock of loss she felt over something she'd never had.

"What's wrong?" Mara said softly as they followed Iris to the examination room.

"Nothing," Cherime muttered, telling her wolf to settle down. "Just thinking about something."

In the examination room, Iris handed Mara one of those horrible blue paper gowns and told her to strip. "Opening to the front, so Dr. Cooper can examine your breasts."

"This is gonna get weird," Cherime mumbled as Iris left.

"Why?" Mara heaved herself up onto the examination

table. "It's just Coop." She seemed one hundred percent better since she'd unburdened herself of her secret and realized she had everyone's support.

"It's not just—" Cherime clamped her lips shut as Coop glided into the room with an air of professionalism. He looked from Mara to Cherime, then down to his chart, his face reddening.

"Hello, Mara," he said, then quickly composed himself as he turned to Cherime with a charming smile. "Nice to see you, Cherime. Been a while."

Cooper was super sexy, and they'd played doctor a few times in the past. He was more into her than she was into him, but to be fair, he wasn't the problem. No one held a candle to Ren, and Cooper, though awesome mate material for someone else, didn't have what she needed. The way he was grinning at her, though, looked like he wanted to get reacquainted.

He turned to Mara. "What's going on?"

Mara took a deep breath and then spilled out her story minus the emotional stuff that she and Cherime had shared earlier. Pregnant with her dead mate's baby, too devastated to come in before, Cherime forced her hand, and now here she was.

Coop seemed understanding enough, nodding as Mara talked, interrupting with a question here and there, probing her belly. "I'll want to do an internal exam, make sure everything is okay inside." He opened the door and called for Iris. When she arrived, he said, "Call the hospital and set up an emergency appointment for an ultrasound." He checked his watch. "4:30 this afternoon if they can squeeze her in."

He returned his attention to Mara. "Nothing to worry about, but I want to make sure everything looks as healthy from the inside as it feels from the outside." He glanced at Cherime. "If you don't mind stepping into the hall…."

Cherime almost protested, in part because she tended to be contrary, but also because Mara had already tasked her to be the birth coach. She caught herself before she opened her mouth, deciding she didn't need to see Mara's goods until absolutely necessary.

She exhaled a relieved breath as she returned to the waiting room and leafed through a fashion magazine so old it made Mrs. Beckett from English class look like an *it-girl.* A half-hour later, mom-to-be emerged with papers in her hand, smiling in a way that tore at Cherime's heart. It had been a long time since Mara smiled like that. Maybe just after she and Connell mated. It hadn't been an ideal pairing and Cherime never understood why the two mated, but who was she to talk? Wait until the world found out about her and Ren.

Coop followed Mara out and said a few last words to her before turning to Cherime. "Got a few minutes?"

Shit. "Sure." She stood. "Be right back," she mumbled to Mara and followed Coop to his office.

"Nice digs," she said as she glanced around the room. It was a typical doctor's office, white walls, a desk, a coatrack, some big heavy uninteresting books. Cooper's credentials hung on the wall in three separate frames. Big degrees with shiny round stickers on them. She was impressed. "Not many shifter doctors."

He waved to a chair and sat in the one next to it. "How's Mara really doing? She seems emotional."

Cherime had trouble meeting Coop's eyes. "Yeah. She kind of slipped through the cracks this winter. You know what it's like: we go into hibernation and get together only when there's a need. Mara didn't reach out after Christmas and I didn't check on her."

Coop nodded. "Best keep an eye on her going forward. If you can't, get someone else from the pack."

Cherime thought that was a good idea since she was sure to be side-tracked with Ren. "I'll talk to Trist. It might be good for Mara to have the babies around to get used to them."

Coop grinned in a way that made him sexy and handsome at the same time. "You look good, Cherime. Been thinking of you."

Cherime drew a jagged breath into her lungs. "Thanks." She didn't know what else to say.

"I know neither of us is interested in long-term with each other, but maybe we could get together again. We can be discreet."

Her wolf rolled its eyes. *Damn girl, that was almost as romantic as something Ren would say.*

Cherime asked herself if she'd be into Coop if Ren wasn't in the picture.

Her wolf said, *nope.*

Coop was good at the sex part, but there was no connection between them, no electricity. No nothing. "I'm… uh… flattered, but…"

He looked dejected, embarrassed as he stared at a file on his desk. "But you're not interested."

Fuck, when had she lost her backbone? "It's not that. I'm… with someone. Think it might be long-term."

Cooper's eyebrows shot up. "Never thought I'd live to see the day. Who's the lucky guy?"

Okay, what to do? Tell him?

Her wolf agreed. *Why not?*

It was right. Aubrey and nine teenage girls knew about Ren, so the secret was likely out by now. "Ren," she mumbled.

"Ren?" Coop raised his voice, realized he was too loud

and dropped it an octave. "Ren as in Mountain alpha, Ren?"

"Yeah."

Coop was incredulous. "Jesus, Cherime, are you nuts? Tell me you're just getting your jollies. You can't possible be thinking long-term with that prick."

She certainly was thinking about it, even though she felt the same sense of the ridiculousness as Coop did. "I haven't decided yet. He's thinking about it and he's kind of hard to say no to."

Cooper's face registered disgust. "He hasn't done anything against your will, has he? Not tried to mark you?"

Other than coercing her into returning with him to his cabin, he'd more or less respected her wishes. "Of course not. You know me, Coop. I'd cut his balls off if he tried anything I didn't want."

Coop blew out a puff of air. "I'm worried about you."

His statement irritated and gratified Cherime all at the same time. "I'm a big girl. You know I can look after myself." She wanted to leave but she had this urge to let Coop down easily. After all, of the men she had been with, Coop was one of the good ones. "I gotta go. But thanks Coop, for everything – squeezing Mara in, your concern for me. You've been a good friend."

"So it's like that, hey? I've been friend-zoned." He chuckled indulgently as he stood and gave her a warm hug. "I'm not counting myself out yet, Cherime. You can't know what the future holds."

Cherime quickly returned his hug and stepped back, knowing it was too late – his scent was already clinging to her. Ren would go ballistic if he ran into her smelling like Coop. The good doctor might not survive the day. "Better get Mara home."

The waiting room was empty when she walked into it. "Where's Mara?" she asked Iris.

Coop's assistant looked up from her computer monitor. "Mara told me to tell you she was going to get some groceries, then to the hospital for the ultrasound. You should catch up with her at the IGA."

"Thanks." Cherime offered a fake smile as she left the clinic fuming. The IGA was at least a couple kilometres away and stilettos were not exactly the shoes one used to hike that far.

CHAPTER TWENTY-FIVE

After Ren left, Eva returned to the cop shop feeling guilty about talking to the Mountain alpha behind Jackson's back. Frustrated too, because her acting chief rebuffed her attempt to talk to him about the oddness of Dexter's unannounced appearance.

When she'd cornered him this morning, he practically bit her head off. "I'm not stupid, Eva. I don't need you telling me what's up with my brother. I got it handled."

Yeah, handled alright. Jackson had a temper, but it wasn't hair-trigger, and he didn't usually blow up unless he thought it had strategic value. This morning had been an anomaly and Eva wasn't exactly thrilled at being on the receiving end of it.

She had a suspicion that his crankiness was also related to the bombshell Leah had dropped a few days ago. After trying to chase down Leah, Eva had returned to the precinct, neither confirming nor denying as Jackson, Dagmar and Adam stared at her like she had broccoli in her teeth.

Dagmar, the fuck, was openly checking out her breasts,

asshole probably thinking they would be bigger if she were pregnant. He spent so much time talking to her chest anyway that he probably knew it better than Aztec.

Fucking Leah! Eva was going to rain holy hell down on the little latent when she caught up to her.

She shook her head at the awkwardness of the prior day as she wandered back into the building. Adam Cole was manning the on-duty officer's desk, and she could hear Jackson and Ivan talking in the chief's office. She needed to get out on patrol. Today she was partnered up with Dagmar because someone above her pay grade had a cruel sense of humour.

She hardly ever had to partner up, but a new RCMP regulation made it a requirement for officers to pair up on the afternoon shift, after a cop in Halifax was caught masturbating in a squad car in the parking lot of a local kiddies park, shortly after school had let out. It was a typical organizational move to punish everyone for the actions of one stupid jerk. And thanks to Ivan's obtuse scheduling, she'd pulled the short end of the straw.

She was still pissed that Jackson had given the temporary staff sergeant position to Ivan instead of her. Sure, Ivan was already a Sergeant, so it kind of made sense, but he was also the precinct's forensic specialist and kept busy between that and major crimes investigations. Mind you, other than the deaths of Tia and Adrienne, there hadn't been many recent major crimes in Darkness Falls. Still, he could have done something useful like putting away the Christmas ornaments that were still scattered around.

She sighed as she stared at the fake Charlie Brown tree. It had become a battle of wills among the cops as to who was going to break first and stow them for the summer. Jackson was a little OCD about shit like that, but Eva knew him well enough to know that he was waiting for someone to piss him off so he could punish him or her with the task. She hoped she hadn't made herself a target by attempting to talk to him about Dexter.

Dagmar came out of the conference room, chewing his cud or something equally disgusting, then swallowed and used his thumbnail to pick a piece of it out of his teeth.

"Ready, Officer Judson?" Eva tried not to judge the jackass – lots of men were pigs, but Dagmar seemed to have mastered it.

"At your service, Officer Blakely. Or is it Reeves yet? Thought you guys were getting married in the spring. Probably gonna want to soon, so your kids aren't born bastards."

"My business is none of yours, you asshole," Eva snarled too loudly, prompting Jackson to stick his head out of his office doorway.

"Shouldn't you two be out cruising?"

Fuck, she missed Chief Levesque. "Going now," she muttered.

At the same time, Dagmar said, "On it, boss."

Dagmar insisted on driving and Eva didn't fuss about it. She had seniority over him, so she could have overruled him, but didn't mind the asshole chauffeuring her around. At least he was a decent driver.

"We pulled the downtown core. Why're you headed to industrial?" Eva asked when Judson steered the car southwest.

Judson glanced over at Eva. "It's the only way I can get you alone."

"You asked to partner with me?" Eva felt the steam rise to her ears.

"Yeah." He smirked as he made a right turn. "Told Polski that you and I got off on the wrong foot and I thought it was high time we reconciled."

"You're full of shit!" A tingle of fear got her alarm bells ringing and she wondered if she should be wary of Dagmar. They'd been enemies since he stepped into the precinct two years ago. The guy was good enough looking that he turned a lot of women's heads, which made him think he was a hotshot with the ladies. He propositioned Eva the first week he was there.

How about you and me go somewhere and fuck?

She shot him down spectacularly. *Not in this fucking lifetime if you were the last man on earth.* Kicking the shit out of a man's ego was a stupid thing to do, but Eva wasn't one to shrink from confrontation. It was her life's goal to prove she was as good as the men she worked with.

Dagmar nodded his agreement. "I am. I wanted you alone to talk to you about something."

The tingle gave way to a frission of fear, but she wasn't the kind of girl to duck and cover. "I should kick your ass."

"Fuck!" He sounded frustrated. "See, right there. That's why we can't talk at the station."

She scrunched her eyes shut for a moment, then nailed him with a glare. "We can't talk at the station because you are a giant-sized prick."

"I have one, so thanks for that." Yep, that was Judson, turning everything sexual.

"Take me back to the precinct. Now!"

Judson pressed the gas peddle harder, taking them further out of town. "Could we call a truce, Eva. At least for now. I want to run something by you."

Eva crossed her arms over her chest as she gazed out the window. The sun was already dropping behind the trees and she didn't want to be isolated with Judson somewhere out of town. "Okay. Turn the car around though. Then say what you have to say."

"Thanks," he mumbled, and she knew it had taken a

lot for him to say that. He flipped a U-turn and headed back towards Darkness Falls. "Here's the thing. I'm having a little trouble with the Chief's bro arriving in town the way he did."

Eva absolutely did not want to ever be on the same page as Dagmar Judson, but it looked like they might be reading the same mystery book. "How so?" she asked cautiously.

"Well, I didn't initially, even if the guy comes off a little shifty and Jackson doesn't seem all that happy to see him. But I was bored yesterday; cruising around can be mind numbing. I saw Dexter on foot so I decided to shadow him. Just… you know." He shrugged and glanced at Eva. "An exercise."

Eva did know. She did it too. Darkness Falls could be sleepy at times and entire shifts came and went with little to do but chat up the townsfolk or run drills. "Yeah, I know."

Dagmar turned into the industrial area, slowing the car, rolling slowly. "So, he meets up with this guy. I didn't know who he was, but they're friendly, shaking hands and giving each other back slaps, like they know each other. Then they get in the new guy's truck and head out towards the industrial section." He tapped his fingers on the steering wheel as he talked. "I followed but had to keep my distance. Cop car's kind of like a beacon, so I gave them a few minutes and then cruised the area, looking for the truck. It's a new Ford. Red and shiny, so it should stand out. Lost it though – I'm thinking they must have parked it inside one of the buildings."

"Okay. So far I don't hear a crime being committed."

"Yeah, not so far. Funny thing is, this afternoon, after the ITCU meeting broke up, I saw him again. Coming out of the conference room with the rest of you guys."

Eva dragged in a shocked breath. "Who?"

"Well I know Ivan and Jackson, Ren and Raff." He made a left and cruised down an empty street. "That only leaves the one guy."

Eva filled in the blank. "Weston Hawke."

"Never heard of him."

Eva wasn't surprised that Dagmar didn't know Gideon's new beta – she hadn't either. Hawke didn't hang in the same circles she or her shifter friends did. Becker's was not his tavern of choice. He preferred the Zoo, which was a little less savoury. Didn't matter though. The guy was charming and smart, and it was none of her business if he liked to party harder than she did.

"He keeps his head down around town. Never been in trouble, doesn't mix it up like other male shifters do."

Dagmar cruised past a big empty parking lot. "Doesn't seem like beta material."

Eva was about to agree when something in the lot caught her eye. "Turn in there." She pointed to an access. "There's something over against the building."

Judson made the right and headed towards the building. "Looks like a shopping cart."

"Simon's." Eva felt her pulse speed up as she searched the parking lot for the mentally ill young man. "Wonder where he is?" She had a soft spot for Simon, not only because he'd saved her life last year, but because his trust and affection were reserved only for her. They considered each other friends, and Eva was the only one who could bridge Simon's paranoid walls.

"Want me to stop?" Judson was already braking the car.

"Yeah. Not like him to leave his shopping cart. Let's check around. See if we can find him."

As she walked towards the cart, Eva's heart pumped harder than usual.

The shopping cart held the usual assortment of stuff Simon dragged around. Cans and bottles, an old waffle iron without a handle, a faded red umbrella, a huge box of green apples, and a one-eyed teddy bear.

"All the comforts of home," Judson mumbled as he pulled his flashlight from his belt so he could better see the contents. "Want to split up?"

Eva felt her belly flip. She hated to show vulnerability in front of Judson because he lapped up that shit like it was ice cream on a hot day, but too much had happened to her in the past year, and alleys and shadowed dead ends, even in daylight, made the scars on her right arm ache.

Don't worry, the little darling inside of her said. *You're not alone.*

That's exactly why I am worried. "No. You might spook Simon if you find him first."

It was a half-truth, and one Judson easily accepted. "Makes sense."

They swept the parking lot they were in as well as the nooks and crannies of the building, then moved onto the next lot, and the next. No Simon, no nothing. A few cars were parked in some of the lots, but apparently the business day was over. She glanced at her watch. Just after 5pm. "Seems a little early in the day for everyone to already be off work."

Judson had wandered away from her towards a bunch of wooden crates stacked together, disappearing from Eva's sight. She glanced around the lot as her brain searched for an answer. Maybe someone had taken Simon for a meal. That happened. People knew him, knew his issues, and tried their best to look out for him.

"Eva," Judson called, his voice an octave lower than

usual and hollow as an echo. His head popped up from behind a crate as he gestured at her. "You better come over here."

Eva felt her pulse accelerate as she walked with lead feet towards Judson. Whatever he'd found wasn't going to be good news. When she reached him, her fears were confirmed.

Someone was huddled in a fetal position on top of snow that hadn't yet melted because it was protected from the sun by the crates. A blanket covered the body and all she could see was the shock of mousy brown hair at one end, and tattered, worn out running shoes at the other, no socks. Dirty jeans had slid up the exposed flesh on the legs until it was masked by the blanket.

She crouched down and flicked the blanket off the face. Simon, ash grey, not breathing. Dead. She glanced at Dagmar, whose pale face and dull eyes reflected how Eva felt.

He swallowed. "I don't see blood."

She carefully brushed the hair from his face and pointed to his neck. "Ligature marks."

"Strangled."

Eva's gaze settled on Simon's face, her stomach threatening to purge its lunch. "Looks like." She stood and took a step back. Never good to vomit on the crime scene.

Judson followed her lead and backed away several steps. "I'll call it in." He sounded like someone had taken something precious from him.

Eva understood. That's how she felt.

After Judson made the call and returned with the squad car, they stood next to the crates, wordless and motionless as they waited for Ivan and Jackson.

Dr. Jared Cooper was with them when they arrived. He nodded at Eva as he followed Dagmar to the crime scene.

"Why Cooper?" Eva said as she approached her boss.

"Wanting someone with a nose to tell us if a shifter's been around," Ivan replied as he heaved his crime scene kit from the back of the SUV.

She liked Ivan, but he was always poking his nose into business he wasn't invited to. "He died by strangulation not blood loss from having his throat torn out. Think that's fairly obvious."

"Doesn't mean anything," Jackson defended Ivan, his tone almost scolding.

Eva tilted her head but zipped her lips. Seemed like she couldn't say or do anything these days without Jackson snapping at her.

"What're you and Dagmar doing out here anyway?" he asked.

She had figured that question would come, since she and Dagmar had been assigned the downtown core. "Following a hunch." She decided to throw Dagmar under the bus, but not in a mean way. "Dagmar actually had a thought."

Jackson nodded his head as Dagmar approached. "You'll take the lead on this, Judson, so hang around until Ivan's done here."

Eva's blood pressure went through the roof. "What the hell!"

"Like you said, his hunch, he should run with it." He tossed her his keys. "You can drive me back to the station and then grab a squad car and get on your assignment for the day."

They locked eyes, but Jackson wasn't backing down and Eva wasn't going to argue with him. Simon was dead and that made her grief palpable. If she started talking, she'd start crying, and she couldn't fucking cry in front of these jerks.

CHAPTER TWENTY-SIX

Cherime stood outside the clinic fuming as she pulled out her phone and called Mara's number.

No answer and Cherime huffed. Dammit. She dialled again. Still no answer. She walked a few more blocks and tried Mara's number again.

Third time was the charm as Mara finally picked up. "Hi."

"What the fuck, Mara? I wasn't in there with Coop that long."

Mara seemed distracted. "Well, how would I know that? I wouldn't put it past you and him to be bumping uglies in his office."

Cherime pulled the phone away from her ear and glared at it. "We were talking, that's all. Come back and get me."

"Okay." Mara's exasperation was coming through loud and clear. "I'm in the middle of shopping, so I'll be a half hour and then I have the ultrasound, which I can go to on my own, if you don't want to go."

Yeah, good old Mara. Now that her crisis was over,

thanks to Cherime, she was back to being the bossy big sister. "Right. I'm meeting a friend later anyway. I'll catch up to her and bum a ride." She hit the end button and shoved her phone into her purse.

Now what? She looked around while her wolf pranced inside of her, begging for a run. *Settle, princess. We're not going to run through Darkness Falls with my purse around your neck. We'd end up on the front-page news and not in a good way.*

She slipped out of her stilettos and started to walk. She wasn't that far from Aubrey's apartment and decided she could walk there and hang out for a while. Maybe get Aubrey to give her a ride.

Or maybe not.

The outcome kind of depended on how pissed off Aubrey was. As Cherime strolled towards the apartment building, she concocted a plan to get back in Aubrey's good graces. It wasn't much of a plan – more like the right thing to do. Apologize.

Karma chose that time to mock her and she stubbed her toe on a rock. "Fuck!" she muttered. After she blew on her toe and imagined the rock apologizing to her, she felt better.

That's all she had to do; pretend she was the rock.

When she reached the apartment building, she stood on the third floor beside Aubrey's apartment door and listened while she put her shoes back on. The low murmur of the television confirmed a presence inside. Nice being a schoolteacher, finishing work half-way through the day.

She knocked and a minute later, Aubrey opened it wearing a bathrobe and towel around her head. "Cherime," she said, ice in her voice, a frown on her face.

Cherime was once again transported back to high school. Goddamned schoolteachers. "Aubrey," she replied trying to appear contrite. "I came to apologize for Monday."

Aubrey tilted her head as she crossed her arms. "Okay. Apologize then." Her stance was straight, her legs parted and stiff. She would have seemed intimidating if she hadn't had to tilt her head back to glare up at Cherime's face.

"I did. That was the apology."

"That's not an apology," Aubrey scoffed.

What did the little freak want from her? "I'm not getting down on one knee and asking forgiveness."

Aubrey rubbed the back of her neck like she was deciding, then stepped back, holding the door and motioning with her head for Cherime to enter.

Cherime had never been to Aubrey's place before because the two were friends through their mutual friendship with Eva. Other than the glamping trip, they had only ever talked at Becker's during girl's night out.

First thing she noticed was the tidiness, then the goldfish. Then the fucking cat, who was standing on the back of the couch, its back arched, its teeth bared, hissing like a tire with a hole in it. Cherime stopped cold. "You have a cat."

Aubrey looked at the cat. "Yeah. His name's Moses. He's usually friendly to people, so I guess he's reacting to you."

Cherime shuddered. Cats were her nightmare, her phobia, the one thing in life she couldn't deal with. "Cats hate shifters." Her voice wobbled as she tried to place the blame for their enmity on Moses. "We're predators. They're prey. They know that."

Aubrey paled. "Don't you dare eat my cat."

Cherime momentarily forgot the vicious feline as she turned to Aubrey in astonishment. "Why would I eat your cat? What do you think I am?"

It was Aubrey's turn to be contrite. "Sorry. That was uncalled for. It's just that Leah ate Eva's goldfish so I thought...." She let her words trail off as a blush suffused her face.

Cherime couldn't concentrate on Aubrey's words while the cat was meowing from the couch. "Could you maybe put it in a room?" Cats were not rabbits, which had no clue how to fight back. Cats scratched eyes out, bit ears off, dug their claws into the tops of heads and hung on like they were riding a bull.

Aubrey picked up Moses and gave it a kiss on its lips, making Cherime shudder. It was like watching a horror movie. Any second now, the cat would devour Aubrey's face.

The woman didn't seem at all perturbed by her imminent disfigurement as she carried it to another room, pushed it in, patted its head, and closed the door. "That should settle him."

It certainly settled Cherime. She closed the front door and moved further into the apartment. "Thanks," she mumbled.

Aubrey opened the fridge and pulled an uncorked bottle of chardonnay from it, setting it beside a little spinner that held stemmed wineglasses. "Help yourself. I'm going to put some clothes on, then we can talk."

Cherime poured the wine into two glasses and carried them to the sofa, setting Aubrey's glass on the coffee table as she settled onto the sofa, which smelled too much like cat. The apartment was cozy, neat, and feminine. Almost too neat, but it had all the little touches that women like. A few pictures on the wall, framed prints mostly. A few knick-knacks here and there. Some books neatly lined up on a shelf. Aubrey's backpack was on a barstool next to the open counter that separated the living room from the kitchen.

Cherime took a sip of her wine and imagined living here. It pulled at her human side and even her wolf was interested. Aubrey didn't really have anyone she could call family, but she certainly understood the value of having a home.

Aubrey came out the bedroom dressed in a loose-fitting summer dress that fell slightly above her knees. It was pale yellow and stood out against the human's lightly tanned skin. Small but shapely, Aubrey attracted her fair share of interest from men, though she never seemed to reciprocate. "Pretty," Cherime remarked as Aubrey caught her looking.

Aubrey tossed her a secretive grin and sat down on the other end of the sofa, curling her legs under her as she reached for her wine. She took a sip and sighed in satisfaction. "One more day of school, thank god. I love the little miscreants, but June is the worst."

Cherime laughed, taking another hit of wine, wishing it were of the red varietal. "Anytime is the worst time with kids." Then she swallowed, tears brightening her eyes.

"What's wrong?" Aubrey reached out and touched her arm gently, her empathy flowing into Cherime.

Cherime sucked in a breath. "I'm sorry about yesterday. Really sorry." She realized that she was. She needed a friend like Aubrey. "These last few days…." She shuddered.

"What did Ren do to you?" Aubrey had the no-one-fucks-with-my-friend scowl on her face.

"Nothing." She needed to talk to someone and thought Aubrey would be a good listener. "If I tell you something, you're required to keep it confidential, right?"

Aubrey lips turned up a little. "I'm not your teacher so

I don't have to respect your privacy, but as a friend, I'd never betray a confidence."

Cherime felt sheepish, recalling the conversation she had earlier with Mara about Coop. "I believe you. Ren didn't do anything to me I didn't want. We're what shifters call pair-bonded."

"Wow! That means you're meant to be together." Aubrey's eyes danced with excitement and Cherime realized she had a romantic on her hands.

"It means we have highly compatible DNA that makes us desire one another. It doesn't mean we're perfect for each other, but it's hard to deny the attraction."

"Oh." Aubrey seemed disappointed. "I thought once you met your mate, it was a happy ever after."

"Fate has a hand in bringing mates together, but free will determines the level of happiness. Look at me and Ren. We're nothing alike. Complete opposites, both so strong-willed that we'd rather have our toenails torn out than give into one another." She took a sip of the Chardonnay, despising the oaked taste. "But he's alpha, the male, so my wolf will concede to him, no matter if it works for me or not."

"Your wolf?" Aubrey bunched her eyebrows together.

"Yeah. It's not like I'm half human and half wolf, though that's how shifters often describe themselves. We're one and the same; our wolf guides the human side and the human side guides the wolf. But the wolf is far more in touch with instincts, which is why mine will kneel before Ren."

"That's so crazy." Aubrey stood and retrieved the wine bottle, emptying it into Cherime's glass, then carrying it to the kitchen. She dropped it into a closed bin and grabbed a full bottle from the fridge.

Cherime decided it was a good day to learn to like

Chardonnay. "It is and it isn't because I can resist the call of nature by avoiding Ren. The problem is, I don't think I want to."

A huge smile creased Aubrey's face. "You love him!"

Cherime stared down at her wineglass. "We met when I was 18. He was my first." She closed her eyes as she remembered the craziness between them. He'd had a voracious appetite and she couldn't deny him. Didn't want to. "We had a few crazy days together, then he rejected me." She blinked at the painful memories.

"What the hell was wrong with him?"

Cherime lifted her shoulders and sighed. "I was a teenager in love, so that wasn't the question I asked myself. It took a couple of years before I quit wondering what the hell was wrong with me."

"Bastard!" Aubrey gulped down the last of her wine, unscrewed the fresh bottle and dumped a good measure of its contents into her glass. "He doesn't deserve a second chance."

"That's what I keep saying to myself. How can I trust him? What if rejects me again?"

"So that's why the blow-up at the school. I understand now."

Cherime shook her head. "Not entirely. I got pregnant while I was with Ren, so my emotions were fucking with me. I lost the baby a couple of days ago."

Aubrey straightened her shoulders and narrowed her eyes. Clearly confused, she took another gulp of the wine, maybe to help her mind sort it out. It apparently didn't work as she shook her head slightly. "That doesn't equate, Cherime. You were with him three days, right?"

Cherime nodded. "It only takes once, isn't that what they say?"

"Well, yes, but…."

"Female shifters know almost from the point of conception. Their wolves do anyway. I'm maybe not as in touch as most female shifters, so I didn't realize I was pregnant until after I cornered you at school." She twisted her lips to one side. "But when I got home and had a few minutes to settle, I knew. The next morning it was gone."

"I'm sorry." Aubrey had tears in her eyes. "It happens, Cherime. To all women. Most don't even realize they were pregnant."

Cherime sighed. "The curse of being a shifter. We're not delicate except when it comes to carrying babies. It's partly why our population is dwindling."

Aubrey's big eyes settled on Cherime, a withered sadness to her gaze. "Are you okay?"

Cherime wrinkled her nose. "Yeah. It wasn't like I'd already decorated the nursery." She drained her wine and refilled the glass. "Mara's pregnant."

"Your sister?"

She nodded. "Turns out her asshole husband planted a little Connell in her belly just before he kicked off. She's been keeping it secret from the pack."

"Shit, Cherime."

"Yeah. She wants me in the delivery room." Cherime shuddered at the thought. Now that she was away from Mara, the whole idea seemed ridiculous. "What does one even wear to a birthing?"

Aubrey grinned, not realizing it was a serious question. "You've had a rough couple of days. How can I help?"

Cherime set her glass down on the coffee table. The wine just wasn't doing it. "Mind if I light up a blunt?"

"Can't. Non-smoking building, but I have a better idea."

"Better than a blunt?"

"Better and compatible. Let's go to Becker's and get buzzed."

Cherime grinned at the little human, who rarely had more than a drink or two during girls' night out. "It's a school night. Don't want the principal calling you to his office and punishing you."

Aubrey laughed too hard at the feeble joke. "It's June. He's too tired to lift the whip, let alone use it."

Why not go to Becker's? Cherime was always up for a rousing game of *who's more wasted*. "Let's do this!" She grabbed her purse on her way to the door.

"I'll be right behind you." Aubrey tossed her keys to Cherime, who caught them deftly. "I have to let Moses out of the bedroom, and you won't want to be here when that happens. He gets a little cranked when he's been locked up."

Cherime couldn't disagree, closing the door and heading to Aubrey's Honda Civic, which had to be at least 15 years old. Why was teach driving this bucket of bolts? At least it was clean, she thought as she leaned against the hatchback and closed her eyes, scenting the air around her.

She caught the freshness of June breezing by and the domesticated varieties of flowers like dahlias and hydrangea lingering in the air, their spirit overcoming the recent snow dump. Trees too, pine and cedar, some oak. But there was also the residual odor of gasoline and exhaust and the cooking of food with too much garlic in it. And a sweet spicy scent that Cherime had come to associate with Aubrey.

"All done," Aubrey announced as Cherime opened her eyes and grinned at the little woman.

Cherime palmed the keys as Aubrey reached for them. "I'll drive. You're half drunk already."

"I know," Aubrey giggled. "I haven't done this in forever. I am so overdue."

Cherime folded herself into Aubrey's car and started it up as Aubrey belted herself into the passenger seat. "First thing I'm going to do when we get to Becker's is light up. I need to catch up to your buzz."

"How're we going to get home?" Aubrey rolled her window down and stuck her head out like a dog, letting the breeze rifle through her short, brown curls.

Cherime shrugged. "Someone will give us a ride. We'll have to leave the car at Becker's"

"I don't care," Aubrey purred like a relaxed little kitten.

Not now, Ms. School teacher, but tomorrow, be prepared to be mortified. And hungover.

Cherime smirked.

CHAPTER TWENTY-SEVEN

Cherime still wasn't picking up Ren's calls, not answering his texts. She was pushing all his fucking buttons, which annoyed the hell out of him. It was one thing to need a little space, another to ignore him altogether. His feisty little female was playing games with him, and when he caught up to her, he'd make her regret it. The only game he was playing right now was for keeps.

Yeah, he'd fucked up eight years ago. He should have kept her with him. Maybe then she wouldn't have embraced all that glamour bullshit. But Christ, she had been so young. No life experience, stars in her eyes, so not ready for a life with him in the mountains. How could he make her see that what he'd done was in her best interest?

He checked the time as his stomach growled. He'd agreed to meet Jackson at Becker's for dinner at 6:30. Eva's words about Dexter had resonated with him. Dexter and Jackson were blood, so it would be impossible for Jackson to be impartial. Ren would feel him out over dinner, see where his head was at.

Jackson was already seated when Ren stepped inside.

The cop was on the phone, an almost empty mug of beer in front of him, and a full one next to it, indicating he'd been there a while. The bar was busy enough for a Thursday night and people were sitting and standing everywhere, drinking too much and talking too loudly. Nevertheless, they parted like the Red Sea as Ren stalked his way towards Jackson.

He'd shut down his smeller the moment he stepped inside. All the fucking perfume and body odor was too much for him to handle.

A few brave voices greeted him, and he nodded slightly in acknowledgement. He'd never understood the attraction of bars, the need to gather together to drink too much and become jackasses. Maybe that's what set his Mountain pack apart from others. None of them were interested in that type of social bullshit.

He slid his bulk into the booth opposite Jackson as the cop nodded his greeting and held up a finger, indicating he'd be a moment.

The human female, Lowry, stopped at his table. "Hi Ren," she said shyly. "What can I get you?"

He nodded at Jackson's mug. "Beer'll do."

"On its way." She turned, and he watched as Jackson's eyes followed the barmaid. She was nice enough looking, but she had three strikes against her. One, she was human, two, she was far too interested in him, and three, she wasn't Cherime.

The only woman Ren had ever wanted was Cherime, and that sentiment had never wavered over the years. He didn't engage with a woman who wanted more than a good fuck. Too much drama when it started to get domestic.

Sure, his wolf sneered. *Because Cherime is all sunshine and daffodils.*

He grinned at the thought and then brought his attention to Jackson, who had ended his call.

"Sounded serious. Who died?" he grunted.

"Exactly that. Between us, Simon Flanagan was found dead by two of my officers a couple of hours ago. Preliminary cause of death is strangulation."

Ren raised his eyebrows at the news. "This town is becoming quite the crime mecca. Doesn't sound like shifter work, though."

"Doesn't sound like it isn't." Jackson raised his beer to his lips and took a long pull. "Ivan is still at the scene and he hasn't conclusively ruled out anyone."

They stopped talking as Lowry approached and set Ren's beer down in front of him. He nodded in acknowledgement, his attention on Jackson. After she left, he said, "Three bodies in less than a year."

"Four if you count Connell."

"Yeah." The shifter that tried to kill Eva, the one Simon Flanagan killed. "Think there's a connection?"

Jackson shrugged as he pulled his menu towards him. "Too soon to say."

Ren glanced at the menu though he didn't have to. Everything on offer was overcooked shit except the steak, which he had control over providing the cook didn't fuck it up. "Gonna attract the attention of the feds."

Jackson sighed as he waved Lowry over. "Already has."

Ren order the 12-ounce ribeye blue rare, and Jackson grinned wryly as he ordered a burger. "You should mix it up once in a while."

Ren smirked. "I do. When I'm feeling particularly civilized, I order the steak tartare."

His wolf whined – it didn't like when Ren tried to be funny.

Jackson laughed. "I think you have to go to the Zoo for that level of sophistication."

Ren smirked and took a long swallow of his beer. "You were saying about the feds?"

A frown played at Jackson's lips. "I've had a few conversations with the feds but managed to convince them we're on top of everything." He raked a hand over the top of his head. "Four fucking deaths now. Doesn't make us very on top of anything, does it?"

"Maybe Simon's murder is unrelated."

A roar in the corner near the door drew their attention. A fucking group of teenagers, old enough to drink, but too stupid to do it responsibly, had a bottle of tequila on the table and were slamming shots. Jackson dismissed them. "Maybe. But that screws things up on a grand scale if it is. Bad enough we've got some guy preying on the women around here, but then to have this happen." He rubbed the back of his neck. "Who the hell would want to kill Simon? He was less than harmless."

"You sure?" Ren said, catching a whiff of another alpha shifter as the front door opened. The independent alpha, Ulrich, entered alone. He glanced around, his eyes settling first on Jackson and Ren, then past them, fixating on someone. Ren checked over his shoulder.

Aubrey, the schoolteacher who had taken up lodging in his community centre, was sitting alone drinking white wine, but there were two other drinks on the table. A mug of beer and something green in a martini glass. He glanced back to Ulrich, who had taken a seat at the bar.

Lowry showed up with their meal, stopping Ren from asking what the deal was with Ulrich. "Want another?" She nodded at Ren's beer and he flicked his eyes to hers, which he shouldn't have done because she froze for a few seconds, then dropped her eyes quickly. Perfect little alpha's mate. Shit, he thought as his wolf sat up and took notice.

"Yeah," he said, shooting her a withering glare. Not her fault for being interested, but he wanted her and her thoughts about him gone.

She pouted and looked at the chief. "Jackson?"

He shook his head as he popped a fry into his mouth. "No. Two's my limit tonight."

She gave him a half-smile and left them alone.

Jackson ate another couple of fries, chewed and swallowed. "Maybe you should do what you do best and break her heart. That way, the rest of us might stand a chance."

Ren scowled at Jackson despite knowing the cop was joking. "No. I've already got a girl."

Jackson's eyebrow's shot up. "Does she know?"

Ren chuckled as he cut a big chunk of red meat off the bone. "Yeah, she does. Playing hard to get, but she'll come round."

CHAPTER TWENTY-EIGHT

Cherime was standing with Leah, outside in the shadows near the back of the building. She lit up a joint, took a puff, then passed it to the latent. They'd run into Leah on the way to Becker's and picked her up.

"I don't really smoke pot," Leah said as she took a deep draw of the blunt, then hacked up half a lung. She passed it back to Cherime.

"Why not?" Cherime demanded. It didn't make sense to her why a shifter wouldn't want to get buzzed like everyone else, but then, was Leah really a shifter if she couldn't shift?" She drew the smoke deep into her lungs, held it there for a few seconds, then blew it out in a visible stream.

"Well, for starters, it stinks, clings to your clothes." Leah took the joint and sucked in another toke, coughing it out. "The buzz makes me careless, and my wolf goes all stupid."

Little Leah. Leah the Devil. The Devil's helper. "Are you sure it didn't start out stupid?"

It was meant to be insulting, but Leah laughed, maybe more than she should have. "It's hard to tell if it's the stupid one or I am." She took another long pull of the joint.

Cherime took it from her, smoking down the last bit, then tossing it into a puddle of what used to be snow. "That's a little harsh."

The latent giggled. It didn't matter if she didn't like the pot, the pot clearly liked her. "Maybe it's both of us."

Fucking Leah was killing Cherime's buzz. "Stop making me gag. We both know you're the least stupid shifter around these parts."

Leah threw her head back and barked a loud laugh. "Wow! That means a lot coming from you!"

So much for self-esteem Thursday. "You're mean when you're high."

Leah agreed. "Another reason I don't like pot." She took a couple of steps towards the door. "Let's go in and play with the human. We can pretend she's a kitten, bat her around a bit, then I'll bite her head off."

Cherime followed Leah inside. "You'll do nothing of the sort. We like Aubrey, remember?" Cherime was feeling mellow, relaxed and in the mood for some hot, hot sex with a certain alpha shifter. Her body felt alive, and her wolf was belly up batting at flying unicorns. It was almost like Ren was in the room with her.

The too-sexy-to-be-true human bartender, Harris Palmer, bumped against her as he headed back to the bar.

"Sorry, gorgeous." His smooth voice was like warm brandy as he slid his fingers down her arm.

"Hands off, buddy," she cooed, stepping back from him and running her hands down her body, caressing her neck, her breasts, her stomach. "This bod's taken."

"Really?" Leah sidled up to Harris and grabbed his bicep to keep him from touching Cherime. "Who's the frisky fella?"

Harris grinned down at Leah, almost wolfish, and drew her hand into his, kissing her on the knuckles. "You high, little wolf?"

Cherime gave him a push, separating the two of them. "Hand's off the puppy while she's buzzed, Harris. She's not used to being under the influence."

Leah giggled in a very un-Leah-like way. "Of weed or love?" She added an exaggerated sway to her hips as she danced her way back to Aubrey.

Cherime rolled her eyes and followed Leah back to the table where Aubrey was sipping her fourth glass of wine. Coupled with the drinks she'd had at her apartment, the schoolteacher was clearly feeling no pain.

"This was so the right thing to do!" Teach's loud exclamation made Cherime wince. "I love you guys!"

"We love you too!" Leah shouted. "Group hug, darlin's."

Cherime gave Leah a shove when she tried to climb on Aubrey. "Don't be so quick to love Leah. Just a moment ago, she was talking about biting off your head."

Aubrey scowled at Leah. "Why? What did I do?"

Cherime hoped Aubrey wasn't one of those mean drunks.

"You," Leah pointed a finger at Aubrey, then watched it while it moved back and forth. She blinked and refocused. "You," she stabbed her finger again, "were born human. That's your mistake."

Aubrey drained her wine glass and waved at Lowry, drunkenly motioning for another round. "You're not kidding there. I am a fucking mistake."

Cherime dropped her jaw. "What is it with you two and you're self-esteem issues? Grow some backbones."

Aubrey glared at Cherime, then grinned. "I have one, thanks. It's under repair." She turned to Leah. "I've never been gnawed on by a shifter. You could chew on my ankle a little, but don't bite it off."

"She can't," Cherime announced. "She can't shift."

"Why the hell are you obsessed with my inability to shift?" Leah snarled too loudly, drawing the attention of those closest to her. Not Aubrey, Leah was the mean… uh…. pothead.

"Hush," Cherime admonished her. "I'm not obsessed. It's just that you're short on physical and shifter skills and loud on mischief and snark. It's gonna get you hurt someday."

Leah tipped her head to one side. "Awwwe, you love me. I knew it!" She tried to crawl onto Cherime's lap.

Lowry arrived with their drinks. "You girls look like you're having fun tonight."

Cherime gave an exaggerated nod. "Yeah, we're having a man-free night."

"That reminds me." Leah leaned on the table and twisted her head Cherime's way. "You never said who you were giving out your blowies to."

Fucking Leah, master stirrer of the pot. "That's right, bitch. I never said."

Lowry sighed as she rested her tray on the table, setting the empties on it. "I wouldn't mind a few nights with a certain man." Her eyes drifted behind her. All three women stretched their heads around Lowry's body to see who she was looking at.

"Ren?" Leah gasped, again too loudly.

Lowry furrowed her forehead. "Shh. He'll hear you."

"Tabernacle!" Cherime swore the Quebecois way as her heart started hammering in her chest. Ren, who had indeed heard Leah, was throwing Cherime a mean glare, or maybe it was a hard stare. Maybe a mean, hard glare-stare. Yeah, definitely that was it.

Before she had time to brush her hair behind her ears, check her lipstick, and straighten her blouse, the alpha was on his feet, stalking towards the four women.

Leah giggled. "He did hear me. He's coming our way."

"Thanks Captain Obvious," Cherime muttered as she nervously twisted the grasshopper she'd ordered.

Aubrey giggled too. "There's going to be a cat fight."

Cherime narrowed her eyes at Aubrey. "Call me a cat again and I'll let Leah bite your head off."

"What's he doing now?" Lowry murmured breathlessly her eyes glued to the tray on the table.

Aubrey seemed not to care if Leah bit her head off. "Breaking your heart, Lowry. He's Cherime's beau."

All heads swivelled towards Aubrey. "Who the fuck says beau?" Leah slurred.

Aubrey drew her eyebrows together. "Schoolteachers do. All the fucking time."

Ren had arrived, brushing up next to Lowry but ignoring everyone but Cherime. "I've been calling."

Cherime looked at the green froth in her glass. "I've been busy." She picked up the glass and raised it to her lips, but Ren deliberately bumped the bottom of it, causing it to spill down her chin and onto her sheer white blouse, soaking through to her tank and bra.

"You asshole!" Cherime exclaimed as she jerked to her feet, baring her teeth.

"Tabernacle," Lowry mumbled as she moved away.

"You broke Lowry's fucking heart, Mountain man."

Leah knelt up on her chair, so she was peering into his face. "The least you could do is not make a mess."

Aubrey stood too, sort of, swaying on her feet. "You're mean."

"I did you a favour, didn't I?" He spat back at Aubrey. Then to Cherime, he said, "What the fuck are you doing hanging out with the human?"

They had the entire bar's attention including the independent shifter, Ulrich, who was striding towards them like a lion with a toothache.

Ren caught his approach. "Back the fuck off, asshole," he snarled.

Jackson was on his feet too, moving fast to intervene before Ulrich reached Ren. "Nope. Not here," he said aggressively as he shoved himself between the two.

"What the fuck do you mean, you did her a favour?" Ulrich snarled over Jackson's shoulder.

"No!" Jackson's voice reverberated through the bar. "Outside, all of you."

"Fuck," Leah moaned. "I hate when we have to go outside. Somebody always makes me go home."

"Time to go home anyway," Ren said to Leah. "You fucking trouble-maker."

She stood on her chair so she was taller than Ren. "I don't think this was my fault, you fucking alpha."

Ren's eyes turned amber at her disrespect and Cherime grabbed his arm as Jackson snatched Leah around the waist and carried her over his shoulder out of the building.

Ren stalked after them with Cherime in tow, his hard grip bruising her wrist.

She clawed at his hand, trying to untangle herself. "Leah's high. And she can say what she wants to you. You're not her alpha."

He wasn't listening though. She glanced behind her.

Ulrich had his hand wrapped around Aubrey's arm the same way Ren was holding Cherime and was dragging her to the door. "Let her go!" she yelled at Ulrich, who ignored her.

Fuck, she was saying important stuff. Why wasn't anyone listening!

CHAPTER TWENTY-NINE

"Fucking trouble, the whole lot of you!" Ren cursed as he stepped out of Becker's, Cherime in tow.

Cherime was fighting him every inch of the way, but between her buzz and her high heels, she wasn't much of an opponent. "Then why bother, Ren? If I'm so much goddamn trouble."

"Because you're a good lay," he snarled as he rounded on her, his temper overriding his good sense.

"You're such a shit." The she-wolf smacked him before he had a chance to stop her.

He grabbed her wrists and yanked her flush to his body. "Do that again, Cherime. I dare you."

Leah jumped on Ren's back, grabbing him by his hair and riding him like he was a wild horse. "Do not threaten Cherime, you fucking alpha!" She looked around Ren's bicep and said to Cherime. "Don't know why you're so mad. It sounded like a compliment."

Ren dropped his grip on Cherime, reaching behind him and grabbing Leah by the waist, hauling her over his head and thumping her ass-down on the ground in a puddle of water. "Go the fuck home, Leah!"

Leah crawled out of the mud, her teeth bared. "You don't tell me what to do, asshole! And you don't hurt my friends!"

Jackson pushed his way between Leah and Ren. "Go home, Leah, before I have you arrested for public intoxication."

"I'm not drunk!" Leah snarled.

"I don't know that!" Jackson returned her snarl and raised her a growl. "You got three seconds or I'm going to cuff you."

Leah peered at him, her eyes curious. "Maybe I want to be cuffed – last time was kind of fun."

"One—"

"She shouldn't be walking out here alone," Aubrey gabbled, staggering into Ulrich, who still had a grip on her arm. She tried to wrench it away with a weak jerk that almost knocked her on her ass.

Ulrich pulled her upright. "Stop wiggling."

"Aubrey's right," Cherime agreed. "It's late, dark, and Leah's little."

Leah glared at Cherime. "Stop with the little shit!"

Cherime rolled her eyes. "I didn't call you a shit!"

Ulrich cursed under his breath. "I'll take them both home."

"I'm not going home with you," Leah bared her teeth at Ulrich.

Aubrey giggled as she staggered two steps towards Leah before Ulrich yanked her back. "I think he meant he'd drop us off at our homes." She stretched her head back as she looked up at Ulrich. "It's what you meant, right big guy? I'm not really into threesomes."

Leah widened her eyes. "Neither am I, you pervert. I'll find my own fucking way home."

"Christ," Jackson muttered as he scrubbed at the back of his head. "I'll drive you home, Leah."

Leah shook her head and stepped away from Jackson. "No, nope. No way am I arriving home in a cop car."

"We're leaving," Ren growled, pulling Cherime towards his truck.

"Hold the fuck up!" Ulrich growled. "I'm not done talking to you."

Aubrey tried to straighten her back and stand still, but she was rocking like a boat on a stormy sea. "Yeah, and no one's taking Cherime unless she wants to go." She pointed an unsteady finger at Ren.

Jackson turned to Ren. "Aubrey's right. Cherime doesn't go with you unless she wants to."

Ren felt the savage inside him grow out-of-control. "Who's gonna stop me?" he boomed. "This is shifter business, you fucking cop!"

He had to give Jackson credit for holding his ground. "Consider me off-duty, alpha. She's not fucking getting in your truck unless she wants to."

Ulrich stepped up next to Jackson. "I got your back on this one."

Cherime rolled her eyes. "Stop with the pissing contest. Let's agree you all have big dicks." She grinned at Ulrich and Jackson. "Thanks for being all gallant and shit, but I can take care of myself."

Ren didn't know whether to hug Cherime or drag her off by her hair. The caveman inside him grunted. "Are we done here?"

"Not done." Ulrich had a dangerous edge to his voice but kept his distance, probably because Cherime was between them.

Ren moved in front of her as Ulrich handed Aubrey off to Jackson. "You got something to say, you motherfucker, get it said."

"Fuck," Jackson muttered as he shoved Aubrey towards Leah. They were practically the same size, but Leah staggered under Aubrey's drunken weight.

Ulrich ignored everyone but Ren. "I asked you a question inside that you didn't see fit to answer. What the fuck favour did you do for Aubrey?"

Jesus Christ, he hated independents. Especially the alphas. They were always trying to prove a point. "Why the hell is that your business?"

Ulrich took a threatening step towards Ren. "I'm making it my business. You have a hate on for humans, and you aren't going to make Aubrey a target for your bigotry."

Cherime wiggled out of Ren's grasp and pushed herself between the two Alphas. "Ren's not prejudiced against humans. Just Aubrey."

Ren tried in vain to yank Cherime behind her where she was safe from the fucking independent. "Not really helping, Wolverine."

"For god sake's you guys!" Cherime exclaimed as she shrugged Ren off. "When the snowstorm hit, Aubrey and I got stranded with some high school girls on the mountain and took shelter in the Mountain's pack's community centre."

"Yeah," Aubrey added. "He didn't throw us out even though he wanted to."

Cherime glared at Aubrey. "I've got this covered, Aubrey."

Ren pulled Cherime behind him again. "I'm gonna say this once, you rogue shifter. What I do is none of your fucking business. Not now, not ever. You question me again and I'll turn you into fucking bear bait."

Ulrich inhaled deeply. "Go home to your mountain and stay there." The threat was clear in his underlying tone. He stalked over to Aubrey and Leah. "Let's go."

This time Leah didn't protest as she looked up into the Ulrich's face. "Okay. But I want my own bedroom."

Ren couldn't make out the muttered response as Ulrich herded the two females into his truck and drove away. Even though the independent had backed down, his words were no concession to Ren's status. Ren decided he needed to watch his back around Ulrich. He turned to Jackson. "Going to call another ITCU meeting?"

"Yeah, going to have to," Jackson replied over his shoulder as they parted ways.

Ren flipped open the passenger side door on his truck. "Let's go," he said to Cherime, trying to keep his anger at her out of his voice.

Cherime didn't move from where she was standing. "They're right, Ren. I don't have to go with you."

So fucking contrary, turning everything into something more than it had to be. "We gotta talk, baby."

She tugged a lank of her hair as she narrowed her eyes. "That's the problem, Ren. We don't talk. We either fight or fuck. There's no in-between."

He leaned threateningly into her. "By tomorrow, everyone in Darkness Falls is going to know about us, so we gotta figure this out. We're either together or we're not, and whatever we decide, there'll be no turning back." His heart hurt at the thought of not being with Cherime, but he had his pride. He wasn't about to beg.

Cherime seemed to understand that this was a turning point for them, though she huffed an exaggerated sigh of irritation to try to cover the panic that had her heart pumping faster. It didn't work; he heard it loud and clear.

She climbed into his truck and belted herself in. "How're we going to do this?"

Ren slid his bulk into the driver's seat and pulled out of Becker's parking lot. "Let's establish some rules of engagement."

"Sure, because we'll totally agree on those." She crossed her arms as she looked out the window into the blackness of the night.

Darkness Falls disappeared behind them as Ren headed into the mountains. "Okay. We decide the rules, but we each have one veto."

Cherime seemed to mull this over. "Fine. I'll go first. No touching."

Of course, that would be the first thing she'd choose. "Veto. We need to fuck and get it out of our systems, so we can have a conversation without screaming at each other."

Cherime's brow drew together. "You've got such a way with words. I can't believe you haven't already been snatched up, the way you charm women." She turned her body more towards him. "I'm using my veto."

Well shit. "You're vetoing my veto? Is that even allowed?"

"I was vetoing your 'fuck first' rule. You know that touching leads to kissing and then fucking. Then after we've done the deed, you'll fall asleep or say something insensitive and everything will blow up again."

Ren had to concede her point. "Okay. I take back my veto. No touching until we've talked." He turned off the main highway onto a secondary road, gearing down on the steep incline.

"We both have to be happy with the outcome of the conversation before we stop talking. You can't decide it's done unless I agree."

That made sense. "That applies to both of us. No pouting or silent treatment, Wolverine."

"No calling me Wolverine."

Ren shifted as the incline steepened. "Not sure I can help myself."

"You still have a veto. Use it."

He glanced at her. "Trying to trick me into using my veto?"

Cherime shrugged. "Just pointing out the facts."

Ren nodded, trying to think of another rule. "No standing and pacing around the room."

"We've got to be honest with each other. No hiding our feelings and no getting mad at each other for saying them."

Ren raised his voice. "Well how the hell can we honest and not get about mad about it? All I gotta do is open my mouth and your feelings get hurt."

"No yelling at each other," Cherime yelled.

He was a fucking alpha – he didn't talk feelings and he didn't think Cherime was a fan of sappy conversations either. "Guess it means we have to stay civilized."

"Yeah, we do. No being mean."

"Intentionally. Sometimes I say things that are meant to be nice and you take them the wrong way."

"Give me an example."

"Well, back at the bar, when I said you were a good lay."

Cherime sucked in a breath as she looked at him like he was an alien. "Jesus, Ren, you don't really think before you talk, do you? It's one thing to say, *Cherime, you're a good lay*, after hot sex when we're alone together. It's another thing yelling it in the parking lot for everyone to hear after you called me a trouble-maker. What you did back there was retaliation against me fighting back."

Ren thought about this. She was right about his

behaviour outside of Becker's, but the words had popped out of his mouth before his brain caught up to them. Reluctantly, he had to admit he shouldn't have said them. "I'll try not to retaliate by saying nice things."

She didn't return his smirk. "No retaliating at all. You'll hurt my feelings and I'll get mad, which will make you mad."

Ren wondered how she became so good at negotiation. "Okay," he conceded. "No retaliation."

"Besides," Cherime muttered as she turned back to the window, staring out at the darkness. "You don't tell a woman she's a good lay. It's not romantic. You say things like, *Cherime, I love making love to you*. Stuff like that."

"I'm not ever going to say stuff like that." He stopped and thought about it. "Here's what I will say. You have a tight pussy, best tasting in the world. Your tits are amazing, great nipples. And your ass, made for fucking, girl."

"You're not fucking my ass."

Ren thought back to the ITCU meeting when Jackson handed out the sheet of paper with the list of discussion points. "Let's put that on the agenda."

"We're having an agenda?"

Ren nodded, taking a sharp right off the road without signaling. No point wearing out the blinkers for no reason. "Why not? We got ourselves a list of topics. Makes sense, doesn't it?"

"Fine." Cherime tucked her bottom lip between her teeth, making Ren's cock become a little more attentive. "We gotta talk about the past."

No fucking way! It wouldn't get them anywhere rehashing it. "I'm using my veto."

"The veto is for the rules of engagement, not the topics. No topic is off-limits."

Okay, if that was the case.... "Then we're talking about fucking your ass."

"Jeeeesussssss. Fine!"

Ren smirked in the dark. He was going to get his way on this one. "Gotta talk about being together. Mating."

"We can't talk about mating without talking about that hovel you call a home."

A hovel! That was taking it too far. "I thought we weren't being mean."

Cherime shrugged. "The meeting hasn't started yet. We're still making the rules and building the agenda."

Fuck, things were getting out of control. "Now we're calling it a meeting? Should I wear a suit and tie?"

Cherime seemed to take him seriously. "No. But you gotta keep your clothes on. No distracting me with your body."

"Agreed. Likewise, baby. You stay dressed." He glanced at her. She was wearing the drink-soaked blouse that was too sexy for being out in public to begin with. "You can put on one of my T-shirts when we get to the cabin."

"I'm taking my shoes off. Is that okay?"

"Me too, we'll both get more comfortable." He glanced at her again. "The way you dress goes on the agenda."

She huffed. "What the hell's wrong with the way I dress?"

Nope. She wasn't going to fool him into talking about it in the truck. "We'll discuss it at the meeting."

They finally passed the community centre, and Ren drove the gravel road maze back to his cabin. It was dead dark as he pulled into yard. "I'm using my veto on not calling you Wolverine." He got out of the truck.

CHAPTER THIRTY

Cherime followed Ren inside, her stomach feeling all wobbly as she recalled the passion they'd shared a few days ago. It led to her thinking about the baby, their baby. If she hadn't lost it, everything would be different now. But maybe this was better – *not better,* her guilt interrupted – because now they were going to talk. And maybe after, they could be together.

The cabin smelled better – Ren had aired it out enough that the stink of the deer hide was almost undetectable. And it was still neat, in the same condition it had been in when she left.

Ren went into the bedroom, emerging with a T-shirt, which he tossed at her, then shut himself inside. Cherime kicked off her heels, then stripped off her blouse, camisole, and bra. The blouse was ruined – she didn't see how it was possible to get the lime-coloured stain out of it – so she balled it up and shoved it into a trash bag.

Sliding the T-shirt over her head, she inhaled deeply. Perhaps it wasn't the best idea to put on something that was covered in sexy Ren-smells. It was distracting, but everything in this cabin smelled like Ren. She wouldn't be able to avoid it. Too bad she hadn't thought about having this conversation on neutral grounds.

Too late, and Ren probably would have used his veto on that anyway, she thought as she filled the percolator with water and coffee grounds and set it on the wood burner. Straightening up after she lit the fire, she noted that the dishes she'd washed earlier in the week were still on the towel, but the only dirty ones in the sink were a cup and one plate.

The bedroom door opened on a creak and Ren stepped out wearing low-hanging sweatpants and a T-shirt that hugged his chest and biceps. No shoes or socks.

Cherime's eyes swept him. "You may as well be bare-chested for all that T-shirt does to hide your body."

Ren grinned. "What can I say? I'm a big guy. Hard to find T-shirts my size that drape on me." He rounded the cabinets and approached her. "Thanks for making coffee, Wolverine." He grinned as he reached for her.

"No touching."

"The meeting hasn't started yet," Ren complained.

Cherime skirted around him. "The rules apply from now until the meeting's over."

Ren contemplated her for a few seconds, then nodded, his expression serious. "Okay. I'll behave." He pulled two cups off the towel and turned them upright. "You sit down. I'll get the coffee."

Cherime wasn't sure if he was being genuine or still playing, but made her way over to the sofa, curling up against one arm.

Ren puttered in the kitchen, then brought the coffee over and handed one to Cherime. He sat down at the other end of the couch, keeping the space of a cushion between them. As they sipped their coffee, an awkward silence grew.

Finally, Ren cleared his throat. "Where do you want to start?"

"The beginning," Cherime replied softly because it was time for him to understand how devastated she'd been. "I need to know why you rejected me eight years ago." She felt the burn of tears and blinked rapidly. "I was so hurt, Ren. You have no idea the wreck I was." She couldn't look at him, so instead, she stared at the fireplace. "I loved you so much. Still do." A tear spilled over and down her cheek. "It took so long to force you into a corner of my mind so I could move on. I tried to hate you, but I never could. All I felt was this empty ache that I couldn't fill no matter how I tried. My pull to you is so strong. For the longest time I thought you'd change your mind, come find me, and make me your own."

"I did. You're here now. I thought we were in a good place when we fucked, but then I woke up and you were gone."

Cherime shrugged, trying her best to ignore the pang of guilt in her gut. "Sorry."

Apparently sorry didn't cut it. "Why'd you leave?" Ren growled.

"Because I have this thing called free will." Damn, it was hard to be nice. "Sorry," she said again. "I left to get the glampers home before the parents started their witch hunt." He didn't need to know that glampers were already home when she arrived at the community centre. He didn't need to know that she could have come back.

Ren didn't appear to buy it anyway. "You didn't answer my texts or calls. Didn't reach out. No explanation of why you didn't stay with me."

Cherime felt the familiar flare of irritation at him, but

swallowed it down, keeping her words gentle so she didn't have to apologize again. It wasn't easy. "Our getting together was serendipitous, Ren. If it hadn't stormed, we wouldn't be having this conversation."

He shuffled around on the couch, then put his feet on the coffee table and crossed his ankles. "So you're saying that if it hadn't stormed, we'd never get back together." He shook his head as he took a swallow of coffee. "You're blaming me for all these years of us being apart. You could have come to me."

Such a fucking stubborn man! "You don't get it, do you?" She heard the hint of shrillness in her voice and tried to temper it as she turned towards him, searching his face for some hint of understanding. "You destroyed me, humiliated me. We were… are pair-bonded, and you rejected that, rejected me. I gave you my heart and you shattered it. I can't go through that kind of pain again."

She was met with stony silence and so she added. "Maybe it's because I'm a woman. We love more deeply, need more than sex. Or maybe it's because you're an alpha. Maybe love isn't natural to you." Her voice cracked on the last word. The thought of him incapable of love haunted her, mocked her. Made her hate herself for still wanting him.

He cleared his throat. "I want to touch you, baby."

She denied him. "I'm too brittle right now. No breaking the rules."

He pulled a breath into his lungs as he gripped his coffee cup so tight, she feared he'd shatter it. "I was lured by your scent. It was like sunshine, a fresh kill, a heavy snowfall. It was irresistible. And then when I saw you, fuck, I was lost. I wasn't looking for a mate, but there you were. I knew we were pair-bonded before I touched you." He looked at her. "You knew it too or you wouldn't have followed me back here."

She touched the tips of her fingernails one by one as she focused on her hands. "Yeah, I knew."

"Every moment of every day I spent with you was fantastic." He drew a deep breath. "We were so different back then."

"You don't like the older me?" Cherime tried to invoke the rule about not getting savage when her feelings were hurt.

"I like the older you even more that the younger you." He paused. "No. I don't."

Cherime swallowed as her lower lip trembled. "You don't?" she croaked.

He stared down into his coffee cup, then rubbed a hand over his beard. "I love you, Cherime. I loved you then and I love you now."

Cherime squeezed her eyes shut, trying to stem the flow of tears leaking over her lashes. "Fuck." It was all she could say. She had longed to hear him say those words for so many years, and him saying it now, when she was on the verge of falling apart, was like salt in her emotional wounds.

"I want to touch you," he said softly.

Nope, no. No touching or this conversation would be over. She shook her head. "Tell me why you broke up with me, Ren. I need to know."

Ren turned to face her. "It was right around the time that Tess's husband died. I had just taken on the alpha role and was feeling my way through things. Overwhelmed, and all the shit I was feeling for you was getting in the way of me doing the things I needed to do for the pack. I couldn't seem to separate them, and you were young and high-maintenance."

"That hasn't changed," Cherime said on soft laugh.

He tossed her a grim smile. "I decided I needed to get some space between us while I found my bearings; otherwise the pack would lose confidence in me. I needed their respect and they needed my guidance."

"You chose your pack over me." It hurt, Cherime had to admit, but she kind of understood. Only kind of…. "But you were so brutal about breaking it off."

Ren's gaze rested on her. "I wasn't at first, if you think about it. I tried to tell you that you needed to grow up and I needed some space to sort out my life. I know I can be blunt and insensitive, but fuck, Cherime, back then you were out-of-control. You wouldn't accept what I was saying, refused to leave. Don't you remember?"

Her lips tugged down, her face heating in embarrassment. "Yeah, I do. I thought someone was pressuring you to get rid of me. I thought your pack didn't want me."

"They didn't even know about you."

"I know. But you couldn't have convinced me of that. It was easier to blame someone else than to think you made this decision all on your own." She swiped at her tears. "And you know me. I don't take prisoners. I wanted you and fuck everyone else, including you, I guess."

Ren rubbed at his eyes as if he were weary of this conversation. "Your behaviour reinforced my decision. Back then, being together would have destroyed both of us."

Cherime knew he was right, maybe had always known. Still… "Being apart destroyed me, Ren. No one ever measured up to you. No one ever will."

"Same." He dropped his chin to his chest and peered at his hands. "Everything I wanted to do with you was gone." He waved a hand around his cabin. "What was the point in fixing this up? I was never going to bring a woman here who wasn't you."

His words lightened her heart, but she still needed an answer to her question. "Why wait so long, Ren? Why didn't you try to reconnect with me?"

Ren stood and retreated to the kitchen, picking up the percolator and bringing it over to refill the coffee cups. He set the pot on the coffee table and turned to her, still standing. "I thought about it, but once my pack stabilized and I was on solid ground, you'd moved on with your life and I wasn't about to disrupt it again."

"You could have reached out."

He shook his head as he returned to his seat. "Maybe, but you seemed happy, always had a guy around. It killed me, but I had no right to interfere, pair-bond or otherwise. Besides, I didn't think you were cut out for life with me." He took a sip of his coffee, then ran his hand over his moustache. "When I saw you last week, everything I had decided flew out of my head. It was like the first time I laid eyes on you. You make me crazy, Wolverine. All I can think about is you. It makes me savage, and I can't control what I do or say."

Cherime let her eyes wander over Ren, his long hair, his untidy beard. Coffee-brown eyes that pierced through to the soul. His dark skin, hard body, his size, his presence. She shivered. "Okay."

He narrowed his eyes. "Okay, what?"

She wet her lips with her tongue. She was about to dive off the edge of the cliff into a bottomless sea. One that she could drown in, float in, or swim in. But if she didn't take the leap, she'd never experience any of the wonders. "Promise me that you'll put up with me despite my craziness. Promise me we'll always be together."

He tilted his head as a sexy smile spread across his lips.

"I promise, though I can't promise I won't call you out on your craziness."

"Promise me you'll fix the cabin." She set her coffee cup down on a side table and inched closer to him.

"Promise me you'll hunt with me." He held her eyes as he set down his mug.

"Promise me you'll be nice to my human friends."

"I'll try." He wrinkled his nose. "Promise me you'll be nice to Felan."

"I'll try." She closed the distance. "I move that we hold over the rest of the agenda items until next meeting."

He pulled her into his arms. "I second that."

She curled her fingers into his hair and brought her lips to his. "Meeting adjourned," she murmured, and pinned him with a savage kiss.

CHAPTER THIRTY-ONE

Cherime was on top of Ren, grinding herself against the fabric of his jeans. He knew wearing clothes was a bad idea and wished he had vetoed that rule. Her long silky hair was splayed across his face and he gathered it with his hands until he had it all wrapped in his fist. He held it tight as he pressed his mouth to hers, taking over the kiss she initiated.

Their tongues duelled, but this time it was a tango, each touch, each sweep taking them further from the world around them. He had tunnel vision, just the two of them, dancing to a beat no one else could hear.

Her fingers clutched the fabric of his T-shirt and her silky thighs hugged his hips. Not enough room on the couch, so he wrapped his arms around her and stood. She circled his hips with her legs as he carried her to the kitchen counter, sweeping the clean dishes onto the floor.

The shattering of glass wasn't enough to break through their fog. As he dropped her curvy bottom onto the countertop, she pulled her head back and looked down, fumbling at the buttons on his jeans.

"Take them off!" Her breaths were heavy and uneven, and her chest rose and fell in tandem. He grasped the hem of her T-shirt and pulled it over her head, tossing it onto the floor next to the broken glasses, then her hands were back at the opening of his jeans, drawing his zipper down and grabbing hold of him in both hands.

It wasn't that he didn't love the silky grip of her hands on his cock, but his self-control was wire-thin. "It doesn't need a handi-wipe to get ready, Wolverine. I've never been so hard in my life."

"So hard." Her hands went up and under his T-shirt, stroking across his chest, pinching his nipples.

He jerked as her teasing stroked down to his cock. "Hard for you." His hips shoved forward of their own volition.

"God," she moaned as she clutched at him and ground her pelvis against his. "I need you inside me, Ren. Now!"

"Not yet." He wanted to prolong this because he was a greedy bastard who wanted it all. Also, in Cherime's arms, he felt like a teenage boy, not sure he could last long enough to give her the pleasure she deserved.

He shoved as much of her breast into his mouth as he could and clamped down as his hands roamed over her. Every curve of her body was soft and supple, her long legs hugging him, her crossed ankles pressing on his ass. A flush of need enhanced her gorgeous face as she kissed along the top of his head, then gasped and grabbed his beard when he bit down on her breast, dragging his face to hers.

"Stop biting me," she moaned without conviction.

He gripped her hair and yanked her head back, kissing her voraciously. "I'll do whatever I fucking want to this body. It's mine. You're mine."

"Promise me!" she shrieked and widened her thighs as

he dropped to his knees and nuzzled his face into her pussy.

"Promise." His reply was muffled as he sucked and nibbled his way up and down her folds, his tongue stroking her, fucking her, tasting her. He breathed her in – her desire, her uniqueness. He'd missed her so much – this scent, this taste, this woman.

She was writhing on the countertop, pulling at his hair. "Oh god, Ren. A little more."

He stood, licking his lips, then rubbing his beard on her chest. "I want to see you painted with my cum." Then he shoved his dick inside until he was buried in her tightness.

They groaned together, their bodies a frenzy of movement. She twisted under him when he shoved her down on the counter and gripped her ankles, holding them in the air while he thrust. "*Fuck!*" she screamed as her orgasm shuddered through her, her pussy pulsing around his cock, dragging him deeper until he exploded.

He knew that scream; it was indelibly imprinted in his memory. Over the years, he'd begun to doubt he'd ever hear it again, ever have her again. It buckled his knees that they were back together, that he didn't fuck up so badly that he couldn't turn it around.

Anything. He'd do anything for his precious Wolverine.

AFTER, they lay on the cool hard surface of the wood floor, somewhere between the kitchen and living room, Cherime curled on top of him, still panting.

Struggling to get his emotions under control, he tightened his arms around her and rocked her. She was wild and crazy, difficult and contrary. And the only women in the world for him. It was more than a pair-bond. It had to be fate bringing them together. No one else could be his mate and survive him. No other woman was strong enough to take him on and bring him to his knees.

"You okay?" he said, his voice a blend of chainsaw and cheap bourbon.

"I will be." Her soft giggle brought back the good memories of the girl he'd once known. His heart grew two sizes bigger.

He held her tighter. "We should mate."

She lifted her head and gazed at him, confusion in her eyes. "Now?"

"Soon," he replied.

She sighed as she settled her head back on his chest. "Not in this dump."

He grabbed her shoulders as he rolled, flattening her on the floor with his heavy body. His cock was hard for her again and this time, he shoved inside without any foreplay. His difficult little female needed a good fucking to remind her who her alpha was.

CHAPTER THIRTY-TWO

In the morning, Cherime woke first, turning her head to gaze at Ren. He was on his side facing her, his huge hand draped over her belly, his breath deep and even. The blanket was low on his hips, covering his goods.

He gave her chills and a fever all at the same time. Heaven and hell combined. A devil with a halo. He was a good man, had a good heart, not good with words but he didn't have to be. His actions were proof enough. Pretending to be angry at her last night for calling his cabin a dump, he'd worked her into a frenzy of need, making sure she was pleasured several times before he let himself come.

One more round of lovemaking after that and they were finally sated. Cherime was so exhausted that when he lifted her in his arms and carried her to bed, she didn't complain that the sheets needed changing.

Now, as dawn broke, she hovered her fingers over his belly, not quite touching it, and air-traced the contours of his pecs, the valleys of his abs, and the sexy vee that disappeared under the blanket. Checking to see that he was still asleep, she gently lifted the blanket and tugged it down so that it rested on his thighs.

His flaccid cock was impressive enough and she inspected it closely, her pussy warming up at its appearance. His foreskin hid the prolific hood, which, when hard, was like a mushroom with a super long and wide stem. His penis seemed lighter than the rest of his skin, but the helmet, when exposed, was as a dark as he was. Erect, the flesh on his shaft was silky to the touch, the root of it nestled in dark curly hair.

His thighs were open enough that she could see his heavy sac, his balls hard against the skin. Some hair on them, and saliva formed in her mouth as she thought about taking a taste.

She wet her lips, then dipped her head down until her tongue touched his flesh. She licked gently, like she was painting a canvas, easy strokes, tucking into the nooks and crannies around his thighs and under his sac.

His cock stirred, started to harden, which made room for her to tackle the area where penis met pelvic bone. She licked quickly at it; the texture of the coarse pubic hair against her tongue made her shiver and her nipples perk up. Pleased with the effect she was having on herself, she tongued the underside of his cock like she was eating a chocolate covered banana, making sure she got all the chocolate before she devoured the fruit of her labours.

A groan filled the room and Cherime peeked up to capture Ren's dark gaze stroking over her. He'd snaked one hand behind his neck and his other slithered down to his cock, which he grabbed and tapped against Cherime's lips.

Since she already up at the top, she slid her wet lips around the crown and sucked it into her mouth, tasting the pre-cum, teasing the shallow underside of it with her tongue. Sucking at it, holding it in her mouth, swiping over the top of it, which made it jerk.

"Fuck!" Ren grunted as he tugged at her hair.

You taste good, baby. She pushed herself higher on her elbows so she could take more of him, finally touching his cock with her hand, sliding it down the shaft, her lips following it as much as she could take, then back up, her head bobbing along with it. She hollowed her cheeks as she went down again, and Ren jerked upwards, his cock hitting the back of her throat.

She took him deeper, holding on to her gag reflex, trying to swallow all of him, but there was no way something that big was going down all at once. She held him at the base of her throat for a moment and then popped her head up and off his cock, gasping for breath. It was a veined, steel rod in her hand, pulsing and bobbing in front of her, and her pussy was wet with want, her clit begging to get in on the action.

She climbed to her knees, looking at his dick like it was her favourite new toy, and really it was. A vintage collectable and it was time for a good polishing. She grinned at Ren, then straddled his hips, groping behind her for his rod, then carefully pushing herself down on it.

His size split her apart. No matter how wet she was, he stretched her out and made her ache. It was good, all of it, as she drove deeper on the shaft, taking as much as she could.

Ren gripped her waist as she flattened her palms against his chest, thrusting her breasts at him. He sat up so that he could suck one of her nipples into his mouth, his hand squeezing the softness of it. "You are so fucking perfect, baby."

"Oh my god," Cherime breathed as she groped her way to the apex of her folds, her needy button demanding attention. "How much more, Ren? I want us to come together." She stroked herself lightly so that she could hold on.

He took the hand she was using and sucked her fingers into his mouth, then brought his thumb to her little pleasure nub. "Keep moving that ass, morning wood doesn't pop off quickly."

"Well, if you're going to take your time, I'm gonna have to come twice."

He grabbed her wrists. "Know what will make me come faster? If I bend you over backwards and treat you like a whore."

What the hell? "What?"

But that was all she managed to squeak out, because he jerked her off him, then turned her around, bringing her down so she was riding him reverse cowgirl. He shoved her thighs wider and forced her head down to his knees. "Stretch your arms straight out in front of you and grab my ankles," he demanded through heavy breaths. He didn't stop thrusting his hips.

"If I do that, I can't touch myself," Cherime whined, not liking this turn of events.

"That's the fucking point, babe," Ren growled. "Do it!"

Thanking nature for her being so flexible, she pushed her arms out in front of her and gripped Ren's feet, then hung on as he pounded into her. He was a champion – this ride was going to last longer than eight seconds. "Ren!" she shouted, her body burning out of control.

His rough hands on her ass, squeezing her flesh, and his commanding voice made her desire spiral upwards. The sweet spot inside her was begging for more as his cock brushed back and forth over it as he thrust. It was enough to bring to her the edge, but not enough to topple her over. "Fuck me harder!"

He walloped her ass. "You don't fucking order me around! I'm your alpha. Best you remember that."

She shrieked and bucked her body, the sting of the slap mixing with pleasure and making her quiver, her need for release becoming almost painful. "It was my idea to tap you," she gasped. "Not fair you taking over."

He growled and smacked her ass again. "Tell me who I am, baby." His husky voice rubbed like sandpaper on her needy little lady bits.

"Alpha," she rasped. She could barely put two words together she was wound so tightly.

"Whose alpha?" Another stinging slap across her ass.

Fuck! He was a bastard, getting her to this point and not helping her over the edge. "My alpha!" she screamed.

He swatted her again, then his enormous hand snaked around her throat and lightly squeezed. His other hand fisted her hair as his breathing got deeper and faster. "You sure you wanna come?"

She gasped out as her desire spiked with his rough handling, the depth of his cock, his possessive demands. "I have to come."

"I wanna hear you beg, baby."

She was so out of her mind she'd do anything he wanted. "Please, Ren. Please let me come."

His moved his hand from her neck to her belly, the rough pad of his fingers fumbling for her clit, then pinching painfully. "Who am I, Cherime!" he shouted at her as he thrust deep inside her.

"Oh my god!" she screamed at the pain, her body almost leaping off the bed. "My alpha. You're my fucking alpha!"

He released her clit and returned his hand to her throat, yanking her hair so she was looking at his face. "Fuck!" he roared. "Don't you fucking forget it!"

Her orgasm thundered through her like a tidal wave, devastating every nerve in her body. "Ren! Ren! Ren!" She was shaking all over, pulsing in places that didn't actually pulse.

His grip on her tightened as she strangled his cock. He was so deep that she felt the warmth of his release as it hit up against her cervix and bathed her walls. "Fuck, Cherime."

He yanked her up so that he had her back pressed against his chest, his giant arms circling her, one hand cupping her chin, forcing her face to his. The warmth of his tongue stroked over her lips, then his mouth crashed down on hers, taking her in a possessive primal kiss. She was too boneless to kiss him back, too boneless to do anything but sag in his arms.

He broke the kiss and tossed her on her back then dropped to his back next to her. No words marred the quiet as their heavy breaths slowly evened out.

Finally, his deep rasp broke the impasse. "You're a fucking dream come true, Wolverine."

He was a fucking dream come true. "Tell me you love me, again."

The silence stretched for a moment, then his husky voice traced over her. "I've always loved you." He wrapped his arm around her shoulders and tugged her to him, his tight grip squeezing. "Even when I didn't."

"Same," Cherime blew a breath of warm air on his nipple as she teased it with her fingers. It puckered and she grinned in satisfaction. "That was really good. What you did." She looked up at him. "I don't think I've ever come that hard." She tilted her head to see him looking down at her.

"There's plenty more where that came from." He paused as he stroked up and down her arm. "And, yeah, you're the best I ever had too."

CHAPTER THIRTY-THREE

Ren carried the big tin bathtub down to the stream and rinsed it of dirt, the bodies of bugs, and other debris that had collected over the winter. He rarely bothered to use it himself, either dunking his body in the deep part of the stream and cleaning up that way or heating some water on the stove so he could soap himself up and wash his hair.

Cherime wanted a warm soak to ease the soreness of her muscles, and he was fine with that. He'd even get in with her and help her out if she asked. His cock and wolf perked up at the thought, though his wolf didn't much like water, but it liked Cherime enough to tolerate a bath.

After the fun this morning, Cherime was walking around in a happy daze. He loved how wild she was, how unrestrained. He loved how she spoke her mind, wasn't shy about giving him shit. She knew what she meant to him, knew how to respect him. Knew when to back off. Most of the time anyway.

She was more than anything he dared to hope for. Far more than he deserved.

After a second round this morning, this time gentler and more intimate, they talked over coffee. He was surprised at how much he enjoyed sharing his morning with someone else. Used to be, he hated talking to anyone before lunch, but Cherime wasn't anyone. She was his fated mate.

He sighed as he swished the tub in the stream. They hadn't yet talked about making it official – Cherime side-stepping the topic when he'd broached it last night. He'd wanted to do it this morning. It was the perfect time for them; her yelling his name and calling him alpha had made him harder than he'd ever been in his entire life.

That was the difference between then and now, right there. Teenage Cherime wouldn't have been able to handle his darker urges, wouldn't have known what to do. But mature Cherime was all in, understood his desires and embraced them. Not that she had a choice. He grinned. But she wasn't mad. Nope, she was thanking him and wanting more.

He picked up the clean tub and put it on the top of his head, his long arms reaching up and grasping the rim on each side to balance it. He was wearing faded jeans and his trail boots; no shirt, but the sun was doing a good enough job of keeping him warm. Shifters didn't feel the cold like humans did, though there were plenty of them missing and fingers toes from frostbite. Miraculously, he still had 10 of each.

The cabin came into sight and he tried to see it through Cherime's eyes. It was a dump, which was to be expected considering he'd neglected it for eight years. What was the point? It was just him, and in his mind always would be, unless he found his way back to Cherime.

His stomach lurched at the thought. Not only had that happened, but she was willing to let go of the past, and even went so far as to acknowledge her role in their relationship blowing up.

He kicked a rusted shovel as he entered the overgrown yard. He'd fix this up, make it perfect for her or he'd move and build something new, where they could easily hook into electricity. Some place where he could drill a viable well and get water piped in.

The new place needed better access to the secondary highway so they could get into Darkness Falls in the winter. A big yard for the children, a fenced patch for a big garden like Tess had. That way they'd have stores for all year round.

Maybe they should wait to make it official until he built Wolverine a proper home. She was as posh as female shifters got, and he was going to have to compromise. He couldn't expect her to embrace his lifestyle and leave hers completely behind.

His wolf rolled its eyes. *Are you a pansy or an alpha?*

He dropped the tub on the porch and frowned at his thoughts. What were his expectations of her, and how far was she willing to meet him mid-way? She didn't cook, didn't hunt. Of course, those were skills that could be learned. She coloured her hair and wore heels. Guess she could still do both, though he never could understand what the draw was.

He stroked his beard, then did a double-take when the screen door banged and the woman of his thoughts stepped up beside him, stark naked, with a grin on her face. His cock took a stand, saluting her body out of respect. "I like the outfit, Wolverine. Hugs you in all the right places. Not sure if it's right for this weather though. Still a bit cool."

She laughed, her snark set to low this morning.

"Thought I'd take a run before the bath. Roll around in the mud, get myself good and dirty."

"I like you dirty." Ren smirked. "I'll come with you."

Cherime shook her head. "Nope. I need a little me-time and besides, I want that tub full of hot, steamy water when I get back." She teased the hair on his chest with her fingers. "You're just the man to make that happen."

No fucking way. "Nope. It's not safe out here for you to be on your own. What if a bear attacks?"

She rolled her eyes at him and he decided that was something that would have to stop. He liked her spirit, liked when she was playful, but he wasn't used to being disrespected.

"My sniffer is good enough to scent a predator, so you don't have to worry about me accidentally tripping over one. And my pretty beast is as savage as any other shifter. She knows how to scrap."

Ren didn't want to concede, but the wild woman beside him wasn't going to back down and he didn't want this day to turn bad. Besides, he lived in the mountains and he couldn't expect her to never go outside alone. He tucked his hands into his jean pockets and tilted his head at her. "I'm not comfortable with you traipsing around by yourself."

She placed her hands on her hips. "Get used to it, big guy. I'm going on a solo run. You're going to stay here and draw me a bath. Maybe, if you behave yourself, I'll bring back a rabbit for breakfast." She stopped, perhaps realizing that telling him what to do wasn't the best way to get what she wanted. She batted her long dark eyelashes at him. "Pretty please."

He grinned at her antics. "Begging only works in the bedroom, Wolverine." He sighed, looked at the sky. "Don't be gone too long, because if I gotta come find you, I'm gonna turn your pretty ass a nice shade of red."

"I won't be gone long despite your promises." She winked at him, then shifted. Her wolf was fucking amazing. Snow white, no markings, pale blue eyes. Strong, sturdy, sleek. Large enough to own her place at his side. His pack might grumble because Cherime was a princess, but she wouldn't take shit from them. They'd quickly find that out and the respect would grow from there.

She glided up to him gracefully, then nipped his knee hard enough to break skin. "You little bitch," he roared as she scrambled away, her tail high in the air, that last flash of white before she disappeared into the trees.

CHAPTER THIRTY-FOUR

Cherime hadn't intended to bite Ren, but her wolf brought out her playfulness and he was standing there like a prey animal asking to be mauled. She was happy to oblige.

She thought he'd chase after her and was almost disappointed when he didn't come roaring through the trees to tackle her. She decided to be happy he showed some restraint instead of cranky about his lack of attention.

Her first stop was at the shallow creek that ran behind Ren's cabin. The water was cool, clean, and crisp. Perfect, the way water was meant to be, and she stepped into it with her front paws as she lapped at it. She didn't often shift in front of other shifters or humans. She didn't join in pack runs unless Lucien insisted, and had shifted only once over the winter, during a showdown with the brother of her former packmate, Honi, and his group of murderers. She'd killed one of the shifters to save Lucien and it had felt fantastic. She rode that high for months.

Other than that, she let her wolf out when it needed a run, some fresh air, to touch base with nature, but always alone so she could savour the gifts of the earth. Of course, now that she was with Ren, there'd be more shifting. The mountains were much easier to traverse as a wolf.

It was important to shifters not to suppress their wolf or human sides. Shifters that stayed in wolf form too long struggled to shift to human and vice versa. It was like meditation – as long as you did it regularly it was effective. Shifting to wolf form was subline, orgasmic even. Wolves were graceful, fearless, apex predators, especially as a pack. And they needed their packs to survive, to have their backs, to nurture the pups, to be a community.

Yeah, Cherime loved the wolf side of her, but unlike most other shifters, she embraced her human side too. She didn't find her body graceless or awkward as many other shifters complained. She loved her long legs, her feminine curves and all the wonderful products out there that enhanced what mother nature had given her.

She grinned inwardly at the lingerie she had at home and wondered what Ren would think when he saw her in her black lace corset, skimpy panties, and thigh highs. And of course, her 4-inch stilettos to finish it off. Maybe he'd grow a new appreciation for her heels.

She hadn't ever spent much time thinking about shifters and why they were the way they were. Their human side governed their wolf. They fucked as humans, got pregnant as humans, and had human babies. The shift didn't start until they reached puberty, and like humans, that's when they were most out-of-control and vulnerable. Shifting took practice and for young shifters it was hard to shift or maintain wolf form under stress. She'd never had that problem though.

She stopped and scented the air. Not much of a breeze, but nothing in the vicinity that seemed threatening, so she loped ahead, her nose and eyes alert for rabbits. Her plan was to catch a nice big one that she could bring home to Ren. Yeah, it was a puppy dog ploy, but she wanted to give him something he'd appreciate. The rabbit would fill his belly, but more importantly, she'd show him she had game.

As a predator, she was out of practice. Okay, that was being generous. She'd never actually bagged a rabbit or deer. Just that one mean shifter dude, though feasting on other shifters was frowned upon.

Still, if she could kill a male, surely she could track and kill Bugs Bunny.

She lingered until she spied a rabbit and gave chase. The pursuit lasted less than a minute as the fucking rabbit unexpectedly sprinted around a tree and she didn't. Damn rabbit, she thought as she bounced off the hard trunk of an old growth redwood. She scrambled to her feet and shook her body. A little bump to her forehead was not going to put her off her plan, and she scuttled deeper into the woods as she caught a whiff of escapee number one.

The second round ended in a stalemate, and the rabbit outsmarted her in round three.

An hour later, the score was rabbits: six, Cherime: zero. Fuck it, she thought after falling off a large log into a puddle of melted snow, mud clinging to her fur. Ren would start to get growly if she didn't return soon. She shook herself off and headed towards the cabin, sniffing the air. She wanted one last go.

She stopped in her tracks when she drew a blank on the scents. She couldn't smell anything, let alone a bunny. It was weird to have nature become odorless. She swiped a paw across her nose. Maybe the last fall had jarred something in her nasal passage. She hoped not – a shifter who couldn't scent was pretty fucking vulnerable. Speaking of which, without being able to smell, she was now lost. She couldn't pick up the scent of her trail and unlike humans who would mark their trail (well, the smart ones would), shifters used their noses as their markers.

Unless of course they lost their sense of smell, which she had never heard of. She sat on her haunches and let out a defeated whine, thinking about alternatives. Howling was probably the best thing to do. Wolves had unique howls that carried a long way. Even if Ren didn't hear her, other wolves would pick up on it, and they'd reply and relay it forward.

She raised her snout in the air and let out of a single tragic howl, hoping Ren heard and understood she was in trouble. She pulled air into her lungs, starting to follow the first howl with another one, when something slammed into her back and flattened her.

Teeth tore into the nape of her neck and she rolled quickly, scrambling to her feet, gaining distance, and turning. A huge grey wolf stood before her, snarling and snapping its teeth.

Holy shit!

At least it was a wolf and not a bear.

Cherime retreated a few steps, her tail drooping as she emitted a whine. She might be able to beat it in a scrap, but if she let it think she was submissive to it, it might be enough to get it to back off.

The wolf took another step towards her, still growling like she'd insulted its mother, and she backed away, keeping her hackles down even though she was becoming less afraid and more pissed. Fucking wolf! Who the hell did it think it was dealing with?

She thought it was a male because it was so big, but she couldn't really tell, couldn't scent whether it was a shifter or a wolf. If she survived this encounter, she was probably going to need brain surgery to get her nose working again.

The wolf leaped and so did she as her adrenaline

soared. At least her reflexes were intact. No point in turning tail and running. She didn't know where she was going, and in the mountains, it was too easy to run off the side of a cliff.

She went for the wolf's throat, trying to get a grip, while it flipped her in the air and body slammed her to the ground. Its teeth gouged her side, the pain momentarily paralyzing her. Her attacker must have thought it had won as it eased up on her.

This was her chance to show the dude that she didn't fucking take a mauling laying down. She scrambled from beneath it, then twisted her body, her wolf all fur and teeth, flying at the asshole like a nuclear missile, grabbing its ear as she passed it and ripping it as she landed on its back.

This big boy was all male, she realized as her teeth clamped down on the back of its neck. *Take that you fucker!* But wolf-boy wasn't impressed, and it whipped around so fast she lost her grip and hit the ground hard. She was stunned but her wolf knew the danger it was in and rolled away several feet until it came to rest against the side of a rock.

She tried to stagger to her feet, but she was bleeding, her adrenaline was ebbing, and her wolf was retreating inside her. *Don't,* she moaned to her wolf, willing it to crawl forward on the earth until she was next to a decent-sized rock. Then she let go and returned to her human form, her fingers curling around her new weapon.

Her attacker didn't leap at her like she expected. Instead, it sauntered over like a bully on a playground and pawed at her back, splitting more skin with its claws.

She moaned and it lowered its head and lapped at the open wound in her side. What the hell was it doing? Wolves didn't play with their food, and she was definitely steak at this point. She needed it to come a little closer to her head, maybe clamp down on her neck, which was what wolves did to hold their prey.

Like she had willed it to happen, the wolf sniffed up her spine until it got to her hair, which it inhaled deeply. It was go time, and she was thankful that even in human form, she was stronger and faster than humans. She yanked the rock from the ground as she twisted her body, then slammed it into the head of the wolf.

It yelped and leapt back as Cherime struggled to her knees and heaved the rock straight at the wolf's head, catching it square between the eyes. The wolf dropped to the ground, writhing, pawing at its face. Her head was swimming and she willed herself not to black out. It wasn't dead, which meant she was still vulnerable. She crawled towards it, searching the ground for another rock to finish it off.

It was creeping on its haunches, away from her, then it staggered to its feet, turning towards her, holding her eyes with its vicious amber orbs. It bared its teeth and let out a serious of yips and growls that had her shuddering, then it turned and limped away, disappearing into the forest.

Cherime buckled, covering her face with her hands as she started to sob. Darkness tugged at the edges of her vision and she struggled to stay conscious, but her brain shut down and she collapsed on the ground, thinking this might be the last time she thought anything.

CHAPTER THIRTY-FIVE

Ren was in mid-pour when he heard Cherime's howl of distress. He dropped the bucket like acid had eaten through it and ripped off his jeans and boots, tearing out of the house and shifting as he ran.

That single yowl made his adrenaline surge through him and his heart drop to his toes as he picked up Cherime's trail. That single howl meant she was in danger, somewhere in the forest, and he was fucked if he could sort out where she'd gone. Her scent was all over the place, taking him in circles, stopping up against trees and rocks, in underbrush and deadfall.

He raced around like a goddamn headless chicken until he was out of breath. Finally, he stopped and drew in some air, settling his panic. If he was going to find her, he needed to get in touch with his instincts. He raised his nose and sniffed the air, tracing her path, his ears straining to hear something other than bird calls and rustles.

His wolf stiffened, the predator inside catching a whiff of blood. He almost collapsed on himself as he raced towards it, his heart thumping faster than it was built to beat. As he got closer, he scented Cherime: Cherime and blood, a lethal mixture that had him steeling himself for what he might find.

He skidded into a small clearing and saw her limp body laid out on her side, eyes closed. On his last stride, he shifted and dropped to his knees beside her body. His eyes raced over her – a slash in her side, claw and bite marks on her body, the nape of her neck had been pierced, a deep gash on the left side of her forehead.

"Cherime!" he shouted as he hugged her body to him. "Cherime, baby. Talk to me."

She moaned and opened her eyes. "Ren," she croaked, raising a bloodied hand to his beard and stroking it. "I'm okay."

"You're not fucking okay!" It came out too loud and harsh and she winced. "Sorry, baby. Your bleeding everywhere. We gotta get you to the hospital."

"No," she weakly protested.

Always a fucking fight with her. He stood and gathered her in his arms before plunging into the trees like a madman. He knew his way around this area, knew that it was a good hour's walk in human form, but he had to hope that the slashes didn't go so deep she'd bleed out.

"I can shift," she mumbled and then passed out.

By the time Ren got back to the cabin, his feet were torn to bits. That mattered far less than Cherime moaning every time he jostled her. Both of them were bloody, but he only stopped long enough to throw on his jeans and a T-shirt, force his mashed-up feet into his boots. He slid Cherime's panties and T-shirt on her, then wrapped her in a blanket and laid her on the bench in the crewcab of his truck.

His stomach in knots, he barrelled down the mountain like it was spewing lava behind him.

At the hospital, he raced inside with Cherime in his arms. "I need help!" he yelled. "She's been attacked."

A red-headed nurse came running towards him, took a quick assessment and led him into an examination room. "Put her down there," she ordered as she motioned to a padded table.

Cherime moaned as her eyes fluttered open. "Where are we?"

He brushed her hair back from her forehead as a doctor entered. "Hospital, baby."

"No." She struggled to get up. "I'm okay."

The doctor took a single glance at her. "No, you're not." Her voice lacked warmth, but her cool efficient tone was reassuring. She pulled on latex gloves as she looked at Ren. "I'm Dr. Phillips."

"Where's Cooper?" Ren demanded. He didn't trust human doctors; didn't believe they knew a goddamned thing about treating shifters. "I want him here."

"Call Dr. Cooper," Phillips said to the nurse. "Tell him it's an emergency."

The nurse scurried away as Dr. Phillips assessed the damage on Cherime's body. "Can you help me roll her over?" she said to Ren, and when he did, she swallowed a gasp. "Who did this to her?" Her gaze held shock, anger, and accusation.

"I don't know. Found her like this." He was used to seeing shifter wounds. "These aren't defensive. She fought back hard."

Dr. Phillips nodded her agreement. "A wolf attack?"

Ren glanced at the lacerations on Cherime's back. "Lone wolf by the looks of it. They're the only motherfuckers crazy enough to take on a shifter."

She glanced up at him, the frown an indication that he had shaken her up. A different nurse entered the room and began preparing a tray for the doctor. "Gillian's on her way back but told me to tell you that Dr. Cooper is in Vancouver at a conference. He's the keynote apparently."

"Fucking figures," Ren growled.

Dr. Phillips touched the bump on Cherime's forehead. "Looks like she hit her head, but she's in and out of consciousness, so probably just the body dealing with the shock. We'll do a cat scan to make sure that's all it is."

Ren didn't care for the doctor's casual attitude. He pointed an aggressive finger at her. "Don't you fucking let her die!"

Dr. Phillips threw him a withering glance. "She's not going to die. Why don't you take your big-ass self to the front desk and fill out the forms so I can get on with my work."

Ren narrowed his eyes, but swallowed the growl forming inside his chest. "I'll be back."

"Fucking terminator," he heard her mutter as the door banged shut behind him.

Gillian, the bad news nurse, caught him as he stalked towards the nurses' station. She indicated a room with several couches and chairs, a coffee maker, and a shelf of books. "Let's go in here, and I'll help you go through the paperwork."

Ren followed her in and slumped down on one of the sofas, too small for his frame, but that was pretty much the case with most furniture. "Let's get on with this."

"Can I get you some coffee?" The redhead asked as she headed towards the machine.

"No," he barked. He didn't want fucking coffee. He wanted Cherime to open her eyes and smile at him.

"Okay," Gillian said quickly, moving from the coffee machine to the couch opposite Ren. She pulled a pen from the top of the clipboard and hovered over the form. "Name?"

"Cherime Montana," he muttered. She would take his name after they mated.

She scribbled a note. "And yours?"

"Ren Ketkah."

She looked at him, catching his eye, then dropping hers quickly. She focused on the clipboard. "You're the Mountain pack alpha, aren't you?"

"Yep." He popped the *p*.

"What's your relationship to Cherime?"

He leaned towards her, not liking her line of questioning. "We're together."

"But not officially mated?" She kept her eyes glued to the pen in her hand.

"So what?"

She sucked in a breath. "Cherime's from the Lodge pack and federal law requires us to inform the pack alpha when a member of his pack is admitted to hospital. And she's got blood kin, too. They need to know."

"So call them," Ren said as mildly as he could. What the fuck were they thinking? That he had a hand in Cherime's injuries?

"Right," she nodded. "Can you tell me what happened?"

He felt like this was an inquisition – since when did the hospital need the details on the attack? "No. I wasn't there when it happened." He crossed his arms over his chest, realizing that the second Gillian called Lucien, the Lodge pack would swarm the hospital and blame him. It would get ugly, and the cops would be called to shut things down.

He could tell by the nurse's expression that she was thinking the same thing.

"I'm not leaving." He narrowed his eyes at her and

watched as the blood drained from her face. "I don't give a fuck if you call in the armed forces, I'm staying here until Cherime is cleared to go."

She fussed with her pen as she nodded. "I'll make the call." She almost ran out of the room.

Once Ren was alone, he called Jackson. "Got a problem," he grunted when Jackson picked up. "I'm at the hospital. Can you come up?"

"On my way," Jackson ended the call.

Ren rested his head against the wall, thankful that Jackson was smarter than the average cop. If Ren was calling, Jackson knew that whatever the problem, it was big enough to blow the lid off the hospital.

Cherime had been right. He shouldn't have brought her to the hospital. Instead, he should have taken her to Tess, who would have known what to do. The female wasn't a healer, but she had enough experience to nurse a shifter back to health. Ren had even seen her stitch up a few.

One of the nice things about Darkness Falls was that it was small, so it didn't take more than 10 minutes for Jackson to show up. One of the shit things about Darkness Falls was that it was small, and Eva was trailing behind Jackson, the look on her face telling him she already knew about Cherime.

"Where is she?" Eva demanded. Cherime and Eva were pack mates, and worse, friends.

"Settle down," Jackson said to Eva as he took the same seat Gillian had earlier occupied.

Eva sniffed. "I don't have to settle down. This is pack business."

Ren almost rolled his eyes. A fucking human pretending to represent a shifter pack. "Fuck off, Eva," he said bluntly. "You want to know where Cherime is, go ask a fucking nurse. No one's telling me anything."

Eva huffed out of the room as Ren turned to Jackson. "This is going to get ugly."

"What happened?" Jackson rested his elbows on his thighs and clasped his hands as he leaned forward.

"She went for a run by herself and was attacked. Wolf I think."

"Wolf or shifter?"

Ren rubbed the back of his neck, trying to recall the scene. Bits and pieces, his focus on Cherime, not his surroundings. "I heard her distress call, so I lit out to find her, but she'd been running around in circles, so I had trouble following the trail. Then I smelled the blood and tracked it back to her. The wounds are wolf."

"Not shifter?"

Ren narrowed his eyes, thinking about it. "Don't fucking know. The scent was missing."

Jackson straightened up, his face a mix of excitement and concern. "Sounds like our guy."

Ren gazed at Jackson, good cop, but lousy sympathizer. "Try to bottle your enthusiasm when the Lodge pack arrives. Don't think they'll be celebrating the fact that you got a break in the case."

Jackson offered a chagrinned smile. "Sorry. Not the way I wanted it to happen and we won't know for sure until we talk to Cherime."

Ren felt himself deflate. "Don't think anyone is letting me near her. They think I did this."

Jackson shook his head. "Pretty sure it wasn't you."

"Thanks for the fucking vote of confidence, asshole."

The words were barely out of his mouth when Lucien stalked into the family waiting room. "What the fuck did you do?" His anger was barely constrained, and Ren had to hold his wolf back from taking a run at the Lodge pack's alpha.

Ren stood and stretched to his full height. "I didn't do a fucking thing except let Cherime talk me into letting her take a run by herself."

Lucien glanced at Jackson. "Why are you here?"

Jackson seemed pissed at the hostile question and refused to answer it. Instead he said, "Have you checked on Cherime yet? How's she doing?"

Lucien stalked closer but kept a good six feet between himself and Ren. "Raff's checking on her." He turned to Ren. "Want to explain why the hell you're down off your mountain, fucking around with one of mine?"

Ren tried to quell the instinctual hostility that was overflowing inside him. "Cherime and I are planning on mating," he said quietly. Ren hated having to explain his business, but the bastard was Cherime's alpha. Raff was her brother. They were going to find out eventually.

Raff walked in at that moment. "Over my fucking dead body."

Ren had never liked the aggressive hostile beta, so he grinned maliciously. "That can be arranged."

Jackson finally got to his feet, brave fucker, putting himself in the centre of the antagonistic male shifters. "How's Cherime?"

Raff glared at him. "She's awake but groggy. Eva's with her."

Ren started forward but Lucien and Raff blocked his path to the door. "No fucking way you're going near her," Lucien snarled.

Ren was done playing nice. "I will throw both your asses off the rooftop if you don't get out of my way."

"All of you stop!" Jackson growled, his face creased in

anger. "The attacker sounds like it might be our guy, so it's my business until we know otherwise."

"Eva can conduct the interview." Lucien's eyes pinned Jackson in place.

Clearly, Jackson was having none of Lucien's attitude. "Eva reports to me when she's on duty, and she'll fucking do as I say or she'll find herself suspended."

CHAPTER THIRTY-SIX

Cherime never really passed out, though she struggled to open her eyes. She blamed it on the fight and the depletion of her adrenaline. She was exhausted, but more upset that Ren hadn't listened to her when she told him not to bring her to the hospital. Some fucking alpha he was, unable to keep his head under pressure.

She was in a hospital bed, also ticked that Coop chose that time to go to Vancouver. If she was going to be in a hospital getting stitched up, she didn't want a human doctor poking and prodding her. Her vision swam as she peeked her eyes open. So fucking bright in here. What was wrong with these people? It was like looking directly into a solar eclipse.

"You're awake." It was Eva's voice.

"I was never asleep," Cherime grumbled. "I didn't feel like to talking to anyone." She took a breath and realized her ability to scent had returned. What a time for that to happen. All she could smell was antiseptic, blood, and urine.

"Dr. Phillips stitched you up and says you can go home

once you can walk steady. Nothing else wrong with you that she has the credentials to fix." Eva smirked at her little joke.

Cherime didn't find it funny. She struggled to sit up, shrugging Eva off when the cop tried to help. "Where's Ren?"

"Uh, he's in the waiting room."

"Why?" Cherime demanded. She already knew why. It was because he brought her to the freaking hospital and someone called Lucien and Raff, who would prevent Ren from seeing her. "And why are you here?" Eva was in uniform, looking too freaking good for a pregnant woman. Why the hell was everyone pregnant but her?

"Just making sure you're okay. That's what friends do."

"Yeah," Cherime barked weakly. "And they prevent other friends from coming in the room."

Eva flushed. "We wanted to make sure that Ren didn't do this to you."

If Cherime wasn't so sore, she would have knocked Eva on her ass. "Are you freaking kidding me! Why the hell would make anyone think Ren did this?"

"Hey, settle down." Eva reached out to touch Cherime and she slapped the cop's hand away, regretting it immediately as the sutures in her side screamed at her.

"We're only looking out for your best interest," Eva continued. "And Ren doesn't exactly have a good track record."

Cherime was seething. Every fucking asshole that got between her and Ren was going to regret that they woke up this morning. "And you know this how? Because you've seen him beat the shit out of a female? Or even a male?" It was the same way she was treated. She was easy in everyone's eyes because she dressed seductively, flirted, and liked to have a good time.

"No… uhm…, but he has a reputation."

"For beating on women?" Cherime slid off the edge of the bed and swayed a little as she got her bearings.

Eva tried to defend herself. "He's aggressive, Cherime. Mean."

"You don't even fucking know him, and here you are deciding things based on his size and crankiness? Like Aztec's any different."

Eva's bottom lip wobbled at the mention of her mate. "Lucien asked me to stay with you."

"I bet he did." She looked down at herself, dressed only in a hospital gown, but at least it was tied shut at the back. Fuck modesty anyway. She took a few tentative steps towards the door, making sure her legs were going to hold her, and her brain wasn't going to shut down.

Eva rushed to her side, trying to stop her. "You need to be in bed, Cherime. You've been through a trauma."

Cherime turned to the human cop. "So I'm not thinking straight? Is that what you're implying? Or maybe you think I'm a battered woman who doesn't want to get her honey in trouble." She'd found her voice and her fury, raging at Eva. "Or maybe you're a narrow-minded weak Stepford wife who obeys her pack leader and her boss over her common sense!"

Eva's face turned beet red as she glared at Cherime, her eyes bright with tears. "You know I'm not! I'm the only female cop in this town and so I'm the one who deals with woman who have been raped or beaten up by those near and dear to them. And I'm a friend of yours so I was concerned."

Cherime almost felt bad for Eva. Almost. "Yeah, well if we're such good fucking friends, then you would know that no man does something like this to me and gets away with it. Ren saved my fucking life!" She tried to make a dramatic exit, but she was still too weak to do anything but shuffle out of the room.

"Shit!" Eva clenched her teeth as she followed Cherime. "I don't know why you're so mad. I was protecting you!"

Cherime had enough of the conversation. "Where is he?" she demanded loudly.

Gillian came rushing over. "Cherime, you should be in bed."

"And Ren should be looking after me, not this spineless cop. Where is he?" She bared her teeth at the redhead.

Gillian took a step back. "In the family waiting room, but you need to settle down or we'll have to call the police."

Eva raised her hand. "Uh, police already here."

"So cuff me or shut up," Cherime grumbled and shuffled her way to the waiting room she'd been to a few months ago when her former pack mate, Honi, had been injured trying to escape her deranged brother.

Her body protested every move she made. Muscles that she didn't know she had ached, and the stitched cuts stretched, sending feelers of pain to all her nerves. Fuck it all. She'd sit when she saw Ren. She slammed into the waiting room to see Ren and Jackson facing off against Lucien and Raff. "Ren," she said weakly. Seeing him stole her strength and she felt her knees buckle, but she willed herself to stay standing. Until Ren was holding her, she'd hang on.

All heads swivelled towards her and Ren tried to step around Lucien and Raff, but they blocked his path. "Get the fuck out of my way," Ren growled. "Or I'll forget where we're at."

Cherime saw the subtle movement of Eva's hand going

to her gun. "Let's stay calm, boys." Eva's voice held authority.

Cherime's voice held derision. "Quit being a fucking cop, Eva and start being a friend."

She shuffled towards Lucien and Raff. "Get out of my way," she snarled at them. "You have no business getting between Ren and me."

Raff mistook her anger. "You're too weak to take him on, Cherime. Let us handle this."

She stared at her brother. "You think Ren did this to me." The tears pricked her eyes at how unfair they were all being. "Ren saved my life, brought me here even though I told him not to." The muscle in her jaw ticked. "Because I knew this would happen!" She shoved Raff with her hands, then immediately regretted it as her muscles reminded her why she was here. "I hate you all." Her knees buckled, but Ren leapt forward and caught her, pulling her into his embrace and lifting her in his arms.

"It's okay, Wolverine. I got you." His warm breath brushed her ear as he took a few steps back until he was pressed against the wall.

Jackson created a barrier with his body, so that the Lucien and Raff couldn't get past him without physically moving him. "Enough. Ren and Cherime are clearly together, want to be together, so everyone needs to stand down."

"This is shifter business," Lucien said, a warning growl in his throat.

"You're in my town, Lucien. Maybe it's shifter business, maybe it's not, but you're not fucking brawling in the hospital, so back the hell off."

Eva sidled up to Raff, and Jackson's eyes flicked to her. "While you're on duty, Corporal Blakely, you represent the RCMP, not your pack or family. Think you need to spend some time figuring that out. Go back to the station house. You're officially on desk duty."

"C'mon on, Jackson," she seethed. "Everyone's on edge right now. Don't be making snap decisions."

"That how you address your chief, Blakely?" Jackson tone was ice cold. "Get going!"

Eva huffed, tossed him a derisive salute, and bolted from the waiting room.

Jackson turned his attention back to Lucien and Raff. "We'll get Cherime back to bed, then, if she feels up to it, we'll listen to what she has to say about the attack."

Cherime'd had about enough of all men except Ren, but she owed Jackson because he booted Eva out. "I'm not going back to my room. I'll tell you all what happened and then I'm leaving." Ren tightened his hold on her as she added, "With Ren," to make sure everyone understood what was going on.

"Can we all sit and try being civilized?" Jackson again.

Lucien breathed in through his nose as he considered Jackson, then Cherime. "Yeah," he finally said.

That was a big concession for Lucien, and Cherime appreciated it. Raff would follow Lucien's lead, at least for now. After all, when Cherime and Ren mated, they would all be family. Raff would struggle to accept it, mostly because it was Ren, who challenged every male shifter he encountered simply through his size and power. He didn't even have to open his mouth to get his point across. All he had to do was scowl. Like he was doing now, she thought, as he sat on one of the couches and settled her firmly on his lap.

Jackson seated himself on the other end of the couch, while Lucien and Raff sat across from her. "You okay to do this now, Cherime?" Jackson asked.

She nodded, then wished she hadn't as a wave of dizziness hit her. "First, Ren had nothing to do with this." She glared at Raff, who narrowed his eyes in return. Stubborn asshole. "Ren and I have been spending time together." She glanced at Ren trying to gauge his comfort level at her revealing their relationship.

He helped her out by saying, "Cherime and I are together. Planning on mating."

"Fuck that," Raff exploded, but Lucien held his hand up.

"You can't stop her from doing what she wants, Raff."

Raff shook his head at Cherime, a look of betrayal in his eyes. "Christ, Cherime. Of all the fucking shifters, why him?"

Shit, Raff. Why can't you be human just once? "I gotta explain it to you? You mated with a fucking omega! And don't look at me like I've done this to you on purpose. It isn't about you, except that we're family and you should be supporting me, not treating me like I've done you wrong!"

"Let's get back to the attack." Jackson kept his tone mild, but authoritative.

"Right. I was with Ren last night and we were talking about mating." She peered up at him. "I know I'm not good Mountain shifter material, so I wanted to hunt and bring you some food."

Raff growled, staring too aggressively at Ren. "So you let her go out there alone."

Cherime felt Ren stiffen under her and not in a good way. They were never going to get through this conversation if Raff didn't back down. "He didn't let me, Raff! Not everyone's a caveman like you. I told him I was going for a run, he wanted to come with me, and I told him I wanted alone time, which he respected."

"I shouldn't have let you go," Ren muttered, not helping his case.

"I would've gone anyway. It should be safe to run in the forest for any shifter, and you all know I'm more than capable of looking after myself." She took a breath as the males settled down. "I tried to chase a rabbit down, but it zigged and I zagged and slammed into a tree. I think that's when I lost my sense of smell."

"What?" Lucien interrupted. "You've lost your sense of smell?"

Cherime nodded. "Temporarily. It's back now."

Jackson and Raff exchanged uneasy glances. "Keep talking," Raff said, his tone a little more civilized.

"I was trying to track back home, but because I couldn't scent my original path, I got disoriented. That's when the wolf showed up."

"Wolf or shifter? Male or female?" Jackson asked.

Cherime tried not to point out the stupid questions. "I lost my sense of smell, so how would I know?"

Jackson grinned wryly at her tone. "Couldn't tell the difference any other way?"

"Let me finish," Cherime said crossly. "It grabbed me by the nape of my neck and bit down hard, but not before I sent out a distress call." She looked up at Ren, a soft smile forming on her lips. "You heard."

"Yeah, baby, I did." He gently touched her cheek with his finger, moving it down until it was at her lips, which he traced.

"Can we get on with it," Raff grumbled, glaring at the two of them.

"Yeah." Cherime decided to throw Raff a bone and not be a bitch. "I fought back as much as I could, got the wolf good a couple of times, ripped its ear." She smiled maliciously at the memory of it yelping like a pussy. "But the bastard was big and powerful."

"Male then," Jackson decided.

"I didn't have a chance to get between his legs to check out the goods, but yeah, I think so." She paused as she thought about it. "Had to be because I haven't yet met a female shifter who could take me."

"All around vicious, aren't you?" Lucien's face was a mask of indifference, but Cherime could sense the anger below the surface. Not aimed at her, she didn't think, but at what happened.

Cherime tossed him a half-smile. "I wasn't strong enough to win and I tried to hold onto my wolf but couldn't. I shifted." She swallowed the hurt in her throat. "I thought I was going to die."

Ren felt her distress and tightened his hold. "I got to you in time."

"So you saw the wolf?" Jackson said to Ren, a hopeful inflection in the words. He was like a terrier with a bone.

"No. Just Cherime when I got there."

Cherime nodded. "Once I shifted, the wolf started licking at my wounds." She shivered. "He traced his nose up my spine and inhaled the scent of my hair."

"Wolves don't do that," Raff grumbled.

"No, they don't, but shifters might," Lucien observed. He focused on Cherime. "Why'd it leave?"

Now that she was safe in Ren's arms, she allowed herself a moment to enjoy the win. "I nailed it in the head with a rock, then when the bastard staggered away from me, I caught it in between the eyes with the same rock. Stunned it, I guess. It took off after that."

Ren hugged her tighter. "My girl." The pride in his voice made her giddy.

Jackson made a note in his book, then asked Ren, "When you got there, what did you scent?"

Ren hooded his eyes. "I had trouble following Cherime's trail." His half-lidded gaze made her shiver as her need for him snaked downwards. "You didn't make it easy with all your circling around."

"Sorry," she whispered as she stroked her palm over his beard.

He grinned and despite the pain in her body, her stomach clenched. "I finally caught a whiff of blood in the breeze and was able to follow that," he said. "When I got there, Cherime was laid out in human form, cut up, bloodied and bruised." He seemed agitated, rubbing her arm up and down as he recalled the scene. "I picked her up and carried her back."

"Bareass naked?" Raff asked. "Must have fucked with your feet."

Cherime gave Raff a side-eyed glare. "It sounds like you're wanting proof."

Raff returned her hostility. "Maybe I am."

"Well, too fucking bad," Ren spat. "I'm not taking off my boots for you or anyone else."

Jackson ignored the byplay. "So you could scent the blood. What else?"

Ren closed his eyes for a few seconds. "Cherime. I could scent her, could scent everything."

"The bastard that attacked her?" Lucien leaned forward.

"No." He massaged Cherime's scalp gently.

She knew her hair was disaster, needed washing and probably detangling. Maybe a hot oil treatment. "You couldn't scent him either?"

"No. Just you, baby. And trees, dirt, decay and all the other shit in the forest. But you were the only wolf I could smell."

"Okay." Jackson stood, tucking his notebook away and digging his phone out of his pocket. "I'm going to get Ivan out to the scene." He turned to Ren. "Going to need you to take him out there. Raff, maybe you want to tag along?"

Cherime frowned. "What about me?"

"I can take her home," Lucien said.

No, nope, not going to happen. "I want to go with Ren!"

"No," all the men protested including Ren.

Traitor!

Ren's arm's tightened around her. "Not safe at my place alone right now, baby."

A miracle happened; Raff and Ren were on the same page. "And you'll be alone for hours," Raff said.

Cherime so hated men telling her what to do. "Well, I'll be alone at my place, too. Just because I'm on pack land, doesn't mean he won't take another run at me. It happened to Trist and Honi."

That argument held no water with the males surrounding her. "You can stay with Mara. Safety in numbers," Lucien said.

Jesus. "Yeah, she's preggers and I'm stitched up to my eyebrows. I'll scare the baby right out of her."

Ren stood his ground. "Stay with Mara until I get back to get you."

Lucien tilted his head. "How're you going to do that?"

Ren turned to him. "Raff and I'll drive up together. I'll pick her up when I bring him back to the Lodge."

Jackson, Lucien and Cherime raised their eyebrows. "You sure it's safe to be riding in the same vehicle together?" Jackson said.

Ren flashed an insane Jack Nicholson smile. "We're gonna be brothers, time to get to know each other better."

"Fuck," Cherime said under her breath.

CHAPTER THIRTY-SEVEN

It was set. Jackson made the phone call to Ivan while Cherime stubbornly argued against the logic of going with Lucien to stay with Mara.

Raff solidly shut her down. "You're going to do as your told or I'm gonna take you over my shoulder and dump you at her feet."

Jackson observed the myriad of emotions on Ren's face. The big guy looked like he wanted to simultaneously punch Raff in the mouth and applaud him for going toe-to-toe with Cherime. Jackson figured that the two would never be friends, but they'd work out a way to co-exist. Male shifters were highly protective and possessive of their females, but Ren would be able to handle Raff being around Cherime, because the two were siblings.

Lucien, on the other hand, was not only an unmated male, but alpha of Cherime's pack. It must be killing Ren to let Cherime leave with Lucien. He was handling it though, even if, judging by the fire in his eyes, he'd rather kill Lucien than let him step outside with Cherime.

Ren took Cherime aside before she left and kissed her

deeply, making Jackson envious. Not over Cherime because, while the woman was gorgeous, she was as high maintenance as women came. But it seemed like Ren couldn't deny Cherime's vulnerability and anyone watching them now would know the Mountain shifter would never hurt her. She was precious to him, and as Jackson watched their interactions, he realized he wanted that in his life.

The lovefest was broken up by Lucien, who approached them with an air of authority. "Let's go, Cherime. I gotta get back to the Lodge."

Cherime clung to Ren. "Let me go with you."

He peeled her hands off his arms and set her back. "It's already decided. I'll be back before the end of day."

"Fine," she sulked. "Don't kill Raff," she called over her shoulder as Lucien herded her away.

Jackson stepped up beside Ren, watching Cherime leave. "Probably should have checked her out from the hospital and got her some clothes and shoes." He snorted his laughter at how casual shifters could be as the hospital gown Cherime was wearing flapped open in the breeze revealing her pale bottom.

Ren frowned. "Get your fucking eyes off her ass."

Jackson chuckled. "That's the problem with hospital gowns, isn't it?"

The big guy narrowed his eyes and Jackson dropped his smile. Fucking shifters had no sense of humour.

Raff stalked toward them, the scowl on his face like a permanent etching. "Told Mara what happened. She's freaking out." He viciously kicked the building. "I'm going to tear that fucker apart when I get my hands on him."

Jackson scrubbed at the back of his head, the bristles of his short haircut brushing his palm. "Ivan's on his way here. He'll follow you up to Ren's in his cruiser. Adam Cole's coming along to assist him."

"How're we going to deal with this?" Raff rumbled. "ITCU meeting?"

Jackson nodded as a myriad of details flashed through is head. "Tomorrow afternoon? I'll have Eva put the word out. We'll have to do the rounds again, checking alibis." He let the silence dangle, then added, "Good thing Cherime's a fighter."

"Yeah," Raff and Ren said at the same time.

Jackson thought of what had happened to Adrienne and Tia and fear slammed into him at what might have been. "Fuck," he said softly.

Ren followed Jackson's profanity up with an aggressive, "Goddamn sonofabitch." Jackson couldn't recall a time when he saw Ren looking so helpless, but the idea of losing Cherime seemed to cripple him.

Jackson's stepfather, Sandy, would say that it was typical shifter behaviour. A pair bond made shifters both weaker and stronger, though Jackson thought it weakened the male shifter, at least until he marked his mate. Until then, Ren would be aggressive and reckless, especially when it came to Cherime, especially because she'd been attacked.

Jackson turned to the two shifters. "I hate that this happened, but there's a silver lining."

Ren glared at him for daring to find a positive in the attack on Cherime. "What fucking silver lining?"

"Not many shifters were aware of Cherime and you," he said to Ren. "It might make it easier to narrow the suspect list."

He was dragged from his thoughts by the sight of Ivan pulling into the hospital parking lot. The big bearded Russian was going have another one those days he hated. Last time the forensic specialist was out with shifters, he not only had to endure a swim under the crushing weight of the Darkness Falls waterfall, but he spent much of the day alone in a cave with a naked alpha shifter.

Jackson approached the squad car that Ivan was driving. Ivan was Russian, his accent pronounced when he was agitated or drinking. A big, bearded softie with a dry wit, a funny sense of humour, and a quick orderly mind.

Adam Cole was a rookie cop, fresh out of training. Despite his awkwardness, he had first class honors when he graduated university with a criminology degree. Ivan brought him along to crime scenes and so far, had no complaints, which was high commendation because Ivan bitched about everything.

Jackson thumped the top of the car a couple of times as he bent towards the open window. "All set?"

"Yeah. What'd you say to Eva? She's steaming."

Of course, she was. Eva was a good friend, but since she'd mated with Aztec, she was blurring too many lines. "I'll talk to her. Get up there, process the scene and get back. I want a preliminary report on my desk first thing tomorrow, so I have some information going into the ITCU meeting.

Ivan glanced at his watch and groaned. "I had a date with a six-pack tonight. Need you to authorize overtime."

"Consider it done. I want you to sit in on the ITCU meeting tomorrow."

Ren approached. "Let's go," he said in greeting, then headed towards his truck. He climbed behind the steering wheel, waiting for Raff to close his door before heading off. Ivan trailed him out of the parking lot.

Jackson watched until they were out of sight, then got in his cruiser and headed back to the precinct. Ivan wasn't wrong about Eva. As soon as he entered the bullpen, Eva approached him.

"We need to talk!" she seethed as she stomped off to his office, not waiting for an invitation.

Oh yeah, they did.

He followed her in and closed the door. The office had big windows so whatever was going on inside was highly visible. It didn't matter. He was sure he and Eva were the only two currently in the precinct. He turned to her, determined to get the first word in. "What's your rank, Eva?"

"You know bloody well what my rank is."

"Say it anyway."

She stood toe to toe with him. "I'm a corporal, Jackson. I'm still a corporal because you promoted a *man* over me to fill your sergeant shoes."

"Not the topic of discussion right now," Jackson retorted. "What's my rank?"

"Acting Chief." She folded her arms protectively over her chest.

Jackson slumped down in his office chair, realizing he really didn't want this showdown with Eva. "Then is this attitude of yours because you don't respect authority?"

"I respect authority!" Her jaw tightened.

"I see." Jackson contemplated Eva's response, feeling almost hurt by it. "Then I guess it's because you don't respect me."

His statement seemed to steal her thunder as tears flooded her eyes. She flopped into a chair on the opposite side of the desk. "I respect you, Jackson." Her husky whisper betrayed her emotions. "We're friends."

Jackson considered the pretty blonde officer sitting across from him, practically crumpled into her chair. She was right, they were friends. When she had joined this precinct almost four years ago, she had been young and eager, but brainy too, with a sharp analytical mind. It had been her first posting and she was determined to be the woman who could make the difference in this male-oriented profession. Four years of experience matured her, but the past year had been hard on her – attacked twice, mated to a shifter, and now, though they didn't speak of it, pregnant.

"Then what's going on, Eva?" He wanted to be grumpy with her, but he didn't have it in him today. "Back at the hospital, your conduct was over-the-top."

She rubbed at her face. "I know," she squeaked. "I don't know what's going on. Everything, I guess. I don't understand why Ivan got to take over for you. He's already a sergeant; he didn't need the opportunity."

She paused and he waited for her to express *everything*.

"Simon," she whispered. "You gave Dagmar the lead on his murder, not me." She blinked rapidly as a couple of tears trickled down her flushed cheeks. "It should have been me. I was his friend."

Jackson belatedly realized that Eva was grieving for Simon. Insensitive ass that he was, he hadn't anticipated the degree of Eva's sorrow. She and Simon had a strong connection; the schizophrenic man trusted her over everyone else and because of that, he had been with Eva when Connell tried to kill them both. Simon had saved Eva's life. "I'm sorry about Simon." More than that, he was sorry he was such a thoughtless prick.

She nodded, the words spilling out of her like a dam had broken open. "It's not just Simon. It's Dexter too. There's something off about him – everyone thinks so but you."

He blinked and bit his tongue as all traces of empathy disappeared at her holier-than-thou opinion of his brother. He nodded for her to continue.

"I hate being in a pack. I always feel torn about where my loyalties lie. Like at the hospital." She stopped, clearly wanting to say something else.

Jackson prompted her. "And?"

"And I'm pregnant." Her voice cracked. "I feel like shit all the time, I'm scared of raising a shifter, and Aztec is treating me like I'm a delicate porcelain doll." She inhaled deeply. "I'm afraid the pregnancy is going to derail my career."

As tears spilled down Eva's face, Jackson thought of the bottle of scotch in the bottom drawer of his desk. It would be impolite to have a shot in front of Eva, knowing she couldn't join him, wouldn't it? Maybe just a sip. No, not even that.

He scrubbed at the back of his head. Where to start? "Let's tick off each one starting with why I asked Ivan to take over for me when I stepped into the Chief's shoes."

Eva nodded. "Okay." She snatched a tissue from the box on his desk and swiped at her eyes. He knew she thought tears were a sign of weakness, especially on the job. It wasn't easy being a woman trying to navigate in a traditionally male profession. Or a shifter's world.

"This is a private conversation, yeah?"

Eva blew her nose. "Yeah."

"The Chief won't be returning to work. That has huge implications for me. I've been offered this position permanently but haven't decided whether to take it. It's not as much fun as it looks."

He got a soft laugh out of Eva and was grateful for it.

"I like being in the trenches, and the Chief position pretty much shoves me behind a desk. I have to deal with the bullshit. Politics, press. Pressure."

"You're a good chief, Jackson." Eva's voice was still reedy, but her tears were drying.

Jackson half-smiled. "I think of the alternative. Chief Levesque was a good leader for us, but there are so many assholes in our world. What if we got one of them? Our lives would be intolerable. Imagine if it's someone from Toronto coming up here, thinking he—"

"Or she—"

"—knows everything about everything, looking down on our community, on the shifters. Better it's me."

"I agree," she concurred.

"I didn't hand my job to Ivan when I took over for the Chief. My superior didn't want to fill my position because we already had a sergeant on staff. It was decided he could do double-duty. We could manage while short an officer in the interim."

"Oh." Eva's voice was small. "Why didn't you say?"

Jackson stretched his neck from side to side. Why didn't he say? "Don't know. I shouldn't have to explain everything I do, but maybe in this case, I should've told everyone."

"You used to be more approachable. You used to tell us everything when you were the staff sergeant."

He tapped his fingers on his desk as he considered her words. "You don't know that."

She stared at him, her eyes blinking in surprise. "You're right. Maybe I don't know you as well as I thought."

"Careful, Eva. I'm not the one disrespecting my superior officer in front of alpha shifters."

She stared down at her hands. "It seems like every time I turn around, I'm answering to some man. Either you or Lucien or Raff." Her bottom lip trembled. "Aztec."

"This one's easy. When you're on-duty, you answer to your superior officers. When you're off-duty but acting in the line of duty, you answer to your superior officers. When you're off-duty generally, who you answer to is none of my business." He gauged her reaction to his hard tone. "But don't forget you're a cop in this community first and foremost. We run into each other in Becker's and you haul off and slug me because you don't like what I said, that earns you an automatic dismissal from the force. You hit anyone, on- or off-duty, it gets investigated. You know that, and if it were a colleague doing it, you'd be reading him the same riot act I'm reading you now. Yeah?"

Eva blew out a breath as she rubbed at the corner of her eye. "Yeah. Seems so easy when you're saying it."

"It is that easy, Eva." Jackson was done with the topic. "Dagmar's the lead on Simon's case because you're too close to it. You're grieving his death, calling him a friend. Dagmar has as much right to lead this case as you do. I don't care if you don't like each other, the two of you managed to work together to track down Simon and I expect you both to continue being professional."

"I disagree," Eva replied, her chin jutting stubbornly. "Because I care, I'll investigate more carefully."

"More emotionally, you mean." Jackson was losing his patience. "You're a good friend, but we both know you sometimes let your feelings rule your judgement."

She looked at him sharply. "When have I ever done that?"

Jackson sighed. When hadn't she? "When Gideon reported his truck stolen."

Eva shook her head at Jackson's reference. "I wasn't emotional when I suggested Dagmar handcuff Trist. I was… uh…." She pressed her lips together and flailed her hands helplessly.

He could see he'd scored a point. He moved on. "You're lead on Tia's murder and you did a fine damn job of investigating her disappearance. I've already told you that. What else do I need to do? Stroke your ego everyday?

Five minutes before your shift starts, so you can feel good about yourself?"

A frown creased her face. "You're getting personal."

Speaking of personal. "Dexter is none of your business."

She thinned her lips. "Respectfully disagree, Chief. The reason we were at the warehouse was because Dagmar saw Dexter and Weston Hawke together in the industrial section. If Dexter had anything to do with Simon's death, that makes him my business." She held his eyes as she used his words against him. "You're emotionally involved because he's family. He plays you like a puppet because you're his big brother and maybe because you're the Chief. You're too close to see what he's really like."

Jackson slapped his hand down on the desktop, causing Eva to startle. "Don't be telling me what my brother is and isn't. I already know he's not a saint, but don't go judging him until you have some hard evidence. And if you think Dexter has something to do with Simon's death, why am I just hearing about it now?"

Eva sat back and held his eyes. "Because it's a theory, a thought without hard evidence. It's something we cops talk about in the bullpen all the time. But when it's family, it's different, isn't it? You just told me not to be accusing your brother without evidence, but now you want to know. Which is it, Jackson?"

Jackson thumped back in his chair as he glared at Eva. "Is this what everything's about, Eva? You didn't know how to tell me about Dexter?"

"No." Eve sat back too. "Dagmar's the lead on the case, so it's his responsibility to report to you." Her voice cracked. "And no, this isn't what everything's about. It's because I'm pregnant and I don't know what to do."

Jackson shuddered internally at the turn of conversation. "Talk to a girlfriend, Eva. Or Aztec. I can't discuss this with you, because I'm your senior officer. It's not appropriate."

Eva stood, shoving her chair back. "Or is it because you're a man, so anything like this is beyond your realm of comprehension." She huffed as she headed for the door, but turned back to him, her hand on the knob. "Respectfully request returning to active duty, Sir!"

"Denied," Jackson snapped.

Eva looked like she was about to argue as her lips pursed and her face flushed, but after a moment, she turned on her heel and stomped from the office.

Jackson's temper was fraying, and he needed to get some air before Eva and he said words they couldn't take back. He scooped his car keys off the desk and walked out of the office. "I'm going for lunch," he shot at Eva, then left through the back door.

Fucking goddamn everything! Why the hell was Eva going on about Dexter? She hadn't said anything he wasn't already thinking. But Jackson already knew the answer, knew why she was accusing him of protecting Dexter. It was because the asshole showed up at the precinct unexpectantly, acting all sheepish and telling them all a bullshit story about how Felan Xoloti came to be dropping him off.

Jackson knew Eva well – she had been excited to finally meet his brother, then pissed at Leah for spilling the beans on her pregnancy, then embarrassed when she returned after dragging Leah out of the building.

Dexter was still talking when she re-entered, her colleagues hanging on every one of his charismatic words. He was in the middle of making a good-old-boy remark about Felan's ass that got Dagmar and Adam laughing. That's when Eva's cloudy eyes sharpened with suspicion.

She'd thrown an annoyed glance at Jackson with a tilt

to her head that told him she saw through Dexter's lies and charm. At the time, it made Jackson irritable that she was already judging Dexter's character, and he responded defensively, which of course made him appear clueless about the kind of man his brother was.

Now, everyone was going around acting like they were an expert on Dexter, but not talking to Jackson about it. He wondered what Ren thought of his brother, and Cherime and Felan. Were they thinking the same thing as Eva and Dagmar?

He climbed into a cruiser and headed to Becker's. On his way, he called his stepfather, Sandy Ivers, and asked him to lunch. Sandy was a good guy, married his mother when Jackson was young, best stepfather he'd had. Unfortunately, his mother was fond of weddings, but not so great at marriage part, and Sandy only lasted a couple of years.

That hadn't stopped Jackson from keeping in touch with the man, not only because he was a friend, but also because Sandy was the local expert on shifter history and behaviour. It was why he'd originally come to Darkness Falls. The town and surrounding wilds were like the epicentre for shifters in the north. Something attracted them to this area, made them want to stay.

Most humans and even some shifters would deny that it was supernatural, but Jackson believed it to be the case. There was somcthing spiritual about the massive waterfall that the town was named after, the wild untouched land, the First Nations' traditional beliefs. It all acted as a magnet that lured shifters to the area, grounded them, made them want to settle. It was home for them.

Jackson arrived at Becker's before Sandy and found a booth that was facing the door. He ordered a beer while he waited. Legally, RCMP officers were not supposed to drink while in uniform, but Chiefs had some discretionary licence. After all, as Chief Levesque was fond of saying, the role of the Chief was to schmooze and booze. Jackson wasn't much of schmoozer, though he could fake it just fine. Booze, on the other hand, was his specialty.

Sandy strolled into the pub as a waitress that Jackson didn't know set his lager on the table. Grey hair, straggly beard, thick black glasses, and rumpled clothes lent credibility to Sandy's reputation as a nutty professor, though he was anything but. The man was sharp, inquisitive, and orderly.

Jackson waved to Sandy and asked the new girl to bring a beer for his stepfather. The smile she threw was meant to be seductive, but he didn't bite. He figured she was barely legal, and cute as she was, nothing about her rocked his boat.

"Hi son," Sandy said, as he grabbed Jackson's hand and gave him a hearty pat on the back. "We don't do this enough."

"Yeah." Jackson felt annoyed at himself for neglecting the old man. "Things are a little crazy right now."

The waitress set Sandy's beer in front of him and said, "I'll be back in a few minutes to take your order."

Sandy murmured his thanks as he picked up the mug. "Congrats on your promotion, kid."

Jackson grinned as he clinked glasses with the old man. "Thanks. It's temporary."

Sandy gulped down a huge swallow. "Bullshit. Francois Levesque is not coming back. Magalie won't let him." He pulled the lunch menu towards himself and flipped it over to the sandwiches.

Magalie was the Chief's wife and very committed to her family. "So I've heard."

Sandy snorted. "His heart attack scared all us old guys. I'm off sugar and refined carbs thanks to him."

Jackson took a careful drink of his beer as he considered Sandy. He was about to share secrets with his stepfather because there weren't that many people in this small community that he could trust not to pay it forward. May as well start with the truth about the Chief's job. "Between you and me, I've been offered Francois's position."

Sandy grinned through the thin line of foam on his moustache. "Congratulations! I figured it was going to happen sooner or later. A couple of years and the chief would've retired anyway if his health hadn't forced him to."

Jackson picked up the menu though he already knew what he wanted. It gave him something to do with his hands. "Yeah. I'm taking some time to think about it, but I'll accept the offer. It puts me behind a desk and I'm not loving that idea, but it's better than some new guy coming in thinking he knows everything."

"Good. Darkness Falls has a delicate balance and needs the right handling. You've got that in you better than anyone I know."

The waitress approached with a coy smile on her face that Jackson refused to return. "Steak sandwich, medium rare. Fries."

She pouted at him then turned to Sandy, who winked at her. "Beef dip and fries."

Jackson raised his eyebrows. "What happened to being off the carbs?"

"Didn't realize there were carbs in beef." The corners of Sandy's eye crinkled as he grinned.

Jackson laughed, appreciating the old man's sense of humour, then he sobered as he thought about his morning. "Dexter's in town."

"I heard."

News travelled fast in Darkness Falls. "Has he dropped by to see you yet?"

Sandy shook his head as he played with a coaster, spinning it with his fingers. "Nah. Don't think he will either. Never has in the past."

"As far as I know, he hasn't been to Darkness Falls in a while."

"Why do you say, as far as you know?" Sandy pulled a draw of beer.

"He wasn't exactly walking through the front door. Got caught in the snowstorm and was rescued by Felan Xoloti." He didn't mention Cherime because that would lead to other questions that he had no business sharing. "Says he was coming to Darkness Falls to see me, decided to take the lazy drive in."

Sandy shrugged. "Never could figure that kid out."

"You heard Simon was killed?"

Sandy's eyes lost their brightness. "Sad day when someone's attacking the vulnerable and harmless."

Jackson grimaced. "Yeah. Maybe the death is related to the other two killings. I brought Jared Cooper in to check the scene."

Sandy scratched at his beard as he studied Jackson. "Just Cooper? No one else to validate him?"

Jackson narrowed his eyes at the line of questioning. He didn't need the old man to tell him his job. "I trust him."

"Not saying you shouldn't, but seems like something like that wouldn't hold up in court if you didn't have another shifter supporting Cooper's findings."

The waitress brought the meals. "You're new here, aren't you?" Sandy said to her.

Her perfect set of pearly white teeth flashed as she grinned, seemingly happy that someone at the table acknowledged her. "Yeah. I'm visiting my grandparents for the summer. Grandpa got me this job."

"You're doing a fine job of it," Sandy replied, then offered his hand. "I'm Sandy Ivers. I teach at the local college." He motioned to Jackson. "This here's my son, Jackson. If you haven't already guessed it, he's the Chief of Police in Darkness Falls."

"I'm Addie." She shook Sandy's hand smartly, then turned to Jackson who had no choice but to grasp her fingers. "My grandparents are Barry and Diane Hall."

"The Halls!" Sandy exclaimed. "They're good people. Had Diane in my class last semester, taking a course on Northern BC indigenous history."

Jackson tried not to snort out loud. The Halls were well-to-do by Darkness Falls standards and more than a little bit entitled, which explained Addie's perfect teeth and new job.

"Yeah, grandma's always doing something like that." Addie glanced at another table, someone waving to get her attention. "Gotta run. Nice meeting you." She held Jackson's eyes a few seconds too long before walking off.

"She seemed nice," Sandy casually said.

His stepfather was trying to play matchmaker. "She's too fucking young, Sandy," Jackson grumbled. "And I wouldn't touch Barry Hall's granddaughter with a 10-foot pole.

Sandy grinned widely at him. "I was thinking for Dexter," he teased.

Jackson shoved a couple of fries into his mouth and changed the subject. "Here's the thing, and this is confidential."

Sandy nodded as he took a big bite of his sandwich.

"These killings have a couple of things in common. Unmarked girls are marked before they're killed. Raped maybe, or it could be consensual, but no semen. Hair is cut, so the killer is taking trophies. Tia's body was discovered in a cave behind the falls. Nothing indicating it was a shifter other than the mark on her back. Adrienne Powell's throat was ripped out, but the mating mark occurred enough in advance that it was healed before she was killed. Two other women have been attacked by the same guy." He leaned towards Sandy. "Want to know how I know?"

"Yeah, I do." Sandy rubbed a napkin over his mouth and beard, then took a guzzle of his beer.

"No scent at the scene. Girls couldn't scent him or anything else. It was like an odorless bubble wrapped itself around the guy."

Sandy leaned back and stared past Jackson, his eyes unfocused. "That why you're worried about Dexter?"

"Yeah. He rarely comes to Darkness Falls that I'm aware of. Except he's caught coming in this time, and right on the heels of it, a female shifter gets attacked. Says she thought she'd lost her sense of smell."

"So you got a witness."

Jackson shook his head. "The fuck was in wolf form, but the lack of scent leads me to think he had a partner. Someone who can manipulate nature."

"Like you and Dexter," he mumbled as he chewed a bite of his sandwich.

Jackson stabbed his fork into a slice of steak. "Yeah. And I know it isn't me. That leaves Dexter. Serial killers working together is more common than you'd think."

Sandy swallowed his mouthful and reached for his beer. "You're missing the obvious."

"Which is?" Jackson grunted, aware he was starting to sound like a fucking male shifter.

"That your shifter is also a windwalker."

Jackson shoved his partly-eaten meal toward the edge

of the table. All this murder talk had messed with his appetite. "That isn't a thing."

"You don't know that," Sandy argued as he wiped his fingers on his napkin. "Windwalkers aren't a thing either, and yet, here you are."

"Are you saying Dexter is also a shifter?" It was possible. Jackson and Dexter had different fathers, and Jackson would have been too young at that time to know if Dexter's dad was a shifter.

The typically supportive Sandy wrinkled his forehead. "Maybe you're not Chief material after all."

Ouch.

"Dexter doesn't have shifter blood. I'm saying that it's possible that there's a shifter in these parts who's also got windwalker blood."

That seemed unlikely. "He'd have to have our blood running through him." Jackson meant his Nation's blood. To his knowledge, his people were the only ones who had the gene, and he and Dexter were the only two he knew about.

"Easier to hide being a windwalker than keeping shifter blood a secret." Sandy looked at his watch and drained his mug. "After all, only three people know about you. Me, you, and Dexter."

"And the old woman." Georgette was the wise woman on the reserve. The woman was ancient, no one knew how old, but she seemed timeless.

"I can guarantee that she isn't a suspect."

Jackson pulled a reluctant smile. "Wolf's big and grey, so that narrows it down."

"Maybe someone new to these parts? Killings started last summer, didn't it?" He dug in his pocket and slapped some bills on the table. "I'll cover lunch." Sandy always paid for lunch.

"Thanks, I'll get it next time," Jackson mumbled his usual response, his mind churning with all the possibilities.

The old man stood and clapped his hand on Jackson's shoulder. "I'll be holding you to that, kid. See you soon."

Jackson watched Sandy leave. His stepfather seemed more jovial than usual; the last time he was this relaxed he had a woman warming his bed. Jackson wondered who she was.

He let the thought go as he pulled his phone from his pocket, opened his contact list, and scrolled to Ulrich Calhoun's number. Ulrich Calhoun had come to Darkness Falls last summer before Adrienne Powell turned up dead. The independent alpha's background was a mystery because he never offered up details and ignored Jackson when Jackson tried to draw it out of him. However, he had shared his reason for being in Darkness Falls. He was a federal agent following a lead in a case he was tasked with, though he didn't share the specifics.

Of course, Jackson checked his credentials, had a long chat with Ulrich's superior. He'd even tried to bully Ulrich into spilling the beans, but that hadn't worked. Feds trumped the RCMP and Chief Levesque told Jackson to back down. He followed Levesque's orders and kept his mouth shut but his eyes were wide open. Whatever the subtext of Ulrich's mission, Jackson would root it out eventually.

Jackson pressed Ulrich's number and listened as it rang. Shifters didn't share the same social conventions that the rest of the planet embraced. They spoke their minds, were often blunt and one of their overused phrases was, *none of your fucking business*.

He got exactly what he expected when Ulrich picked up. "Ulrich Calhoun." The big motherfucker sounded like he'd rather eat Jackson than talk to him.

Jackson decided to play good cop. "Hi Ulrich, it's Jackson Hayes."

"What do you want?" Straight to the point, though less hostile than his greeting.

Ulrich was a big, mean motherfucker only to be handled wearing kid gloves. "Got time to come to the station to talk?"

"Can't," Ulrich grunted. "I'm out of town."

Ice slithered down Jackson's spine thinking about last night in Becker's parking lot, the big guy driving off with Aubrey and Leah. And now he was gone – maybe licking his wounds after losing the fight with Cherime. He steadied his voice despite the drum beating in his chest. "Didn't know you were leaving."

"Personal business. Didn't know I needed permission."

Ulrich was supposed to be one of the good guys, but that didn't make him clean. "I'll catch you when you're back." He ended the call before Ulrich could ask questions.

He immediately called the station house.

"Eva Blakely, Darkness Falls RCMP." Eva's tone was businesslike but a whole lot friendlier than Ulrich's had been.

"It's Jackson."

There went the friendliness. "What do you want?" Ice dripped from her words as she channelled Ulrich.

Jackson frowned into the phone. The woman was spending too much time around male shifters. "I need you to call Leah and Aubrey and make sure they made it home safely last night."

"Why?"

Of course, she'd ask. Jackson blew out a frustrated breath as he quickly conjured up a reasonable justification. "They were at Becker's with Cherime. I want to make sure they weren't targeted."

"Unlikely—" Eva started, but Jackson interrupted.

"Could you do it, please, Eva. Just this once without turning it into a debate."

Her voice was faint and bitter as she said, "Sure. No problem."

"I'm on my way back to the precinct. If you can't get hold of them, call me and I'll try to track them down."

"I'm on it, *Chief*," she snapped, then ended the call.

Jackson sighed as he tucked his phone away. Could the day get any worse? Apparently, it could, as he saw Addie approaching him.

"Can I bring you another beer, Chief?" Her smile was shy but there was nothing timid about the way she arched her back to get her breasts to jut out. Jackson glanced at the pert round mounds that were slightly too big for her frame. She knew he was looking and rocked forward on her toes, the result of which was a gentle jiggle that had Jackson thinking things he shouldn't.

Fucking Sandy, he griped to himself as he shifted his gaze to her face. "No thank you, Addie. I'm on duty."

He stood and she brushed up against him as he slipped by her. "You look good in uniform, Chief," she cooed.

He had to shut this down right fucking now, before the town started speculating about the two of them and her grandfather came gunning for him. Things like this destroyed careers. "You should meet my younger brother." He clipped his words. "He's better looking."

He turned and raced out of Becker's like a moose was chasing him.

CHAPTER THIRTY-EIGHT

Mara practically tackled Cherime as she stepped inside. "Oh my god, what the hell happened to you?" She was crying, grabbing Cherime in a too tight hug, pulling at sutures, forcing a flood of pain.

Cherime gave Mara a gentle push. "Let go. I kind of hurt all over."

"Of course," Mara fretted as she released her hold. "Stupid me. Come sit down." She clutched Cherime's hand and led her to a chair.

Cherime contemplated her situation as she sat. She would have rather gone to her home and slept it off, but still, it was nice to have someone care.

The fussing had already started as Mara shoved a pillow behind Cherime's back and threw a thin faded quilt over her lap, tucking it in like she was wrapping up a caterpillar. "I'll make some tea." She bustled from the room into the kitchen as quickly as she could, which wasn't very fast given her bulk.

"Bourbon please," Cherime called as she shoved the blanket off her lap. A week ago, it was storming, and now it was too damn hot. Daddy nature was having a good giggle at her expense.

Mara returned to the living room. "Are you kidding me? You can't have bourbon in your state." She waddled to Cherime and awkwardly crouched to pick up the blanket, tucking it around Cherime again.

Cherime swatted the air to wave Mara off. "I'm not an invalid and I don't need a blanket."

"Fine!" Mara harrumphed as she headed back into the kitchen.

Cherime heard the filling of the kettle. Fuck, she hated tea. "Coffee then, if I can't have bourbon."

"Caffeine isn't good when you're on pain pills," her stubborn sister's muted voice called back.

That was a new one and most likely bullshit. "Don't make me tea. I won't drink it."

Mara stuck her head into the living room. "How about iced tea?"

How about that shot of the bourbon? "Sure." Or a joint, which she knew Mara wouldn't have. Cherime's purse was at Ren's and her hospital gown didn't seem to come equipped with a pocketful of weed.

Mara returned with two glasses of iced tea, condensation dripping down the sides. She handed one to Cherime than struggled to keep the tea from sloshing over the top of her glass as her ungainly form sank into the cushions on the sofa. "All Lucien told me was that you were attacked and needed to stay at my place. What happened?" Mara's voice was full of worry.

Cherime felt guilt at being so cranky. Mara wasn't herself right now and Cherime pined for the sister she knew before Connell's death. That Mara was tough, held her emotions inside, held her own against Lucien, Raff, and Cherime. The Mara sitting on the sofa was fragile and vulnerable, fear and sadness her primary emotions.

Cherime took a breath and retold the events of the day. Mara didn't interrupt as Cherime relayed the entire story, though her face went through several iterations of surprise, panic, and shock.

After she finished, Mara held the cold glass of tea against her temple. "You're with Ren?" Her tone was disbelieving.

The hackles on Cherime's wolf rose and rightly so. "That's your takeaway from this conversation?"

Mara sucked a shaky breath into her lungs. "I just can't imagine the two of you together. He's… big and… primitive and… and… well, savage." She twisted the glass like she needed something to do with her hands. "If he did this—"

The words were like a hot poker to her gut and Cherime felt a deep scowl furrow her face. "He fucking didn't do this!" She slammed her glass on the coffee table and cautiously stood, which undermined her attempt to be dramatic. "Why does everyone think the worst of him?"

"I'm sorry," Mara mumbled. "Sit down before you break open your stitches."

Cherime reseated herself, but she wasn't done with the conversation. "Explain to me, Mara, why everyone, and I mean everyone, thinks Ren abused me."

"He's got a reputation—"

"For beating on women? That's bullshit! Raff is a total asshole, and no one accuses him of slapping Trist around."

"Let me finish," Mara said crossly.

Cherime pursed her lips. "Finish then."

"He's a bit of a mystery, isn't he? He doesn't come into Darkness Falls very often, and when he does, he's all hostile and aggressive." She paused, seeming to choose her words carefully. “And he’s huge and I’ve heard he knocks around his pack, including the women.”

“Who’d you hear that shit from?”

Mara tried to shrug off the question as unimportant, but at least had the decency to appear sheepish. “Around.”

“Fucking gossips.” Cherime was well aware that she was being a hypocrite because she was a fan of sharing newsworthy chatter, but she didn’t spread lies. She knew what it felt like to be the subject of malicious rumors and it wasn’t a nice takeaway. “Ren’s a bastard, but not that kind of one. Besides, you know me better than that. How can you even think I’d take a beating from any male and then protect him? That’d be the day.”

Mara looked down at her hands. “Love makes people do stupid things.”

Cherime stopped her rant as she realized they weren’t talking about Ren anymore. “Like what?”

“Like staying with a cheater even when I knew the truth. Like putting up with his bullshit.” Mara stared across the room, her eyes bright with tears.

“Did you hit you?” Cherime ached for her sister, for all she’d been through.

“A couple of times when our fights got out of control.” She shrugged like it was nothing. “Not like what happened to you.”

“Why’d you stay?” Cherime was careful to keep judgement from her voice, but she was curious. Mara wasn’t nearly as challenging as Cherime, but the woman had a backbone and knew how to use it. Or at least, she used to.

Mara lifted her shoulders. “Don’t know. I guess because if I left him, Lucien and Raff might have made him leave the pack and I didn’t want that for him. His upbringing was not kind to him.”

Cherime snorted. “That’s no excuse for bad behaviour.

Look at Honi. She had the worst childhood, and yet, she's one of the best there is."

Mara nodded. "Yeah, I know. Doesn't matter now, does it? He's gone and every person in Darkness Falls knows he cheated on me."

Cherime looked down at her iced tea. "Getting cheating on sucks big time."

"Makes you feel inadequate."

"Yeah."

"You ever been cheated on?"

Nope, she never had, mostly because she didn't stick around long enough for that to happen. And Ren, he wouldn't cheat. She wasn't sure how she knew that, but she knew. Would it devastate her if he did? Yes, but Cherime didn't feel inadequate, not anymore. She knew where to place the fucking blame. She'd chew Ren's balls off and swallow them before kicking him to the curb.

Mara didn't need to know any of that right now. She was too vulnerable. Cherime changed the subject. "I guess the attack on me lets Connell off the hook for Adrienne's and Tia's murders. Whoever the killer is, he's still out there."

Mara seemed to be thinking the same thing. "That's not good news though, is it?"

Weariness washed over Cherime as she shook her head. "I need to lay down for a while. I'm so tired."

"Of course." Mara held her belly as she struggled to her feet. "Crawl into my bed and get some sleep. When you wake, help yourself to my clothes."

"Thanks." Cherime followed Mara into the bedroom. Everything was as neat and tidy in there as it was in the rest of the house. A little stark, but most shifters didn't like clutter or too many possessions. It tied them down, made them feel suffocated. Not Cherime, though. She loved shopping and owning stuff.

Mara pulled down the bedding, then moved to the window and drew the curtains. "I need to know something, Cherime," she said, watching as Cherime climbed into the bed and nestled under the blankets.

"Sure. What?"

"How serious is this thing with Ren?" Her voice was paper-thin, crumbling around the edges.

Vulnerable as Mara was, Cherime wasn't about to lie. "It's serious. We're going to mate."

Mara's dull eyes matched the desolation in her face as she nodded. "Congrats, Cherime," she whispered and left the room, closing the door softly behind her.

The guilt that Mara's sadness evoked wasn't enough to stop Cherime from dozing off as soon as her head hit the pillow. When she woke a few hours later, she was in the same position she'd been when she fell asleep, and her body had stiffened up like a three-day old gingerbread woman. She took a careful stretch as she opened her eyes, remembering where she was.

The fogginess in her head had dissipated and she felt whole again, her body quickly knitting itself together like a shifter's body should. Her muscles ached, and the sting of the bites and deep slashes still pinched at her. The pain had become an old memory, pulsing in the background, but not nearly as present anymore.

She slowly sat up and dropped her feet to the floor, then awkwardly stood. The crack in the drapes beckoned so she hobbled to the window and held the fabric back to see outside. The westward moving sun told her that it was getting towards evening. She opened the curtains wider and let warm sunlight flood the room. It was a good salve for her weariness.

As she shuffled across the room to Mara's closet, she wondered how Ren was doing. Had he returned from the mountain? Was he waiting for her at the Lodge? Her heart pinged in her chest at the thought of him.

The hangers screeched against the rod as she considered Mara's wardrobe. Mara and Cherime were physically similar but their differences were pronounced. Cherime was taller and curvier while Mara's body was more conservative, smaller breasts and hips, slightly thicker at the waist. Cherime's feet were bigger, not by much, but proportionate to her height.

Thus, Cherime had trouble finding anything of Mara's that fit her frame. After trying on several skirts and tops, she had no choice but to settle on a large faded lime green T-shirt with a logo that read *I woke up like this*, and a flowy printed white skirt that draped to her knees and sank to her hips because the waistband was slightly too big.

She borrowed a pair of underwear from the dresser. Not sexy, though Mara owned some, but the only pair large enough for Cherime's hips was granny panties. What the hell was Mara doing with them? None of the bras came close to fitting so Cherime was forced to go au natural in that department. She wouldn't generally have minded, but the T-shirt pulled across her breasts making it clear that they were two sizes too big.

The only shoes that would remotely fit her feet were a hot pink pair of flip-flops. Her foot extended past the back of the heel, but at least she had something to walk in.

She stared at herself in Mara's mirror, equal parts dismay and embarrassment creeping through her. Add to that the stark white gauze on her forehead, which stood out against her pale skin, and the dull tangled lifeless mess that was now her hair, and she was mortified. At least if she let her hair hang in the front, it curtained the bruises on her face and partially concealed her bobbing tits.

Her wolf was belly up laughing its head off.

Bitch.

There was no way on earth she was going to let Ren see her like this. She'd have to risk the wrath of everyone and go home and change before he got back.

Her stomach chose that time to growl loudly and she placed a hand over it. She hadn't eaten all day, so it was small wonder her belly felt hollow. She hoped Mara had fixed dinner, but as she scented the air, she couldn't smell food.

She opened the bedroom door to Mara's pale face, sitting on the sofa, her hands clasped between her knees. "What's wrong?" Cherime felt irritated that Mara was so high-maintenance.

Pot calling kettle black again? her wolf observed. It was clear the nap had also refreshed her inner beast.

"I'm in labour," Mara blurted.

"What? No!" Cherime hadn't meant to shout, but Jesus, could this day get any worse?

"Yes." Tears glistened in Mara's eyes. "I wasn't sure at first because the cramps were so faint, but they've been coming regularly for the past hour."

Cherime's stomach twisted into a seething mass of panic-induced vomit and a little came up her throat. She swallowed it down before she spewed. "You can't be in labour. I'm not ready!"

Mara ignored her. "It's early, but it's labour. The contractions are about 15 minutes apart. I think there's still time enough to get to the hospital, but we should leave right now."

Cherime yanked on her hair as she paced the floor. "Why didn't you wake me up?"

"Because this is my first baby and I might be in labour a long time. You needed your rest."

"Fuck, Mara. It's an hour drive. What if you have the baby in the car?" Cherime had to swallow down the bile again as she conjured an image of her kneeling between Mara's legs and helping the kid out of its mother's vagina. "I can't deliver a baby!"

Mara struggled to her feet. "Let's go then."

Cherime yanked out her phone and opened the contact list. "Not yet," she said as she pressed Eva's phone number.

Eva picked up on the second ring. "Cherime, are you okay?"

"No," she shrieked into the phone. "I'm not fucking okay. Mara's in labour."

A short pause sent Cherime's blood pressure through the roof.

"Mara's pregnant?" Eva sounded confused.

Oh yeah, not general knowledge yet. "Yes! I'll explain on the way to the hospital. We're at her house, but I need you to come with us. If she has the baby in the car, I can't deliver it."

She could hear Eva shuffling around in the background. "Okay, get her in the backseat and pick me up."

"Thanks." Cherime ended the call as Mara moaned. "What?" she shouted.

"Hurts when I have a contraction."

Cherime didn't think it was possible, but her heart rate notched up higher. "Let's go! You have like a baby kit or something to take with us?"

Mara creased her forehead as she clutched her belly. "A baby kit?"

Good god. Did Mara not know anything? "A baby kit! You know! You put stuff in a bag like a change of clothes, earrings, maybe a nail file and polish. I have no idea what goes in one."

"No, I don't have anything prepared. I don't even have a nursery ready." A loud sob fell from her mouth as she struggled into a pair of canvas shoes. "The spare room is still full of Connell's stuff." She picked up her car keys, which Cherime snatched from her hand.

"I'm driving. We want to get to the hospital before the kid turns 10." Mara drove like an old lady,

"Funny," Mara muttered, but didn't deny Cherime's words.

Cherime jerked the back door of Mara's car open and helped her in, then circled around and got in the driver's side, her fingers shaking as she fumbled with the car keys. Finally, she got the car started and ripped out of Mara's driveway down the road to Eva's and Aztec's cabin.

Members of the Falls Lodge pack lived in isolated cabins that dotted the Lodge property, but Eva's and Aztec's home was in the far reaches of the territory. It took 10 freaking minutes on the rutted road to finally get there. To Eva's credit, she was already outside with a backpack on her shoulder and raced over to the car as Cherime braked.

She yanked the driver's side open. "I'm driving," she said. "I'm not risking my life, not even for Mara."

Cherime huffed as she climbed out. "What if she has the baby in the car?"

Eva nudged her out of the way as slid behind the steering will. "I pull over, climb in the backseat and deliver it." She did up her seatbelt as Cherime got into the passenger seat. "What did you think we were going to do? Let Mara deliver while you drove like a maniac?"

It made sense now, but Eva was too fucking calm. "Well then, get going, copper."

Eva didn't get going. She turned to Mara. "Hi Mara. You okay?"

Mara nodded as she hugged her belly. "I think so."

"How far along are you?"

"Are you fucking kidding me?" The urgency Cherime was feeling was so high, she thought her head might explode. "She's eight months!"

Eva tossed Cherime a narrow glare, then returned her attention to Mara. "And the contractions? How far apart?"

"Fifteen minutes!" Cherime said. "Go! Go! Go!"

"I'm talking to Mara," Eva snapped.

"I think they're getting closer now," Mara said helpfully.

"Oh my god! Can't you drive and talk? The baby's coming!"

Eva rolled her eyes to the ceiling. "This isn't about you, Cherime."

Cherime wanted to kick Eva but restrained herself because her toes were bare, and she feared breaking one. "It *is* about me. I'm supposed to be helping deliver the baby and I'd rather do it in a hospital where I don't have to put my hands inside her twat."

Mara huffed from the backseat. "Jesus, Cherime. Could you tone it down just a little?"

Cherime frantically shook her head. "I don't think I can! Please can we go!"

"Fine!" Eva shoved the car in drive and headed out. "Has your water broke?"

Good question. Cherime didn't know the answer so she looked back at Mara.

Mara's hand stretched across her belly. "Not yet."

Eva acknowledged Mara with a nod. "How much pain? On a scale of one to ten."

"Uhm… maybe four or five when a contraction hits."

"Okay. That's good." Eva glanced at Cherime. "She's fine, so you can settle down. We should make it to the hospital no problem." She glanced at rear-view mirror. "Does your doctor know you're on your way?"

"Fuck, this is a disaster." Cherime swore. "Coop's in Vancouver at a conference."

"I want Coop!" Mara wailed from the backseat, sounding a little too much like Cherime.

"You can't have Coop. He's out of town!" Cherime snapped, thinking she now sounded like Mara.

"It's okay," Eva stressed soothingly as she rolled to a stop at the intersection where the Lodge property hooked up with the highway. "There'll be someone to back Cooper up." She checked for traffic, then turned left after an old beat-up Chevy passed by. To Cherime, she said, "Call the hospital and tell them we're coming."

Cherime opened her phone, googled the hospital, and pressed the number. When the receptionist or desk nurse, or whatever, picked up, Cherime explained the situation. She was asked the same questions Eva had and was reassured that they should make it to the hospital, no problem.

She ended the call and looked at Eva. "Okay, what now?"

Eva shrugged. "Maybe Raff should know."

"Yes." Cherime nodded, annoyed that Eva was outthinking her.

At the same time Mara said, "No."

Cherime ignored her sister and made the call. If she didn't, she'd have to deal with both Raff and Lucien and no way she was taking heat for this. Raff's phone went to voicemail. "He's not answering."

"Good," Mara huffed. "He doesn't need to know until it's all over."

"Yes, he does," Eva said. "You can't put Cherime and

me in the position of not telling him, and besides, what difference does it make if he knows now or not."

"I don't want him in the delivery room."

The idea of Raff being in the delivery room with Mara was ludicrous and both Eva and Cherime broke into laughter. "Can you imagine?" Eva snickered.

Cherime snorted. "Mara, Raff won't come near you while you're having the baby. He'll be cowering in the waiting room with Lucien."

"He was with Trist when the twins were born," Mara argued stubbornly.

Cherime was still giggling. "That's because she's his mate and he's very familiar with that part of her anatomy. I doubt very much he wants to see his sister's vagina."

She called Trist. "Hey," she said when her sister picked up. She could hear the cry of babies in the background and cringed.

Trist seemed a little frazzled. "Hi Cherime, I can't talk now. Scout's being fussy, and Shadow is being the supportive big brother, so I have a mutiny on my hands."

"S'okay. I tried to call Raff but he's not answering. Hope Ren didn't kill him." She clamped her lips together. That was probably the wrong thing to say to Raff's fated mate. "Just kidding. If you see him first, tell him Mara's in labour and we're on our way to the hospital."

"Shit," Trist swore. "Are you okay, Cherime?"

Cherime felt the kinship with the little omega she had initially rejected when the two had first met. Trist had a pure heart. "Yeah, at least with Mara going into labour, I don't have time to think about myself."

Mara and Eva both snorted as Cherime rang off. "Fuck off, both of you," she said on a pout.

They made it to the hospital without incident, but as Eva parked the car, Cherime saw Leah, Aubrey, and Honi scurry towards them. She slid out and turned to them. "What are you doing here?"

"Trist called me and told me to meet you here. She thought you might need some support," Leah said. She pointed a thumb at Honi. "I thought I might need some support, so I brought Honi."

Honi's face matched the colour of her red hair. "She insisted. And you know…." She shrugged helplessly.

Eva was opening the backdoor to help Mara to her feet. "I'm here to support Cherime."

"You didn't tell Trist that, did you?" Leah stood next to Eva, her unwavering gaze on Mara's belly. "Besides Supergirl, I need to be here to make sure you behave. If I seem to recall correctly, you have a fetish for pregnant women in handcuffs."

Eva glared at Leah. "I have already apologized for getting you all cuffed. Over and over again. What do you want me to do, convert to Catholicism and confess to a priest?"

Leah stroked her hands over Mara's baby bump like she was warming up a crystal ball. "No. I don't want the priest to have all the fun." She held tight when Mara tried to push her away. "You know you're having a boy, right?"

Cherime turned to Aubrey. "Leah call you?"

Aubrey nodded. "She thought I could help keep you calm better than she could."

Why did they all think she couldn't handle the pressure? "I am fucking calm!" Cherime shouted at everyone.

Aubrey tilted her head. "What are you wearing and what happened to your head?" Her critical schoolteacher eyes touched on every inch of Cherime.

Everyone turned their attention to Cherime except Mara, who gave out a little moan and clutched her stomach.

Fuck. Cherime had forgotten about the ridiculous clothes she had on. "It's complicated," she muttered. "Shouldn't the spotlight be on Mara?"

Eva rolled her eyes as she gripped Mara's arm. "Sure princess. If you say so."

Leah grasped Mara's other arm and marched along with Eva. "Okay, but we want all the dirty details once the pregnant girl is settled."

The front-desk nurse was efficient, getting a wheelchair for Mara and checking her in. "You women wait in the family room until the doctor's been through to check on her, then it's okay to come in."

"No," Mara pouted. "I want my sister with me."

The nurse stared at Cherime like she was a lime jello parfait. "Of course," she replied with a superior tone. "Are you all sober?"

"Yes!" came an outraged chorus of voices.

All except one. "No."

Everyone turned to stare at Leah, who innocently shrugged. "I might be. How would I know?"

"Drinking alcohol usually precedes drunkenness," Aubrey dryly counselled.

Leah widened her eyes and moved them around their sockets. "I drank alcohol yesterday, so it's possible."

"Leah, enough," Eva snapped, then to the nurse she added, "She's not drunk. Just nuts."

"Hey!" Leah shoved her hands on her hips as she looked up into Eva's face. "No getting personal at a birthing."

The desk nurse rolled her eyes and called for another nurse as Leah, Eva, and Aubrey bickered. Honi wandered away to view a poster on STDs.

The desk nurse shooed them to the waiting room a few minutes later when a young nurse in Winnie-the-pooh scrubs arrived. "I'm Jaime," she introduced herself. Cherime followed as Jaime pushed Mara down the hall. "Your friends can't be in the labour room," she said in voice far too enthusiastic for any occasion.

That didn't deter Mara. "But Cherime can, right? She has to be there when I have the baby." She indicated with her hand that Cherime come to her side.

Cherime picked up her pace and threw a wistful half-smile at Jaime. Maybe she should have gotten drunk before she came, then Eva could have taken over.

Coward! her wolf sing-songed, mimicking Jaime.

The nurse gave Cherime a side-eyed glance as if she wasn't quite in agreement with Mara. "Of course, if that's what you want."

"I do want," Mara replied as she was wheeled into a private hospital room. "She's my sister."

Everything was bright and white, and smelled like antiseptic, but nothing much else. Not at all like Cherime's hospital room earlier in the day. "This is nice," Cherime said as she gave the bed a bounce with her ass like she'd do in a hotel room.

Jaime smiled brightly. "I'm going to get the doctor. Do you want to take a shower to make yourself more comfortable before you change into the hospital gown?"

"God, yes!" Cherime decided she could overlook all that positivity that spouted from Jaime – the woman was a superstar. "I could so use a hot shower and shampoo."

A grin teased Mara's mouth. "I think she was talking to me."

Cherime frowned, not sure Mara was right… but she probably was. Yes, she was right, but fuck it. To Jaime, she said, "Could I take a shower too?" She pointed to the gauze on her head. "I was in here earlier today getting stitched up, and I didn't check out so technically, I'm still a patient."

Jaime cracked a huge smile that made Cherime's pupils dilate. "Why don't you go first. That way you're out of the room when the doctor checks Mara."

"Thank you!" Cherime breathed in relief. "I don't suppose I could have a hospital gown too. Won't I have to wear one in the delivery room anyway? It's gotta be better than the fashion statement I'm currently making."

The nurse looked Cherime up and down. "You aren't wrong about that. Be right back."

When the nurse left, Mara said, "I don't know if I can handle this, Cherime."

"Of course, you can," Cherime replied as she tugged the curtain aside and peeked out the window. It was overlooking the parking lot. No sign of Ren's truck yet, so maybe she'd have time to clean up before he got here. She turned back to Mara. "Those women in the waiting room are pretty fucking great and they'll support you until that kid is in college. You'd know that if you came to girl's night out once in awhile."

Mara ran her hands over her belly. "I was kind of being pregnant, Cherime. And there was no girl's night out before you got arrested."

"Kind of true," Cherime admitted as regret flashed behind her eyes. "And then I got sidetracked with them and forgot to make sure you were okay."

Mara shrugged like it didn't matter. "I didn't reach out to you for support."

"Also, true," Cherime agreed, then thought maybe those were wrong words. "But you were in a bad place, so you have an excuse."

Mara dropped her eyes to her hands, which were folded in her lap. "I still am."

Cherime touched Mara's shoulder. "Well I'm here now."

"Until you mate with Ren." Mara rubbed her stomach and moaned as a contraction hit. "We better get sorted. I don't think this kid's going to wait for us to get our shit together."

The nurse returned with a hospital gown and pointed to the bathroom. "All yours, Cherime. I'll get Ms. Mara ready. Doctor Phillips is on her way."

Cherime groaned as she closed the bathroom door behind her. Why the hell wasn't Coop here where he belonged. Bloody doctors!

She stripped and stepped under the warm stream of water, sighing as it pelted down on her. She probably should have taken the gauze off her forehead and waist, wasn't sure she should even be showering with all the stitches, but it felt so good. She shampooed her hair twice, then soaped her body, carefully avoiding the sutures. There was no hair conditioner and that spelled doom and gloom for her tresses, but still, it was better than before.

She stood in the shower for a few minutes with her eyes closed, thinking about Ren, his panic when he'd found her. The manic drive to the hospital. Good thing she was a shifter, or she might not have been able to handle all the bumping and thumping.

Speaking of bumping and thumping, her hand strayed to the little button between her folds, which was throbbing at her thoughts of Ren. She kneaded it, bringing herself up, feeling the tension rise, almost there, then a knock on the door had her desire scurrying away.

"Yeah," she called hoarsely.

"Time to finish up," Jaime said in her sweet nurse voice. "Doctor Phillips wants to talk to you."

"Be right there." Cherime turned off the shower, dried

off with a rough towel and dressed quickly, then slipped the blue gown on so that the opening was at the front. She grinned at herself in the mirror, thinking she looked a little like a doctor. Then she frowned. She had no makeup, no comb, not even lotion to moisturize with. At least the hospital gown kind of hid the T-shirt and her braless state.

"I'm here!" she announced gaily as she left the bathroom.

Dr. Phillips frowned as she stared at Cherime. "What are you doing back here?"

Mara looked between the two of them. "Cherime's my birth coach."

The doctor unsuccessfully tried to keep a neutral expression as she glanced down at Cherime's feet. "She can't wear flip-flops into the delivery room."

"It's all I have," Cherime protested, hoping the footwear would get her banned from the delivery room.

"Eva will trade with you." Mara clearly didn't know Eva well.

Cherime tried to remember what Eva had on her feet. Probably leather boots or sneakers, but whatever it was, it couldn't be worse than her current hot pink number. "She'll say no if I ask her. You have to ask her."

The doctor interrupted. "Why don't you have gauze on your sutures?"

Cherime waved towards the bathroom. "I was taking a shower."

Dr. Phillips narrowed her eyes at Jaime. "Why is she showering in the hospital?"

"Because I haven't had a shower all day!" Cherime exclaimed as her stomach growled. "Or food. Could we have some food?"

"No." The doc shook her head. "Mara can't have food right now and you are not going to leave her to go eat."

Doctors were so fucking unreasonable. “Fine. Then bring me some food.”

Dr. Phillips tilted her head at Cherime. “I’m not a serving wench.”

“You’re barely a doctor,” Cherime muttered.

“Stop it, Cherime,” Mara groaned as another pain hit her. “Can we get along until the baby’s born?”

Cherime felt herself flush. She really had to work on her civility. Maybe take a finishing class or something fun like that. “Sorry, sister. I’ll try to focus.”

Dr. Phillips nodded too, but clearly she wasn’t about to concede the round to Cherime. “Get Mara’s friends to grab something for you.” She turned to Jaime. “Look at Ms. Montana’s stiches once you’re done prepping Mara. She needs them disinfected and covered.” Back to Cherime, “I said no showering for a couple of days. Getting the sutures wet creates a breeding ground for bacteria.”

“I’m a shifter, doc. I’ll survive.”

“I don’t care what your genetic makeup is. You’ll do as I say until Dr. Cooper is back to take over.” Then her bedside manner kicked in. “How are you feeling otherwise?”

Cherime hated being told what to do. “Bruised and sore, but don’t let that stop you from running my life.”

The doctor patted Mara’s shoulder in what appeared to be sympathy and left the room.

Jaime prepped Mara, then fixed up Cherime. “I’ll let your friends know they can come in now.”

As she left, Cherime said to Mara, “Don’t forget to ask Eva about the shoes.”

CHAPTER THIRTY-NINE

Somehow Ren and Raff managed to get through the day without killing each other, although Ren didn't like Raff any better than he had five hours ago. Still, the Mountain alpha decided to consider it a step forward as the trip back to town was mostly made in silence.

On the other hand, Ivan Polski made a career out of finding fault as they trekked to and from the crime scene. Right from the start, the Russian bitched and moaned as he and the other cop, Adam Cole, pulled equipment from the trunk and backseat, Ivan handing a case off to Ren.

Ren passed it back. Loathe as he was to admit it, his feet were too tender to walk into the bush. "I'm gonna shift and lead you in. Can't walk that far in human form."

Ivan Polski wrinkled his nose. "Bad enough I had to go deep diving with you animals, now I have to follow the two of you into a forest. You better not be thinking about making me your next meal."

Raff crossed his arms. "I wouldn't eat you if you were the last man on earth. Russians are all gristle."

Ivan glared at Raff. "And I hate the way you guys

prance around naked with your big pricks hanging out. Makes us mortals feel inadequate."

Ivan also hated the soft moss under his feet, the over-powering scent of pine, the bear scat, the uneven surface of the forest floor, and… well… by then Ren had tuned him out.

When they arrived at the scene, Ren had the chance to examine the area without the panic he'd had earlier. Trees and rocks were blood-spattered as well as a portion of hard-packed earth, which seemed to be the only thing that made Ivan happy.

"We might actually get some samples of the attacker's blood."

Raff said what everyone else was thinking. "That would be the biggest break we've had."

Ivan agreed. "We can check it against the international database. Even if we don't get a hit, at least we'll have it on hand. Any shifter who turns up hurt should give us enough cause to get a court order to check their DNA."

Ren sat and watched, not shifting back to his human form. They were deep in the forest where the smell of copper infused the air. It could attract predators, but the scent of his wolf form would discourage bears and wolves from dropping by for a snack.

It took an hour to process the scene, then another hour to walk out because Ivan was trudging and stopping every few minutes to complain. By the time Ren and Raff were on their way down the mountain, the sun was setting and Ren was grumpy. His need for Cherime was so intense he felt like he was going insane. They'd have to mate soon because he couldn't stand being apart from her.

As Ren turned left onto the main highway towards the Lodge, Raff's phone rang.

"Hey, baby," he said softly. Ren had never heard Raff

use that tone of voice and felt his lips tug up for maybe the first time that day. Trist was Raff's Achilles heel.

The softness didn't last as Raff frowned at Trist's words. Then he said on a grumble, "Because I didn't think about checking my voice mail. What's going on?"

Trist's garbled words flew too fast for Ren to make out more than a few phrases, but he picked up one that made his heart pound in his chest: Cherime at the hospital. He bit his tongue to keep from demanding an immediate explanation.

"Fuck!" Raff snarled as he ended the call. To Ren, he said, "Turn around. We gotta get to the hospital."

Ren checked the traffic as he slowed enough to make a dangerous U-turn. "What happened to Cherime?" All he could think about was that he'd left her vulnerable, left her behind. He fucking shouldn't have done that.

"Not Cherime."

Relief flooded his body. "Then what? Where's Cherime?"

"At the hospital with Mara. She's in labour."

Ren narrowed his eyes. "I'm not following you. Mara's pregnant?"

Raff grinned maliciously. "Cherime forget to mention it to you?"

Ren thought about clipping Raff a good one in the temple. "We don't do a lot of talking when we're together."

"You fucking better not be stringing her along," Raff growled from the back of his throat.

Ren huffed an aggressive snarl. "Give you sister some fucking credit, you mangy asshole. She can take care of herself."

Raff clearly wasn't going to let the topic go. "She did a bang up job of it this morning, didn't she?"

Ren felt defensive of his woman. "She did! She won the fucking fight. Your sister is the strongest woman I've ever met."

"You must have it bad if you're interested in that crazy, self-centred wildcat." Raff shook his head in disbelief.

Rage shook Ren to his core, and he considered pulling over to the side of the road and having it out with his brother-to-be. "You talk about Cherime that way again and I'm going to mess you up good." His voice was a low growl of barely contained aggression. "Problem with you is that you're so busy being a fucking male shifter, you don't spend anytime getting to know her. She's mine, you asshole, and maybe that's a good thing, considering your shitty attitude."

Ren pulled into the parking lot at the hospital and got out of the truck, slamming the door, not waiting for Raff as he stomped towards the hospital. He was steaming. He didn't care if Raff was family, big brother, or beta of Cherime's pack. The prick had no right talking about Cherime that way.

He stopped, thinking about the truth of that statement, then turned and glared at Raff as the asshole strode towards him. He curled his fingers and as Raff got close enough, sucker-punched him in the jaw, sending him flying backwards, landing on his ass on the pavement. "That's the only warning you're gonna get, you motherfucking beta."

He didn't get far inside the hospital before Raff caught up with him. "Outside, you fucker!" he shouted.

Three women at the front desk threw them the stink eye, one the doctor who treated Cherime earlier in the day. "Shush!" she declared.

"Why are you here?" A nurse the size of fly said with authority that was likely going to get her swatted someday.

Raff elbowed his way past Ren. "I'm Mara Montana's brother."

"Of course, you are," Dr. Phillips said drily. "Both your sisters are here." To Ren, she narrowed her eyes. "Did you hit him?"

Here we go again. "Yep." That was all the explanation anyone was going to get from him.

The doctor narrowed her eyes. "I don't care if you have unresolved shit. This is my hospital and Mara is my patient. The two of you had better respect that."

It's not actually her hospital, Ren's wolf observed.

"Where the fuck is Cooper?" Raff growled.

"Conference in Vancouver," Ren muttered. "Where's Mara?"

"You're not going in there," Raff snarled.

Ren was a few seconds away from belting the beta again. "I don't want to fucking go in there. I want to see Cherime."

A nurse with the nametag Jaime, got between them. "Follow me, boys. I'll take you to them." She scurried down a hall and rounded a corner, then pointed to a room with the door closed. "It's getting late, so say hello and goodbye. Send the other girls home too."

"What other girls?" Raff rumbled. "I thought Cherime was staying with Mara through the birth."

"She is. All the other girls but Cherime."

Raff and Ren exchanged glances. "What the fuck is Cherime doing? Throwing a party?"

That was almost the same thought Ren had, but he couldn't let this teachable moment pass by. He grabbed Raff by his T-shirt and slammed him against the wall as Jaime scrambled back. "See right there. That's what I'm talking about. Give Cherime the fucking benefit of the doubt."

A burst of laughter filtered through the door, not helping Ren's case in the least. He released Raff and banged open the door to Mara's room. He got everyone's immediate attention. "What the hell?"

Raff brushed by Ren and hurried to the bed. "Mara, you okay?"

"Yeah," Mara said on a groan. "Labour pains are hurting more, but nothing's happening down below."

"She's not dilating," Eva announced as if it weren't clear the first time.

"Jesus Christ," Ren groaned as he rubbed at his forehead.

"I'm alright too," Cherime said to Raff, hands on her hips. "Thanks for asking."

"You're old news, Cherime. Looks like you're surviving just fine, though that knock on your head clearly fucked with your fashion sense."

Ren caught Cherime's eyes and lifted the corner of his mouth. "You look better than fine, Wolverine. Come talk to me." He crooked a finger.

Leah rolled her eyes as Cherime gave Ren a sultry smile and sashayed her way to him. He had to admit, the outfit she was wearing was a little out of the norm for his girl and maybe all other woman in the world. It didn't matter to him, though. She could have been dressed in a sack and he'd still want her.

She is dressed in a sack, his wolf muttered, covering its eyes with its paws.

Good thing it was colorblind.

Cherime stepped into his arms, wrapping her arms around his waist, and resting her chin on his chest so she could peer up at him. He bent his head and brushed his lips across hers while grabbing her ass and pulling her flush to him.

"Get a room!" Leah catcalled.

"Get the fuck off my sister!" Raff snarled.

"Outside with the hanky panky, you pervs!" Eva commanded.

Aubrey stood and scratched at her ear. "I should go."

Honi said nothing.

"No!" Mara wailed. "She can't leave!"

All eyes turned to Mara for clarification.

"Cherime can't go. Aubrey can leave."

"No!" Leah glared at Mara. "If she leaves, Honi and I have to go. Aubrey's our ride."

"You really need to get your licence," Eva observed.

Leah wrinkled her nose at Eva. "So you can handcuff me again? Speaking of pervs."

"Enough!" Aubrey said softly, stepping up to Leah and gripping her arm. "You owe me for locking me out of my classroom, so let's go before I kick your ass."

"Somebody got detention," Eva singsonged.

Honi followed as Aubrey dragged Leah out of the room.

Leah shook her fist at Eva. "One of these days copper, I'm going to get the last doughnut!"

Mara groaned as she gripped her belly, grabbing Eva's and Raff's hands and squeezing. "Hurts every time I have a contraction but doesn't seem to go anywhere."

Ren tugged Cherime towards the door. "I want Cherime for a few minutes, Mara. You don't need me in here, invading your privacy."

"That's for fucking sure," Raff muttered.

"Okay," Mara said, her eyes tearing up. "I need my sister."

"You should go too, Eva," Cherime smiled wickedly as Ren hauled her from the room. "You need your rest now that your preggers."

"Are you fucking kidding me?" Ren heard Raff exclaim as the door shut behind him.

"Let's get some air." He grabbed Cherime's hand and dragged her out a back door before she could protest. They were in an isolated area of the hospital and he barely had to move to get away from the dim lightbulb that lit up the doorway. He took a deep pull of the night air before pushing Cherime up against the wall. His eyes stroked over her body. "You're pale."

"Been a long day." Cherime gave him a weak grin. "But I'm okay. The doc looked at my stitches and Jaime replaced the bandages." She touched his arm, her fingers exploring the dip of his bi-ceps. "How'd it go for you?"

He didn't want to talk about his day. "Good enough, but too fucking long away from you."

"I know that feeling. I missed you like crazy."

Ren crushed his mouth to hers as she pushed into him. The kiss went from gentle to savage in less than 10 seconds, their tongues warring with each other. When he came up for air, he said, "Tell me if I hurt you." His hand found its way up her skirt and his fingers dug into her ass.

Cherime pushed at his chest. "Not here, Ren. Everyone will know."

He raised an eyebrow. "Since when does something like that stop you?"

She gave him a harder shove. "Since my sister is in there having a baby. Fuck, even I'm not that insensitive!"

He laughed. "I'm playing with you, Wolverine. You're still healing from the attack. I'm not going to mess with you against a brick wall, no matter how alluring you are in those clothes."

She landed a hard punch to his chest. "It was all that fit me at Mara's. She's smaller than I am, in case you hadn't noticed."

He pinched her chin and raised her face to his. "You're the only woman I notice, and I don't give a fuck what you're wearing as long as I can take it off you."

She threw her head back and laughed as she clutched his T-shirt. "I so want to get horizontal with you."

His eyelids drooped when she grinned up at him with her beautiful bright eyes. Lust snaked its way through his body, making him think they could do a quickie right there and now, as long as he handled her gently. He traced the edges of her full lips. "What if I want to stay vertical?"

As if reading his mind, she glided under his arm and reached for the door. "You can do it anyway you want to later."

His thoughts wandered to her curvy tight ass. "It's a date."

She took his hand and pulled him inside with her. "Mara's labour could take all night," she said as they walked together down the hall. "You should go home and get some sleep."

Not a fucking chance in hell was he leaving this hospital without her. "I'm staying until you're done here."

"Okay." She smiled up at him. "But you know that means you and Raff are going to spend more quality time together."

Yeah, he realized that. "I'll try not to fuck him up."

Cherime didn't seem at all concerned about Ren's penchant for knocking around her brother. "Well, if you do, take it outside. Dr. Phillips gets cranky when we fight inside."

He chuckled. "I noticed."

When they entered the hospital room, Raff was the only one in it besides Mara. He jumped to his feet when he saw them, a look of relief on his pale face. "You stay here with Mara. I'll be down the hall in the waiting room." To

Ren, he said, "If you aren't going home, then you'll want to come with me." He almost ran out of the room, to Ren's disgust. Shifter males should be able to easily handle a birthing.

Mara let out a long loud shriek that made his wolf howl in distress. Maybe Raff had the right idea, he thought, as he edged from the room.

CHAPTER FORTY

Cherime slid into the chair Raff had vacated and held Mara's hand through the contraction. After it passed, she stroked the hair off her sister's forehead. "How're you doing?"

"The doctor came in while you were gone and checked. Labour pains are coming closer and I'm dilating more. They're prepping the delivery room now."

"Okay." Cherime's stomach lurched as she squeezed Mara's hand. *You can do this, you can do this, you can do this.* "What do I gotta do?"

Mara wiggled her fingers. "For starters, loosen your grip. I need to squeezc tightly not you."

That seemed like bullshit, but Cherime complied. "What else?"

"Breathe." Mara sucked in a deep breath, then held it a few seconds, then exhaled. "Like that or you'll faint."

Cherime aped Mara and it settled her enough to be contrary. "I'm not going to faint."

"Good." Mara curled around herself and wailed, "*It hurts so fucking much!*"

Mara wasn't joking about her tight grip, but Cherime held steady as Mara squeezed through the pain. It seemed to last forever, and Cherime breathed in and out, though she didn't think that helped Mara much. "How the hell am I going to do this?" Mara moaned.

Cherime wondered the same thing. Her sister was alone in this world, having a baby without a mate to support her. And worse, the circumstances around how she lost Connell were enough to shrivel any woman's soul.

Cherime made a silent promise to Mara that she would be there to support her through what would be the next few rough patches. And the pack, they would rally around her. Cherime had a brief bout of homesickness at the thought of leaving everyone behind, but it passed as she thought of Ren and where she was going.

A bowl with water and a wet cloth sat on the nightstand and Cherime wiped Mara's face as the pain released. "How're you now?"

"Same as before. Thank god there's just one baby."

Cherime nodded in agreement. "Trist's a trooper, isn't she?"

Mara laughed. "She deserves a medal for pushing Scout and Hunter out of her vagina."

"I can't even imagine." A shudder ripped through Cherime at the thought, but she knew she wanted babies with Ren. More than one, though maybe not at the same time.

Another labour pain hit, then another and another.

Finally, Jaime and a new nurse entered the room. "Cherime, come with me so I can get you a gown and mask. Mara, Pat is going to get you ready."

By the time Cherime was gowned up, with booties on her feet and a mask on her face, Mara had been taken to the delivery room where Dr. Phillips was seated on a stool between Mara's legs, which were propped up in stirrups.

Cherime scrambled over to Mara and held her hand. "How're we going to do this?"

It seemed like a reasonable question, but Dr. Phillips furrowed her forehead. "Jaime will assist me, Mara will push, I'll catch the baby, and you'll stand there and look pretty."

Cherime returned the doctor's glare. "At least I've mastered my job."

Any retort the doctor might have had was lost in the noise of Mara's wail. "I wanna push," Mara gasped as grabbed Cherime, dragging her down so her face was almost mashed between Mara's breasts.

"Not quite yet, Mara," the doctor gently murmured.

"What do you mean, not quite yet?" Cherime's voice was muffled as she noted for the first time that her sister's breasts had increased significantly. "When a baby wants to come, why not let it out?"

"This isn't like letting a dog out of a kennel," Dr. Phillips snarked. "We want the baby out with minimal damage to Mara's vagina. Keep it nice and tight for her future man."

"There will never be another fucking man!" Mara screamed as she squeezed Cherime so hard that a couple of the sutures in Cherime's side popped.

"She's killing me here!" Cherime cried. "Let her push!"

Mara grabbed Cherime's hair and yanked on it like it was worry beads. "Let me push!"

"Okay, you can push, but gently, Mara. The baby's perfectly situated, so we want the head out first, then you'll breathe through the rest of the contraction, and push again on the next one.

Mara growled deep in her throat as she pushed. She let

go of Cherime's hair and grabbed her arms for leverage. Cherime straightened her back and stretched her neck in time to see a tiny head emerge. After she panted with Mara through the rest of the contraction, Mara pushed again on the next one, and the baby slipped out.

"Oh my god!" Cherime watched as the doctor raised it in the air. "It's so tiny."

"It's a boy." Dr. Phillips announced. "And he looks perfect." She passed the baby on to Jaime, who set it on Mara's chest while the cord was clipped off.

Mara's tears were infectious and Cherime scrubbed at her eyes with the sleeve of her gown. "Look at him, Cherime!" Mara exclaimed. "He's perfect."

"Yeah," Cherime sniffled. "Don't you just love him?"

"Oh my god," Mara sobbed as she hugged him close. "I do! I love him so much."

CHAPTER FORTY-ONE

Mara named her boy Roman and Cherime, Raff, and Trist gave their blessings. The four of them sat together in the hospital room, Mara in the bed holding Roman to her in a desperate hug. She and Trist were weepy, and Cherime's eyes kept stinging. Raff remained gruff but kept clearing his throat.

"He's beautiful," Trist said as she pulled back the blanket and peeked in at the baby. "I'm so happy for you. And Scout and Shadow are so excited to have a cousin to play with.

"Where are the little guys anyway?" Mara asked, her eyes never straying from Roman's face.

"In the family room with Honi, Aubrey and Leah."

"What?" Raff said, his eyes narrowing at his mate.

"What?" Trist said defensively. "They're friends and they love the boys. They're perfectly capable of looking after them."

"What do they know about babies?" Raff seemed determined to ruin the family moment.

"About as much as we did when we had ours." Trist

mock-glared, then turned her attention back to Roman and Mara.

"Ren's there too if they need help." Cherime was tearing at a fingernail. She needed a manicure and worried they might become a thing of the past once she and Ren mated.

"That fucking animal is in with my boys?" Raff bolted to his feet.

Cherime scowled at Raff, thinking she had to quit scowling before the lines became permanent. "For god's sake, Raff. It's not like he's going to eat them."

Trist jerked her head towards Cherime. "Why would you say such a thing?"

Cherime shrugged, not at all understanding Raff's and Trist's drama. "To reassure you!" She rolled her eyes. "Fuck."

Mara covered Roman's ears. "No swearing, Auntie Cherime."

Cherime smiled tenderly at mother and child. "Sit down, Raff. I'll go rescue Ren. It's late, or early, or whatever. I need to catch myself some zeds."

"Not on Falls Lodge territory," Raff barked as he took a seat and pulled Trist onto his lap.

Despite having a handsome little nephew, Raff was still an asshole. "Wouldn't think of it, big brother." She drifted out of the room but didn't have to go to as far as the family room find Ren. He was hovering in the hall, a few metres from Mara's door.

Relief flooded her body when she saw him, and she walked straight into his arms. "I have three nephews now, which might explain my exhaustion."

He pulled her to him, tightening his embrace enough to make her wince, but she didn't protest. Ren's hugs were the best thing ever, well… except for his kisses and his touches and his sexiness. A sizzle of energy perked her up.

"Let's go," he said gruffly into her ear.

Aubrey wandered towards them. "I'm going too. Leah and Honi have the twins and said they're okay."

Cherime felt her throat tighten. "Thanks for hanging around. You didn't have to, though."

Aubrey shrugged. "I feel like we've bonded these past few weeks. It's good to have a purpose occasionally."

"You do have a purpose. You teach children."

A faint smile crossed Aubrey's face. "That I do." With a small wave, she headed towards the exit.

"Be careful on your way home," Cherime called after her, worried for Aubrey's safety.

"We can give you a ride," Ren said, causing Cherime to feel both relief and possessiveness at the same time. She didn't want Ren anywhere near Aubrey, despite the little schoolteacher's discomfort with the Mountain alpha.

Aubrey refused, a flash of panic in her eyes. "My car's in the lot, and I need to get it home." She quickly left the hospital, not giving Ren or Cherime a chance to work on their persuasive skills. Cherime was relieved that she didn't have to suppress more emotions than she had already done for the day.

"Let's go," Ren said, capturing her hand in his as he tugged her out of the hospital.

"Where're we headed?" She didn't want to go up the mountain. "I want to stay close to Mara."

"I've been up and down that fucking mountain twice today. Besides, there's an ITCU meeting tomorrow."

Cherime glanced at him as he rubbed the back of his neck. Her man was as worn out as she was. "I don't think we should go to my place. Don't want to stir up more stuff right now." She paused, her tired mind trying to come up with solutions. "We could crash at Aubrey's." She paused, thinking Aubrey would say yes despite her discomfort with Ren. It wasn't a good solution, however. "She's got a cat though."

Ren snorted a laugh. "How about the Heritage Hotel?"

Darkness Falls had only two hotels, the other being the Imperial Hotel, which was attached to the Imperial Bar, otherwise know as the Zoo for its well-earned reputation. Of the two hotels, the Heritage was a much better choice. "Yeah, that'll work."

Ren helped her into his truck, then rounded it and climbed behind the steering wheel. "We have a lot of shit to talk about, Wolverine." He sighed. "But it can wait until tomorrow."

The clerk who checked them in was Kenny Hutchins, a jerk back in high school and apparently still one as he smirked at Cherime when Ren handed him a credit card. "Ren Ketkah. Wow, Cherime you've hit the jackpot this time."

Ren tugged her to him. "Just give us the fucking room and leave the editorializing to the newspaper."

Kenny was also not the brightest. "The best room in the house for the lovely Cherime. Gonna be an expensive night for you, fella." He winked as he slid the access card to room 110 towards Ren.

Ren reached over the counter, grabbing Kenny by the throat and dragging him across the top, their faces inches apart. "Apologize you fucker, before I make dinner out of you."

Kenny wrapped his hands around Ren's wrists as his face turned the colour of beets. "Sorry, Cherime," he choked. "Just a joke. Didn't mean to imply anything."

Cherime picked up the room card with a sigh. "Let

him go, Ren. You can't choke the loser out of him and I'm too tired to eat anyway."

Ren snapped his hands from Kenny's neck and pushed him back to his side of the counter. Kenny pulled a deep breath of air into his lungs as he slid down the other side until he was out of sight.

"I'm calling Axel, you bitch!" he croaked from the floor.

Neither Cherime nor Ren bothered to respond as they left the lobby. Kenny was a trouble-maker, mean and difficult, but compared to Kenny's brother, he was a puppy dog. Cherime decided not to share that information with Ren. Unlike Kenny, Axel knew how to pick his fights and he wouldn't take on Ren.

The room was a typical hotel room. A king bed smack dab in the centre, two basic night tables flanking it, a dresser with a TV inside, a small closet, a desk with a cheap coffee maker and an uninteresting bathroom. Ren bolted and chained the door behind him, then stripped off his shirt. "I'm gonna take a shower. Want to join me?"

Cherime gazed at his chiselled chest. She was torn between climbing his body under a warm stream of water and crawling between the hopefully clean sheets and closing her eyes. Her muscles were still aching, and she didn't want to get the gauze over her sutures wet again because she didn't have the supplies that she needed to fix herself up. She pointed to her forehead. "Can't."

She was surprised when he flushed. "Forgot that you're hurt, princess." He gently pulled her against his chest. "You're such a remarkable woman."

Oh god, he was being all mushy and stuff. And he smelled incredible; even his sweat from the exertion of the day stroked all of her lady bits. She hugged him back and then stepped away. "Go take your shower before I change my mind. I don't want to have to get Dr. Phillips to fix my sutures again. She gets all grumbly around me."

He buried his nose in her hair. "Your hair smells like antiseptic and I'm still horny for you. You could be wearing granny panties and it wouldn't matter."

Shit, she was wearing granny panties, but it wouldn't be the fucking day Ren would see her in them. "Go shower. I'm crawling into bed." She squirmed out of his arms.

He smirked as he let her go, then stripped free of his boots and the rest of his clothes and disappeared inside the bathroom.

As soon as she heard the bang of the bathroom door, she stripped off her clothes and crawled between the sheets. They were cool and crisp and smelled like industrial detergent. Reassured they were clean, Cherime laid her head on the pillow and her brain shut down almost immediately.

She was drifting when she felt Ren beside her, pulling her to him until she was cradled in his arms. How did she get so lucky? As he kissed her head, she mumbled, "Good night." Then she was out.

CHAPTER FORTY-TWO

Morning came too soon. The sunlight leaked through the crack in the curtain and sent a laser beam across Ren's face. He rubbed at his eyes as his pupils adjusted to the brightness. Cherime was already up, if the running water in the bathroom was any indication. Her side of the bed was cool to his touch and he wished she were still next to him so he could utter sweet nothings to her pussy.

He adjusted his morning wood as he swung his feet to the floor, thinking about the plan for the day. First thing was to drop Cherime off at Falls Lodge so she could greet Mara and the baby, who were coming home today.

Acid burned his stomach and the contentment he'd felt when he awoke disappeared. He recognized it as shifter instinct, allowing his woman onto another pack's territory without his protection. Except it was still Cherime's pack until she officially declared that it wasn't. And she hadn't done that yet, though he wasn't feeling insecure about the state of their relationship.

They had already fallen into an easy way of being with each other, but they hadn't spent as much time together as he wanted. The universe was a prick sometimes and wasn't ready to let them have some peace.

At least he didn't have to wait around for her and stew about what she was doing and who she was talking to. There was another meeting of the ITCU, and he had to attend because Oz still wasn't back. No word from him either and Ren was trying not to read anything into it. Oz needed some time to get over his guilt and grief at what had happened to Aubrey's sister, Adrienne, so that when he returned, he'd be the shifter he used to be.

At least Ren hoped that's all it was. Oz was his beta, but more than that, the brother he never had, the friend who always had his back. He missed the fucker and worried that Oz might be hurt or permanently gone.

That line of thinking had him spinning his wheels, so he switched gears to the ICTU meeting. The killer of Adrienne and Tia had made it personal when he attacked Cherime. Ren wouldn't rest until he got his hands on the fuck and tore him limb for limb.

He was distracted by Cherime, who came out of the bathroom, gloriously naked, her wet hair leaving waterdrops on her fine breasts. Fuck, she was gorgeous. "Those tits, Wolverine. Can't keep my eyes off them."

"Good morning to you, too, Ren." She strolled over and stood between his parted thighs, looking down at him while he examined her curves. "You really know how to charm a girl." Her touch sent a sizzle of heat downwards as she massaged the contours of his shoulders like she was moulding clay.

"Better get some gauze on your cuts." His dick was thinking other things and his hand automatically reached for it. The five-finger salute would have to do.

"Let me help you with that," Cherime cooed as she took over the stroking of his cock, bringing his hand to her lips, and kissing the palm.

Fuck, nothing ever felt this good – he had to stop it now or they'd be back at the hospital getting her stitched up again. "No, baby. You're bruised and battered. Not going to do anything to hurt you."

"I've got an ache, Mr. Wolf." She pointed to the strip of dark hair at the apex of her thighs. "Right here. Maybe you could help me out with it."

He needed to get her to listen to reason before the tight tether of his resolve snapped. "No means no, baby. I said no." Why was his voice so raspy?

"Sure, your lips are saying no, but your cock…." She looked down at his hard, aching erection like she was worshiping it. "It's speaking my language."

He grasped her waist to steady her as she climbed onto his lap facing him, her knees straddling his hips as she lowered herself on his dick. "See?" She breathed carefully as she filled herself with him. "Hold my hips. There's no damage there."

She was fucking right about that. He loved her hips, and he traced his palms over the flare of them, then dug his fingers into the cheeks of her shapely ass. Arching her back, she raised herself up several inches, using his shoulders for leverage, then moved down again slowly. It was clear she was in pain.

"We shouldn't be doing this."

She kissed him gently on his lips, then wrapped her arms around his neck and dropped her head down in the cradle of his shoulder. "Just let me fuck you like this until you need more. Then you can take me from behind."

Her words inflamed him, her breath on his neck, the warmth of her arms as they hugged him, her tits bobbing against his chest. And her ass, thrusting steadily up and down, her sweet moans of pleasure each time she dropped down on his cock. "Fuck," he groaned, his hands helping her thrust.

"This is so amazing. You're so amazing." She pushed her face against his skin, and he felt the wetness of her tears.

Oh shit, he was hurting her, or no… maybe she was getting emotional. "Are you crying?" Stupid question, but he wasn't used to Cherime being all vulnerable and soft. Not that it bothered him. In fact, it brought out his protective side, but he knew the extent of his sensitivity and worried he'd say the wrong thing, she'd stop the lap dance, and he'd get blue balls.

"No," she sniffled. "I'm happy, Ren. I have a new nephew, and a new best friend, and a man who loves me. Everything else is background noise."

He shoved his face into her nape as his hands crept up her back, skin so smooth and silky. Unblemished until yesterday. How to respond? Who was the new best friend?

His wolf growled as it rolled over onto its back and covered its eyes. *Who cares who her new best friend is? You're fucking embarrassing.*

Then what, asshole?

Try saying nice stuff.

Now was not the best time to come up with something clever, he thought as his breathing deepened and his mind got stuck on the silky heat of Cherime's pussy. "I love you, baby," he growled deep in his throat. "You're the sexiest fucking female in the world."

She let out a moan as she moved her ass faster. She was getting close to coming, which got Ren overexcited. "I'm going to shoot, baby," he growled as he met her thrusts. Yeah he was, right fucking now as his balls tucked up.

"Me too," she shrieked and bucked. "Now! I'm coming now!"

He felt her pussy tighten around his dick, pulsing fast, strangling him. "Jesus fuck!" he roared as he released inside her. "Fuck. Fuck!"

He toppled backwards onto the mattress, pulling her with him, his breathing uneven, his body shaking from the force of his orgasm.

Cherime curled into his chest, her heart beating rapidly. "It keeps getting better and better," she mumbled, and he felt the wetness leaking from her eyes again.

He scrubbed her back up and down. "Are they good tears?"

"My eyes are watering is all." She licked at a tear that slid to her lips. The dart of her pink tongue proved his cock was a greedy bastard as it tingled.

Fucking stand down! He squeezed her gently. "It's okay to cry." That sounded pretty fucking good.

"I'm emotional I guess." She plucked at his chest hair. "I'm happy for Mara. Something good in her life that she really needed."

"Me too," Ren said, then clarified. "Happy." He didn't know Mara well, but he wasn't completely heartless. This baby might be the blessing the female needed to make her whole again. If only Oz could find something like that.

After lingering for a few more cuddles, they dressed and packed up what little they had. Cherime called Lucien on the way, letting him know that Ren was dropping her off at the Lodge. It was a courtesy when a male shifter crossed into another shifter's territory. The plan was for her to change, then head into town to bring Mara home.

After the ITCU meeting was over, he'd reluctantly agreed that he'd head home. When Cherime got Mara settled in, she'd follow in her SUV.

"A day or two," she said as she stepped from the vehicle.

"Stay with Mara. Don't stay alone."

"Planning to." She gave him a last peck on his lips, then a deeper one when he refused to let her go. It took him back eight years, to that day when he forced her out of his life. He'd been so fucking brutal and he realized how lucky he was that she had given him another chance.

He let her go when she wriggled in his grasp. "Might have to come up tonight." Her voice was raw and raspy.

"Go," he urged before he changed his mind and kept her with him. "Gonna miss you."

"Me too," she called as she closed the truck door.

He got hard as he watched the sway of her ass under that ridiculous skirt. He wasn't lying. He already ached for her.

After a quick lunch at Becker's, he joined the rest of the ITCU at the precinct. Everyone was seated in their usual chairs as Jackson recapped the facts of the case.

The cop started with the common factor in the two deaths and two attacks: the lack of scent. Jackson's eyes were focused on his hand, which was on the table, fingers tapping. Not generally the way Jackson related to others. He was omitting something, Ren thought.

He glanced across the table and caught Raff's eye. Looked like brother-to-be was thinking the same thing as he lifted an eyebrow.

"I think we can agree that the wolf was grey," Jackson continued. "Cherime saw him in broad daylight, so that back's up other reports."

"Right. Like Trist's," Raff grumbled.

"Maybe there are two shifters," Eva posited. "The grey one and a second one."

"How'd they hide their scents?" Ren asked.

"Maybe one of them has the ability to do that." She caught Jackson's speculative gaze and raised her eyebrows. Looked like there was still trouble in paradise.

"Seems farfetched," Jackson muttered.

Eva took offense. "Maybe, but what else do we have? Or maybe it isn't even one of ours."

"Has to be," Raff argued. "Knows the coming and goings of his victims too well."

Eva conceded his point. "I kinda agree, just wanted to throw it out there." She toyed with the agenda on the table in front of her. "I had one other thought. We all talk about what the attacks have in common. Something we haven't talked about was why these particular women? They had one more thing in common besides being unmarked."

"Yeah, and…?" Weston finally joined the conversation.

"They were about to be marked." She held Jackson's eyes. "Think about it. Adrienne was with Oz—"

"He wasn't going to mark her," Ren growled, not really knowing if that was the case, but it was Adrienne they were talking about. He was aware that he was in full denial of the extent of Oz's relationship with her and probably always would be.

"So you say." Eva turned towards him. "But we don't know that for sure. Oz isn't saying and maybe her killer decided the two were planning to mate. Maybe something she said." She took a sip of water and licked her lips, making Ren miss Cherime. "Trist was attacked just as she and Raff were getting closer. Tia was leaving town, talking about returning home to be mated. And Cherime… well…." She turned to Ren. "You two had a very public fight at Becker's and you left together. Gossip doesn't procrastinate."

Ren reluctantly nodded as Weston said, "Okay, I hear you."

Eva glanced at the beta dismissively, returning her attention to Jackson. "And there's a weirdness going on too. Adrienne's body was left out, meant to be found, but Tia's body was shoved in a cave. If Honi hadn't swam there to get away from her brother, who knows when the body would have been discovered."

Raff huffed out an impatient breath. "Tia was tortured to death. Starved and frozen, which tells us how sick the fucker is. Maye he was keeping her on ice for the winter and then going to dump her outside with the spring thaw."

Raff's point was astute, so Ren decided to muddy the waters. "Or maybe something happened with Adrienne that the killer hadn't expected. Like she managed to get away."

Ivan cleared his throat. "The site where her body was found was a dump site. The murder took place elsewhere."

Ren wasn't ready to let go of the line of argument. "So she got away and he brought her down somewhere, but couldn't leave her there because it would expose him. Too close to where he kept her or his scent was all over things, so he decided to dump her somewhere else."

"We weren't able to track down the place of the killing," Ivan grumped. "And now, there'll be nothing to find after the winter, unless she died inside."

Jackson glanced at Ivan, then back to Eva. "So how does Simon's death figure into this?"

Eva lifted her shoulders in a half-shrug. "Maybe it doesn't. Maybe it's something else entirely. Or maybe Simon saw something or overheard it and needed to be shut down."

"Like what?" Raff growled. "The kid was nuts. Nothing he said made sense."

Ivan seemed to get on the Eva bandwagon, ignoring Raff and talking directly to her. "Agree, Eva. We ignore what he's telling us because he's paranoid, but he says something that gets back to the killer, who can't risk someone taking the kid seriously."

"Have we tracked Simon's movements the 24 hours prior to his death?" Ren asked Eva.

She nodded. "Dagmar's on it, got our guys going door to door, starting at the obvious places first, like the shelter."

Jackson stretched his back as he responded to Eva. "Good. We need to know what Simon was talking about, even if it seems whacked or insignificant. He talked a lot to you. Spend some time thinking about the things he said to you over the past several months. You might come up with something that makes sense."

Eva nodded and made a note on her agenda. "Will do."

Ren was growing impatient, tired of listening to people talking. "What's next, Jackson? We wait until the fuck takes another woman?"

Jackson dropped his chin to his chest as he thought. Then, "We pound the pavement, ask the questions, check alibis. Time to draw up a list of suspects."

"Make sure you include Oz on the list." Raff held Ren's eyes as he said it. "This is twice he was out of town."

"Fuck off, Raff. I was with him when Adrienne died."

"So you say, but you've made no secret about how much you disliked her," Raff snarled aggressively. "Convenient that Cherime was attacked by a shifter with no scent while she was on your mountain. Maybe it was your partner that did it so you could swoop in like a hero and save her."

Ren swivelled his head towards Jackson, his rage

making his vision swim. "This meeting over?" he snapped with a dangerous edge to his voice.

"Yeah." Jackson barely had the words out of his mouth before Ren shoved back his chair and stalked from the room.

CHAPTER FORTY-THREE

Cherime was missing Ren like nobody's business. Two days apart, and while they talked and texted, it wasn't the same as snuggling into his body and listening to his reassuring heartbeat. But time and distance from him helped her body heal. She was limber again, her muscles no longer ached, the bruises on her skin faded and her stitches, well they were fucking itchy. While every day was a good day to be a shifter, the ability to quickly heal made the universe that much brighter.

She was sitting on the deck of Mara's cabin, the sun caressing her as Mara handed her off a glass of lemonade. "Thanks," she said as she took a swallow. "The little freak-show settled down?"

"Finally!" Mara giggled as she sat in the chair next to Cherime.

Cherime grinned at her sister. Mara's carefree laugh was one she hadn't heard in such a long time. "Momhood looks good on you, sis."

Mara sipped at her lemonade as she patted the loose skin on her belly. "It feels good, too. I was so afraid I'd resent the baby for being half Connell, but one look at those innocent blue eyes and I forgot all about who his daddy was."

"He's beautiful," Cherime said as jealousy poked at her. "Looks exactly like you."

Mara grinned. "Thanks for that." She glanced at Cherime's SUV. "You headed to Ren's?"

"Yep. Meeting Eva for lunch at Becker's and then I'm on my way." She took a swallow of her lemonade. "Unless you need me here." She so didn't want to stay, but even she could be selfless sometimes.

"Nope," Mara said to Cherime's relief. "Thanks for keeping me company and for all your help, but I really want to spend some alone time with Roman. Just me and him for awhile." Her lips quirked up. "Besides, Raff and Trist are nearby if I need anything, and Eva keeps texting wanting to come over."

Cherime drained her lemonade, then stood. "I'll check in on you in a week or two. Going to find my man and fuck his brains out."

Mara shook her head in exasperation as she got up. "Jesus, Cherime."

"What? Roman can't hear me out here." She gave her sister a hug and headed to town.

When she pulled into Becker's, Eva was already there, in full uniform, leaning against her squad car. Before Cherime could cut the engine, the cop popped into the passenger seat of the SUV.

"What are you doing?" Cherime felt the usual irritation at her human packmate. She never fully explored why she and Eva couldn't get along. Possibly because they were both strong women, or Eva had this holier-than-thou attitude or maybe... it was because the fucking cop got her arrested and handcuffed. "I thought we were having lunch."

"We are, but while I was waiting for you, I saw Dexter Hayes and Weston Hawke together. They were headed to the industrial area of town. I want to know what they're doing, but don't want them to see a cruiser in the area. Your SUV looks a lot more innocent."

Going undercover and playing spy? That was right up Cherime's alley and her heart kickstarted in excitement as she headed south towards the industrial area. "We have to keep this on the down-low, good buddy." She tried to sound like Leah as she talked. "You don't want to take any chances, being preggers and all."

Eva pouted. "Really, that easy to convince you? I thought you'd argue with me and I was all set to make a good case over why you should do this."

Cherime grinned as she turned left, which took her out of the town proper. Playing detective and annoying Eva at the same time made her day. "I like to think of myself as a private dick."

That elicited a laugh from her passenger. "Fine by me. I'll hang on to my convincing argument for when I need another favour from you."

Cherime grinned. "Is it transferrable?"

The cop nodded. "I think it applies to any situation."

They chatted without the usual rancor about girl stuff and shifter men as Cherime slowly cruised around the industrial area following Eva's directions. Nothing much was going on: several cars were parked next to warehouses, a few men stood outside talking and smoking, light traffic in and out of the area.

"There!" Eva pointed to a bright red truck sitting in an otherwise empty lot, next to a warehouse.

"That Weston's truck?" She steered towards the big Dodge Ram.

"Yeah. I wonder what's going on?"

Cherime rolled her eyes at the coppish clip to Eva's words. "The easiest way to find out is to knock on the door and ask them."

The sneer on Eva's face seemed mocking. "If they're doing something they shouldn't be doing, they won't tell us the truth."

Cherime looked down at her filmy blouse and popped another button, then cupped her hands under her breasts and shoved them up one at a time. "Pretty sure I could get the truth from them." She smirked as she admired her cleavage. No doubt about it, her chest took men's minds off lying.

Eva shook her head, a hard line of authority in her voice. "You're a civilian. I can't put you in the line of fire." She pointed to an abandoned warehouse with overgrown grass. "Park over there. I'll sneak up on them."

Cherime decided the cop was crazy… or reckless. Or both. Yeah, that's what she was – crazy-reckless. "Not without me! You and your gun don't stand a chance against Weston. Have you already forgotten what happened with Rusty?"

Eva pursed her lips. "Don't you dare go there. It's my job to check on suspicious activity."

Cherime raised her eyes to the sky as if appealing to the universe would stop the flow of bullshit. "And it's my job to protect members of my pack, of which you are one."

"Not while I'm on duty."

Jesus woman. Cherime was getting a headache. "Any fucking time. Quit arguing and get the hell out of my SUV. We're going in together."

Eva huffed as she softly closed the car door and joined Cherime as they jogged towards the building. The prairie-like grass between the warehouses was high and unkempt but offered good cover as they bent at the waist and approached from the west. That side of the building had a single window next to the entrance. Two big roll-up doors took up the rest of the space.

As they sidled up to the warehouse, Cherime turned to Eva. "What's the plan, Einstein?"

Eva tried the handle of the door. It was locked. "Fuck!"

Cherime sighed as she opened her purse and pulled out her hair kit. "I can pick it."

Eva studied Cherime. "Why do you know how to pick a lock?"

Cherime had the bobby pins out and was crouched, already working the lock. "For times exactly like this." The bolt slid open. She stood and dusted her knees off, though they hadn't touched the ground. "Follow me."

"I should go first," Eva said, jostling for position.

"Because you have superior eyesight, hearing and strength? Or because you have a gun, which you won't use anyway."

"Fine, but you're undermining my authority," Eva snarled, though it lost something in translation because it was whispered.

"Every chance I get, copper." Cherime opened the door and slipped inside, Eva on her heels.

The warehouse was big and empty, which meant that even whispers would be easily heard in the cavernous space.

Cherime blocked out the rapid pulsing of Eva's heart as she listened for movement. Upstairs, she heard the voices. She scented the air. Yep, definitely Dexter and a shifter that she assumed was Gideon's new beta. She knew

Weston Hawke, but not well enough to internalize his scent. She pointed to the stairs and Eva pulled her gun as they trotted silently across the floor, which Cherime made look easier than it was with stilettos on.

At the bottom of the stairs, Cherime set down her purse, removed her heels from her feet, then pulled off her blouse. Eva shook her head and mouthed a silent, *no*, then turned and headed up the stairs before Cherime could wiggle out of the rest of her clothes.

"Wait for me," Cherime whisper-growled. The voices upstairs halted. Shit, they were made. Small wonder since Weston was a shifter too and had all the working parts. Eva had already reached the top of the stairs as Cherime hurried to unhook her bra and drop her cut-offs.

As she kicked off her panties, she caught the whiff of wolf and stared up as it came out of the dark, knocking into Eva and sending her tumbling down the stairs. "Fuck!" Cherime shouted as Eva landed hard on the floor, her head bouncing off the cement.

Jesus Christ, how many times could one woman get hurt in the line of duty? The wolf that hit Eva was already gone as Cherime grabbed her phone and called 911. "I need an ambulance. And better send the cops too. An officer is down."

The dispatcher had a deep sexy voice that made Cherime wish for Ren. "What's your location, ma'am?"

"Don't call me ma'am. We're in the warehouse district. I don't know which building. Can't you track me on the phone?"

"Of course." The click of a keyboard sounded in the background. "I've got your location and have dispatched units. Are you in any immediate danger?"

Cherime peered around the empty space and opened her ears to sound. "I don't think so. I think we're alone."

"Okay, that's good. I need your name and the name of the officer down."

Eva was a menace, Cherime thought as she felt her pulse pick up speed at her friend's prone body and bloodless face. "I'm Cherime Montana. Eva Blakely is the officer down." Cherime sounded breathless and wondered if she was panicking.

"Thank you. Stay on the line and talk to me. My name is Gary."

Nope, no. That wouldn't work. "I won't hang up, Gary, but I'm not talking to you. I've got to tend to my friend." She set the phone next to her bag and knelt beside Eva.

The blonde was unconscious, but at least still breathing and there was no sign of blood under her head. Still her pulse was thready, and she wasn't waking up. Cherime glanced into the shadows at the top of the stairs, getting creeped out by the lack of scent, movement, and noise. Her instinct was to shift and nose through the dark corners to make sure the assholes had left the building, but she didn't dare leave Eva alone and helpless.

She picked up Eva's hand and squeezed it, thinking she could be the next Mother Theresa with all the nurturing she'd been doing lately. Except for the celibacy, of course. And the outfit.

When she heard the sirens in the distance, she put her clothes on, not out of modesty, but because humans got uncomfortable talking to a naked shifter. Especially the men. She smirked.

She retrieved her phone. "Hey Gary, you still there?"

"Yes, I can hear the sirens."

"Tell them there's a door on the west side, next to a couple of big bay doors. They'll find us by the staircase. They don't need to come in with weapons drawn."

Turns out Weston Hawke and Dexter Hayes had still

been in the warehouse and showed themselves almost immediately after the cops arrived. Cherime was unnerved by their sudden appearance. "You assholes!" She shrieked at them. "Look what you've done to Eva!"

Weston's face creased with regret. "I thought someone had broken in, then I saw the gun. Didn't know it was Eva. I shifted, naturally, thinking I would tackle her to disarm her. Nothing else. But she lost her balance and fell down the stairs." His explanation was aimed at Jackson, and Cherime's temper went into overdrive at how easily he had dismissed her.

"So why the hell didn't you make yourself known?"

Weston's turned to Cherime with an angry glint in his eyes. "Because this is my property! Names on the title, doors were locked. Someone trespasses with a gun and what the hell do you think I'm going to do? How would I know you weren't going to shoot me the minute I walked into your line of sight?"

Cherime froze at his words. Fuckity fuck. She and Eva had been breaking and entering. She turned to Jackson. "Uh...." Fuck, she could throw Eva under the bus. Should, actually. The cop deserved it, but she was hurt and preggers and didn't deserve a berating. "Eva and I were going for lunch, a picnic. We thought the warehouse was empty. I picked the lock although Eva said not to. It's my fault. We heard talking and Eva went to check it out."

Jackson's face suggested he didn't believe a word of what Cherime was saying, but he turned to Dexter. "And you? What are you doing here?"

Dexter walked in a circle around Jackson, then stopped when they were face to face. "Not really any of your business what I do in my spare time with my friends, *Chief,* but since we're brothers, I guess I can tell you. Weston and I are partners."

Cherime crossed her arms and watched suspiciously as Dexter and Weston talked to Jackson. She wondered if Gideon was aware of his beta's extra-curricular activities. From what she knew of the Dominant pack, they bought property as a community, assigning one of theirs to manage it. Still, it wasn't unheard of individual pack members investing their own money, but Dexter seemed an unlikely partner. "What are you planning on doing here?"

Weston took an aggressive step towards Cherime. "None of your fucking business. Get the hell off my property before I have the Chief arrest you."

Jackson raised his eyebrows at Weston as Cherime sucked in a breath. Somehow, she managed to hold her pissiness inside, but that didn't sway Jackson from biting back at Weston. "You don't decide who I arrest, Hawke." His words were accented by a deep growl. "I have a hurt officer, and until I determine if she had cause for entering the premises, back off."

Dexter was grinning widely. "Big bro doesn't like being told what to do."

"He'll get used to it." Hawke waved a dismissive hand and turned to Cherime. "Get the fuck out of here."

Eva was being loaded into the ambulance, so it was time to go anyway. As Cherime walked away, she slid her hand behind her back and stuck her middle finger in the air.

At the hospital, she called Ren and let him know that Eva had been hurt, though she held back most of the details. The story was that Eva fell down some stairs and knocked herself out. It wasn't a lie, simply an omission of details. She'd fill in the blanks later if Ren wanted to know.

It took several minutes of back and forthing before she finally convinced him not to come into town. She promised she'd leave just as soon as Aztec arrived. Then she promised she wouldn't talk to Aztec. Also, she promised not to be alone with him.

After she hung up, Gillian pointed to the waiting room with a smirk. "This hospital's fast becoming your second home."

The nurse was right. Cherime had been at this hospital more times in the past week than in her entire life. She hoped three was the charm.

She was in the waiting room, finishing up a cup of the hospital swill, when Aztec arrived. "What happened?" Eva's mate was a man of few words, even fewer than Ren, who talked in grunts but had no problem expressing himself.

"She fell down some stairs."

"Pushed," Jackson corrected as he walked in. To Aztec, he said, "She's awake and asking for you."

Aztec seemed torn between wanting more information and wanting to get to his mate. "Who pushed her?"

"Go talk to Eva; she'll tell you."

Aztec headed to the door, but Jackson called to him.

"Letting you know there'll likely be disciplinary action taken against her. She violated a direct order from me, trespassed on private property, and drew her gun without cause."

Aztec pulled in a deep breath. "Fuck."

After the door swung shut, Jackson turned to Cherime. "What were you doing with her?"

Cherime didn't like the tone of Jackson's voice. It was like he was an alpha shifter talking down to a female. "We're pack mates. I was meeting her for lunch before heading up to Ren's."

"Eva told me what happened, so you can cut the bullshit."

Cherime straightened her back. "Consider it dropped,

big chief." Then she decided to drop the attitude too. "Is Eva okay?"

"So far, so good. She's under observation, since apparently it's risky for pregnant women to tumble down a set of stairs."

Maybe she deserved that dose of sarcasm. "Are you trying to guilt me?" It was working. Cherime felt culpable even though this was all Eva for the most part. Cherime only picked the lock.

"If the shoe fits."

"You know she's right about Dexter and Weston. I could scent it when they came down to talk to you. Lies, is what I think."

Jackson's face held anger. "Ren's waiting, Cherime. Suggest you go now or I'll call him and tell him what went down today. He won't like hearing it from me."

"Love you too, asshole," she said snidely as she brushed past him. At the door, she stopped and turned. "After I called for help, I tried to work out where they were. I thought they'd left the building because I couldn't hear them or scent them. Imagine my surprise when they strolled out of the building after you arrived." She tried to get in touch with her sensitive side, but it seemed to evade her. "Is it because you're a misogynist asshole who doesn't like when Eva has some intelligent thoughts in her pretty little head, or is it because Dexter's your brother and you're unwilling to let a little thing like being the Chief of Police get in the way of looking out for your family?"

"Go home, Cherime!" Jackson snarled.

The drama was right up Cherime's alley as she straightened her back, slammed the door open, and exited the hospital like a member of the royal family.

She ruminated on what had happened the entire drive up the mountain, but it fell away the moment she saw Ren.

He stepped outside, shirtless and with a broad grin on his face, as she drove into the yard. She shivered at his sexiness, which did nothing to cool the heat between her legs.

He opened his arms and she couldn't get her seatbelt off fast enough. She scrambled into his embrace and he swooped her up with a tight hug.

She was home.

CHAPTER FORTY-FOUR

"Where are we going?" Cherime asked as they stepped out of Ren's cabin.

"Stop talking and follow me," he grunted as he shifted. The sun was dropping in the sky and he wanted to get to the place before it got too low.

He headed towards the community hall, not checking to see if Cherime was behind him. He knew she would be. Everyday that passed, they became closer, working as an entity, together instead of against each other. It surprised him how easy it had been. There was only one more thing that needed to happen.

He waited for Cherime to catch up when he got to the secondary road leading down the mountain. He wanted to cross together, make sure she was safe from vehicles. When she reached him, she sat next to him and nuzzled her neck to his. This was his life now and he wondered how he ever got so lucky. He was so fucking in love, more even than he had been eight years ago.

This Cherime, the mature one, was everything to him and it was time for him to show her that. He loped across the empty road and into the trees on the other side, tracing the path he had made eight years ago, the first time he caught her scent. It was where he fell in love with her, even if he denied it to himself. And it was where he was going to now consummate that love.

In the clearing, the rock still stood, the one she'd been sitting on, her long tanned shapely legs stretching out and her eyes closed, her face tilted towards the sun. She stole his breath that day, and now, as Cherime shifted to her glorious human form, she did it all over again.

Tall and proud, the waning sun lighting her up, and Ren's emotions were too strong to put into words. She was magnificent, her long dark hair trailing down her back, the purple dye long since washed out, one hand on her hip as she coyly grinned at him. "Ren," she purred. "What's going on?"

He shifted then and walked up beside her, sliding his arm around the small of her back and digging his fingers gently into her waist. He'd brought supplies out earlier in the day. A soft blanket covered the ground with several unlit candles on the sitting rock. A cooler with beer, scotch, and a bottle of champagne sat next to a second cooler with roasted rabbit, a fresh baked loaf of Tess's bread, a brick of gouda, and some grapes and strawberries. He didn't need to bring flowers because they were already here. Fireweed, dogwood and forget-me-nots scattered across the space and combined with Cherime's natural scent to create an intoxicating blend of sweetness.

He'd also dug a new firepit closer to the rock and had logs piled up. They were going to spend the night here under the stars.

At the now-fenced edge of the cliff, the vista spread out like a perfect painting. The massive waterfall the town was named after swept down the cliffside and mist rose from the lagoon. They were too far away and too up high to hear it, but that didn't stop him from imagining its thunder. The sky was cloudless, becoming a dusky blue as the sinking sun created a watercolour of soft pinks and yellows.

Ren kissed the side of Cherime's hair as he felt her tremble next to him. "I love you, Cherime."

She looked up at him with trusting eyes. She knew. "I love you too, Ren. So much."

He struggled to find the right words, not that he worried she'd say no, but he wanted to make this day one they would both remember for the right reasons. "Will you let me mark you?" Yeah, not really Hallmark calibre, but by the smile on Cherime's face, he knew it was enough.

"You did all this for me?"

He'd do it a million times over for another glimpse of the joy on her face. "Yeah." He followed her gaze to the blanket, a faded quilt that Tess had given him when she took him in as a teenager. "For us. I wanted it to happen in the place I first fell in love with you. I can't erase the past, but I promise I'll do everything in my power to make our future perfect."

She pressed her body into his. "It doesn't have to be perfect, Ren. As long as I'm with you."

"Is that a yes?"

"It's always been a yes," she said breathlessly.

Ren swept her into his arms and lowered his lips to hers, kissing her softly, his dick fighting for control. It could bloody well wait a few minutes. He carried her to the blanket and gently set her down, then pulled matches from a bag and lit the candles.

Cherime was kneeling on the blanket, her beautiful face flushed as she zeroed in on Ren's erection, making it jerk under her scrutiny. "Fuck, Cherime. Keep it in your pants for a few minutes more."

She shuffled forward and grasped his shaft with both hands as she brought her lips to his cock. "Just a taste," she mumbled as she swiped her tongue over the pre-cum that was leaking from him.

He groaned. "I want this to be special for you."

She stuffed the head of his cock in her mouth as she looked up at him. He almost rocketed right then and there, her warm brown eyes locking onto his as she mouthed him. Goddamit, she was fucking trying to take control. That's not how it was going to happen. He needed to pull her off him, right now!

Her tongue travelled up and down the underside of his cock as she mouthed him, still peering innocently up at him. Heat coiled its way through his body. Fuck, he needed to stop this… soon.

She gently squeezed his balls one at a time as she carefully raked her bottom teeth up his shaft until she reached the head of it, then, as she went down, took as much as she could to the back of her throat.

Shit! Fuck! Sonofabitch! He tried to step away, but his hands had other ideas as they gripped her head, roughly yanking her hair and holding himself deep in her throat until she struggled. "Again," he demanded as she gasped for air.

She complied, and he lost the civilized part of him as he fucked her mouth aggressively. To hell with control. "I'm coming!" he shouted as he unloaded into her mouth. So much semen, some leaked down her chin as she swallowed.

He dropped to his knees, kissing her voraciously, his tongue sweeping her mouth. The taste of the two of them together solidified their unity. If they lived to be a hundred, he would never get enough of her. "You're fucking this up, Cherime," he whispered as he flipped her to her back and held her down with his big hands on her waist. "I wanted to make love to you."

"Are you saying you don't have more than one round in you?" She arched a teasing eyebrow.

He growled, despite knowing she was playing with him. "Maybe we should see who has more rounds." He nestled between her legs, his hardening cock rubbing along her pussy, which was already soaked with need. A slight breeze followed him as he moved down until he could bury his face between her legs and scrape his beard against her sensitive parts.

She shrieked at the friction and grabbed his hair, tightening her grip while lapped her up. Fucking amazing. He tugged his arms around her thighs and laced his fingers through hers as he ate her. Compared to him, she was a tiny thing and it fucking turned him on that he could dominate her with his size. He shoved himself up her body and took her mouth, their tongues clashing as he fed her juices to her.

"So good, baby," she moaned as she bucked her hips.

"Want more?"

She gasped as he returned to her pussy, stroking her with his tongue, sucking at her, nipping the insides of her thighs and her delicate folds. "I want everything!" she screamed.

"You're going to fucking get it, princess." He pressed his tongue against her clit as he slid a finger into her. So wet, so warm, so tight. He was relentless as she exploded under him, crying out as her pussy contracted around his finger. Fuck he needed to bury himself inside her.

He raised himself up on his knees and flipped her to her stomach like she was a rag doll, grabbing her hips and hauling her ass up, enough that he could sink inside the tight warm depths of her body. She was still pulsing, embracing his cock, shoving her ass back at him.

He was frenzied, forgetting to be gentle, his narrow focus on marking his mate. Making sure the world understood she was his. Making sure she understood she was his.

His grunts synced with her cries as he battered her pussy with his thrusting. He found her clit and thumbed it as he rode her, bringing her up with him. She was folded under him, not able to do anything but take what he gave her. Submissive posture, her cries loud and vulnerable – his primacy roared.

His wolf was feral now, savage, ready, waiting for the moment. And then as she came, as her pussy gripped his cock, he bellowed and spurted his seed into her. So fucking perfect, the heat of his orgasm numbed his body and he dropped down on top of her, his weight pressing her to the ground. He stayed seated for a moment, his cock pulsing, wanting more.

He felt savage, the apex predator who could take what he wanted, own it, force his will. The awareness of how badly he could hurt her was barely a footnote in his brain, too far away to fully invade his consciousness. He pulled out and hovered over her on his hands and knees, then shifted into his savage beast.

He clamped down on her neck first, his jaw locking so hard his teeth broke skin and dug deep. Enough to scar her, enough to show the world who she belonged to. He raked her back with his nails, and she jerked at the pain. She was shaking under him, but also frozen like a prey animal, and he scented both her fear and arousal. She knew better than to scream or fight him. So fucking perfect.

His licked at her neck, tasting the sweetness of her blood, and it broke his fragile leash. The nails on her back were replaced by his teeth, sinking deep into the muscle of her shoulder. He tried to rein in his wolf. It was frenzied now, he was frenzied, the scent of her sweet body invaded his nostrils and the taste of her blood on his tongue incited him. Her whimpers, her sweet breath, her racing heart – he lost control.

She screamed as he savagely tore into her, chilling and frightened, but it was what he needed to hear to settle his beast. The scent of the mating mark, overpowering the scent of her blood, soothed him. He pressed down on her back as he raised his snout towards the moon and howled, a singular joyful announcement that Cherime was now his.

He ran his tongue over the wound, tasting her, cauterizing the wound, his shifter saliva both healing and numbing. She trembled, not saying a word, but also not crying. She was a marvel, the strongest woman he'd ever encountered and now she was truly his.

When the storm of his emotions fully subsided, he shifted to human form and lay down beside her, his face next to hers.

"Wolverine. Are you okay?" he softly asked.

She opened her eyes, a grimace teasing her lips. "Don't ever fucking do that again."

CHAPTER FORTY-FIVE

When Ren's teeth ripped into her back, Cherime believed he was going tear her body apart. In that moment, her stupid mind wondered at the wisdom of marking the left side of the back, which was so close to the heart, but then all thoughts disappeared as the hot lash of pain battered her.

She wasn't exactly thrilled about him biting her neck. He'd done it once before, but they were both in wolf form when it had happened. His teeth on her human form was more frightening than anything else she'd experienced in her life.

Her wolf was inside, shaking like a leaf, and though she wanted to run, she realized that her submission to his aggression was necessary. It showed she trusted him not to take the marking too far. After, though, she couldn't stop trembling, not even when he shifted to human form and pulled her to him.

"Wolverine. Are you okay?" he asked, a soft growl to his voice.

She opened her eyes and even managed a tiny pain-filled smirk. "Don't ever fucking do that again."

His grinned and kissed her lips, a soft press, gentle nibbling, not seeking the heat of her mouth. "I won't." The warmth of his breath stroked her cheek. "I'm sorry I hurt you."

"Was that an apology?" Cherime wanted to lighten the mood so she could get a handle on her emotions, but Ren didn't crack a smile.

"Don't get used to it." His serious eyes held hers. "You're still trembling."

"It was so intense." All her nerves were pulsing. "I need a few minutes."

He seemed disappointed. "Alone?"

"No." Fuck, if he left her in the state she was in, she'd kick his ass. "Shut up and hold me."

He tugged her tighter, his arm cradling her neck so he could press her head against his chest while he stroked her waist with his other hand. "I love you."

It was what she needed to hear. She blinked her eyes as the sting of tears threatened. "Stop saying shit like that. You'll make me cry."

"You're mine, Wolverine, to love and protect. You're my heart's one and only. Always have been, always will be." He mapped her body with his fingers, skirting the wound on her back.

Tears trickled down Cherime's face. It was the best speech ever and she loved him for saying it. She tried to respond, but her throat closed on her.

He didn't seem to notice. "We'll have children. I'm thinking maybe a half-dozen; or we could round it up to 12."

She tilted her face to see his smirk, and sniffled as she

thought of the little bean that never was. "What if I can't carry a child?"

He kissed her wet cheek, his tongue swiping gently at the tears. "Then we'll steal one."

She jerked her head back and a ripple of pain scolded her for not taking care. "You're not serious?"

He laughed then, a joyful chortle that thundered around them. "What if I can't make 'em?"

You can, Cherime thought, but didn't say. Someday she'd tell him, but this wasn't the day. "I'd love you anyway."

"There's your answer. We're mates through good times and bad. We'll deal with whatever comes our way."

Cherime struggled to sit as her tears dried. The pain in her back was throbbing through her body, and not in a good way. "This marking shit is pretty primitive. The humans have it right – spend too much on a wedding, wear virginal white even if you've banged the entire hockey team, and sign legal papers that chain you for life. No savaging the bride."

"Tell me you haven't banged the entire hockey team." Ren lent her a hand to get her upright, then reached for the cooler and pulled out a bottle of champagne.

"That's your takeaway? My point is that this is scarring, not only on the body, but on the psyche."

Ren popped the cork on the champagne and poured a measure into plastic cups. "It's meant to be, for both of us. I might not be feeling your physical pain, but I can feel you hurting. We're connected now, even more deeply than before." He tilted his face up and breathed the night air. "Don't you feel it?"

Cherime punched him in the jaw, mollified when his head whipped back. "Yep, I feel your pain now." She felt hers too as her mark protested the movement.

His forehead bunched as he glared at her. “Don’t do that again.”

She grinned widely. “I hope I don’t have to.” She raised her glass, her emotions tucked safely back inside. “I love you, Ren Ketkah. I’ve always loved you. I can’t wait for our new home to be ready; I can’t wait for the Wi-Fi and electricity and a bathroom with running water. I can’t wait to share your life.”

He touched his glass to hers. “May we always find middle ground.”

“That’s asking a lot,” Cherime said as she took a sip of the bubbly.

Ren took a large swallow, then turned his head and spat it out. “This is like drinking piss.”

Cherime laughed as she drained her glass and pulled the bottle towards her. “More for me then.”

They drank, ate, and talked into the night, then Ren shifted and licked her wounds again. After, they spooned on the blanket, Cherime finding a comfortable angle to lean against his chest. She gazed at the stars, brilliant against the backdrop of the inky blackness. The night-sky was infinite, awe-inspiring, and comforting. In a world that was ever-changing, it was a constant. Even on cloudy nights, it was there, dark and brooding, unwavering in its loyalty.

Like Ren.

She fell asleep to the cool breeze stroking her mating mark. It had to stay exposed to the elements, was meant to heal ugly. It was a sign to other male shifters that she belonged to Ren. A promise by Ren that he would always protect and care for her. She’d wear it proudly because it was her pledge to Ren that she was his until the end of time.

EPILOGUE

Cherime walked through the framed structure that was to be her new home. The Western Red Cedar logs were massive, tightly woven together in a natural dance of grace and beauty. The perfume of the cedar mingled with the scent of freshly dug soil and Ren's alluring aroma as he stood outside, sweating under the hot August sun, talking with the men who would ultimately create their home.

These men understood nature, worked in harmony with it. Log smiths, timberwrights, and carpenters carefully constructed the frame of the lodge, which was visually harmonious with the landscape, an extension of the durable and stable land they inhabited.

Ren made this happen. For her, for them. Big and luxurious to cater to Cherime's human desires, a home for their family, a haven for their love.

The sun was setting and the last of the men had gone for the day, leaving the two of them alone. Cherime met him at the doorway. "How's everything going?"

Ren gave her a wide smile. "It'll be complete before first snow. That's the promise they gave me."

"Can we sleep here tonight?" That's what they'd been doing since the day they chose the lot. Each night, after they made love, they shifted to wolf form and slept huddled together in the trees or near the massive pile of logs. At dawn, they'd rise and drive to Ren's old cabin, where they washed, changed clothes, and returned to their soon-to-be home.

Ren pulled her close to him, his arms tightening around her. "Yeah, we can sleep, if that's what you want."

She rested her chin on his massive chest as she peeked up at him. "Do you have something else in mind?"

He gripped her around the waist and lifted her into his arms. Her legs circled his torso and she felt his desire for her straining against the material of his jeans, pressing against her heat.

He carried her up the skeleton of the stairs to the second story platform and deposited her gently on the floor. "This is as close to heaven as I'll ever get – you, the stars, the smell of cedar surrounding us."

Cherime pulled her tank off and opened her arms, an invitation wrapped in a promise of eternity.

THE END

BONUS CHAPTER

Leah, Trist and Honi sat cross-legged on the ground in the shadows of the trees near Eva's cabin. "Did you bring everything?" Trist whispered.

"Yep." Leah pulled two sets of police-issued handcuffs out of the pack she was carrying.

Honi's green eyes narrowed. "How'd you get them?"

Leah tilted her head. "I'm very good at getting things. I'm like Stuart Little that way."

"Everything else good to go?" Trist turned to Honi.

"Yeah, Gideon's at Becker's keeping an eye on Raff, Lucien, and Aztec. He'll call me the minute they leave. That'll be our cue to get this done and get home."

Leah tugged on Honi's red hair. "You got game, sister. I can't believe you talked Gideon into helping us."

Honi's flush started at her chest and rose all the way up to her forehead. Even her ears were red. "You would not believe the things I had to promise to get him—"

"Stop!" Leah grabbed her throat and made a retching sound. "I do not need that visual in my head."

Trist seemed bemused. "What did you have to do?"

Leah fake-gagged. "Stop, both of you!"

Trist glanced at Leah with a grimace. "I just thought maybe...."

Honi shook her head. "I'm not talking about it. The important thing is that Gideon is helping us out."

"Too bad Cherime couldn't join us," Trist said as Leah dug deeper into her pack and produced a bottle of scotch.

"She and Ren have been incommunicado. My theory is that her legs are stuck open," the little shifter said. "Girl can't walk."

Trist giggled. "Is that what we're drinking?"

Honi glanced at the bottle. "Whoa, that's expensive stuff. You go all out, Leah."

Leah shrugged as she peered at the house. "I wouldn't know what it costs. I stole it from Gideon."

Honi's jaw dropped. "You did what? Fuck, Leah. One of these days you're going to cross the line with him."

Leah wrinkled her nose. "I cross the line with him, he'll cross the line with me."

"What's that even supposed to mean?" Honi curled her lip.

Trist got to her feet, wiping the cedar needles from the back of her jeans. "Time to go. Remember the plan. We feed Eva the scotch until she's too drunk to resist us and then we strip her bare and cuff her to the bed."

"Hey, cop buddy!" Leah yelled as she flung open the door to Eva's cabin without knocking and stormed inside. "We brought scotch!" She held the bottle up in the air and did a little jig.

Eva peeked up from behind a kitchen counter. "You're going to have to drink it yourself. I'm pregnant, remember?"

"Shit," Leah said as she exchanged glances with Trist and Honi. "Forgot about that."

"Of course you did," Eva muttered as her head disappeared.

Trist brushed past Leah and headed to the kitchen. "What are you doing down there?"

"I dropped the fucking popcorn," came the muffled reply.

Trist rounded the cabinet and stopped short. "Wow did you ever." Popcorn was scattered everywhere, including under the stove and butcher's block.

Leah dropped down next to Eva and tossed a few popped kernels into her mouth. "Yum. Lots of butter too."

"Leah," Honi said, her tone like a disapproving parent. "Don't eat food off the floor."

Leah ignored her as continued to graze on the popcorn. "Eva's not drinking. Gonna be hard to have a game of strip poker if the cop won't down the shots."

"You can play strip poker whether you're drinking or not." Trist's voice was muted as she pulled popcorn out from under the stove.

"I like it down here on the floor." Leah snagged a few popped kernels from Eva's hand. "Honi, grab the scotch and the cards. We'll play here."

"No, we won't." Eva climbed stiffly to her feet and dusted off the knees of her jeans. "We'll play at the table, and I don't get why we're playing strip poker. It's weird unless there are men."

Honi laughed as she set out four glasses, pouring a shot of scotch into three of them. "It would be worse if there were men. Gideon would freak out if I started taking my clothes off in front of Aztec and Raff."

"Ditto," Trist giggled.

"Oh yeah," Eva said, then in a bad imitation of Aztec's voice, added, "Nobody sees you naked but me!"

"What're you drinking, Eva?" Honi asked as Leah finally climbed to her feet and ambled to the kitchen table.

Eva washed her hands as she jerked her head towards the refrigerator. "Soda water. It keeps my tummy settled."

Honi grabbed a half-empty bottle from the fridge and passed it to Trist, then pulled out a plastic wrapped plate of cheese. "This for us?" She raised the plate towards Eva.

Eva nodded as she dried her hands and headed to the table.

While Leah waited for the others to get organized, she pulled a neat stack of U.S. dollar bills from her pack. "Doesn't matter whether the boys are here or not, Eva. I have plans to see you naked before the end of this evening." She slammed her scotch, coughed, and pounded her chest. "Another please," she croaked and slid her glass towards Honi.

Honi complied as she eyed the stack of bills in front of Leah. "Where'd those come from?"

Leah fluttered her eyelashes. "Printing press is my guess."

"Why do you even have them?" Trist grabbed a slice of cheese and placed it on top of a cracker from a bowl Eva set next to Leah.

"For when you get down to your underwear. Then I want dancing so I can put these bills in your G-strings."

Honi tilted her head as she picked up the deck of cards and started shuffling. "I wonder if our government was trying to shut down strip bars when they introduced the loonie and toonie. After all, you can't really stuff a loonie into a G-string."

Eva disagreed. "You could stuff one in there, maybe two, but more than that, and the coins would fall out or weigh the panties down."

"Maybe that's the whole point," Leah said after she

took a conservative swallow of scotch. "Maybe the government really does want to be in the bedrooms of the nation."

"Is that a Canadian thing?" Trist asked as she took a cut of the deck that Honi offered her and showed the 10 of spades. "Or an American thing?"

"I think Justin Trudeau said that the government needed to stay out of the nation's bedrooms." Honi moved the deck over to Eva, who drew a two of hearts.

"Crap," Eva muttered as she threw down the card in disgust.

"Nope. It was his dad," Leah said, showing her queen of hearts. "Back in the day before he was Prime Minister, he introduced the Omnibus bill in the House of Commons, which would decriminalize homosexual acts performed in private." She took the deck of cards and reshuffled them. "He said there is no place for the state in the bedrooms of the nation and what's done in private between adults doesn't concern the Criminal Code."

"High card deals first," Honi said, sliding her seven of clubs towards Leah.

"How do you know that shit?" Eva said with a doubtful frown.

Leah shrugged. "I know a lot of shit. Nobody ever asks me." Dealer was responsible for collecting the blinds, so she tapped the table, the signal for anteing up. After the girls tossed their loonies at her, she dealt the cards.

Of the many times they had played poker together, Leah often took home the pot, although Eva gave her a run for the money. Trist and Honi didn't have the competitive nature to win against the other two. Tonight though, Eva was playing with pregnant brain and even Trist came out ahead of the cop.

Two hours later, Honi got the text the three of them

had been waiting for. She threw her cards down in disgust. "I'm done!" she exclaimed, the code words they decided on when it was go-time. She stood and made an exaggerated show of stretching her back. "Where's the bathroom?"

Eva pointed with her head. Honi already knew where the bathroom was because the Falls Lodge cabins were for the most part identical, unless pack members rebuilt, like Raff had. He and Trist lived in a big log home with a one-bedroom loft, but Raff was in the process of adding an addition because the twins needed space of their own. Or maybe mom and dad did.

Leah knocked her drink over and it landed on Eva.

"Leah!" Eva shrieked as she stood and pulled her shirt away from her body. "I smell like a brewery now."

Leah fake-frowned. "Distillery, not brewery. Better go change before Aztec gets back."

Eva's shifter man was so over-protective that he got pissed at everything that affected Eva. "Yeah, he'll decide that the alcohol can move through my belly and get the baby drunk."

She padded to her bedroom, yanking her T-shirt over her head as she went.

"Better change your bra too! Looks like some scotch soaked through to it," Leah called as she pulled the cuffs from her bag and followed Eva. Honi was already waiting and Trist blocked the bedroom door in case Eva try to flee.

Eva had her back to Leah and Trist, so she only saw Honi. "Why're you in here?" she asked as she snapped off her bra. "Thought you needed the bathroom."

Eva was fast becoming a shifter's mate, less shy of showing her birthday suit than she had been before she got with Aztec. Honi grinned viciously as she looked over Eva's shoulder. "Want to discuss a little BDSM topic with you."

"I don't do that stuff," Eva mumbled, a flush creeping into her face.

"You do now, copper," Leah yelled as she snapped a cuff onto one of Eva's wrists.

Eva twisted towards Leah, her eyes wide with surprise. "What the fuck are you doing?"

Trist had the other cuff and sailed it over Eva's head to Honi, who snared it from the air and hooked it on Eva's other wrist. "On the bed with you!" Trist yelled as Honi and Leah tackled Eva.

Eva was a tall woman, well-built and in good shape, but she wasn't a match for three female shifters, even if one was latent. Honi positioned her in the middle of the bed and clamped her right wrist to the wrought-iron headboard while Leah straddled her body and held her down. Trist was giggling as she pulled two silk scarves from her purse.

"Hold still," Honi bitched as Eva bucked her body and slapped at the redhead until Honi finally got a good grip on Eva's left wrist, pulling it to the headboard and clipping it in place.

"You fucking bitches!" Eva shouted. "Get these handcuffs off me!"

Trist shushed her as Leah leapt to the floor and slid Eva's pants and underwear down her legs and over her feet. "We're not going to hurt you. You're a friend and we love you."

"Yeah," Honi said as she grabbed one of Eva's kicking legs and held it close to the footboard. "Consider this an intervention."

Leah wrapped the silk around the ankle Honi was holding and secured it. "Behaviour modification."

Trist had the biggest smile on her face as she watched

Leah and Honi wrestle Eva's other ankle into place. "Payback for getting a pregnant woman cuffed."

Leah and Honi were huffing a little as they stepped back to admire their handiwork. Trist was proud of Eva. She hadn't gone down without a fight.

Eva thumped her head on the mattress. "Okay, you've had you're fun. I totally deserve this. Now let me up."

"Should we?" Trist said to the other two.

"Do you think she's learned her lesson?" Honi said.

Leah narrowed her eyes and looked speculatively at Eva. "Nope, she hasn't." She turned to leave, then stopped, approached the bottom drawer in the dresser and pulled Eva's police gear out.

"How the fuck do you know I keep it there?" Eva snarled, thrashing on the bed as if that would break her out.

Leah shrugged as she took the handcuff key off Eva's ring. "I have eyes everywhere. They don't call me a mutant for nothing."

Honi wrinkled her nose. "It's latent, Leah. Don't be hard on yourself."

"Whatever." Leah turned towards Eva. "Point is, I've got your handcuff key, but don't worry, I'm not taking it with me. I'm going to hide it somewhere in the house. Aztec won't find it on his own so the only way you'll get loose is if he calls me."

"You don't have a fucking cell phone," Eva spat.

Leah yanked a phone from her pocket. "I do have a cell phone."

Eva's eyes widened. "That's mine, you little thief!"

Leah grinned smugly. "Yeah. That way it'll be easy for the big lug to find me." She turned to the girls. "We should go before hubby gets home. I don't think we want to witness the aftermath when we can get free porn elsewhere."

The girls giggled as they left the bedroom. They swiftly cleaned up in the kitchen, turned off the lights and fled the scene.

Aztec was both surprised and relieved that the lights were out in the cabin when he pulled into the yard. He thought he'd be walking into a houseful of females. Instead, it looked like Eva was already in bed.

His next emotion was panic. Why was Eva already in bed? It wasn't like her to go to bed without him. What if there was something wrong with her or the baby? He quickly unlocked the door and stepped inside. "Eva?" he called.

"In here!" The pitch of her voice was too high.

Aztec's heart thumped in fear. She was definitely not all right. He barrelled into the bedroom, then brought himself up short at the scene before him. "What the fuck?" His blonde beauty was tied down, spread-eagled, and naked.

He grinned widely as he flipped on the light switch. "Is this for me?"

Eva flushed and bit her bottom lip. "Untie me, Aztec. Please untie me."

Aztec kicked off his boots and drew his T-shirt over his head, dropping it on the floor. He made short work of the rest of his clothes while Eva watched him with pursed lips.

Lust hit him hard, his erection pulsing its eagerness at sinking into her welcoming body. "Is it my birthday?"

"Of course, it's not your birthday. C'mon Aztec, don't play games. My three former friends thought this was good payback for when I got them cuffed."

Aztec threw back his head and laughed. It felt good to feel this joy, this sense of belonging with Eva, with this pack. Something he'd never wanted until he had it. He crawled up her body, hovering over her. "The only thing missing is a big red bow around your waist." He dropped his mouth to hers, kissing her until her lips parted and she let him in. "Best birthday present ever," he murmured as he came up for air.

ABOUT THE AUTHOR

Jasmin Quinn is an international bestselling author who embraces her dark side like a storm trooper wearing a G-string.

She's authored a shitload of steamy standalone romances including her Running with the Devil mafia series and the well-loved Shifters of Darkness Falls paranormal series.

She's also partnered with her good friend and international best-selling author, Nikita Slater, to write the After Dark series, which comprises five take-no-prisoners novellas. If you're looking for unforgiving sexy men who take command and make their women bow to their wishes, you'll find them here.

Jasmin's books are a feast of romance with a side-dish of suspense, and hot steamy sex for dessert. Her guys are perfect male specimens with prickish behaviour that matches the size of their dicks but become putty in the hands of their kick-ass heroines.

Not literally putty – more like glazed pottery that resembles big steel rods.

Her biggest regret is not adding an e to Jasmin when she chose her pen name. It's fucking confusing.

Jasmin believes in good manners, compassion for humans and animals alike, and Canadian maple syrup on vanilla ice cream. She generally disregards other people's opinions of her unless they're complimentary, in which case she fully embraces them. She stays in shape by exercising her right to her opinion.

She lives in beautiful British Columbia, Canada with her husband, Mr. Quinn.

Are you following Jasmin's Blog? Check it out at: www.jasminquinn.com

When Jasmin isn't writing about sex, she's most likely blogging about it on her website. Here she lets down her hair, releases her pent-up passions, and embraces her wild side.

Jasmin's blog is a safe outlet for her naughty side – sometimes she interviews her characters, other times, she harasses authors she loves, and she even occasionally writes public letters to Mr. Big (Facebook, not Chris Noth).

---

facebook.com/Jasminquinnwritesromance
twitter.com/JQWritesRomance
instagram.com/jasmin_writes_romance
goodreads.com/Jasmin_Quinn

OTHER SHIFTERS OF DARKNESS FALLS BOOKS

Basic Instinct
Shifters of Darkness Falls Book 1

Primal. Savage. Untamed. The Shifters of Darkness Falls will leave you breathless!

Trist liked her life. Middle of the pack, no pressure, no expectations until she's traded to a new pack.

Now she's the omega, bottom of the pecking order and

has the attention of not only Raff, the savage, unfiltered beta of her new pack, but also a stalker who wants to make Trist his own.

Raff doesn't play nice, ever. And he gets what he wants. Right now he wants Trist and he'll take out anyone who gets in his way.

As the two follow their hearts, dangerous forces are at play that threaten not only their love but also Trist's life.

Basic Instinct is Book 1 of Jasmin Quinn's Shifters of Darkness Falls Series. All books are standalone but are connected by common characters and theme

---

Fierce Intentions
Shifters of Darkness Falls Book 2

"I feel broken, Aztec. I don't know if I can give you what you want."
Aztec leaned into her, his hot breath caressing her neck. "I can make it easy for you, Eva. I can take it."

Aztec has loved Eva since she arrived in Darkness Falls three years ago as a rookie cop, but she's human and he worries that he won't be able to control his wolf around her.

Eva's recovering from a shifter attack that's left her physically and emotionally scarred. Her strength of will helps her healing process, but it's still a daily struggle.

When she realizes that Aztec wants her as his fated mate, she's forced to face not only her fears but also her desire for him. As Eva heals, she and Aztec must make some hard decisions that have dangerous consequences.

Fierce Intentions is Book 2 of Jasmin Quinn's Shifters of Darkness Falls Series. All books are standalone and can be read in any order.

This is a contemporary paranormal romance with suspense and intrigue. No cliffhanger. No cheating. HEA. Contains mature themes including explicit language, violence, and descriptive sex scenes. 18+

Alpha's Prey
Shifters of Darkness Falls Book 3

"I can have anything I want," Gideon said, his warm breath brushing the shell of Honi's ear.

Honi pressed her back into the hard wall. "No, you can't, Gideon. You can't have me."

As Alpha of one of the biggest wolf shifter packs in North America, Gideon has power, respect, wealth, and any woman he wants. Until he lays eyes on Honi, a beautiful redheaded shifter from a rival pack who won't give him the time of day.

Honi is on the run, hiding from an abusive pack that wants her back, when she catches the eye of Gideon, the only man who makes her heart beat faster. But Gideon is aggressive, dangerous, and alpha, a reminder of the brutal life she left behind.

When her former pack hunts her down, she turns to Gideon for help. The fire that ignites between them unleashes Gideon's possessive protective side - he will burn down the world to keep Honi safe.

Alpha's Prey is book 3 of Jasmin Quinn's Shifters of Darkness Falls Series. All books are standalone and can be read in any order.

Savage Hearts
Shifters of Darkness Falls Book 4

"I thought about you a lot over the years, Wolverine. Of how we ended things."

"You ended things! It was your choice!" Cherime didn't need this blustering fool talking about the feels with her. "Are you on some sort of 12-step program?"

Eight years ago, Cherime spent a wild weekend with Ren, Alpha of the Mountain pack, but it ended badly when he literally threw her out of his cabin.

Now, the arrogant jackass is back, thanks to a late spring snowstorm that strands Cherime and her glamping group of teenaged school-girls in his territory.

Ren has spent a long winter isolated in the mountains and he's lonely for a little female companionship. When he comes across Cherime breaking into his community hall, he can't resist the pull of nature. Not only is Cherime his fated mate, but she's still the fearless sexy vixen who stole his heart eight years ago.

He gets way more than he bargained for when he offers shelter to the girls in exchange for Cherime's company for a few days. As their mutual passion explodes into a war of epic proportions, Cherime's life is threatened by a predator in his territory.

While cops and shifters hunt for the serial killer in their midst, Ren and Cherime have battles of their own to fight. Will they find their way back to each other?

Savage Hearts is book 4 of Jasmin Quinn's Shifters of Darkness Falls Series. All books are standalone and can be read in any order.

Primal Heat
Shifters of Darkness Falls Book 5
Coming February 26, 2021

PreOrder your copy today!

Ulrich has his hands full with his job, his crazy ex-wife, and his 12-year-old son, Tag, who recently moved in with him. He doesn't need more complications, which is exactly what he gets when he discovers that Tag's teacher is none other than Aubrey Powell, a woman he's tried to avoid since he first laid eyes on her.

Aubrey has a secret crush on a man… no, shifter male… who has secrets that he won't share, a resentful pre-teen son, and an air of authority and danger that gets her heart racing and the rest of her body heated. She's human, but she knows she's his fated mate. The problem is trying to convince him of that.

As the universe keeps throwing them together, their lives spin out of control. He's hunting the serial killer that killed Aubrey's sister and fears Aubrey could become the next victim. As he gets closer to the truth, his feelings for Aubrey spill over into uncontrollable passion.

Just as life starts to settle down, Ulrich goes missing, setting Aubrey and Tag on a dangerous course of cat and mouse to find him.

This is a contemporary paranormal romance with suspense and intrigue. No cliffhanger. No cheating. HEA. Contains mature themes including explicit language, violence, and descriptive sex scenes. 18+ In other words, bad language, murder, mayhem and hot, hot sex. For adults only.

Primal Heat is book 5 of Jasmin Quinn's Shifters of Darkness Falls Series. All books are stand-alone, but be aware there are common characters and themes across the books that may result in spoilers.

PRIMAL HEAT (SHIFTERS OF DARKNESS FALLS BOOK 5)

Coming February 26, 2021

Teaser

"You don't understand shifter ways!" Ulrich bellowed at Aubrey. "How the hell can you be a schoolteacher to my son?"

Aubrey dropped her eyes to her hands, which were folded in her lap. She wished she were standing, though that wouldn't give her much height advantage. But still, to have this massive man towering over her, angry at her for reasons beyond her comprehension, made her want to get up in his face and shout back.

Except that she was in the school, in her classroom, late at night, alone. Anything she said or did would only rile him up further, and while she didn't exactly fear for her life, she was highly aware of the damage he could do to her if he lost control.

"I'm sorry," she said, trying to sound conciliatory, but her words fell flat, even to her ears.

He pulled her from her chair, his massive hands wrapping around her biceps. "You're not fucking sorry!" She was in the air suddenly, then her ass landed on top of her desk. That made her tall enough that she could see his mouth if she looked directly at him. He had a luscious mouth, lips full and pouty as they snarled at her.

She blew out a breath to settle her racing pulse, then pushed her hand against his chest, the drumming of his heart beating against her palm. "Back up, please, Mr. Calhoun. I'm feeling threatened."

The words seemed to piss him off even more. "You think I'd hurt you?"

She tilted her chin so she could see his eyes. "Yes."

That seemed to do the trick. He stepped back and raked a hand over the top of his head. "I would never hurt you." The wind had dropped from his sails as his light blue eyes met hers.

The unbidden thought that they would make beautiful blonde, blue-eyed children jumped into her mind. "Your aggression suggests otherwise."

He paced away, his face red. Then as if to justify his behaviour, he said. "My son is the most important person in the world. You upset him."

Aubrey nodded. "Yes. I noted that, which is why I called you." She stayed seated on the top of her desk though she would have liked to pace around like he was. It was better if she stayed more or less eye level with him than to walk out her discomfort. "I agree that I'm no expert on shifter behaviour, but your son punched another boy in class."

"The little shit was fucking with Taggart," Ulrich growled. "Shifters don't take shit like that lying down."

"And nor should they." Aubrey felt like she was lecturing a grown-up child, who had huge powerful arms, sexy lips, and an ass so hard she was sure she could bounce a stick of chalk off it. "But violence should never be the first reaction to a situation. Taggart needs to learn how to negotiate."

He stalked up to her, pushing up against her knees, his fists dropping to the desk on either side of her hips as he leaned in.

Aubrey slanted her body backwards, flattening her hands on the desk to keep her upright. Her pulse was racing again, and she knew he knew the effect he was having on her.

"The kid stole Taggart's lunch." His words were deceptively soft as he stared into her eyes. "Why should he negotiate with a thief?"

She licked her lips as she tried to hold his intense gaze. It was impossible but dropping her eyes to his lips was a big mistake. What were they talking about? Lunch. Right. He kind of had a point, but violence begat violence. She swallowed, thinking she should tell him that. Thinking she should tell him to back away and leave. Thinking nothing about this was right.

Then she thought to hell with it. She grabbed the fabric of his shirt and pulled herself forward, settling her lips on his. They were exactly as she imagined, soft and full, pillowy as they took her kiss, and pressed back, seeking more of the same.

Her hand, the traitorous limb, was all in as it snaked its way to the back of his neck and clung to it. He didn't move, didn't touch her other than to return her kiss, pushing at the seam to be admitted inside. Aubrey opened her mouth and let him in, her tongue seeking his, tasting him.

It was too much, and she let out a soft sigh, her eyes closed, her nipples peaked, her sweet spot throbbed. Her body ached for him in a way she'd never felt before. She was drunk on the scent of sandalwood, high on the idea of him making love to her. He was every fantasy she'd ever had come to life. She couldn't resist him.

Apparently, that was not the case with Ulrich. He pulled himself out of her grip, the heat of his body, the press of his lips gone. Her eyes flew open to see him standing a few feet away, a curious set to his eyes. "Is that how you negotiate?" he said gruffly, sounding both heated and displeased.

She cleared her throat realizing that she'd been less than professional. Schoolteachers did not go around kissing the parents of her students, especially this one.

"I'm so sorry," she blurted breathlessly. "I shouldn't have done that." She hopped down from the desk and walked towards the window. She needed air and space to settle her desire, get her head on straight. More than anything, though, she wished she could escape through the window, hide somewhere, and die of embarrassment.

She turned back to him. "I've never done that before. I promise you. I don't know what came over me." She scratched at the top of ear, then wrung her hand's together. "I… it's just…." She stopped the stammering. What could she say to him that didn't sound insane?

"It's fine, Ms. Powell." He gave her a crooked grin as he headed for the door but when he turned back towards her, his face was serious again. "You realize that you've given me leverage over you, don't you?"

She choked on his words. "Leverage? Why would you need leverage over me?"

He shrugged. "Don't know yet."

She raced to the door as he stepped out of her classroom. "No one would ever believe you," she called to his retreating back. "Not a single soul in Darkness Falls."

RUNNING WITH THE DEVIL ROMANTIC SUSPENSE SERIES

By Jason Quinn

It's so good to be bad!

Jasmin Quinn's steamy romance series takes readers on a thrill ride as the rivalry between Rusya Savisin, Russian Mob Boss and the mysterious Mr. Jackman heats up. Romance blooms with intensity as innocents get drawn into the dark terrifying worlds that Jackman and Savisin rule. Each book in the series is standalone but are connected by common themes and characters.

UNLEASHED

Unbroken Book 1

Buy it on Amazon!

Prologue

Gem

I am a pet. I was taken against my will when I was just 13. A young virgin meant to become a sex slave but bought by Adrian Rodriguez and brought to his house. He kept me six years, but he never touched me, at least not sexually. My job was to be his pet, stay with him when he was home. Go where he went in the house, fetch him what he needed, sit at his feet, sleep in his bed when he was alone, sleep on the floor of his bedroom when he was with a lover. I fed him, served him. When he was entertaining his friends, I helped by serving drinks, readying his toys, cleaning him up, cleaning up after him. It was my job and I was the only one who did it.

When he wasn't home, my job was to prowl the house. Our house, he told me. No one watched over me and I could have walked away at any time. I did once, in the early days, after I was bought, but I was caught and brought back to Adrian. He had me beaten, not by him. He didn't touch me, but he sanctioned it, determined the degree of brutality and watched as Jake, his man, delivered the punishment.

When it was over, he ordered me to the kitchen to help the cook prepare the evening meal and serve it to him and his friends. I could barely walk, could barely manage through my tears. When the meal had been eaten and the dishes cleared, he made me sit at his feet for the evening, and then at the end of the evening, as I cleaned him up and put away the toys, he told me that the beating was a light one. That should I run again, I would be beaten until I couldn't walk.

After that, I didn't run. Because I was afraid, yes, but also because there was no reason to. Adrian treated me well, gave me what I needed to be comfortable, and he didn't touch me other than to sometimes ruffle my hair or give me a small hug. There was no better place for me to be, though I knew that my term as a pet had a short life-span and as the years passed, I was rapidly approaching the end of mine. At 13, I was cute, had plump curves and the roundness of an adolescent girl. But at 19, I am less soft, my body thinner, my face more angular. And I have become more serious and less tolerant of anyone and everyone who isn't Adrian.

Chapter 1

Gem

There is bad news today. Adrian was killed, shot to death by an enemy. The house is in an uproar and I'm more afraid than I've ever been. I never thought to consider what would happen to me should Adrian die. Jake, Adrian's lieutenant, has gathered all of us together in the formal sitting room: Adrian's security team, the household staff and me. Jake is the one who beat me, but it has never been something I held him accountable for. After all, I made the mistake and Adrian ordered the beating.

I am sitting off to the side, on the floor next to Adrian's empty chair, on my knees, alone. It is well-known that I am owned, that I have no rights, but at the same time, I am a pampered pet, not to be kicked around or abused. Not to be touched by anyone except Adrian. I say nothing as the staff mill about, some of the women weeping, but my brain is working overtime. I wonder what will happen to me, to all of us. No one is really talking. They appear to be waiting and so I wait with them. The service staff has made coffee and tea, put out some food and alcohol. I don't touch any of it. Adrian forbade me to take any food that he hadn't explicitly sanctioned. Forbade me to eat without him.

After an hour or so, there's a flurry of activity at the front door and everyone who had been seated stands, except me. The security men straighten; they seem somewhat fearful as deep voices and loud footsteps penetrate the funereal gloom. Several men walk into the room, all of them large, serious, menacing. Four of them forge a path and then step to the side as a fifth man stands at the centre. He's tall, much taller than Adrian and very big, but not fat. He's wearing a dark suit that pulls across his shoulders and tapers to his waist, the seams of the sleeves strain against his strong arms. His brown hair is cropped short and his dark critical eyes give the room the white glove treatment. He looks like Adrian but also not.

"I'm Harlow." His deep, arrogant voice rings in the room, making everyone stand straighter. "Who's in charge?"

Jake steps up, his lips thin, his courage strung tightly. No one has said who this Harlow is, but everyone seems to know but me

Harlow's eyes flick to Jake. "How'd he die?"

Jake closes his eyes briefly, sadness and regret lingering on his face. "A gunman caught him at his club. Two of his friends died too."

Harlow nods and I see something like grief flicker briefly in the set to his mouth before he banishes it. "It was going to happen eventually. He was reckless." His eyes sweep the room again, landing on the service staff, Adrian's men and then me. When he sees me, he stops, stares, his glance narrowing.

"Who's this?" he says to Jake.

"She's Adrian's..."

Harlow frowns, a snarl that makes me cower. "A pet." He steps up to me and I shrink from him as he crouches. Then he reaches out and grasps me by the chin, forcing my eyes to his. "What's your name, kitten?"

I react to his touch, rearing my head back. No one touches me except Adrian, no one since Jake beat me, and it unsettles me. He reaches again and I duck, shuffle backwards on my knees out of his reach. He turns to Jake, a hard glint in his eyes. "Why's she afraid?"

"She doesn't like to be touched."

He laughs like he's just heard a bad joke and straightens up, but his eyes are still glued to me. "A pet that doesn't like to be touched. Only Adrian would own something like that."

He turns to one of his men. Pudge is his name, though I'm not sure why. "Take her. She'll come with us." To Jake, he says, "Make funeral arrangements, get the service staff to close up the house."

As Pudge tries to scoop me up in his arms, I crawl backwards until my back hits a wall. He grabs me with his hands, tries to pull me towards the door and I dig in my heels. His eyes narrow as he catches me by the waist and picks me up. Panic sets in and I start to scream as I struggle in his arms, flailing, kicking, twisting.

Harlow laughs as he watches his man try to contain me. Pudge seems to not want to hurt me, but I don't make it easy for him. He tries to get a solid grip on me, but I'm small, agile and won't settle. His hand strays too near my mouth and I clamp down on it, capturing it between my teeth and hanging on.

He tries to shake me off, but I stay fastened to his hand until he grabs a fistful of my hair with his free hand and yanks my head back. I have no choice but to let go or he'll rip my hair out. He's mad now and backhands me across the face, but he doesn't let me fall. The slap stops my tantrum cold, but he no longer trusts me, so ensures I'm well subdued by wrenching my arms painfully behind my back and pushing me towards the door.

I have been beaten twice now, once because I ran and today because I was defiant. It's a first for me because I'm never unruly. Everyone in the household knows Adrian's rules when it comes to me – hands off. But Adrian's dead and Harlow seems to be in charge.

Pudge looks to Harlow, his voice a growl. "The fucking little thing's not tame."

Harlow frowns as his eyes sweep me, but he says nothing. I have a new owner. And he doesn't know the rules.
